THE TEMPLE OF
THE GOLDEN PAVILION

ALSO BY YUKIO MISHIMA

THE SOUND OF WAVES

AFTER THE BANQUET

*THE SAILOR WHO FELL FROM GRACE
WITH THE SEA*

THIRST FOR LOVE

Yukio Mishima

THE TEMPLE OF
THE GOLDEN PAVILION

Translated by Ivan Morris
Introduction by Nancy Wilson Ross
Drawings by Fumi Komatsu

A BERKLEY MEDALLION BOOK
PUBLISHED BY
BERKLEY PUBLISHING CORPORATION

BERKLEY MEDALLION EDITION, JUNE, 1971
FOURTH PRINTING

SBN 425-02930-1

BERKLEY MEDALLION BOOKS are published by
Berkley Publishing Corporation
200 Madison Avenue
New York, N. Y. 10016

BERKLEY MEDALLION BOOKS ® TM 757,375

Printed in the United States of America

INTRODUCTION

The Temple of the Golden Pavilion is the fourth book to be published in America by Yukio Mishima—the most famous, gifted, and prolific young Japanese writer—who, at thirty-two, already has some fifty volumes of work—novels, stories, essays, poetry—to his credit in his own country. *The Temple of the Golden Pavilion*, under the title *Kinkakuji*, won an important literary prize in Japan, sold over 300,000 copies, and was made into a successful modern play. It has been translated by Ivan Morris, one of the skillful young translators who are, since the war, beginning to make a place for themselves in the niche so long occupied alone by the redoubtable Arthur Waley.

The three other works by Yukio Mishima which preceded *The Temple of the Golden Pavilion* in America were entirely different in character. The first was a deceptively simple and brief novel of life and love in a Japanese fishing village, *The Sound of Waves*. The second, *Five Modern Nō Plays* was a brilliant utilization of old *Nō* drama themes in contemporary settings, published with an admirable introduction by its translator, Donald Keene. The third was a novel, *Confessions of a Mask*. The present novel, *The Temple of the Golden Pavilion*, based on an actual occurrence in recent Japanese history, deals with the complex pathology and final desperate crime of a young Zen Buddhist acolyte, in training for priesthood at a Kyoto temple.

In 1950, to the distress and horror of all art-loving and patriotic Japanese, the ancient Zen temple of Kinkakuji in Kyoto was deliberately burned to the ground. This Golden

Pavilion, a rare masterpiece of Buddhist garden architecture, dated back over five hundred years to the
days of the great Shogun, Ashikaga Yoshimitsu, military
leader, aesthete, and powerful patron of the Zen cult, who,
near the end of his amazing career, abdicated to take the
tonsure. The Kinkakuji, tradition said, had served as a
retreat for this hard-driven Shogun of the fourteenth
century. Here on evenings of music and poetic
composition Yoshimitsu found respite from the constant
internecine warfare and general turbulence of the
medieval period. So revered was this historic and religious
shrine that it enjoyed in Japan the status of a National
Treasure. It was willfully set fire to and destroyed by an
unhappy and unbalanced student of Zen Buddhism.

The newspaper accounts of the actual trial relate how
this young acolyte—born with an ugly face and afflicted
from childhood with a difficult stammer—became
obsessed with "envy" of the Golden Temple whose beauty
daily attracted a throng of admiring visitors. After
establishing a typically neurotic pattern of behavior at the
temple to which his dead father, also a Zen priest, had
taken him for his training—such behavior as stealing,
gambling, cutting classes, frequenting geisha houses—he
finally decided to die a spectacular death by burning down
the Kinkakuji and perishing in the blaze. But when he had
actually succeeded in setting the sacred edifice afire he
lost his courage, ran from the burning building to a hill
near Kyoto, and there attempted to commit suicide.

Failing in this, he gave himself up to the authorities and
asked for his just punishment. At his trial he said: "I hate
myself, my evil, ugly, stammering self." Yet he also said
that he did not in any way regret having burned down the
Kinkakuji. A report of the trial, in explanation of his
conduct, stated that because of his "self-hate and self-
detestation he hated anything beautiful. He could not help
always feeling a strong destructive desire for hurting and
destroying anything that was beautiful." The psychiatrist
who was called on the case analyzed the young man as a
"psychopath of the schizoid type."

This is the incident from which Yukio Mishima has

built his engrossing novel. But although Mishima has made use of the reported details of the real-life culprit's arrogant and desperate history, culminating in the final willful act of arson, he has employed the factual record merely as a scaffolding on which to erect a disturbing and powerful story of a sick young man's obsession with a beauty he cannot attain, and the way in which his private pathology leads him, slowly and fatefully, to self-destruction and a desperate deed of pyromania.

As the setting of this novel is a Zen temple and its writing contains frequent references to Zen training, classes in Buddhism, Zen daily rituals, and in particular to the practical use of, and various interpretations and misinterpretations of, certain famous Zen *koans, The Temple of the Golden Pavilion* is likely to set going among America's new generation of Zen zealots some lively arguments concerning the author's real purposes. Is the burning of the ancient Zen temple, topped by its golden phoenix, a symbolic act—as the novelist uses it —suggesting revolt on the part of young Japanese against the forms and disciplines of the Zen Buddhist way of life: an influence that has for generations laid its powerful spell on the whole range of national behavior and culture from social etiquette to swordsmanship and judo, from theater techniques to flower arrangements, from garden designs to archery, from the formal tea ceremony to literary styles and conventions—most notably, the stripped, evocative forms of Japanese poetry? Or is this novel to be interpreted in rather more general terms as an expression of post-war social revolt, even nihilism, on the part of young Japanese, following in the wake of the defeat and the Occupation? Or, finally, is it to be considered in more simple psychological terms, merely as a detailed, dramatic study of personal pathology?

It is not possible to ignore the fact that the Kinkakuji, around whose "obsessive power" and final destruction the novel's theme revolves, was a sacred Buddhist relic, and must stand, therefore, as a religious symbol. There is also, certainly, significance in the fact that scattered through the pages of *The Temple of the Golden Pavilion* are telling examples of what amounts to misuse of that famed Zen verbal dialectic presumably leading to "self-enlightenment." In *The Temple of the Golden Pavilion* the Zen aphoristic riddle, the *koan*, and the general Zen *Weltansicht* are frequently employed by neurotic characters in ways of rough, or perverted, "therapy." These special Zen techniques are even utilized for ulterior purposes. So openly is this done by some of Mishima's characters that I was reminded of a criticism once written by Gerald Heard about the dangers inherent in the possible malpractice of Zen tenets: "Zen's anxiety to avoid metaphysics and to be purely empiric can end in the forging of an instrument which may be used by a fiend." It is noteworthy that a nihilistic misinterpretation of an old classic *koan* prods on the psychotic hero to his last desperate deed. There are, in Mishima's novel, a few implications—essentially mild, however—of the power and hypocrisy of some Buddhist sects and of the rigidly formalized and dogmatic teaching-methods of these sects in Japan today, as contrasted to the more individualized search for *satori* ("enlightenment") characteristic of the past. Mizoguchi, the young acolyte, himself comments about Zen: "in former times when not yet captured by convention and when the spiritual awakening of an individual was valued above all else. . . ."

Yet the author of *The Temple of the Golden Pavilion* does not give the impression that he is in any way concerned with voicing a philippic against Zen Buddhism. Yukio Mishima appears chiefly interested in the imaginative re-creation of a psychotic acolyte's obsession and a detailed portrayal of the steps that led to his last desperate, destructive act. The emphasis falls on the individual. Even the sociological factors are made subservient to young Mizoguchi's pathology.

It would be all too easy to read into this novel, in several instances, more than is apparently intended. Facile and disturbing interpretations might, for example, readily present themselves around the occasional references to Americans in the pages of *The Temple of the Golden Pavilion*. The most deeply shocking scene in the book

8

takes place in the snow-covered temple gardens between an American soldier, a pregnant prostitute, and the young acolyte, Mizoguchi. It is this occurrence which might be said to have started Mizoguchi—already, however, clearly neurotic and unbalanced—on his dedicated path of willful deceit and wrong-doing. He accepts cartons of cigarettes from the American in return for the shameful part he has played in the garden incident. After accepting the cigarettes he gives them to the Superior of the temple, not so much as a way of currying favor but rather to involve the Zen Master indirectly in a shocking deed of which he is, at the moment, totally unaware. (Once the "figure of authority" represented by the Temple's Superior is besmirched, even if only in Mizoguchi's sick mind, there is no stemming the dark tide of his future actions.) In the novel one looks in vain for any *planted* connection between Mizoguchi's participation in the . American soldier's pathology and the future development of his own psychosis, beyond, of course, the obvious fact—also quite unemphasized by the author—that the American and the Japanese could both be said to share a common physical sadism.

And again, in relation to the indirect role played by the Americans in *The Temple of the Golden Pavilion:* Prior to this garden episode—and thus before Japan's defeat and the Occupation—Mizoguchi has become convinced that the temple, whose Master his dead father and pathetic poverty-stricken mother have fondly hoped he would some day become, will be burned down by the Americans with their incendiary bombs. This thought acts as a "release" to him. He is temporarily freed of the paralyzing beauty of the golden shrine that has been his obsession since childhood; the temple whose image—forever rising in his mind's eye—effectively prevents him from leading a normal life of direct action: in friendship, in the sexual act, in the simplest and most ordinary affairs of everyday existence. Now, at last—it seems to him—he and his beautiful structure with which all worldly beauty is identified, possess something in common; they share a common danger, the same possible fate: "I felt that a

9

bridge had been built between myself and the thing that until then had seemed to deny me, to keep me at a distance. . . . Just like my own frail, ugly body, the temple's body, hard though it was, consisted of combustible carbon."

But "release" from the Golden Temple's obsessive power was not destined to come to Mizoguchi in this manner. (Actually the American Air Force carefully avoided Kyoto, with its ancient Japanese religious and national relics, its temples and art treasures.) The war ended with the Golden Pavilion still standing. Of the war's end the novel's hero says: "I must state what the defeat really meant to me. It was not a liberation. No, it was by no means a liberation. It was nothing else than a return to the unchanging eternal Buddhist routine which merged into our daily life. This routine was now firmly re-established and continued unaltered from the day after the Surrender: the 'opening of the rules,' morning tasks, 'gruel session,' meditation, 'medicine' of the evening meal, bathing, 'opening the pillow.' . . ." There was no way left, then, in Mizoguchi's sick mind but to pursue his mad career through a series of nihilistic, self-destructive actions which his Superior continued to accept without comment or censure. And it was this behavior on the Master's part that the acolyte found unendurable—because it was inscrutable.

Finally, in the novel, as in real life, the tortured young man sets fire to the famed National Treasure, and, managing to escape at the last possible moment from the conflagration (after a special little golden room, in which he hoped to die, refuses to open its door to his insane pounding), he flies to a nearby hill. There, watching the flames roar up, he takes a cigarette from his pack and begins to smoke. The novel ends with the lines: "I felt like a man who settles down for a smoke after a job of work. I wanted to live."

The Temple of the Golden Pavilion has around it an aura of Dostoevskian violence and passion. I found many reminders of Dostoevsky's involved and tortuous struggles with the ageless questions of "forgiveness," "love," "mastery." Yet as the story of *The Temple of the Golden Pavilion* fatefully unwinds, one is strangely free of emotional identification with any character—and here, certainly, the Dostoevskian comparison sharply ends.

This freedom from emotional identification does not, however, lessen the book's power. It seems, in a singular way, to intensify it, almost as though the stuttering Mizoguchi's murky analyses of the nature and conduct of the people he encounters in his daily life become the reader's own astigmatism. The "moral" position from which we, as Westerners with a Puritan tradition, are accustomed to judge behavior both in life and literature is missing from these pages. The episodes are, for the most part, presented free of judgment. In fact there seems to be little, if any, stress on familiar "values." Those dualisms of black and white, body and soul, good and evil that we take so for granted are not found in *The Temple of the Golden Pavilion*. Evil is represented, to be sure, but never with comment direct enough to suggest a tangible attitude toward it. Take as example young Mizoguchi's icily oblique thoughts when he first encounters the black market: "If the people of this world, I thought, are going to taste evil through their lives and their deeds, then I shall plunge as deep as I can into an inner world of evil." This seeming partial justification of his own conduct is, however, in no way emphasized as an explanation of Mizoguchi's subsequent crimes. Rather it is as if the crimes of the black marketeers and the crimes of Mizoguchi all existed in the same great continuum; were, in a sense, *one*.

The Temple of the Golden Pavilion is rich in scenes, incidents, episodes which, though developed in great detail, often leave the reader uncertain as to their meaning and portent in relation to the story's main line. There is in this a similarity to life itself, where the threads of relationship are never neatly woven into a clear and fixed pattern. In reading Mishima's novel, one is not so much baffled as frequently *suspended*. Sometimes Mishima's minor incidents seem not unlike certain discursive, even apparently extraneous, passages in *The Possessed* and *The*

11

Idiot. In both Mishima and Dostoevsky, the reader's response to these minor themes and commentaries will depend on his own personal literary taste. He will consider them enrichment of the central theme or mere excrescences. (The "spun-out" quality in Mishima, as in Dostoevsky, may be partly due to the circumstance of the original serialization form of their novels.)

The Temple of the Golden Pavilion frequently presents, in the course of a single episode, the most highly developed Japanese national traits: refined taste, finesse, delicacy of feeling, along with the most sharply contrasted types of behavior: coldness, ugliness, cruelty. I think in particular of a scene in which Mizoguchi's blackhearted, clubfooted student friend, Kashiwagi, artfully composes a bouquet of flowers after the Kansui style of flower arrangement in the traditional Heaven, Earth, and Man manner. The bouquet is made up of irises and cattails which he has persuaded Mizoguchi to steal for him from the temple gardens. As Kashiwagi deftly and gently arranges the flowers in the *tokonoma* in his room, Mizoguchi plays some melodies on a flute. Kashiwagi also offers at this time his own ingenious and twisted interpretation of several famed Zen *koans.*

The quiet scene is terminated by a moment of penetrating and sadistic cruelty on the part of the crippled Kashiwagi toward a woman visitor who has, during the course of a sexual affair, been teaching him the exacting art of flower arrangement. This woman, noting the bouquet of cattails and irises in the alcove, sincerely compliments the clubfooted Kashiwagi, remarking that the beauty of the arrangement testifies to his new skill. Kashiwagi responds to her smiling praise by replying, with cold formality, that he is glad to hear her say just this. Having learned all she has to offer him, he need never see her again, and does not wish to. At this flatly cruel announcement the woman, without abandoning her ceremonious manner (she has been kneeling just inside the door since her arrival), crosses the room, still on her knees, and, without warning, abruptly overturns and destroys his artful arrangement. Kashiwagi, enraged, seizes her by the hair and strikes her in the face.

This violence affords no relief from the scene's muffled tensions. The refracted quality persists even after Mizoguchi, urged by Kashiwagi to run after the weeping woman to "have" her, accompanies her home. As they sit in her house, quietly talking, following her prolonged bitter outbursts about Kashiwagi's many cruelties and perversities, Mizoguchi, in spite of his handicap of incoherent stuttering, is able to reveal to her what he had just discovered in Kashiwagi's room. She is the same woman he had once seen by chance in a very intimate and tender tea ceremony in a temple tearoom with her dead soldier-lover. Indeed this is the third time this stranger has impinged on his consciousness. Once before a casual "date" told him the woman's story in such a way that he instantly realized the girl was describing the figure from the tearoom pantomime on which, years before, he had spied from a distance.

Such a sequence of events is typical of the design of *The Temple of the Golden Pavilion.* The story unwinds as a slowly moving spiral in which figures originally glimpsed from a distance suddenly, with the passing of time, appear in the immediate foreground. Ghosts of the past also become, momentarily, living realities. In the West such occurrences would be described as "coincidences" or "hallucinations." The East has other interpretations. In this particular scene between Kashiwagi's distraught rejected mistress and Mizoguchi, the woman, deeply moved by the memories that the inarticulate young stammerer has revived for her, cries: "So that's what happened! So that's what really happened, is it? What a strange karma! Yes, that's what a strange karma means." In an uprush of sad-sweet recollection she then offers herself to him. But he cannot take her. Here again, as always, the image of the Golden Temple intervenes to paralyze him. His emotions bind rather than free him.

The entire episode fades away into the mists of "might have been," of "seemed to be." This pervasive fog, in which the hero himself is living, reminds one of a Japanese painting, those subtle masterpieces created with

13

sumi ink on silk which show a world tantalizingly half-revealed, half-obscured; misty landscapes in which trees, mountains, people—all of seemingly equal significance—are presented in a great living emptiness. In *The Temple of the Golden Pavilion* the inference seems to be: Nothing remains what it was. Nothing is really what it seems. Even the death of Mizoguchi's one "good" friend, the unfailingly kind, optimistic, cheerful, and positive Tsurukawa, turns out to have been not an accident as reported, but a suicide brought on by an unhappy adolescent love affair. What is equally significant—or is it so intended?—the "evil" cripple, Kashiwagi, reveals after the death of the "good" Tsurukawa that they too had secretly become great friends—even though Tsurukawa had sought to warn Mizoguchi against the crippled student's friendship. All the last letters written from Tokyo before his suicide had been written to Kashiwagi. Mizoguchi, the old companion, received none. Is this another expression of life's spiral riddle; a further subtle Eastern emphasis on the error of seeing "opposites"? Are the only definable qualities of human existence illusion and evanescence? Mizoguchi muses, at one point: "It is said that the essence of Zen is the absence of all feature, and that the real power to see consists in the knowledge that one's heart possesses neither face nor feature."

The character of the Superior in *The Temple of the Golden Pavilion* is another example of the subtle mystifications that are presented to the Western reader in the pages of Mishima's novel. The Superior is a figure of utmost significance to the young acolyte, Mizoguchi, yet he remains throughout as baffling (deliberately baffling?) to the reader as he is to the novel's hero. This particular Zen Master is hardly, by anyone's standards, a disciplined "holy" man, with his fleshly pursuits, his open enjoyment of the good things of life—fine food, cigarettes, saké—his secret adventures with geishas. Yet there is a scene in which the young acolyte discovers this head priest crouched alone in an isolated room within the temple grounds, bent over "to the utmost possible extent . . . with

14

his head between his knees and his face covered with his long sleeves." An altogether new and different note is lightly struck for a moment; a note of deepened mystery. Here is the Superior in a pose of supplication and abasement quite unlike his usual calm, poised, and powerful self. The plump, self-indulgent, omniscient Master of the temple has been abruptly transformed into a broken figure of suffering humility, kneeling alone in The Tower of the North Star. But the note of mystery is only briefly sounded; indeed it hardly registers, drowned out by the onrolling development of Mizoguchi's pathology. For to Mizoguchi, the Master's crouching figure was only "utterly devoid of pride and dignity. There was something ignoble about it, like the figure of a sleeping animal."

As for the deliberate introduction into the story of the use of Zen *koans*, those aphoristic problems or "riddles" by which Zen aspirants seek to pierce through into the reality of "self-enlightenment"—they too are presented in various interpretations as though allowing the reader to reach his own conclusions. One of the most absorbing and mystifying scenes takes place in the Zen temple the day the war was officially declared lost. To the amazement of all the young acolytes, the Superior appeared at evening services in his most splendid robes, "the scarlet priest's robe which he had kept stored away for years." There was about him a "ruddy air of good health," even a "look of overflowing delight." Without so much as speaking about the war or its tragic conclusion, the Superior, after the sutra recitation, gives a lecture on a classic Zen catechetic problem: *Nansen Kills a Cat*, or as it is sometimes called: *Shoshu Wears a Pair of Sandals on his Head*. The Superior offers an interpretation of this classic *koan* which appears to his young audience in no way to relate to the shameful disgrace of the loss of the war. The boys walk away deeply puzzled. "We felt as though we had been bewitched by a fox. We had not the faintest idea why this particular Zen problem should have been chosen on the day of our country's defeat." Tsurukawa's explanation is: "I think that the real point of tonight's lecture was that on the day of our defeat he [the Superior] should not have said a word about it and should have talked about killing a cat."

This same *koan* reappears later in the book during Kashiwagi's flower-arranging scene, where it is given a twisted interpretation characteristic of the clubfooted student's twisted mind. At this same time an even more fateful *koan* is also quoted by the clubfooted Kashiwagi to the inarticulate, stuttering Mizoguchi. This is a quotation from the famed master Rinzai (here given as Ivan Morris translates it from Mishima): "When ye meet the Buddha, kill the Buddha! When ye meet your ancestor, kill your ancestor! When ye meet the disciple of Buddha, kill the disciple! When ye meet your father and mother, kill your father and mother! When ye meet your kin, kill your kin! Only thus will ye attain deliverance. Only thus will ye escape the trammels of material things and become free." (This stern exhortation brings an echo of Christ's admonition: "He that loveth father or mother, son or daughter more than me is not worthy of me" and that a "man's foes" are "those of his own household.")

The quotation from Rinzai rises to the surface of the acolyte's mind and, in his sick consciousness, seems to command him to commit his final unforgivable crime—this at the very last moment when the temple's compelling beauty in the nighttime garden is about to deprive him of his will to act. With his own nihilistic misinterpretation of the ancient saying about the drastic path one must follow to gain self-enlightenment, Mizoguchi seeks to rid himself of the paralyzing obsession with the Golden Temple that has haunted him since childhood. He sets a match to carefully placed bundles of straw. The Golden Temple is doomed!

One closes the novel with the feeling that this sacred architectural relic from the days of Japan's rich, paradoxical, and turbulent past may well be the true protagonist in these pages, as the book's title suggests.

Two passages from *The Temple of the Golden Pavilion*

linger strongly in my mind; both of them, in a sense, profoundly Eastern and Buddhist—though not particularly Zen in tone.

One of these passages occurs early, on the occasion of Mizoguchi's first visit to the temple with his dying father. He sees a skillfully executed model of the Golden Temple resting in a glass case in one of the rooms. "This model pleased me. It was closer to the Golden Temple of my dreams. Observing this perfect little image of the Golden Temple within the great temple itself, I was reminded of the endless series of correspondences that arise when a small universe is placed in a large universe and a smaller one is in turn placed inside the small universe. For the first time I could dream: of the small, but perfect Golden Temple which was even smaller than this model; and of the Golden Temple which was infinitely greater than the real building—so great, indeed, that it almost enveloped the world."

The other passage occurs near the end, a part of the musings of the young acolyte just before he sets fire to the temple. "When the Golden Temple reflected the evening sun or shone in the moon, it was the light of the water [in the pond before it] that made the entire structure look as if it were mysteriously floating along and flapping its wings. The strong bonds of the temple's form were loosened by the reflection of the quivering water, and at such moments the Golden Temple seemed to be constructed of materials like wind and water and flame that are constantly in motion."

To its invisible basic elements the mad young acolyte—in both fact and fiction—reduced the Golden Temple's gloriously visible form. The rooms in which Shogun Yoshimitsu once sat on a straw mat, drinking tea, listening to the flute, and composing poetry, went up in flames and disappeared in ashes. It is perhaps not irrelevant to state, however, that the Japanese have already rebuilt the Kinkakuji. True to the symbol of the eternally reborn phoenix that surmounts its rooftop, The

17

National Treasure stands again in the famous Kyoto monastery grounds. Some even say it is "more beautiful and more golden than before."

The Temple of the Golden Pavilion is a novel which could only have been written by a Japanese and a member of a race whose cultural heritage is essentially Buddhist. This is one of its great values to the Western reader. The fact that the hero is a Zen acolyte as well as a psychopath, that the book deals with the willful destruction of a famed Buddhist religious monument, that its pages contain many telling examples of the use, and misuse, of Zen techniques—all this is bound to interest the growing body of Zen enthusiasts in America today. But more important—and in a wider context—*The Temple of the Golden Pavilion* offers the Western reader pictures of other ways of life, other world views, differing radically from our own but perhaps of equal validity. The Japanese have developed slowly over the centuries—in part because of their determined isolationism—a truly unique civilization. Through the pages of a novel like Yukio Mishima's, one is able to perceive some of the elements that have gone into the creation of this rare, paradoxical, and long-enduring civilization; elements which well may, in the modern world, face final dissolution. In *The Temple of the Golden Pavilion* a fragment of contemporary Japanese life, with its roots still deep in the culture of the past, is presented not for our judgment but for our observation. The opportunity offered here by Yukio Mishima's special insight and fictional talent is one for which to feel properly grateful.

NANCY WILSON ROSS

THE TEMPLE OF THE GOLDEN PAVILION

CHAPTER ONE

Ever since my childhood, Father had often spoken to me about the Golden Temple.

My birthplace was a lonely cape that projects into the Sea of Japan northeast of Maizuru. Father, however, was not born there, but at Shiraku in the eastern suburbs of Maizuru. He was urged to join the clergy and became the priest of a temple on a remote cape; in this place he married and begot a child, who was myself.

There was no suitable middle school in the vicinity of the temple on Cape Nariu. At length I left my parents' house and was sent to my uncle's home in Father's birthplace; while I lived there, I attended the East Maizuru Middle School, going to and fro on foot.

The sky in Father's home town was very bright. But each year in October and November, even on days when it did not look as if there could be a single cloud, we would have several sudden showers. I wondered whether it was not here that I developed my changeable disposition.

On spring evenings when I returned from school, I would sit in my study on the second floor of my uncle's house and gaze at the hills. The rays of the sinking sun shone on the young leaves that covered the hillside and it looked as though a golden screen had been set up in the midst of the fields. When I saw this, the Golden Temple sprang into my mind.

Though occasionally I saw the real Golden Temple in photographs or in textbooks, it was the image of the Golden Temple as Father had described it to me that dominated my heart. Father had never told me that the real Golden Temple was shining in gold, or anything of the sort; yet, according to Father, there was nothing on this earth so beautiful as the Golden Temple. Moreover, the very characters with which the name of the temple was written and the very sound of the word imparted some fabulous quality to the Golden Temple that was engraved on my heart.

When I saw the surface of the distant fields glittering in the sun, I felt sure that this was a golden shadow cast by the invisible temple. The Yoshizaka Pass, which forms the boundary between Fukui Prefecture and my own Kyoto Prefecture lay directly to the east. The sun rises directly above this mountain pass. Though the actual city of Kyoto lies in exactly the opposite direction, I used to see the Golden Temple soaring up into the morning sky amidst

22

the rays of the sun as it rose from the folds of those eastern hills.

Thus the Golden Temple was apparent everywhere. In so far as I could not actually set eyes on the temple, it was like the sea. For though Maizuru Bay lies only three and a half miles to the west of the village of Shiraku where I lived, the water itself was blocked from view by the hills; yet there always floated in the air a sort of presentiment of this sea: sometimes the wind would bring with it a smell of the sea, sometimes in rough weather flocks of gulls would swoop down into the nearby fields to take refuge.

I had a weak constitution and was always being defeated by the other boys in running or on the exercise bar. Besides, I had suffered since my birth from a stutter, and this made me still more retiring in my manner. And everyone knew that I came from a temple. Some of the more ill-behaved children used to make fun of me by imitating a stuttering priest as he tried to stammer his way through the sutras. There was a story in one of our books in which a stuttering detective appeared, and the boys used to read these passages to me in a specially loud voice.

My stuttering, I need hardly say, placed an obstacle between me and the outside world. It is the first sound that I have trouble in uttering. This first sound is like a key to the door that separates my inner world from the world outside, and I have never known that key to turn smoothly in its lock. Most people, thanks to their easy command of words, can keep this door between the inner world and the outer world wide open, so that the air passes freely between the two; but for me this has been quite impossible. Thick rust has gathered on the key.

When a stutterer is struggling desperately to utter his first sound, he is like a little bird that is trying to extricate itself from thick lime. When finally he manages to free himself, it is too late. To be sure, there are times when the reality of the outer world seems to have been waiting for me, folding its arms as it were, while I was struggling to free myself. But the reality that is waiting for me is not a fresh reality. When finally I reach the outer world after all my efforts, all that I find is a reality that has instantly changed color and gone out of focus—a reality that has lost the freshness that I had considered fitting for myself, and that gives off a half-putrid odor.

As can easily be imagined, a youth like myself came to entertain two opposing forms of power wishes. In history I enjoyed the descriptions of tyrants. I saw myself as a stuttering, taciturn tyrant; my retainers would hang on every expression that passed over my face and would live both day and night in fear and trembling of me. There is no need to justify my cruelty in clear, smooth words. My taciturnity alone was sufficient to justify every manner of cruelty. On the one hand I enjoyed imagining how one by one I would wreck punishment on my teachers and schoolmates who daily tormented me; on the other hand, I fancied myself as a great artist, endowed with the clearest vision—a veritable sovereign of the inner world. My outer appearance was poor, but in this way my inner world became richer than anyone else's. Was it not natural that a young boy who suffered from an indelible drawback like mine should have come to think that he was a secretly chosen being? I felt as though somewhere in this world a mission awaited me of which I myself still knew nothing.

The following episode remains in my memory from this time. The East Maizuru Middle School had spacious grounds, surrounded pleasantly by the hills, and was equipped with bright, modern buildings.

One day in May a graduate of our school, who was now a student in the Maizuru Naval Engineering School, had a holiday and came to visit his old middle school.

He was attractively sunburned and a powerful nose emerged from beneath his uniform cap, which he wore pulled down over his eyes: from top to toe he was the perfect young hero. Now he stood telling his juniors about the rigors of his present life with all its military regulations. Yet, although he was meant to be describing a life that was full of hardships, he spoke in a tone as though he were telling us about the most luxurious and extravagant existence. Every move that he made was full of arrogance, but, for all his youth, he was well aware of

24

the importance of an assumed modesty. His chest, clothed in his braided uniform, was stretched out like the breast of the figurehead on a ship as it cuts its way through the sea breeze. He was sitting on the stone steps that led down to the school grounds. Round about him stood a group of students who listened eagerly to his words, and in the garden beds on the slope the May flowers were in bloom—tulips, sweet peas, anemones, and daisies; and above their heads hung the rich white blossoms of the magnolia tree.

Both the speaker and his listeners were stationary like monuments. I was sitting by myself on the ground a few yards away. Such was my manner. Such was my manner toward the May flowers and toward that pride-filled uniform and toward those bright peals of laughter.

Now this young hero was more concerned with me than with his admirers. It was only I who did not appear to bow before his dignity, and this thought hurt his pride. He asked the others what I was called.

"Hey, Mizoguchi!" he called out; this was the first time that he had set eyes on me. I stared at him without a word. In the smile that he now directed towards me, I could detect something like the flattery of a man of power.

"Why don't you answer me something? Are you dumb?"

"I'm a st-st-stutterer," replied one of his admirers in my stead, and they all doubled up with laughter. What a dazzling thing it was, this scornful laughter! To me there was something brilliant—brilliant like the light reflected from the clusters of leaves—about this cruel laughter of my classmates which was so characteristic of boys of their age.

"What, you're a stutterer, are you? Why don't you enter the Naval Engineering School? They'll flog that stuttering out of you in a single day!"

I do not know how, but at once I gave a clear answer. The words flowed out smoothly, without the slightest volition on my part.

"I won't go there. I'm going to become a priest."

Everyone was silent. The young hero lowered his head,

picked a blade of grass, and put it in his mouth.

"Well, then," he said, "one of these years, when it's time for me to get buried, I'll be giving you some work to do."

The Pacific War had already started.

At that moment I undoubtedly experienced a certain self-awakening. The knowledge that I was to stand waiting in a dark world with both hands stretched out. That some day the May flowers, the uniforms, my ill-natured classmates would all come into my outstretched hands. To be seized with the knowledge that I myself was grasping the world, squeezing it out, as it were, at the base. . . . But such a knowledge was too heavy to become a source of pride for a young boy like myself.

Pride must be a lighter thing, more cheerful, easier to see, more brilliant. I wanted something visible. I wanted my pride to be something that could be seen by anyone. For instance, the sword that *he* wore hanging from his waist was clearly such a thing.

This short sword, which all the middle-school students were admiring, was truly a beautiful ornament. It was said that the students at the Naval Academy were in the habit of using their swords secretly to sharpen their pencils. How elegant, I thought, to use so solemn a symbol for trifling matters of this sort!

It happened that the young man had taken off his Engineering School uniform and hung it on the white fence. The trousers and the white undershirt, as they hung there directly next to all the flowers—yes, it was the smell of a young man's sweat-moistened skin that they gave off. A bee mistakenly alighted on that white, shining shirt-flower. The uniform cap, adorned with its gold braid, rested on one part of the fence; just as if it were on its wearer's head, the cap sat there correctly, pulled down over the eyes. Its owner had been challenged by one of his juniors and had gone to the wrestling-ring in the back to engage in a bout.

Looking at these objects that he had discarded, I had the impression that I was seeing a sort of honorable grave. The abundant May flowers strengthened this feeling. The

26

cap, which reflected the jet black of the visor, and the sword and its leather belt, which were hanging there next to it, had all been separated from his body and exuded an especially lyrical beauty. They were themselves as perfect as my memory of him—indeed, they looked to me like relics left by a young hero who has departed for the battle front.

I made sure that there was no one about. I heard the sound of cheering from the direction of the wrestling-ring. From my pocket I took out the rusty knife that I used for sharpening my pencils; then I crept up to the fence, and on the back of the beautiful black scabbard of the sword I engraved several ugly cuts. . . .

From a description of this sort, people may judge at once that I must have been something of a young poet. But until this very day, far from ever having written a poem, I have not so much as written a memorandum in a notebook. I had no particular impulse to outshine others by cultivating some new ability and by thus making up for those points in which I was inferior. In other words, I was too proud to be an artist. My dream of being a tyrant or a great artist never went beyond the stage of being a dream, and I did not have the slightest feeling of wanting to accomplish something by actually putting my hands to it.

Because the fact of not being understood by other people had become my only real source of pride, I was never confronted by any impulse to express things and to make others understand something that I knew. I thought that those things which could be seen by others were not ordained for me. My solitude grew more and more obese, just like a pig.

All of a sudden my memory alights on a tragic incident that occurred in our village. Though I was not actually supposed to have been concerned in any way with this incident, I still cannot rid myself of the definite feeling that I participated in it.

Through this incident, I found myself at a single stroke face to face with everything. With life, with carnal pleasure, with treachery, with hatred and with love—yes, with every possible thing in this world. And my memory

27

preferred to deny and to overlook the element of the sublime that lurked in all these things.

Two houses away from my uncle's home there lived a pretty girl. She was called Uiko. Her eyes were large and clear. Perhaps because hers was a rich family, she had a haughty manner. Although people used to make much of her, one could not imagine what she was thinking when she was all by herself. Uiko was probably still a virgin, but jealous women used to gossip about her and say that her looks betokened a sterile woman.

Immediately after graduating from the Girls' Secondary School, Uiko became a volunteer nurse at the Maizuru Naval Hospital. The hospital was near enough for her to be able to go to work by bicycle. She had to report very early in the mornings and she left home in the gray light of dawn, some two hours before I set out for school.

One evening I lay sunk in gloomy fancies, thinking about Uiko's body. I could not sleep properly that night and, while it was still dark, I slipped out of my bed, put on my gym shoes and went out into the obscurity of a summer dawn.

That night was not the first time that I had pictured Uiko's body to myself. Something that had occasionally passed through my mind came gradually to adhere to it. Uiko's body, as though it were a coagulation of these thoughts of mine, became immersed in a gloomy shadow, which was both white and resilient; it came to congeal in the form of scented flesh. I used to think of the warmth that my fingers would feel when I touched that flesh. I thought, too, about the resilience which would meet my fingers and about the scent which would be like that of pollen.

I ran straight along the road in the dawn darkness. The stones did not make me lose my footing and the darkness freely opened up the road ahead of me.

I came to a place where the road widened and led into the little hamlet of Yasuoka. Here grew a great *keyaki* tree. The trunk of the *keyaki* tree was moist with dew. I hid at the foot of the tree and waited for Uiko's bicycle to come from the direction of the village.

I had no idea of what I meant to do after I had waited. I had come running along here out of breath, but now that I had rested in the shade of the *keyaki* tree, I did not know myself what I was intending to do. I had, however, been living too much out of touch with the external world, and had as a result conceived the fancy that, once I leaped into the outer world, everything became easy, everything became possible.

The mosquitoes stung my legs. I heard cocks crowing here and there. I peered up the road. In the distances I saw something white and indistinct. I thought that it was the color of the dawn, but it was Uiko.

She was riding her bicycle. The headlight was turned on. The bicycle glided along silently. I ran out from the *keyaki* tree and stood in front of the bicycle. The bicycle just managed to come to a sudden halt.

Then I felt that I had been turned into stone. My will, my desire—everything had become stone. The outer world had lost contact with my inner world, and had once again come to surround me and to assume a positive existence. The "I" who had slipped out of his uncle's house, put on white gym shoes and run along this path through the darkness of the dawn until reaching the *keyaki* tree—that "I" had made merely its inner self run hither at full speed. In the village roofs whose dim outlines emerged in the darkness of the dawn, in the black trees, in the black summits of the Aobayama, yes, even in Uiko who now stood before me, there was a complete and terrible meaninglessness. Something had bestowed reality on all this without waiting for my participation; and this great, meaningless, utterly dark reality was given to me, was pressed on me, with a weight that I had until then never witnessed.

As usual, it occurred to me that words were the only things that could possibly save me from this situation. This was a characteristic misunderstanding on my part. When action was needed, I was always absorbed in words; for words proceeded with such difficulty from my mouth that I was intent on them and forgot all about action. It

29

seemed to me that actions, which are dazzling, varied things, must always be accompanied by equally dazzling and equally varied words.

I was not looking at anything. Uiko, as I recall, was frightened at first, but, when she realized that it was I, she only looked at my mouth. She was, I suppose, looking at that silly little dark hole, that ill-formed little hole which was soiled like the nest of a small animal of the fields, and which now wriggled meaninglessly in the early dawn light—she was only looking at my mouth. And, having satisfied herself that not the slightest power was going to emanate from that mouth to connect me with the outside world, she felt relieved.

"Good heavens!" she said. "What an extraordinary thing to do. And you only a stutterer!"

Uiko's voice carried the freshness and propriety of a morning breeze. She rang the bell of her bicycle and once more put her feet to the pedals. She bicycled round me, as though she were avoiding a stone on the road. Though there was not another soul about, Uiko scornfully rang the bell of her bicycle again and again, and as she pedaled away, I could hear it echoing across the distant fields.

That evening, as a result of Uiko's having told on me, her mother called at my uncle's house. My uncle, who was usually so gentle, scolded me harshly. I cursed Uiko then and came to wish for her death; and a few months later my curse was realized. Ever since then I have firmly believed in the power of curses.

Day and night I wished for Uiko's death. I wished that the witness of my disgrace would disappear. If only no witnesses remained, my disgrace would be eradicated from the face of the earth. Other people are all witnesses. If no other people exists, shame could never be born in the world. What I had seen in Uiko's visage, behind those eyes of hers which shone like water in the dark, dawn light, was the world of other people—the world, that is, of other people who will never leave us alone, who will stand ready as the partners and witnesses of our crime. Other people must all be destroyed. In order that I might truly face the sun, the world itself must be destroyed. . . .

Two months after she had told on me, Uiko gave up her job at the Naval Hospital and stayed at home. There was all sorts of gossip in the village. Then, at the end of autumn, the incident occurred.

We never so much as dreamed that a deserter from the Navy had taken refuge in our village. At about noon one day a member of the *kempei-tai* military police came to our village office. But it was no such rare thing for the *kempei* to come and we did not attach any particular importance to the visit.

It was a bright day towards the end of October. I had attended my classes as usual, finished my evening homework and was ready for bed. As I was about to turn out the light, I glanced out of the window and heard people running along the village street; they sounded out of breath like a pack of dogs. I went downstairs. My aunt and uncle had woken up, and we all went out together. One of my schoolmates was standing at the entrance of the house. His eyes were wide open with surprise.

"The *kempei* have just caught Uiko," he shouted to us. "They've got her over there. Let's go and look!"

I slipped on my sandals and started running. It was a lovely moonlit night and here and there in the harvested fields the rice racks threw clear shadows on the ground.

Behind a cluster of trees I could see the movement of a group of dark silhouettes. Uiko was sitting on the ground in a black dress. Her face was extremely white. Round about her stood some *kempei* and her parents. One of the *kempei* was holding out something that looked like a lunch box and he was shouting. Her father was turning his head from one side to the other, now apologizing to the *kempei*, now reproaching his daughter. Her mother was crouched on the ground and was crying.

We were observing the scene from the far end of a rice field. The number of spectators gradually increased and their shoulders touched each other silently in the night. Above our heads hung the moon as small as if it had been squeezed.

My schoolmate whispered an explanation into my ear. It appeared that Uiko had stolen out of her house with the lunch box and was setting off for the next village when she was caught by the *kempei*, who had been lying in ambush for her. She had clearly intended to deliver the lunch box to the deserter. Uiko had grown intimate with this deserter while she was working at the Naval Hospital; as a result she had become pregnant and had been dismissed. The *kempei* was now cross-examining her about the deserter's hiding place, but Uiko just sat there without moving an inch and remained obdurately silent.

For my part, I could only gaze unblinkingly at Uiko's face. She looked like a madwoman who has been caught. Her face was motionless under the moon.

Until then I had never seen a face so full of rejection. My face, I thought, was one that had been rejected by the world, but Uiko's face was rejecting the world. The moonlight was mercilessly pouring over her forehead, her eyes, the bridge of her nose, her cheeks; but her motionless face was merely washed by the light. If she had moved her eyes or her mouth even a little, the world, which she was striving to reject, would have taken this as a signal to come surging into her.

I gazed at it and held my breath. At the face whose history had been interrupted at just this point, and which would not tell a single thing regarding either the future or the past. Sometimes we see such a face on the stump of a tree that has just been chopped down. Though the cross section of the tree is young and fresh in color, all growth has ceased at this point; it is open to the wind and the sun, to which it should never have been opened; it is exposed suddenly to a world which was not originally its own—and on this cross section, drawn with the beautiful grain of the wood, we see a strange face. A face that is held out to this world just so that it may reject it. . . .

I could not help thinking that never again would there come a time either in Uiko's life or in the life of myself, the onlooker, when her face would be as beautiful as it was at this instant. But it did not last as long as I had expected. For a transformation suddenly came over that beautiful face of hers.

Uiko stood up. I have the impression that at that

moment I saw her laugh. I have the impression that I saw her white teeth glittering in the moonlight. I can say no more about this transformation; for, as Uiko stood up, her face moved away from the moonlight and was lost in the shade of the trees.

It was a shame that I could not see this change that came over Uiko at the moment when she decided on betrayal. If I had in fact seen it in all its details, there might have sprouted up within me a spirit of forgiveness for people, a spirit that would forgive every sort of ugliness.

Uiko pointed in the direction of the mountain cove of Kahara in the next village.

"Ah, so he's in the Kongo Temple!" shouted the *kempei.*

Then I was infused with a childish sense of festive gaiety. The *kempei* decided to split into separate groups and surround the Kongo Temple from all sides. The villagers were called on to give their assistance. Out of spiteful interest, I joined a few other boys in the first party. Uiko walked ahead of our party as a guide. I was surprised at the confidence in her footsteps as she walked before us along the moonlit path, flanked by the *kempei.*

The Kongo Temple was a famous place. It was built in a mountain cove about fifteen minutes by foot from the hamlet of Yasuoka, and was known for the *kaya* tree planted by Prince Takaoka and for its graceful three-storied pagoda attributed to Hidari Jingoro. In the summer we often used to come here to bathe in the waterfall behind the hills.

The wall of the main temple was by the side of the river. The pampas grass grew thickly on the broken clods of earth and their white ears shone brightly in the night. Near the gate of the main temple the sasanqua were in bloom. Our party walked silently along the river.

The hall of the Kongo Temple was above us. When one crossed the log bridge, the three-storied pagoda lay on one's right; to the left stretched the forest with its autumn leaves, and in the depth of the trees towered the one hundred and five stone steps overgrown with moss. The steps were made of limestone and were quite slippery.

Before crossing the log bridge, the *kempei* looked back and made a signal for our party to halt. It is said that in olden times a Deva gate used to stand here which had been built by the famous sculptors Unkei and Tankei. Beyond this point, the hills of the Kujuku Valley belonged to the Kongo Temple grounds.

We held our breath.

The *kempei* urged Uiko on. She crossed the log bridge by herself and after a while we followed her. The lower part of the stone steps was wrapped in shadows, but higher up they were bathed in moonlight. We hid ourselves here and there at the bottom of the steps. The leaves were beginning to assume their russet autumn tints, but they looked black in the moonlight.

The main hall of the Kongo Temple was at the top of the steps. A gallery led from here to an empty hall, which looked as if it was designed for the performance of sacred Kagura dances. This empty hall was modeled on the stage of the Kiyomizu Temple: it projected over the hill and was supported from under the cliff by a number of interjoined pillars and crosspieces. The hall, the gallery, and the wooden frame that supported it were all washed by the wind and rain. They gleamed pure white like a skeleton. When the leaves were in their full blaze of autumn color, their red tints blended beautifully with this white skeletal structure; but at night the blanched wooden frame, dappled by the moonlight, looked mysterious and bewitching.

The deserter was apparently hiding in the hall above the stage. The *kempei* intended to capture him by using Uiko as a decoy.

We, the witnesses to the impending arrest, hid ourselves and held our breath. Though the cold air of the late October night wrapped itself about me, my cheeks were burning.

By herself Uiko climbed the one hundred and five limestone steps. Proudly like some madwoman. The beautiful white of her profile stood out between her black dress and her black hair.

34

Amid the moon and the stars, amid the clouds of the night, amid the hills which bordered on the sky with their magnificent silhouette of pointed cedars, amid the speckled patches of the moon, amid the temple buildings that emerged sparkling white out of the surrounding darkness—amid all this, I was intoxicated by the pellucid beauty of Uiko's treachery. This girl was qualified to walk alone up those white stairs, proudly throwing out her chest. Her treachery was the same as the stars and the moon and the pointed cedars. In other words, she was living in the same world as we, the witnesses; and she was accepting the nature that surrounded us all. She was walking up those steps as our representative. And I could not help thinking breathlessly: "By her betrayal she has at last accepted me too. Now she belongs to me!"

At a certain point, what we call events disappear from within our memory. The Uiko who was walking up those one hundred and five moss-covered steps remains before my eyes. It seems to me that she is walking up those steps eternally.

But from that point on, she became someone entirely different. Perhaps it is that the Uiko who climbed those steps betrayed me, betrayed us, once again. From that point on, she no longer rejected the world in its entirety. Nor did she entirely accept it. She surrendered herself to the order of mere passion; she lowered herself to the rank of a woman who has given herself over to one man alone.

It is for this reason that I can only remember what follows as though it were a scene depicted in some old lithograph. Uiko walked along the gallery and called into the darkness of the temple hall. The silhouette of a man appeared. Uiko said something to him. The man pointed a revolver at the stone stairs and fired. The return fire from the *kempei* came from behind a nearby bush. The man was getting ready to shoot once more when Uiko turned towards the gallery and started to run. He fired one shot after another into her back. Uiko fell down. The man put the muzzle of the revolver to his temple and fired once again.

First the *kempei*, then all the others, pushed their way

up the steps and rushed toward the two dead bodies. I remained hidden quietly in the shadow of the autumn leaves. The white wooden frames of the temple, piled on top of each other in every direction, towered above my head. The sound of people's feet as they walked along the wooden boards of the gallery above me came fluttering down lightly. The criss-crossing light of torches passed over the railing of the gallery and reached the red-leaved branches of the trees.

My only feeling was that all this was taking place in the distant past. Insensitive people are only upset when they actually see the blood. Yet, by the time that blood has been shed, the tragedy is already completed. I dozed off. When I awoke, I saw that everyone had left. They had evidently forgotten all about me. The air was full of the twittering of birds, and the morning sun shone directly through the leaves of the surrounding trees. The skeletal buildings above me seemed to revive as the sun illuminated them from below. Quietly and proudly the temple thrust forth its empty hall into the red-leaved valley.

I stood up, shivered, and rubbed myself to stimulate my circulation. The chill alone remained in my body. All that remained was the chill.

During the spring holidays of the following year, Father visited my uncle's house. Over a wartime civilian uniform he wore his robe. He said that he would take me to Kyoto for a few days. Father's old illness had become much worse and I was shocked to see how he had declined. Not only I, but my uncle and aunt all tried to dissuade Father from the trip, but he would not listen to us. When I thought about it afterwards, I realized that Father wanted while he was still alive to introduce me to the Superior of the Golden Temple.

To visit the Golden Temple had of course been my dream for many a long year, but I did not enjoy the idea of going on a journey with Father, who, for all his stouthearted efforts, was bound to impress anyone who saw him as being extremely ill. As the time approached for me to come face to face with the Golden Temple, which I had never yet seen, a certain hesitation grew within me. Whatever happened, it was essential that the Golden Temple be beautiful. I therefore staked everything not so much on the objective beauty of the temple itself as on my own power to imagine its beauty.

I was thoroughly versed concerning the Golden Temple, in so far as it was possible for a boy of my age to understand it. In an art book, I had read the following perfunctory account of the history of the temple.

"Ashikaga Yoshimitsu (1358-1408) took over the Kitayama Mansion of the Saionji family and turned it into a large-scale villa. The main buildings consist of Buddhist structures, such as the Reliquary, the Hall of the Sacred Fire, the Confessional Hall, and the Hosui-in; and residential apartments, such as the Shinden, the Hall of the Lords, the Assembly Hall, the Tenkyo Tower, the Kohoku Turret, the Izumi Hall, and the Kansetsu Pavilion. The Reliquary was the most carefully constructed of all these buildings, and later came to be called the Golden Temple. It is difficult to determine exactly when it first acquired the name of the Golden Temple, but it would appear to have been subsequent to the Ojin War (1467-77). In the Bummei Period (1469-87) the name was in current use.

"The Golden Temple is a three-storied tower structure overlooking a pond in a garden (the Kyoko Pond). It was probably completed in about the fifth year of Oei (1398). The first two stories were built in the *shinden-zukuri* style of domestic architecture and equipped with folding-shutters, but the third story consists of an eighteen-foot-square apartment built in pure Zen style. The roof, which is covered with cypress bark, is in the *hokei-zukuri* style, and is surmounted with a copper-gold phoenix. The Tsuri Hall with its gable roof jutted out facing the pond and broke the monotony of the surrounding architecture. The roof of the Golden Temple is gently sloped, and made of fine-grained wood. The structure is both light and elegant. This is a masterpiece of garden architecture, in which the residential style has been made to harmonize with the

37

Buddhist style. Thus the temple expresses the taste of Ashikaga Yoshimitsu, who so wholeheartedly adopted the culture of the Imperial Court, and it perfectly conveys the atmosphere of the period.

"After Yoshimitsu's death, the Kitayama Hall was made into a Zen temple, according to Yoshmitsu's wishes, and was known as the Rokuonji. Later, these structures were transferred elsewhere or allowed to fall into dilapidation. By good fortune, the Golden Temple itself remains. . . ."

Like a moon that hangs in the night sky, the Golden Temple had been built as a symbol of the dark ages. Therefore it was necessary for the Golden Temple of my dreams to have darkness bearing down on it from all sides. In this darkness, the beautiful, slender pillars of the building rested quietly and steadily, emitting a faint light from inside. Whatever words people might speak to the Golden Temple, it must continue to stand there silently, displaying its delicate structure to the eyes of the world and enduring the darkness that surrounded it.

I also used to think of the copper-gold phoenix, which crowned the roof of the Golden Temple and which had remained there year after year exposed to the elements. This mysterious golden bird never crowed at the break of dawn, never flapped its wings—indeed, it had itself no doubt completely forgotten that it was a bird. Yet it would be untrue to say that this bird did not look as if it were flying. Other birds fly through the air, but this golden phoenix was flying eternally through time on its shining wings. Time struck those wings. Time struck those wings and floated backwards. In order to fly, the phoenix remained motionless, with a look of anger in its eyes, holding its wings aloft, fluttering the feathers of its tail, bravely stretching its majestic golden legs.

When my thoughts moved in such directions, the Golden Temple would seem to me like some beautiful ship crossing the sea of time. The art book spoke of "draughty buildings with insufficient walls," and this too brought to my imagination the form of a ship. The pond, which this complex, three-storied pleasure boat overlooked, could be regarded as a symbol of the sea. The Golden Temple had made its way through an immense night. A crossing whose end one could still not foresee. In the daytime, this strange ship lowered its anchor with a look of innocence and submitted to being viewed by crowds of people; but when night came, the surrounding darkness lent the ship a new force and it floated away, with its roof billowing like a great sail.

It is no exaggeration to say that the first real problem I faced in my life was that of beauty. My father was only a simple country priest, deficient in vocabulary, and he taught me that "there is nothing on this earth so beautiful as the Golden Temple." At the thought that beauty should already have come into this world unknown to me, I could not help feeling a certain uneasiness and irritation. If beauty really did exist there, it meant that my own existence was a thing estranged from beauty.

But for me the Golden Temple was never simply an idea. The mountains blocked it from my sight, yet, if I should want to see it, the temple was always there for me to go and see. Beauty was thus an object that one could touch with one's fingers, that could be clearly reflected in one's eyes. I knew and I believed that, amid all the changes of the world, the Golden Temple remained there safe and immutable.

There were times when I thought of the Golden Temple as being like a small, delicate piece of workmanship that I could put in my hands; there were times, also, when I thought of it as a huge, monstrous cathedral that soared up endlessly into the sky. Being a young boy, I could not think of beauty as being neither small nor large, but a thing of moderation. So when I saw small, dew-drenched summer flowers that seemed to emit a vague light, they seemed to me as beautiful as the Golden Temple. Again, when the gloomy, thunder-packed clouds stood boldly on the other side of the hills, with only the edges shining in gold, their magnificence reminded me of the Golden Temple. Finally it came about that even when I saw a beautiful face, the simile would spring into my mind: "lovely as the Golden Temple."

It was a sad journey. The Maizuru-line trains went from West Maizuru to Kyoto by way of Ayabe and stopped at all the small stations like Makura and Uesugi. The carriage was dirty, and when we reached the Hozu Ravine and began to go through one tunnel after another, the smoke poured in mercilessly and made Father cough again and again.

Most of the passengers were connected in one way or another with the Navy. The third-class carriages were full of relatives who were on their way back from visiting petty officers, sailors, marines, and arsenal workers stationed in Maizuru.

I looked out of the window at the cloudy, leaden spring sky. I looked at the robe that Father wore over his civilian uniform, and at the breast of a ruddy young petty officer, which seemed to leap up along his row of gilt buttons. I felt as if I were situated between the two men. Soon, when I reached the proper age, I would be called into the forces. Yet I was not sure that even when I was called up, I would be able to live faithfully by my duty, like that petty officer in front of me. In any case, for the present I was situated squarely between two worlds. Although I was still so young, I was conscious, under my ugly, stubborn forehead, that the world of death which my father ruled and the world of life occupied by young people were being brought together by the mediation of war. I myself would probably become an intermediary. When I was killed in the war, it would be clear that it had not made the slightest difference which path I had chosen of the two that now lay before my eyes.

I tried to look after my father when he coughed. Now and then I caught sight of the Hozu River outside the window. It was a dark-blue, almost heavy color, like the copper sulfate used in chemistry experiments. Each time that the train emerged from a tunnel, the Hozu Ravine would appear either some considerable distance from the tracks or unexpectedly close at hand. Surrounded by the smooth rocks, it turned its dark-blue lathe round and round.

Father had some pure white rice balls in his lunch box

and he felt ashamed of opening it in front of the other people in the carriage.

"It's not black-market rice," he announced. "It comes from the good hearts of my parishioners. I can eat it with joy and gratitude."

He spoke so that everyone in the carriage could hear him, but when he actually began eating, he was barely able to finish one rather small rice ball.

I did not feel that this ancient sooty train was really bound for the city. I felt that it was headed for the station of death. Once this thought had come into my mind, the smoke that filled our carriage each time that we passed through a tunnel had the smell of the crematorium.

Despite it all, when finally I stood before the Somon Gate of the Rokuonji, my heart was throbbing. Now I was to see one of the most beautiful things in the world.

The sun was beginning to go down and the hills were veiled in mist. Several other visitors were passing through the gate at about the same time as Father and I. On the left of the gate stood the belfry, surrounded by a cluster of plum trees, which were still in bloom.

A great oak tree grew in front of the Main Hall. Father stood in the entrance and asked for admission. The Superior sent a message that he was busy with a visitor and asked us if we would wait for a while.

"Let's use this time to go round and look at the Golden Temple," said Father.

Father evidently wanted to show me that he exerted some influence in this place and he tried to go through the visitors' entrance without paying the admission fee. But both the man who sold tickets and religious charms and the ticket collector at the gate had changed since the time, some ten years earlier, when Father used to come often to the temple.

"Next time I come," said Father with a chilly expression, "I suppose they'll have changed again."

But I felt that Father no longer really believed in this "next time."

I hurried ahead of Father, almost running. I was

deliberately acting like a cheerful young boy. (It was only at such times—only when I put on a deliberate performance—that there was anything boyish about me.) Then the Golden Temple, about which I had dreamed so much, displayed its entire form to me most disappointingly.

I stood by the edge of the Kyoko Pond, and on the other side of the water the Golden Temple revealed its façade in the declining sun. The Sosei was half hidden farther to the left. The Golden Temple cast a perfect shadow on the surface of the pond, where the duckweed and the leaves from water plants were floating. The shadow was more beautiful than the building itself. The setting sun was making the reflection of the water wave to and fro on the back of the eaves of all three stories. Compared to the surrounding light, the reflection of the back of the eaves was too dazzling and clear; the Golden Temple gave me the impression that it was proudly bending itself back.

"Well, what do you think?" said Father. "It's beautiful, isn't it? The first story is called the Hosui-in, the second is the Choondo, and the third is the Kukyocho." Father placed his ill, emaciated hand on my shoulder.

I changed my angle of vision a few times and bent my head in various directions. But the temple aroused no emotion within me. It was merely a small, dark, old, three-storied building. The phoenix on top of the roof looked like a crow that had alighted there for a rest. Not only did the building fail to strike me as beautiful, but I even had a sense of disharmony and restlessness. Could beauty, I wondered, be as unbeautiful a thing as this?

If I had been a modest, studious boy, I should have regretted my own deficiency in aesthetic appreciation before becoming so quickly discouraged as I did. But the pain of having been deceived by something of which I had expected so much robbed me of all other considerations.

It occurred to me that the Golden Temple might have adopted some disguise to hide its true beauty. Was it not possible that, in order to protect itself from people, the beauty deceived those who observed it? I had to approach the Golden Temple closer; I had to remove the obstacles that seemed ugly to my eyes; I had to examine it all, detail by detail, and with these eyes of mine perceive the essence of its beauty. Inasmuch as I believed only in the beauty that one can see with one's eyes, my attitude at the time was quite natural.

With a respectful air Father now led me up to the open corridor of the Hosui-in. First I looked at the skillfully executed model of the Golden Temple that rested in a glass case. This model pleased me. It was closer to the Golden Temple of my dreams. Observing this perfect little image of the Golden Temple within the great temple itself, I was reminded of the endless series of correspondences that arise when a small universe is placed in a large universe and a smaller one in turn placed inside the small universe. For the first time I could dream. Of the small, but perfect Golden Temple which was even smaller than this model; and of the Golden Temple which was infinitely greater than the real building—so great, indeed, that it almost enveloped the world.

I did not, however, remain standing indefinitely before the model. Next Father led me to the wooden statue of Yoshimitsu, which was famous as a National Treasure. The statue was known as the Rokuoninden-Michiyoshi, after the name that Yoshimitsu adopted when he took the tonsure.

This, too, struck me as being nothing but an odd, sooty image and I could sense no beauty in it. Next we went up to the Choondo on the second story and looked at the painting on the ceiling, attributed to Kano Masanobu, which depicted angels playing music. On the third story, the Kukyocho, I saw the pathetic remains of the gold leaf that had originally covered all the interior. I could find no beauty in any of this.

I leaned against the slender railing and looked down absently at the pond, on which the evening sun was shining. The surface of the water looked like a mirror, like an ancient patinated copper mirror; and the shadow of the Golden Temple fell directly on this surface. The evening sky was reflected in the water, far beneath the water plants and the duckweed. This sky was different from the one above our heads. It was clear and filled with a serene light; from underneath and from within, it entirely swallowed up this earthly world of ours, and the Golden Temple sank into it like a great anchor of pure gold that has become entirely black with rust.

Father Tayama Dosen, the Superior of the temple, had been a friend of Father's when they had studied at a certain Zen temple. They had both spent three years at the temple and during this time had lived together. The two young men had attended the special seminary at the Sokoku Temple (which also was constructed under the Shogun Yoshimitsu) and, after going through certain ancient procedures of the Zen sect, they had entered the priesthood. Apart from all this, I learned much later from Father Dosen, one day when he was talking to me in a good mood, that my father and he had not only shared rigorous days of training, but that on some evenings after bedtime they had climbed over the temple wall together and gone out to buy women and enjoy themselves.

Father and I, having finished our tour of the temple, returned to the entrance of the Main Hall. We were ushered down a lengthy, spacious hall and shown into the office of the Superior, which was in the Great Library, overlooking the garden with its famous old pine tree.

I sat there straight and stiff in my school uniform, but Father suddenly seemed to be at ease. Although my father and the Superior had been trained at the same Zen school, they could hardly have been more different in appearance. Father was emaciated from his illness, he looked poor, and his skin had a dry, powdery quality. Father Dosen, on the other hand, looked just like a pink cake. On his desk lay piles of unopened parcels, magazines, books, and letters, which had been sent from various parts of the country, and which seemed to bespeak the prosperity of the temple. He picked up a pair of scissors with his plump fingers and adroitly opened one of the parcels.

"It's a cake that someone's sent from Tokyo," he explained. "You don't see such cakes very often these days. I'm told they don't distribute them to the shops any

44

longer, but send them all to the forces or to government offices."

We drank delicate Japanese tea and ate a sort of dry Western cake that I had never tasted before. The more tense I became, the more the crumbs dropped from the cake onto my shiny, black-serge trousers.

Father and the Superior were expressing their resentment at the fact that the army and the officials were only giving consideration to the Shinto shrines and were looking down on the Buddhist temples—not only looking down on them, in fact, but actually oppressing them; then they discussed how it would be best to handle the administration of the temples in the future.

The Superior was a plump man. His face was wrinkled, to be sure, but each of the wrinkles looked as if it was thoroughly washed out. His face was round, but he had a long nose, which gave one the impression that the resin which flowed from it had somehow become solidified. Though his face looked easy-going enough, there was a stern air about his shaven head. It was as though all his energy was concentrated in that head: there was a terribly animal quality about it.

The conversation of the two priests now turned to their days in the seminary. I was looking at the Sailboat Pine Tree in the garden. It had been formed by lowering the branches of a great pine and coiling them together in the shape of a boat, with the branches at the prow all trained at a higher level than the rest. A party of visitors had evidently arrived just before closing-time and I could hear a hum of voices from the direction of the Golden Temple on the other side of the wall. Their footsteps and voices were absorbed in the air of spring evening: the sound they made was soft and rounded, without any trace of sharpness. Then as their footsteps receded like the tide, they seemed to me to be truly the footsteps of human beings passing over the earth. I stared up at the phoenix on the summit of the Golden Temple; it was absorbing all that remained of the evening light.

"Now this child, you see . . ." Hearing Father's words, I turned towards him. In the almost dark room, Father was

45

about to entrust my future to Father Dosen.

"I don't think I shall live much longer," Father said. "I want to ask you to look after this child when the time comes."

Priest though he was and accustomed to comforting people at times like these, Father Dosen had no soothing words for this occasion, but simply answered: "Very well, I'll look after him."

What really astonished me was that they then embarked merrily on an exchange of anecdotes about the deaths of various famous priests. One of them had died saying: "Oh, I don't want to die!" Another had ended his life with Goethe's own words: "More light!" Still another famous priest had evidently been counting the temple money until the very moment that he died.

We were offered an evening meal, known to Buddhists as "medicine," and it was arranged that we should spend that night in the temple. After dinner I persuaded Father to come and have another look at the Golden Temple. For the moon had come out.

Father had been overstimulated by meeting the Superior again after so many years and he was quite exhausted; but when he heard me speak of the Golden Temple, he came out with me, breathing heavily and leaning on my shoulder.

The moon rose from the edge of Mount Fudo. The back of the Golden Temple received its light. The building seemed to fold up its dark, complicated shadow and to subside quietly; only the frames of the Kato windows in the Kukyocho allowed the smooth shadows of the moon to slip into the building. The Kukyocho had no proper walls, and so it seemed that this was where the faint moonlight had its dwelling.

From Ashiwara Island came the cry of the night birds as they flew off into the distance. I was conscious of the weight of Father's emaciated hands on my shoulders. When I glanced at my shoulder, I saw that in the moonlight Father's hand had turned into that of a skeleton.

After my return to Yasuoka, the Golden Temple, which had disappointed me so greatly at first sight, began to revivify its beauty within me day after day, until in the end it became a more beautiful Golden Temple than it had been before I saw it. I could not say wherein this beauty lay. It seemed that what had been nurtured in my dreams had become real and could now, in turn, serve as an impulse for further dreams.

Now I no longer pursued the illusion of a Golden Temple in nature and in the objects that surrounded me. Gradually the Golden Temple came to exist more deeply and more solidly within me. Each of its pillars, its Kato windows, its roof, the phoenix at the top, floated clearly before my eyes, as though I could touch them with my hands. The minutest part of the temple was in perfect accord with the entire complex structure. It was like hearing a few notes of music and having the entire composition flow through one's mind: whichever part of the Golden Temple I might pick out, the entire building echoed within me.

"It was true when you told me that the Golden Temple was the most beautiful thing in this world." So I wrote for the first time in a letter to Father. After taking me back to my uncle's house, Father had immediately returned to his temple on the remote cape. As if in reply to my letter, a telegram came from my mother saying that Father had suffered a terrible hemorrhage and was dead.

CHAPTER TWO

Owing to Father's death, my real period of boyhood came
to an end. I had always been astonished at the fact that
my boyhood was so utterly lacking in what may be called

human concern. When I came to realize that I felt not the slightest sorrow over Father's death, this astonishment turned into a certain powerless emotion that no longer belonged to the category of surprise.

I hurried over to Father's village and, when I arrived, he was already lying in his coffin. I had walked as far as Uchiura and from there gone by boat along the bay to Nariu, which had taken a whole day. It was a hot time of the year just before the rainy season, and the sun blazed down day after day. Immediately after I had seen Father's body, the coffin was taken to the crematory on the deserted cape to be cremated by the seashore.

The death of the priest in a country temple is a peculiar business. It is peculiar because it is too pertinent. The priest has been, so to say, the spiritual center of the district, the guardian of his parishioners' lives, the man to whom their posthumous existence has been entrusted. And that very person has died in his temple. It is as though he has acquitted himself too faithfully of his duty; as though the man who went about teaching others how to die has given a public demonstration of the act and by some sort of mistake has actually died himself.

Father's coffin appeared, in fact, to have been placed in too appropriate a place, in which every single preparation had already been made to receive it. My mother, the young priest, and the parishioners were standing in front of the coffin weeping. The young priest recited the sutras in a faltering tone, almost as if he were still depending on directions from Father, who lay before him in his coffin.

Father's face was buried in early summer flowers. There was something gruesome about the utter freshness of those flowers. It was as though they were peering down into the bottom of a well. For a dead man's face falls to an infinite depth beneath the surface which the face possessed when it was alive, leaving nothing for the survivors to see but the frame of a mask; it falls so deep, indeed, that it can never be pulled back to the surface. A dead man's face can tell us better than anything else in this world how far removed we are from the true existence of physical substance, how impossible it is for us to lay hands on the way in which this substance exists. This was the first time I had been confronted by a situation like this in which a spirit is transformed by death into mere physical substance; and now I felt that I was gradually beginning to understand why it was that spring flowers, the sun, my desk, the schoolhouse, pencils—all physical substance, indeed—had always seemed so cold to me, had always seemed to exist so far away from myself.

Mother and the various parishioners were now watching me as I had my last meeting with Father. My stubborn heart, however, would not accept the analogy with the land of the living that the word "meeting" implied. For this was not at all like a meeting; I was merely *looking* at Father's dead face.

The corpse was just being looked at. I was just looking. To know that *looking* (the act, that is, of looking at someone, as one ordinarily does, without any special awareness) was such a proof of the rights of those who are alive, and that this *looking* could also be an expression of cruelty—all this came to me now as a vivid experience. Thus did the young boy, who never sang loudly, who never ran about shouting at the top of his lungs, ascertain the facts of his own existence.

Although in many respects I was lacking in moral courage, I did not feel the slightest shame now in turning a bright, tearless face towards the mourners. The temple was on a cliff facing the sea. Behind the funeral guests, the summer clouds coiled themselves over the open waters of the Japan Sea and blocked my view.

The priest had now begun to chant the special Zen sutra that accompanied the removal of the body, and I joined in. The main hall of the temple was dark. The banner that was suspended between the pillars, the flower decorations in the sanctuary, the incense burner and the vases —everything sparkled brilliantly with the reflected light of the sacred taper. Now and then a sea breeze blew into the temple, puffing up the sleeves of my clerical robe. As I recited the sutras, I was constantly aware of the posture of the summer clouds as they cast a strong glare into the corner of my eyes.

An intense light poured constantly from outside the temple onto one side of my face. How brightly it shone—that insult!

When the funeral procession was only a couple of hundred yards from the crematorium, we ran into a shower. Fortunately we were just in front of the house of a well-disposed parishioner and were able to take shelter together with our coffin. The rain did not look like stopping. The procession had to continue. We were, therefore, all given raingear and, having covered the coffin with a piece of oilcloth, we continued our journey to the crematorium.

It was situated on the small stony beach of a cape that projected into the sea southeast of the village. This place had evidently been used since ancient times for cremations, because the smoke did not spread from here towards the houses.

The sea was especially rough off this point. As the great waves rolled forward, swelling and breaking, the uneasy surface was constantly pricked by the raindrops. In its obscurity, the rain calmly went on piercing the surface of the water, unaware of its extraordinary state of commotion. But now and again a gust of wind would suddenly blow the rain against the desolate rocks. Then the white rocks became as black as if a great spray of ink had been blown against them.

We went through a tunnel and reached the place. While the workmen prepared for the cremation, we stood in the tunnel to keep out of the rain.

I could not catch a glimpse of the sea itself. There was nothing but the waves and the wet, black stones, and the rain. As they poured oil over the light wood of the coffin, the rain beat down on it.

They set fire to it. Oil was rationed, but since this was the funeral of a priest, they had managed to obtain a good supply, and now the flames fought against the rain and rose into the air with the sound of a whip being cracked.

Although it was daylight, the pellucid form of the flames stood out distinctly amid the dense smoke. The smoke billowed up plumply and drifted little by little towards the cliffs; then at a certain moment, the flames rose gracefully by themselves amid the rain.

Suddenly there was a horrible sound of something being torn. The lid of the coffin had sprung open.

I looked at Mother, who was standing next to me. There she stood, holding her rosary in both hands. Her face was terribly stiff; it looked so small and congealed that one felt one could put it in the palm of one's hand.

According to Father's wishes, I went to Kyoto and became an acolyte at the Golden Temple. At this time I was ordained to the priesthood under the Father Superior. He provided me with my school expenses; in return, I attended him and did his housework. My position was equivalent in lay terms to that of a student dependent.

I realized as soon as I took service in the temple that the only people left, after our severe dormitory prefect had been called into the armed forces, were old men and extremely young ones. In more ways than one it was a great relief for me to be here. No longer was I teased for being the son of a priest as I had been by the lay students at middle school; for here everyone was in the same position. The only points of difference were that I was a stutterer and that I was a trifle uglier than the others.

My course at the East Maizuru Middle School had been interrupted before I graduated, and with the help of Father Tayama Dosen it was now arranged that I should continue my studies at the middle school of the Rinzai Academy. I was to start there in the autumn term, which began in less than a month. I knew, however, that as soon as I had started at my new school I would be mobilized for compulsory labor in some factory. I was now faced with a new set of circumstances in my life. I still had a few weeks of summer holidays left. Summer holidays during my mourning period; curiously subdued summer holidays during the last phase of the war in 1944. My life as an acolyte passed smoothly and, as I think back on it, I feel that this was the last absolute holiday in my life. I can still vividly hear the cry of the cicada.

The Golden Temple, which I now saw again after a period of several months, rested peacefully in the light of the late summer days. Having just entered the priesthood, I had a freshly shaven head. I felt that the air fitted tightly on my head; I had a strangely dangerous feeling that the thoughts which existed within my head were kept in contact with the phenomena of the outer world by a single membrane of their sensitive, fragile skin. When I looked up at the Golden Temple with this new head of mine, I felt that the building was penetrating me, not only through my eyes, but through my head also. Just as when my head responded to the sun by becoming hot and to the evening breeze by suddenly becoming cool.

"Finally I have come to live beside you, Golden Temple!" I whispered in my heart, and for a while I stopped sweeping the leaves. "It doesn't have to be at once, but please make friends with me sometime and reveal your secret to me. I feel that your beauty is something that I am very close to seeing and yet cannot see. Please let me see the real Golden Temple more clearly than I see the image of you in my mind. And furthermore, if you are indeed so beautiful that nothing in this world can compare with you, please tell me why you are so beautiful, why it is necessary for you to be beautiful."

That summer the Golden Temple seemed to use the bad war news that reached us day after day as a sort of foil against which it shone more vividly than ever. In June the Americans had landed in Saipan and the Allies were charging through the fields of Normandy. The number of visitors decreased drastically and the Golden Temple seemed to be enjoying this loneliness, this silence.

It was quite natural that wars and unrest, piles of corpses and copious blood, should enrich the beauty of the Golden Temple. For this temple had been constructed by unrest, it had been built by numerous dark-hearted owners who had one general in their midst. The unco-ordinated design of its three stories, in which the art historian could only see a blend of styles, had surely been evolved naturally from the search for a style that would crystallize all the surrounding unrest. If instead it had been built in one fixed style, the Golden Temple would have been unable to embrace the unrest and would certainly have collapsed long since.

All the same, it seemed most strange to me, as time after time I stood gazing up at the Golden Temple with my hand resting on the broom, that this building should really be existing before me. The Golden Temple that I had seen when I had spent just one night here during that past visit with Father had not given me this feeling. Now I found it hard to believe that the Golden Temple would always be here before my eyes while the long years passed.

When I had thought about it during my Maizuru days, it had seemed to me that the Temple stood permanently in one corner of Kyoto; but now that I had come to live here, it only appeared before my eyes when I was actually looking at it, and when I was asleep in the main hall, it ceased to exist. Accordingly I used to go several times a day to take a look at the Golden Temple, much to the amusement of my fellow acolytes. I was always overcome by amazement at the fact that the temple was actually there, and when I returned to the hall after a good look at the building, I felt that if I were suddenly to turn round and look again, its form would vanish exactly like that of Eurydice.

When I had finished sweeping round the Golden Temple, I went to the hill in the back to avoid the morning sun which was gradually becoming hot, and climbed the path towards the Yukatei. It was still before opening-time and there was not a soul to be seen. A formation of fighter planes, probably from the Maizuru air-force squadron, passed overhead, flying fairly low over the Golden

Temple, and disappeared leaving an oppressive sound in its wake.

In the hills at the back there was a solitary pond covered with duckweed, known as the Yasutamizawa. There was a minute island in the pond and on it stood the Shirahebizuka, a five-storied stone tower. The surrounding morning air was noisy with the twittering of birds; none of the birds was to be seen, but the whole forest was twittering with them.

The summer grass grew in thick clusters in front of the pond. The path was separated from the grass by a low fence. Next to it lay a young boy in a white shirt. A bamboo rake leaned nearby against a low maple.

The boy raised his body with such energy that he seemed to be gouging a hole in the soft summer air which hovered about us; but when he saw me, he simply said: "Oh, it's you, is it?"

I had only been introduced to this boy on the previous evening. His name was Tsurukawa and he came from a prosperous temple in the suburbs of Tokyo. He was affluently provided by his family with school expenses, pocket money, and provisions, and had simply been consigned to the Golden Temple through some connection with the Superior, so that he might have a taste of the training given to ordinary acolytes. He had gone home for his summer holiday and had returned to Kyoto late on the previous afternoon. Tsurukawa talked smoothly in a splendid Tokyo accent. He was supposed to enter the middle school of the Rinzai Academy that autumn in the same class as myself, and already last night I had been abashed by his fast, cheerful manner of speech.

Now when I heard him say "Oh, it's you," my mouth lost its words. He seemed to interpret my silence as a sort of criticism.

"It's all right, you know. We don't have to sweep all that carefully. The place will get dirty in any case, when the visitors come. Besides, there aren't very many visitors these days."

I gave a short laugh. This laughter of mine that I used

to emit unconsciously seemed to make some people feel friendly towards me. Thus I could not always be responsible for the detailed impressions that I made on others.

I climbed over the fence and sat down next to Tsurukawa. His arm was bent round his head and I noticed that though the outside was fairly sunburned, the inner part was so white that one could see the veins through the skin. The rays of the morning sun streamed through the trees and scattered light-green shadows on the grass. I knew instinctively that this boy would not love the Golden Temple as I did. For my attachment to the temple was entirely rooted in my own ugliness.

"I hear that your father died," said Tsurukawa.

"Yes."

Tsurukawa quickly turned his eyes to the side and, without any effort to conceal how absorbed he was in his own boyish process of reasoning, said: "The reason you like the Golden Temple so much is that it reminds you of your father, isn't it? I mean, for instance, when you look at it, you remember how much your father liked it."

I was rather pleased that his half-correct reasoning was producing no change whatsoever on my apathetic face. Evidently Tsurukawa accurately classified human feelings in the neat little drawers that he kept in his room, like boys who classify various specimens of insects; and occasionally he enjoyed taking them out for a bit of practical experimentation.

"You're very sad about your father's death, aren't you? That's why there's something lonely about you. I've thought so since I first met you last night."

His remarks did not repel me in any way. In fact, his feeling that I looked lonely gave me a certain freedom and peace of mind, and the words issued smoothly from my mouth: "There's nothing sad about it, you know."

Tsurukawa looked at me, brushing up his eyebrows, which were so long that they seemed to get in his way.

"Dear me!" he said, "so you hated your father, did you? Or at least you disliked him."

"I had nothing against him and I didn't dislike him."

"Well then, why aren't you sad?"

"Somehow or other, that's the way it is. I don't understand why myself."

Faced with this difficult problem, Tsurukawa sat straight up on the grass.

"In that case," he said, "you must have had some other sad experience."

"I really don't know," I replied.

Having spoken, I wondered why I so much enjoyed provoking doubts in the minds of others. So far as I was concerned, there was not the slightest doubt. The matter was entirely self-evident: my feelings suffered from stuttering. They never emerged on time. As a result, I felt as though the fact of Father's death and the fact of my being sad were two isolated things, having no connection and not infringing on each other in the slightest. A slight discrepancy in time, a slight delay, invariably make the feelings and the events that I have undergone revert to their disjointed condition, which, so far as I am concerned, is probably their fundamental condition. When I am sad, sorrow attacks me suddenly and without reason: it is connected with no particular event and with no motive.

Once more it ended by my being unable to explain any of this to my new friend who sat opposite me. In the end Tsurukawa began to laugh.

"You're an odd fellow, aren't you?" he said.

His white-shirted stomach rippled with laughter. The rays of the sun that poured through the swaying branches of the trees made me feel happy. Like the young man's wrinkled shirt, my life was wrinkled. But, wrinkled as it was, how white his shirt shone in the sunlight! Perhaps I too?

Leaving the outer world to itself, the temple continued according to the regular traditions of the Zen sect. Since it was summertime, we never got up later than five o'clock.

58

Getting up is known as the "opening of the rules." As soon as we were up, we started the "morning task" of reciting the sutras. This is known as the "triple return" and we recited them three times. After that, we swept the inside of the temple and mopped the floor. Then came breakfast, known as "gruel session." We ate our gruel while listening to a recitation of the special gruel-session sutra. After breakfast we engaged in such "tasks" as picking weeds, cleaning the garden, and chopping wood. Then, on school days, it was time for us to set out for our place of study.

Soon after returning from school, we had our "medicine" or evening meal. This was occasionally followed by a lecture by the Superior concerning the sacred scriptures. At nine o'clock came the "opening of the pillow," that is to say, bedtime.

Such was my daily routine, and each day my signal for waking up was the sound of the bell rung by the priest who was in charge of the kitchen and of the mealtime rituals.

There was originally supposed to be about a dozen people attached to the Golden Temple, that is, to the Rokuonji. But as a result of conscription for military service and compulsory labor, the only inhabitants, apart from the guide (who was in his seventies), the woman who did the cooking (who was in her sixties), the deacon, and the vice-deacon, were we three acolytes. The old people were moss-grown and only half alive, while we young ones were virtually children. The deacon had his hands full with the temple accounts, which were known as "auxiliary duties."

Some days after my arrival, I was given the duty of delivering the newspaper to the quarters of the Superior (whom we called our "senior teacher"). The paper arrived every day at about the time when we had finished our various morning tasks, including the cleaning. For our small group of acolytes to mop every single passage in the temple, which contained thirty-odd rooms, in the short time that was allotted to us was rough work. As soon as I had finished, I would go to the entrance to collect the newspaper, cross the front corridor where the Envoy's Hall was situated, walk round the back of the Visitors' Hall, and make my way along an intervening passage to the Great Library where my Senior Teacher would be waiting. The passages were all still damp from the mopping, and where there were hollows in the floor boards, puddles of water shone in the morning sun and wet my feet up to the ankles. Since it was summertime, this gave me a pleasant feeling. Then I knelt down outside the library and called: "May I enter, Father?"

"Huh!" came the reply.

Before stepping into the room, I wiped my wet legs with the hem of my clerical robes, a trick that I had learned from my companions. I was aware of the strong, fresh smell of the outside world that came from the newspaper print, and stealing a hasty glance at the headlines, read: "Is the Imperial Capital bound to undergo air raids?"

It may seem strange, but until then I had never thought of connecting the Golden Temple with air raids. Since Saipan had fallen, air raids on the mainland had been inevitable and the authorities were pressing forward with plans for evacuating part of Kyoto; nevertheless, so far as I was concerned, there seemed to be no relation between the semi-eternal existence of the Golden Temple and the disaster of air raids. I felt that the inherently indestructible temple and the scientific force of fire must be well aware of the complete difference between their natures, and that if they were to meet, they would automatically slip away from each other. The fact remained that the Golden Temple was in danger of soon being burned down in an air raid. Indeed, if things continued as they were, *the Golden Temple was sure to turn into ashes*. Since this idea took root within me, the Golden Temple once again increased in tragic beauty.

It was an afternoon in late summer, the day before school was to start. The Superior had gone somewhere to attend a memorial service in the company of the vice-deacon. Tsurukawa had invited me to go with him to a film, but because I was not especially interested in the idea, he immediately began to lose interest himself: such was Tsurukawa's way.

Having received a few hours' leave of absence, we left the Main Hall, wearing our Rinzai Academy middle-school caps and with leggings round our khaki trousers. The temple was bathed in the full heat of a summer day and there was not a single visitor.

"Well, where shall we go?" said Tsurukawa.

I replied that, before going anywhere, I should like to have a thorough look at the Golden Temple, because after tomorrow it would no longer be possible for us to see it at this hour of the day, and because while we were away working in the factory, the Golden Temple might very well be burned down in an air raid. I faltered and stuttered as I explained myself, and Tsurukawa listened to me with an expression of surprise and impatience. When I had finished even this short speech, the perspiration was streaming down my face, as though I had said something shameful. Tsurukawa was the only person to whom I had revealed my strange attachment to the Golden Temple. Yet in his expression there was nothing but the usual fretful look that I was accustomed to seeing in people who were trying to make out my stuttering. These are the faces that confront me. When I reveal important secrets, when I appeal to people about the resounding feelings with which the sight of beauty fills me, when I try to bring my very viscera into the open—what confronts me is a face like this. This is not the sort of face that people usually turn on others. With perfect fidelity this face is copying my own comic fretfulness; it is, so to say, a terrifying mirror of myself. At such times, however beautiful the face may be, it will be transformed into an ugliness exactly like my own. As soon as I recognize this, the important thing that I wish to express collapses into something of no importance whatsoever, like a roof tile.

Between Tsurukawa and myself were the powerful rays of the direct summer light. As he waited for my words to end, his young face gleamed with fat. Each of his

61

eyebrows was glittering gold in the sunlight and his nostrils were dilated from the sultry heat.

I finished speaking. And as soon as I finished, I was overcome with rage. Ever since I had met Tsurukawa, he had not once tried to tease me about my stuttering.

"Why?" I asked him, pressing for an explanation of his forbearance. As I have so often pointed out, derision and insults pleased me far more than sympathy.

An indescribably tender smile passed over Tsurukawa's face.

"I'm the kind that doesn't care about that sort of thing at all," he said.

I was amazed. Having been raised in the rough environment of the country, I was unfamiliar with this type of gentleness. Tsurukawa's gentleness taught me that, even if stuttering were removed from my existence, I could still remain myself. I thoroughly enjoyed being stripped stark naked. Tsurukawa's eyes, bordered with their long lashes, filtered away my stuttering and accepted the rest of me just as I was. Until then I had been under the strange illusion that to disregard my stuttering was of itself equivalent to annihilating that existence called "me."

I felt a harmony of feeling and a sense of happiness. It is little wonder that I have never been able to forget the Golden Temple as it looked at that moment. The two of us passed before the place where the old porter was dozing, walked along the deserted path by the wall, and came to the front of the Golden Temple.

I can vividly remember the scene. We two boys stood there shoulder to shoulder by the Kyoko Pond in our white shirts and our gaiters. And in front of these two figures, not separated from them by anything, rose the Golden Temple. On this last summer, in these last summer holidays, on the very last day of them—our youth hovered dizzily on the edge. The Golden Temple stood on this same edge, faced us, talked to us. To this extent had the expectation of air raids brought us and the temple closer together.

The hushed sunlight of the late summer decorated the

roof of the Kukyocho with golden foil, and the light that poured straight down filled the Golden Temple with a nocturnal darkness. Until now the imperishability of the temple had oppressed me and kept me apart from it; but its imminent destiny of being burned by an incendiary bomb brought it close to our own destiny. It might be that the Golden Temple would be destroyed before we were. At this thought, it seemed to me that the temple was living the same life as we were.

The surrounding hills with their red pines were mantled in the cry of the cicadas, as though countless invisible priests were chanting the vocation for the Extinction of Fires: *"Gya,"* they sang, *"gyakī gyakī, un nun, shifura shifura, harashifura harashifura!"*

This beautiful building was before long going to be turned into ashes, I thought. As a result, my image of the Golden Temple gradually came to be superimposed on the real temple itself in all its details, just as the copy that one has made through a piece of drawing-silk comes to be superimposed on the original painting: the roof in my image was superimposed on the real roof, the Sosei on the Sosei that extended over the pond, the railings and the windows of the Kukyocho on those railings and windows. The Golden Temple was no longer an immovable structure. It had, so to speak, been transformed into a symbol of the real world's evanescence. Owing to this process of thought, the real temple had now become no less beautiful than that of my mental image. Tomorrow, for all we knew, fire might rain down from the sky; then those slender pillars, the elegant curves of that roof, would be reduced to ash, and we should never set eyes on them again. But for the present it stood serenely before us in all its fine details, bathing in that light which was like the summer's fire.

Over the edge of the hills majestic clouds towered up, like those that I had seen out of the corner of my eyes while the sutras were being recited during Father's funeral. They were filled with a sort of stagnant light and looked down at the delicate structure of the temple. Under this strong summer light, the Golden Temple seemed to lose the various details of its form; it kept the gloomy, cold darkness wrapped inside itself, and with its mysterious outline simply ignored the dazzling world that surrounded it. Only the phoenix on the roof fastened its sharp claws firmly to its pedestal, trying not to stagger under the glare of the sun.

Bored with my lengthy gazing at the temple, Tsurukawa picked up a pebble and with the graceful motion of a pitcher threw it into the center of the shadow that the Golden Temple cast on the Kyoko Pond. The ripples spread out through the duckweed and the beautiful, delicate structure instantly crumbled to pieces.

The one year that followed until the war ended was the period during which I was most intimate with the Golden Temple, during which I was ever concerned with its safety and utterly absorbed in its beauty. It was a period during which I had seemed to pull the temple down to my own level and, believing this, was able to love it without the slightest sense of fear. The temple had not yet given me any of its evil influence or its poison.

I was encouraged by the fact the Golden Temple and I shared a common danger in this world. In this danger I had found an intermediary that could connect me with beauty. I felt that a bridge had been built between myself and the thing that until then had seemed to deny me, to keep me at a distance.

I was almost intoxicated with the thought that the fire which would destroy me would probably also destroy the Golden Temple. Existing as we did under the same curse, under the same ill-omened fiery destiny, the temple and I had come to inhabit worlds of the same dimension. Just like my own frail, ugly body, the temple's body, hard though it was, consisted of combustible carbon. At times I felt that it would be possible for me to flee this place, taking along the temple concealed in my flesh, in my system—just as a thief swallows a precious jewel when making his escape.

During that entire year I did not learn a single sutra or

read a book; instead I was busy day after day from morning till night with moral education, drill, military arts, factory work, and training for compulsory evacuation. My nature, which already tended to be dreamy, became all the more so, and thanks to the war, ordinary life receded even farther from me. For us boys, war was a dreamlike sort of experience lacking any real substance, something like an isolation ward in which one is cut off from the meaning of life.

When the first B-29's attacked Tokyo in November of 1944, it was expected that Kyoto would be raided at any time. It became my secret dream that all Kyoto should be wrapped in flames. This city was too anxious to preserve its old things just as they were; the multifarious shrines and temples were forgetting the memories of the red-hot ash that had been born from inside. When I imagined how the Great Battle of Ojin had laid waste this city, I felt that Kyoto had lost part of its beauty from having too long forgotten the unrest of war fires.

Tomorrow the Golden Temple would surely burn down. That form which had been filling the space would be lost. Even the bird on top of the temple would be revived like the classical phoenix and soar away. And the Golden Temple itself, which had until then been constrained by its form, would be freed from all rules and would drift lightly here and there, scattering a faint light on the lake and on the waters of the dark sea.

Though I waited and waited, Kyoto was never visited by an air raid. Even when I read on March 9 of the next year that the entire business district of Tokyo was a sea of flames, and that disaster was spreading far and wide, Kyoto was covered with the limpid sky of early spring. By now I was almost desperate as I waited, trying to convince myself that this early spring sky concealed within itself all manner of fire and destruction, just as a gleaming glass window hides what lies behind it. As I have already said, I was hopelessly weak in human feeling. Father's death and Mother's poverty hardly affected my inner life at all. What I dreamed of was something like a huge heavenly compressor that would bring down disasters, cataclysms and superhuman tragedies, that would crush beneath it all human beings and all objects, irrespective of their ugliness or their beauty. Sometimes the unusual brilliance of the early spring sky appeared to me like the light of the cool blade of some huge axe that was large enough to cover the entire earth. Then I just waited for the axe to fall—for it to fall with a speed that would not even give one time to think.

There is something that even now strikes me as strange. Originally I was not possessed by gloomy thoughts. My concern, what confronted me with my real problem, was beauty alone. But I do not think that the war affected me by filling my mind with gloomy thoughts. When people concentrate on the idea of beauty, they are, without realizing it, confronted with the darkest thoughts that exist in this world. That, I suppose, is how human beings are made.

I remember an episode that took place in Kyoto towards the end of the war. It was something quite unbelievable, but I was not the only witness. Tsurukawa was next to me.

One day when the power supply was cut off, Tsurukawa and I went to visit the Nanzen Temple together. This was our first visit to the Nanzen Temple. We crossed the wide drive and went over the wooden bridge that spanned the incline where boats used to be launched.

It was a clear May day. The incline was no longer in use and the rails that ran down the slope were rusty and almost entirely overgrown with weeds. Amid the weeds, delicate little cross-shaped flowers trembled in the wind. Up to the point where the incline started, the water was dirty and stagnant, and the shadows of the rows of cherry trees on our side of the water were thoroughly immersed in it.

Standing on the small bridge, we gazed absently at the water. Amid all one's wartime memories, such short absent moments leave the most vivid impression. These brief moments of inactive abstraction lurked everywhere, like patches of blue sky that peep through the clouds. It is strange that a moment like this should have remained clearly in my mind, just as though it had been an occasion of poignant pleasure.

"It's pleasant, isn't it?" I said and smiled inconsequentially.

"Uh," replied Tsurukawa, and he too smiled. The two of us felt keenly that these few hours belonged to us.

Beside the wide graveled path ran a ditch full of clear water, in which beautiful water plants were swaying with the flow. Soon the famous Sammon Gate reared itself before us. There was not a soul to be seen in the temple precincts. Among the fresh verdure, the tiles of the temple roof shone luxuriantly, as though some great smoked-silver book had been laid down there. What meaning could war have at this moment? At a certain place, at a certain time, it seemed to me that war had become a weird spiritual incident having no existence outside human consciousness.

Perhaps it was on top of this Sammon Gate that the famous robber of old, Ishikawa Goémon, had placed his feet on the railing and enjoyed the sight of flowers below in their full blossom. We were both in a childish mood and, although it was already the season in which the cherry trees have lost their blossoms and are covered in foliage, we thought that we should enjoy seeing the view from the same position as Goémon. We paid our small entrance fee and climbed the steep steps whose wood had now turned completely black. In the hall at the top, where religious dances used to be performed, Tsurukawa hit his head on the low ceiling. I laughed and immediately afterwards bumped my own head. We both made another turn, climbed to the head of the stairs and emerged on top of the tower.

It was a pleasant tension, after climbing the stairs, which were as cramped as a cellar, to feel our bodies suddenly exposed to the wide outside scene. We stood there for a time gazing at the cherry trees and the pines, at the forest of the Heian Shrine that stretched tortuously in the distance beyond the rows of buildings, at the form of the mountain ranges—Arashiyama, Kitanokata, Kifune, Minoura, Kompira—all of them rising up hazily at the extremities of the streets of Kyoto. When we had satisfied ourselves with this, we removed our shoes and respectfully entered the hall like a couple of typical acolytes. In the dark hall twenty-four straw mats were spread out on the floor. In the center was a statue of Sâkamuni, and the golden eyes of sixteen Arhants gleamed in the darkness. This was known as the Gohoro or the Tower of the Five Phoenixes.

The Nanzen Temple belonged to the same Rinzai sect as the Golden Temple, but whereas the latter adhered to the Sokokuji school, this was the headquarters of the Nanzenji school. In other words, we were now in a temple of the same sect as our own but of a different school. We stood there like two ordinary middle-school students, with a guide book in our hands, looking round at the vividly colored paintings on the ceiling, which are attributed to Tanyu Morinobu of the Kano school and to Hogan Tokuetsu of the Tosa school. On one side of the ceiling were paintings of angels flying through the sky and playing the flute and the ancient *biwa*. Elsewhere, a Kalavinka was fluttering about with a white peony in its beak. This was the melodious bird that is described in the sutras as living on Mount Sessan: the upper part of its body is that of a plump girl and its lower part has a bird's form. In the center was painted that fabulous bird which is supposed to be a companion to the bird on the summit of the Golden Temple; but this one was like a gorgeous rainbow, utterly different from that solemn golden bird with which I was so familiar.

Before the statue of Sâkamuni we knelt down and folded our hands in prayer. Then we left the hall. But it was hard to drag ourselves down from the top of the tower. We leaned against the railing facing south by the top of the steps that we had climbed. I felt as though somewhere I could see a small, beautiful, colored spiral before my eyes. It must have been an after-image of the magnificent colors that I had just seen on the ceiling paintings. This feeling that I had of a condensation of rich colors was as though that Kalavinka bird were hiding somewhere amid those young leaves or on some branches of those green pines that spread out everywhere below, and as though it were letting me glimpse a corner of its splendid wings.

But it was not so. Across the road below us was the Tenju Hermitage. A path, paved with square stones, of which only the corners touched each other, bent its way across a garden, where low, peaceful trees had been planted in a simple style, and led to a large room with wide-open sliding-doors. One could see every detail of the alcove and of the staggered shelves in the room. A bright-scarlet carpet was spread out on the floor: evidently the room was frequently used for tea dedications and rented for tea ceremonies. A young woman was sitting there. It was she that had been reflected in my eyes. During the war one never saw a woman dressed in such a brilliant, long-sleeved kimono as she was wearing. Anyone who went out dressed as she was would almost certainly be rebuked for lack of patriotic sobriety and would have to return home and change. So gorgeous was her form of dress. I could not see the details of the pattern, but I noticed that flowers were painted and embroidered on a pale blue background, and that her vermilion sash was glittering with gold thread: it was almost as though the surrounding air were illuminated by the brilliance of her costume. The beautiful young woman was sitting on the floor in a position of perfect elegance; her pale profile stood out in relief as if it were carved, and at first I could not help wondering whether she was really a living person.

"Good heavens!" I said, stuttering badly. "Can she really be alive?"

"That's just what I was thinking. She's exactly like a doll, isn't she?" replied Tsurukawa, who stood leaning heavily against the railing without taking his eyes off the woman.

Just then a young army officer appeared in uniform from the back of the room. He sat down with stiff formality a few feet away from the woman and faced her. For a while the two of them sat facing each other quietly.

The woman stood up and disappeared silently into the darkness of the corridor. After a time, she returned holding a teacup in her hands; her long sleeves swayed to and fro in the breeze. She knelt directly in front of the man and offered him the tea. Having presented him with the teacup according to etiquette, she returned to her original place. The man said something. He still did not drink the tea. The moment that followed seemed strangely long and tense. The woman's head was deeply bowed.

It was then that the unbelievable thing happened. Still sitting absolutely straight, the woman suddenly loosened the collar of her kimono. I could almost hear the rustling of the silk as she pulled the material of her dress from under the stiff sash. Then I saw her white breasts. I held my breath. The woman took one of her full white breasts in her own hands. The officer held out the dark, deep-colored teacup, and knelt before her. The woman rubbed her breast with both hands.

I cannot say that I saw it all, but I felt distinctly, as though it had all happened directly before my eyes, how the white warm milk gushed forth from her breast into the deep-green tea which foamed inside that cup, how it settled into the liquid, leaving white drops on the top, how the quiet surface of the tea was made turbid and foamy by that white breast.

The man held the cup to his mouth and drank every drop of that mysterious tea. The woman hid her full breast in the kimono.

Tsurukawa and I gazed tensely at the scene. Later when we examined the matter systematically, we decided that this must have been a farewell ceremony between an officer who was leaving for the front and the woman who had conceived his child. But our emotions at that moment made any logical explanation impossible. Because we were staring so hard, we did not have time to notice that the man and woman had gone out of the room, leaving

70

nothing but the great red carpet.

I had seen that white profile of hers in relief and I had seen her magnificent white breast. After the woman left, I thought persistently of one thing during the remaining hours of that day and also during the next day and the day after. I thought that this woman was none other than Uiko, who had been brought back to life.

CHAPTER THREE

It was the anniversary of Father's death. Mother had an odd idea. Since it was difficult for me to go home because of my compulsory labor, she thought of coming to Kyoto herself, bringing along Father's mortuary tablet, so that Father Dosen might chant some sutras before it, if only for a few minutes, on the anniversary of his old friend's death. Of course she did not have enough money to pay for the mass, and she wrote the Superior, throwing herself on his charity. Father Dosen agreed to her request and informed me about it.

I was not pleased at this news. There is a special reason that I have until now avoided writing about my mother. I do not particularly feel like touching on what relates to my mother.

Concerning a certain incident, I never addressed a single word of reproof to Mother. I never spoke about it. Mother probably did not even realize that I knew about it. But ever since that incident occurred, I could not bring myself to forgive her.

It happened during my summer holidays when I had gone home for the first time after entering the East Maizuru Middle School and after being entrusted to my uncle's care. At that time, a relative of Mother's called Kurai had returned to Nariu from Osaka, where he had failed in his business. His wife, who was the heiress of a well-to-do family, would not take him back into their house, and Kurai was obliged to stay in Father's temple until the affair subsided.

We did not have much mosquito netting in our temple. It was really a wonder that Mother and I did not catch Father's tuberculosis, since we all slept together under the same net; and now this man Kurai was added to our number. I remember how late one summer night a cicada flew along the trees in the garden, giving out short cries. It was probably those cries that awakened me. The sound of the waves echoed loudly, and the bottom of the light-green mosquito net flapped in the sea breeze. But there was something strange about the way in which the mosquito net was shaking.

The mosquito net would begin to swell with the wind, then it would shake reluctantly as it let the wind filter through it. The way in which the net was blown together into folds was not, therefore, a true reflection of how the wind was blowing; instead, the net seemed to abandon the wind and to deprive it of its power. There was a sound, like the rustling of bamboo, of something rubbing against the straw mats; it was the bottom of the mosquito net as it rubbed against the floor. A certain movement, which did not come from the wind, was being transmitted to the mosquito net. A movement that was more subtle than the wind's; a movement that spread like rippling waves along the whole length of the mosquito net, making the rough material contract spasmodically and causing the huge expanse of the net to look from the inside like the surface of a lake that is swollen with uneasiness. Was it the head of some wave created by a ship as it plowed its way far off through the lake; or was it the distant reflection of a wave left in the wake of a ship that had already passed this place?

Fearfully I turned my eyes to its source. Then, as I gazed through the darkness with wide-open eyes I felt as though a gimlet was drilling into the very center of my eyeballs.

I was lying next to Father; the mosquito net was far too small for four people, and in my sleep I must have turned over and pushed him over to one corner. Accordingly, there was a large white expanse of crumpled sheet separating me from the thing that I now saw; and Father, who lay curled up behind me, was breathing right down my neck.

What made me realize that Father was actually awake was the irregular, jumping rhythm of his breath against my back; for I could tell that he was trying to stop himself from coughing. All of a sudden my open eyes were covered by something large and warm, and I could see nothing. I understood at once. Father had stretched his hands out from behind to cut off my vision.

This happened many years ago when I was only thirteen, but the memory of those hands is still alive within me. Incomparably large hands. Hands that had been put round me from behind, blotting out in one second the sight of that hell which I had seen. Hands from another world. Whether it was from love or compassion or shame, I do not know; but those hands had instantaneously cut off the terrifying world with which I was confronted and had buried it in darkness.

I nodded slightly within those hands. From that nodding of my small head, Father could instantly tell that I had understood and that I was ready to acquiesce; he removed his hands. And, afterwards, just as those hands had ordered, I kept my eyes obstinately closed, and thus lay there sleeplessly until morning came and the dazzling light from outside forced its way through my eyelids.

Please remember that years later, when Father's coffin was being carried out of the house, I was so busy *looking* at the dead face, that I did not shed a single tear. Please remember that with his death I was freed from the fetters of his hands, and that by looking intently at his face, I was able to confirm my own existence. To this extent did I remember to wreak my proper revenge on those hands, that is, on what the people of this world would call love; but so far as Mother was concerned, apart from the fact that I could not forgive her for that memory, I never once thought of avenging myself on her.

It had been arranged that Mother would come to the Golden Temple on the day before the memorial service and that she could spend the night in the temple. The Superior had written to my school so that they might let me be absent on the day of the anniversary. Those of us who were liable for compulsory labor did not stay at our place of work, but would report there at the appointed time and would then return to wherever we happened to be living. On the day before the anniversary, I was reluctant to return to the temple.

Tsurukawa, with his clear simple heart, was pleased for my sake that I was to see my mother again after such a long time, and my fellow acolytes were curious about her. But I hated to have such a poor and shabby mother. I was at a loss about how I should explain to the kind-hearted Tsurukawa why I did not want to see my mother.

To make matters worse, as soon as we had finished our

work at the factory, Tsurukawa seized my arm and said: "Come on, let's run back!"

It would be an exaggeration to say that I did not want to see Mother in the slightest. It was not that I had no feeling for her. The fact was probably that I disliked being confronted with the straightforward expression of love that one receives from one's blood relatives, and that I was simply trying to rationalize this dislike in various ways. Therein lay my bad character. It was all right that I should try to justify my honest feelings by all sorts of rationalizations. But sometimes the multifarious motives that my brain spun out would force feelings on me that came as a shock even to myself; and those feelings were not originally my own.

Only in my hatred was there something authentic. For I myself was a person who should be moved with hate.

"There's no point running," I replied. "It only makes one tired. Let's take our time going back!"

"I see," said Tsurukawa. "So you want to make up to your mother and get her sympathy by pretending to be too exhausted to walk fast."

Thus Tsurukawa was invariably interpreting my behavior and was invariably mistaken about it. But he did not bother me in the slightest and had in fact become indispensable. For he was truly my well-intentioned interpreter—an irreplaceable friend who could translate my words for me into the language of the real world.

Yes, Tsurukawa sometimes seemed to me like an alchemist who could transform tin into gold. I was the negative of the picture; he was the positive. How often had I not been amazed to see how my dark, turbid feelings could become clear and radiant by being filtered through Tsurukawa's heart! While I hesitated and stuttered, he would take my feelings in his hand, turn them round and transmit them to the outside world. What I learned from this amazing process was that so far as feelings were concerned, there was no discrepancy between the very finest feeling in this world and the very worst; that their effect was the same; that no visible difference existed between murderous intent and feelings of deep compassion. Tsurukawa could never have believed such a thing, even if I had been able to explain it in words, but for me it was a fearful discovery. If it had now come about that I did not mind Tsurukawa's taking me for a hypocrite, it was because hypocrisy had in my mind become merely a relative offense.

In Kyoto I never experienced an air raid, but once when I was sent to the main factory in Osaka with some orders for spare parts for aircraft, there happened to be an attack and I saw one of the factory workers being carried out on a stretcher with his intestines exposed.

What is so ghastly about exposed intestines? Why, when we see the insides of a human being, do we have to cover our eyes in terror? Why are people so shocked at the sight of blood pouring out? Why are a man's intestines ugly? Is it not exactly the same in quality as the beauty of youthful, glossy skin? What sort of a face would Tsurukawa make if I were to say that it was from him that I had learned this manner of thinking—a manner of thinking that transformed my own ugliness into nothingness? Why does there seem to be something inhuman about regarding human beings like roses and refusing to make any distinction between the inside of their bodies and the outside? If only human beings could reverse their spirits and their bodies, could gracefully turn them inside out like rose petals and expose them to the spring breeze and to the sun. . . .

Mother had already arrived and was talking to the Superior in his room. Tsurukawa and I knelt outside in the corridor in the early summer gloaming and announced our return.

The Superior invited only me into the room. In front of Mother, he said something to the effect that I was doing very well at my temple duties. I kept my head bowed and hardly looked at Mother. Out of the corner of my eyes, I could see the faded blue cotton of her baggy wartime trousers and the dirty fingers of her hands that lay on them.

Father Dosen told us that we might retire to our

quarters. We bowed repeatedly and left the room. I lived in a tiny five-mat room, south of the small library and facing a courtyard. As soon as we were there by ourselves, Mother began to cry. Having anticipated this, I was able to remain quite unperturbed.

"I am now under the care of the Rokuonji," I told her, "and I wish you would not visit me until I become a full-fledged priest."

"I understand. I understand," said Mother.

I was pleased that I had managed to receive my mother with such harsh words. But it annoyed me that, just as in the old days, she gave no sign of feeling or of resisting. At the same time, when I imagined the mere possibility that Mother might cross the threshold and penetrate my mind, I felt frightened.

Looking at Mother's sunburned face, I saw her small, cunning, hollow eyes. Only her lips were red and shiny, as though they possessed a life all of their own; she had the strong, large teeth of a countrywoman. She was at an age when, if she had been a city-dweller, it would not have been strange to use heavy make-up. Mother had made her face look as ugly as possible. I was keenly aware that a fleshy quality remained somewhere in that face like a sediment; and I hated it.

Having retired from Father Dosen's presence and having had a good cry, Mother now produced a towel, which she had brought from our home village, and began wiping her bare, sunburned breast. The towel was of the type that one received on the ration and was made of staple fiber. The material had an animalian gloss and when it was wet with perspiration, it became even more shiny.

Then Mother took some rice out of her haversack. She said that she was going to offer it to the Superior. I did not say a word. Next she extracted Father's mortuary tablet, which had been carefully wrapped in a piece of old gray cloth, and placed it on my bookshelf.

"I'm ever so pleased about all this," she said. "Father'll be real happy to know the Superior is saying Mass for him."

79

"Will you be going back to Nariu after the anniversary, Mother?" I asked.

Her answer came as a surprise. It turned out that Mother had already handed over the rights of the Nariu temple to someone else and had sold the small plot of land. She had paid off all Father's medical expenses and had arranged to go and live by herself at an uncle's house in Kasagun near Kyoto. So the temple where I was to return was no longer ours! In that village on the lonely cape there was nothing left to greet me.

I do not know how Mother interpreted the look of liberation that appeared on my face, but she bent close to me and said: "You see, dear. You don't have a temple of your own any longer. The only thing for you now is to become the superior of the Golden Temple here. You must see that the Father really gets to like you, so that you can take his place when the time comes for him to leave. You understand, dear? That's all your mother will be living for now."

I was astounded by this development and tried to stare back at Mother. But I was too alarmed to look at her properly.

The little back room was already dark. My "fond mother" had put her mouth directly against my ear when she was speaking to me and now the smell of her perspiration hovered before my nostrils. I recalled that Mother had been laughing then. Distant memories of being nursed, memories of a swarthy breast—the images raced unpleasantly round my brain. In the flames of the lowly field fires there existed some sort of physical force and it was this that seemed to frighten me. As Mother's frizzy locks touched my cheek, I noticed a dragonfly resting its wings on the moss-grown stone basin in the dusky courtyard. The evening sky was reflected on the surface of the small, round patch of water in the basin. There was not a sound to be heard and at this moment the Rokuonji seemed to be a deserted temple.

Finally I was able to look directly into Mother's face. A smile played in the corner of her glossy lips and I could see her shining gold teeth.

"Yes," I answered, stuttering violently, "but for all I know, I'll be called up and killed in battle."

"You fool!" she said. "If they start taking stutterers like you into the Army, Japan is really finished!"

I sat there tensely, filled with hatred for my mother. But the words that I stuttered out were a mere evasion. "The Golden Temple may be burned down in an air raid," I said.

"The way things are going," said Mother, "there's not the faintest chance of an air raid on Kyoto. The Americans are leaving it alone."

I did not reply. The darkening courtyard had become the color of the sea bed. The stones sank in the gloom, and from their form one might have thought they had been struggling fiercely with each other. Mother stood up, disregarding my silence, and stared unceremoniously at the wooden door of my little room.

"Isn't it time for the evening meal yet?" she said.

When I looked back on it later, I realized that this visit of Mother's had a considerable influence on my thinking. It was on this occasion that I understood that Mother lived in an utterly different world from mine and it was also on this occasion that for the first time her manner of thinking began to affect me.

Mother was by nature the sort of person who would have no interest in the beauty of the Golden Temple; instead, she possessed a realistic sense that was foreign to me. She had said that there was no fear of an air raid on Kyoto and, despite all my dreams, this was probably true. And if there was no chance that the Golden Temple would be attacked, then for the time being I had lost my purpose in living and the world in which I dwelt must fall to pieces.

On the other hand, the ambition that Mother had pronounced so unexpectedly had captivated me, much as I loathed it. Father had never said a word about this matter, but perhaps he had entertained the same ambition as Mother when he had sent me to this temple. Father Dosen was a bachelor. Assuming that he himself had attained his present position on the recommendation of some predecessor who had pinned his expectations on him, there was no reason that I too, so long as I exerted myself properly, could not eventually succeed Father Dosen as Suerpior of the Rokuonji. If that were to happen, the Golden Temple would be mine!

My thoughts became confused. When my second ambition became burdensome, I returned to my first dream (that the Golden Temple was going to be bombed), and when that dream was destroyed by the clear realism of Mother's judgment, I reverted to the second ambition, until in the end I wearied myself by constantly going back and forth in my thoughts and, as a result, a large red swelling appeared at the base of my neck.

I left it alone. The swelling became firmly rooted and began to press on me from the back of my neck with a heavy, hot force. In my fitful sleep, I dreamed that a pure golden light was growing on my neck, surrounding the back of my head with a sort of elliptical halo and gradually expanding. But when I awoke, this turned out to have been merely the pain from my virulent swelling.

Finally I came down with a temperature and had to go to bed. The Superior sent me to see a surgeon. The surgeon, who was dressed in a national uniform with gaiters, diagnosed my swelling by the simple name of Flunkel. Not wanting to use any alcohol, he disinfected his knife by holding it over a flame and then applied it to my neck. I groaned. The hot, burdensome world burst open in the back of my head, and I felt it shriveling up and collapsing.

The war ended. All that I was thinking about, as I listened in the factory to the Imperial Rescript announcing the termination of hostilities, was the Golden Temple.

As soon as I returned from the factory, I naturally hurried to the front of the Golden Temple. On the path that was used by visitors to the temple, the pebbles were baking in the midsummer sun, and one after another stuck to the rough rubber soles of my gym shoes.

In Tokyo, after people had heard the Rescript, they probably went and stood in front of the Imperial Palace; here great numbers went and wept before the gates of the uninhabited Kyoto Palace. Kyoto is full of shrines and temples where people can go and cry on occasions like this. The priests must all have done rather well that day. Yet despite the great role of the Golden Temple, no one came to visit it that day.

Thus it was that only my shadow could be seen on the baking pebbles. To describe the situation properly, I should say that I was standing on one side and the Golden Temple on the other. And from the moment that I set eyes on the temple that day, I could feel that "our" relationship had already undergone a change. When it came to such things as the shock of defeat or national grief, the Golden Temple was in its element; at such times it was transcendent, or at least pretended to be transcendent. Until today, the Golden Temple had not been like this. Without doubt, the fact that it had in the end escaped being burned down in an air raid and was now out of danger had served to restore its earlier expression, an expression that said: "I have been here since olden times and I shall remain here forever."

It sat there in utter silence, like some elegant but useless piece of furniture, with the antique gold foil of its interior perfectly protected by the lacquer of the summer sun that doubled the outer walls. Great, empty display shelves placed before the burning green of the forest. What ornamental objects could one put on such shelves? Nothing would fit their measurements but something like a fantastically large incense burner, or an absolutely colossal nihility. But the Golden Temple had entirely lost such things; it had suddenly washed away its essence and now displayed a strangely empty form. The most peculiar thing was that of all the various times when the Golden Temple had shown me its beauty, this time was the most beautiful of all. Never had the temple displayed so hard a beauty—a beauty that transcended my own image, yes, that transcended the entire world of reality, a beauty that bore no relation to any form of evanescence! Never before

83

had its beauty shone like this, rejecting every sort of meaning.

It is no exaggeration to say that as I gazed at the temple, my legs trembled and my forehead was covered with cold beads of perspiration. On a former occasion when I had returned to the country after seeing the temple, its various parts and its whole structure had resounded with a sort of musical harmony. But what I heard this time was complete silence, complete noiselessness. Nothing flowed there, nothing changed. The Golden Temple stood before me, towered before me, like some terrifying pause in a piece of music, like some resonant silence.

"The *bond* between the Golden Temple and myself has been cut," I thought. "Now my vision that the Golden Temple and I were living in the same world has broken down. Now I shall return to my previous condition, but it will be even more hopeless than before. A condition in which I exist on one side and beauty on the other. A condition that will never improve so long as this world endures."

The country's defeat was for me just such an experience of despair. Even now I can see before me the flame-like summer light of that day of defeat, August 15. People said that all values had collapsed; but within myself, on the contrary, eternity awoke, was resuscitated, and asserted its rights. The eternity which told me that the Golden Temple was to remain there forever. The eternity that descended from heaven, sticking to our cheeks, our hands, our stomachs, and finally burying us. How cursed a thing it was! Yes, in the cries of the cicadas that echoed from the surrounding hills, I could hear this eternity, which was like a curse on my head, which had shut me up in the golden plaster.

During the sutra recitation that evening before retiring to bed, we recited especially long prayers for the peace of His Imperial Majesty and to console the spirits of those who had died in the war. Ever since the war started, it had become customary in the various sects to use simple vestments, but tonight the Superior was wearing the scarlet priest's robe which he had kept stored away for

84

years. That plump, immaculate face of his, which looked as though even its wrinkles had been washed out, had a ruddy air of good health about it today and seemed to be brimming over with satisfaction about something. In the hot night, the cool rustling of his robes sounded clearly in the temple.

After the sutra recitation, everyone in the temple was called to the Superior's room to hear a lecture. The catachetic Zen problem that he had chosen was "Nansen Kills a Cat" from the Fourteenth Case of the *Mumonkan*. "Nansen Kills a Cat" (which also appears in the Sixty-Third Case of the *Hekiganroku* under the title "Nansen Kills a Kitten" and in the Sixty-Fourth Case under the title "Joshu Wears a Pair of Sandals on His Head") has been noted since ancient times as one of the most difficult Zen problems.

In the T'ang period there was a famous Ch'an priest, P'u Yüan, who lived on Mount Nan Ch'üan, and who was named Nan Ch'üan (Nansen, according to the Japanese reading) after the mountain. One day, when all the monks had gone out to cut the grass, a little kitten appeared in the peaceful mountain temple. Everyone was curious about this kitten. They chased the little animal and caught it. Then it became an object of dispute between the East Hall and the West Hall of the temple. The two groups quarreled about who should keep the kitten as their pet.

Father Nansen, who was watching all this, immediately caught the kitten by the scruff of its neck and, putting his sickle against it, said as follows: "If any of you can say a word, this kitten shall be saved; if you can not, it shall be killed." No one was able to answer, and so Father Nansen killed the kitten and threw it away.

When evening came, the chief disciple, Joshu, returned to the temple. Father Nansen told him what had happened and asked for his opinion. Joshu immediately removed his shoes, put them on his head, and left the room. At this, Father Nansen lamented sorely, saying: "Oh, if only you had been here today, the kitten's life could have been saved."

This was the general outline of the story. The part in

which Joshu puts his shoes on his head was known to present a particularly difficult problem. But according to the Superior's lecture, it was not all that difficult.

The reason that Father Nansen had killed the cat was that he had cut away the illusion of self and had eradicated all irrelevant thoughts and fantasies from his mind. Putting his insensibility into practice, he had cut off the kitten's head and had thus cut off all contradiction, opposition, and discord between self and others. This was known as the Murdering Sword, whereas Joshu's action was called the Life-Giving Sword. By performing an action of such infinite magnanimity as wearing filthy and despised objects like shoes on his head, he had given a practical demonstration of the way of the Bodhisattva.

Having explained the problem in this manner, the Superior came to the end of his lecture, without once having touched on the matter of Japan's defeat. We felt as though we had been bewitched by a fox. We had not the faintest idea why this particular Zen problem should have been chosen on the day of our country's defeat. As we walked along the corridor on our way back to our rooms, I expressed my doubts to Tsurukawa. He too was surprised and shook his head.

"I don't understand," he said. "I don't think anyone could understand who hasn't lived his life as a priest. But I think that the real point of tonight's lecture was that on the day of our defeat, he should not have said a word about it and should have talked about killing a cat."

I myself did not feel the slightest unhappiness about having lost the war, but the Superior's look of overflowing delight had made me uneasy. Respect for one's Superior is what normally preserves order in a temple. Yet during the past year in which I had been under the care of this temple, I had not come to feel any love or esteem for this Superior of ours. That in itself did not matter. But ever since Mother had lit the flame of ambition within me, I had begun on occasion to regard the Superior with all the critical sense of a seventeen-year-old boy.

The Superior was fair and impartial. But it was a fairness and impartiality that I could easily imagine displaying myself if I were to become a Superior. This man lacked the characteristic sense of humor of a Zen priest. This was odd, since humor was usually an inseparable adjunct to people as fat as he.

I had heard that the Superior had enjoyed himself to the full with women. When I actually imagined him indulging in these pleasures, I was amused, but at the same time uneasy. What would a woman really feel when she was embraced by a body that was like a pink bean-jam cake? She would probably feel as if that soft, pink flesh stretched to the very ends of the world, as if she were being buried in a grave of flesh.

It struck me as strange that a Zen priest also should have flesh. The reason that the Superior had indulged himself so thoroughly with women could have been that he wished to show his scorn of the flesh by throwing it away from himself. But if that were so, it seemed strange that this flesh which he so despised should have absorbed ample nourishment and that it should be sleekly wrapping itself about his spirit. Docile, humble flesh like some well-trained domestic animal. Flesh that was exactly like a concubine for the Superior's spirit.

I must state what the defeat really meant to me. It was not a liberation. No, it was by no means a liberation. It was nothing else than a return to the unchanging, eternal Buddhist routine, which merged into our daily life. This routine was now firmly re-established, and continued unaltered from the day after the Surrender: the "opening of the rules," morning tasks, gruel session, meditation, "medicine" or the evening meal, bathing, "opening of the pillow." The Superior strictly forbade the use of black-market rice in the temple. As a result, the only rice that we acolytes would find floating in our meager bowls of gruel was what had been contributed by parishioners, or such small quantities as the deacon had bought on the black market. The deacon obtained the rice for us out of consideration for the fact that we acolytes were now at the age of our most rapid growth and needed nourishment; but he always pretended that this black-market rice was part of the contribution to the temple. Sometimes we would go out and buy ourselves sweet potatoes. It was not only at breakfast that we were given gruel; our lunch and dinner too, consisted of gruel and sweet potatoes, and as a result we were always hungry.

Tsurukawa requested his parents for sweets and occasionally they would send him parcels from Tokyo. Late at night he brought his supply of sweets to my room and we ate them together. Now and again the lightning flashed in the dark sky.

I asked Tsurukawa why he stayed here when he had such a prosperous home and such affectionate parents.

"This is all a sort of ascetic exercise for me," he explained. "In any case, when the time comes, I shall be inheriting Father's temple from him."

Nothing seemed to bother Tsurukawa. He fitted perfectly into the pattern of his life, like a chopstick in its box. I pursued the conversation by telling Tsurukawa that some new and quite unimaginable period might come to our country. I remembered the story that I had heard everyone discussing at school some days after the Surrender. It was about an officer who was in charge of some factory and who, immediately after the war ended, had piled up a truckload of goods and driven them to his own house, explaining quite openly: "From now on, I'm going into the black-market business."

I imagined this bold, cruel, sharp-eyed officer as he stood there, about to rush headlong towards evil. The path along which he was going to run in his half-length military boots revealed the precise quality of death in battle; it had a form of disorder that reminded me of the crimson glow at dawn. As he set off, his white silk scarf would be fluttering at his breast, and his cheeks would be exposed to the cold night wind that still lingered in the early morning. His back would be bent double with the weight of the stolen goods: he would wear himself out with magnificent speed. But more in the distance, more lightly, I could hear the bell of disorder ringing in the bell tower.

I was separated from all such things. I had no money, no liberty, no emancipation. But it was certain that in my seventeen-year-old mind the phrase "a new period" involved a firm determination to pursue a certain course, even though it had not yet taken any concrete form.

"If the people of this world," I thought, "are going to taste evil through their lives and their deeds, then I shall plunge as deep as I can into an inner world of evil."

But the type of evil that I envisaged for myself at first did not go any further than a plan to win the Superior's favor by my wiles and thus to take possession of the Golden Temple, or else an absurd dream like poisoning the Superior and supplanting him. These plans of mine even served to ease my conscience, once I had made sure that Tsurukawa did not entertain the same ambition.

"Don't you have any worries or hopes about the future?" I asked him.

"No, none at all. What good would it do if I did?"

There was nothing gloomy in the way that he said this, nor did he speak haphazardly. Just then a flash of lightning lit up his narrow, gently sloping eyebrows, which were the only delicate part of his features. Tsurukawa evidently let the barber have his way in shaving the top and bottom of his eyebrows; as a result his already narrow eyebrows were made even narrower and one could see a faint blue shadow at the ends where the razor had passed.

As I glanced at this blue, I was seized with uneasiness. The young boy who sat in front of me burned at the pure extremity of life. He was different from me. His future was so concealed that he was burning. The wick of his future was floating in cool, clear oil. Who in this world was obliged to foresee his own innocence and purity? That is, if only innocence and purity remained for him in the future.

That evening after Tsurukawa had returned to his room, I could not sleep because of the steaming heat of the late summer. Apart from the temperature, my determination to resist indulging in my habit of masturbation robbed me of sleep . . .

It happened sometimes while I slept that I had a pollution. This did not involve any concrete sexual image. For example, a black dog would be running down a dark

89

street: I could see its panting breath escaping like flames from its mouth, and my excitement grew with the ringing of the bell that hung from its neck; then, as the bell reached its loudest pitch, I would have an ejaculation.

When I masturbated, my mind would be filled with demonic images, I could see Uiko's breasts, then her thighs would appear before me. And meanwhile I had turned into an incomparably small, ugly insect.

. . . I jumped out of bed and sneaked out of the building by the back door of the small library. Behind the Rokuonji and east of the Yukatei stands a mountain called Fudosan. It was thickly covered with red pines, and interspersed among the thick bamboo grass, which stretched out between the trees, grew deutzia, azaleas, and other plants. I was so familiar with this mountain that I could climb it even at night without stumbling. From the top one could see upper Kyoto and central Kyoto, and in the distance the mountains of Eizan and Daimonjiyama.

I climbed the slope. I climbed to the sound of the birds who flapped their wings in fear as I passed; I did not look to the side and managed to avoid all the tree stumps. I felt that I had been instantly cured by climbing like this without a thought in my head. When I reached the top, a cool night wind blew on my perspiring body.

I was surprised by the sight before me. The black-out had long since been suspended, and now a sea of lights stretched into the distance. This struck me almost as a miracle, since I had not once come up to this place at night since the end of the war.

The lights formed one solid body. They were scattered over the entire flat surface, giving no impression of being either near or far; what rose before me in the night was a huge, transparent structure composed entirely of lights, which seemed to be spreading out its winged tower and to have grown complicated horns. Here, indeed, was a city. Only the forest round the Imperial Palace was unlighted, and it looked like a great black cave. Now and then in the direction of Eizan Mountain the lightning would flash in the dark sky.

"This," I thought, "is the mundane world. Now that the

war has ended, people are being driven about under that light by evil thoughts. Innumerable couples are gazing at each other under that light, and in their nostrils is the smell of the *deed that is like death*, which already is pressing directly on them. At the thought that these countless lights are all obstructive lights, my heart is comforted. Please let the evil that is in my heart increase and multiply indefinitely, so that it may correspond in every particular with that vast light before my eyes! Let the darkness of my heart, in which that evil is enclosed, equal the darkness of the night, which encloses those countless lights!"

There was a great increase in the number of visitors to the Golden Temple. The Superior applied to the municipality and was allowed to raise the admission fee so as to keep pace with inflation.

The scattered visitors whom I had seen until now were modest folk dressed in uniforms, work clothes or baggy wartime trousers. But now Occupation troops arrived, and soon the licentious customs of the mundane world began to flourish about the Golden Temple. The changes were not entirely for the worse, however; for the custom of tea-dedication was revived, and many of the women visitors now came to the temple in gay, colorful clothes that they had stored away during the war years. We priests in our dark vestments now began to stand out by contrast; it was just as though we were acting the part of clericals for fun, or as though we were the inhabitants of some district who took special pains to preserve strange old customs for the benefit of tourists who came to observe them. The American soldiers were particularly struck by us: They used to pull the sleeves of our robes without any reserve, and laughed at us. Sometimes they would offer us money so that we would let them wear our robes; thus attired, they would have photographs taken of themselves as souvenirs. This was the sort of thing that happened when Tsurukawa or I had been routed out to use our broken English on foreign visitors, in place of the regular guides, who knew no English at all.

It was the first winter after the war. On Friday evening it had begun snowing and it continued snowing on Saturday. While I was at school in the morning, I was looking forward to returning at noon and seeing the Golden Temple under snow.

In the afternoon, too, it was snowing. I left the visitors' path and, wearing my rubber boots and with my school satchel slung over my shoulders, I walked to the edge of the Kyoto Pond. The snow was coming down with a sort of fluent rapidity. When I was a child, I had often turned my head up to the snow with my mouth wide open. I did so now, and the snowflakes touched my teeth, making a noise as if they were striking a very thin piece of tin foil. I felt that the snow was scattering throughout the warm cavity of my mouth and melting as it reached the red surface of the flesh. At that instant I imagined the mouth of the phoenix on top of the Kukyocho. The hot, smooth mouth of that mysterious and golden-colored bird.

Snow gives all of us a youthful feeling. And would it be quite untrue to say that I, who still had not reached my eighteenth birthday, now felt some youthful stirring within me?

The Golden Temple was incomparably beautiful as it stood there enveloped in snow. There was something refreshing about the bare skin of that draughty building, with its slender pillars rising close to each other, and with the snow blowing freely into its interior.

"Why doesn't the snow stutter?" I wondered. Sometimes, when the snow brushed against the leaves of the *yatsudé*, it fell to the ground as if it were in fact stuttering. But when I felt myself bathed in the snow as it descended mildly from the sky without any interruption, I forgot the kinks in my heart and seemed to return to some more gentle spiritual rhythm, as if I were being bathed in music.

Thanks to the snow, the three-dimensional Golden Temple had truly become a plane figure, a figure within a picture, and no longer did it bid defiance to what existed outside itself. The bare branches of the maple trees that stretched out on either side of the pond were hardly able

92

to support any snow, and the forest looked more naked than usual. Here and there the snow was piled magnificently on the pines. The snow also lay thick on the icy surface of the pond; but curiously, there were places where there was no snow at all, and where the pond was boldly daubed with great, white patches that looked like the clouds in an ornamental painting. Kyusanhakkai Rock and Awaji Island were joined to the snow on the icy surface of the pond, and the small pines that grew there looked exactly as if they had sprung up by chance from the midst of a plain of ice and snow.

Three parts of the Golden Temple were strikingly white—the roofs of the Kukyocho and the Choondo and the little roof of the Sosei. The rest of the uninhabited building was dark, and there was rather something fresh about the blackness of the complicated, wooden structure that stood out in relief against the snow. Just as when one looks at a castle nestling among the mountains in some painting of the Southern School, and brings one's face closer to the canvas to see whether someone may not be living behind those walls, so the fascination of that ancient black wood before me made me feel that I should like to find out whether the temple tower was not, in fact, inhabited. But even if I were to bring my face closer to the Golden Temple, I should only bump into the cold silk canvas of the snow; nearer than that I could not approach.

Today, too, the doors of the Kukyocho had been opened to the snowy sky. As I gazed up at it, I observed minutely how the falling snowflakes whirled round in the small space where there was nothing of the Kukyocho, and how, then, they settled on the old, tarnished gold-foil of its walls and stayed there until they had formed small patches of golden dew.

The next day was Sunday. In the morning the old guide came to fetch me. Evidently a foreign soldier had arrived to look at the temple before the normal opening-hour. The guide had used sign language to ask the soldier to wait, and had come to fetch me because, as he said, I knew English. Surprisingly enough, my English was better than Tsurukawa's and I never stuttered when I spoke it.

A jeep was standing by the entrance. A dead-drunk American soldier was leaning against one of the pillars. When I appeared, he looked down at me and laughed scornfully.

The front garden was dazzling from the recent snowfall. Against this dazzling background, the young soldier's face with its fleshy folds blew white clouds of steam towards me, mixed with the fumes of whisky. As usual, I felt uneasy as I tried to imagine what feelings must move within a person who differed so enormously in size from myself.

As I made it a habit not to oppose people, I now agreed to show him round the temple, even though it was before opening-time. I asked for the entrance fee and the guide's fee. Rather to my surprise, the great drunken fellow made no trouble about paying. Then he looked into the jeep and said something to the effect of "Get out!"

Because of the dazzling snow, I had so far not been able to see into the dark interior of the jeep, but now I noticed that something white was moving behind the window in the hood. I felt as though a rabbit were moving about in there.

A foot shod in a slender high-heeled shoe was planted on the step of the jeep. I was surprised that despite the cold it was not covered in a stocking. I could tell at a glance that the girl was a prostitute who catered to foreign soldiers: for she wore a flaming-red overcoat and her fingernails and toenails were painted the same flaming color. When the bottom of her overcoat opened, I noticed that underneath she was wearing a soiled nightgown made of towel cloth. The girl, too, was fearfully drunk and her eyes were set. The man was properly dressed in his uniform; but she had merely thrown an overcoat and scarf over her nightgown, having evidently come directly from bed.

In the reflection of the snow, the girl's face was terribly pale. On the white skin, which showed hardly the slightest trace of color, the crimson of her lipstick stood out harshly. As soon as she stepped on the ground, the girl sneezed; tiny wrinkles gathered about the slender bridge of her nose, and her tired, drunken eyes gazed into the distance for a moment, before sinking back into a deep, leaden look. Then she called the man's name.

"Jaak, Jaak!" she said. "*Tsu kōrudo, tsu kōrudo!*" The girl's voice wandered sadly across the snow, as she announced how cold she was. The man did not reply.

This was the first time that I had found a professional woman like this to be actually beautiful. It was not because she looked like Uiko. She was like a portrait that had been drawn with the greatest care so as not to resemble Uiko in any single feature. This girl partook of a fresh, defiant beauty that somehow seemed to have come into being as a reaction to my memory of Uiko. And there was something flattering in this resistance to those carnal feelings of mine that were the aftermath of my very first experience of beauty.

She had only one point in common with Uiko. This was that she did not so much as glance at me as I stood there. I had left my clerical robes behind, and was wearing a dirty sweater and rubber boots.

Everyone in the temple had been out since early in the morning shoveling snow, but they had only just managed to clear the visitors' path. Even now it would have been difficult if an entire party of visitors had come, but there was enough room for a small number to walk along in single file. I walked ahead of the American soldier and the girl.

When the American reached the pond and the view opened before him, he held up his hands and yelled out a cheer in words that I could not understand. Then he shook the girl violently. The girl knitted her eyebrows and simply repeated: "O Jaak, *tsu kōrudo!*"

The American asked me about the shiny red *aoki* berries that one could see behind the heavily snow-laden leaves, but I could think of nothing to say except "Aoki." Perhaps a lyrical poet lurked within that huge body of his, but I felt that there was cruelty in his clear, blue eyes. The Western nursery-rhyme "Mother Goose" refers to black

95

eyes as being cruel and malicious; the fact is that when people imagine cruelty, they normally assign some foreign character to it.

I started explaining the Golden Temple according to the standard guide's formula. The soldier was still terribly drunk and he was very unsteady on his feet. With my benumbed fingers I extracted from my pocket the English text about the Golden Temple that I usually read on these occasions. But the American snatched the book from me and began reading in a comic tone. I could see that my explanations were no longer required.

I leaned against the railing of the Hosui-in and looked at the fantastically glittering surface of the pond. Never had the interior of the Golden Temple been exposed like this to the light—so brilliantly that it made one uneasy.

When I looked up, I noticed that a quarrel had started between the man and the woman, who were now walking towards the Sosei. The quarrel gradually became fiercer, but I could not catch a single word. The girl answered something in a harsh tone; I had no idea whether she was speaking English or Japanese. The two of them walked back to the Hosui-in, still quarreling. They seemed to have forgotten about my existence.

The American thrust his face up to the girl and began abusing her. She slapped his cheek with all her strength. Then she turned round and ran away in her high heels towards the visitors' entrance. I did not understand what was happening, but I, too, left the Golden Temple and began running along the edge of the pond. When I reached the girl, the long-legged American had already caught up with her and was grasping her by the lapels of her red overcoat.

As he stood there holding her, the young man glanced at me. He loosened his grip on the girl's flaming-red lapel. There must have been some fantastic strength in that hand of his; for, when he released it, the girl fell gently backwards on the snow. The bottom of her red coat opened and her bare white thighs were spread out on the snow.

The girl did not even try to stand up. From where she

96

lay she was glaring up into the eyes of the giant who towered high above her. I could hardly avoid kneeling down and helping her to her feet. As I was about to do so, the American shouted: "Hey!" I turned round. There he stood above me, with his legs spread wide apart. He made a sign to me with his fingers. Then in a completely changed voice—a warm, sweet voice—he said in English: "Step on her, will you! Try and step on her!"

I could not understand what he meant. But there was an expression of command in his blue eyes as he looked down on me from his height. Behind his broad shoulders, I could see the snow-covered Golden Temple glittering under the dull, blue, washed-out winter sky. There was not the slightest cruelty in his blue eyes. I do not know why, but at that moment I felt that they were exceedingly lyrical.

His great hand descended, seized me by the scruff of my neck and pulled me to my feet. But the tone in which he commanded me was still warm and gentle.

"Step on her!" he said. "You must step on her!"

Unable to oppose him, I raised my booted foot. The American clapped me on the shoulder. My foot descended and I stepped on something as soft as springtime mud. It was the girl's stomach. The girl shut her eyes and groaned.

"Keep on stepping on her! Keep it up!"

I lowered my foot onto the girl. The sense of discord that I had felt when I first stepped on her gave way now to a sort of bubbling joy. "This is a woman's stomach," I thought. "This is her breast." I had never imagined that another person's flesh could respond like this with such faithful resilience.

"That's enough," said the American distinctly. Then he courteously lifted the girl to her feet, wiped the mud and snow from her clothes, and helped her back to the jeep. He walked ahead of me, without looking in my direction; the girl herself had not once turned her eyes on me. When they reached the jeep, he let the girl get in first. The effects of the whisky seemed to have worn off; the American turned to me and with a solemn expression said: "Thank you." He wanted to give me some money

97

but I refused. He then took two cartons of American cigarettes from the seat of the jeep and pressed them on me.

With burning cheeks I stood at the entrance in the strong reflection of the snow. The jeep jogged steadily into the distance, raising a cloud of snow, and disappeared from sight. My body was throbbing with excitement.

When eventually the excitement subsided, I thought of a scheme that would allow a delightful exercise of hypocrisy. The Superior loved cigarettes. How pleased he would be to receive this present! *Remaining utterly ignorant.*

There was no need for me to confess anything that had happened. I had only acted as I had because I was ordered and constrained. If I had opposed the American, I do not know what plight I might not have suffered myself.

I went to the Superior's office in the Great Library. He was having his head shaved by the Deacon, who was very adept at such things. I waited at the edge of the veranda, where the morning sun was shining with full strength. In the garden the snow was piled up on the Sailboat Pine Tree and glittered brilliantly; it looked exactly like a brand-new folded sail.

The Superior kept his eyes closed while he was being shaved. He held a piece of paper to catch the hair that fell off his head. The raw, animalian outline of the Superior's head emerged more and more distinctly as the Deacon continued his shaving. When he had finished, the Deacon wrapped the head in a hot towel. After a while he removed it and there emerged a glowing, newborn head, which looked as if it had been boiled.

I managed to deliver my message and handed over the two cartons of Chesterfields with a bow.

"Ha!" said the Superior, "Thank you for your pains."

He smiled slightly, as if he were laughing with only the extremity of his face. That was all. Then in a businesslike way the Superior took the two cartons and placed them at random on his desk, which was piled high with papers and letters of every description. As the Deacon now started to massage his shoulders, the Superior once more closed his eyes.

I had no choice but to retire. My body was hot from dissatisfaction. The mysterious, evil action that I had committed, the cigarettes that I had received as a reward, the Superior receiving them in ignorance of why I had obtained them—all this should have added up to something more dramatic and violent. That a man of the Superior's stature should have been utterly unaware of what had happened became a further important reason for me to despise him.

Just as I was about to leave the room, the Superior stopped me.

"Look here!" he said. "I'm planning to send you to Otani University as soon as you graduate from school. Now you must study hard, my boy, so that you'll have a good record when it comes to matriculating. That's what your late father would have wanted. He'd be worrying to see that you got good marks at school."

This piece of news was immediately spread through the temple by the Deacon. For an acolyte to have a university course recommended for him by his Superior proved that he must be quite a promising lad. It frequently happened in former times that an acolyte would go night after night to his Superior's room to massage his shoulders, all in the hope of being recommended for a university education, and in many cases these ambitions were realized. Tsurukawa, who was expected to enter Otani University at his parents' expense, slapped my shoulder with delight when he heard the news. Another of the acolytes, however, to whom the Superior had said nothing about entering the university, would not speak to me after this.

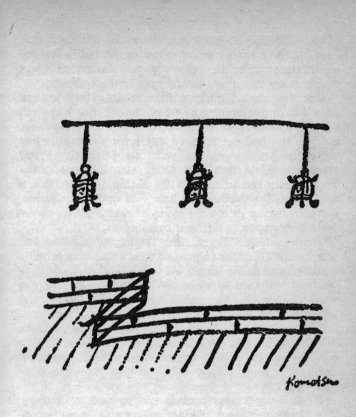

Komatsu

CHAPTER FOUR

In the spring of 1947, the time came for me to start on the preparatory course in Otani University. But my entry into the university was no triumphant event attended only by the unswerving affection of the Superior and by the envy of my colleagues at the temple. From the outside it may have appeared to be a proud event for me, but in fact my advancement into the university was beclouded by a circumstance that it was hateful even to think about.

One day when I returned from school, about a week after that snowy morning on which the Superior had given me permission to go to the university, I saw that other acolyte who had not received any word about attending university looking at me with an extremely happy expression. Until then, this young man had not said a word to me. The attitudes of the Sexton and the Deacon also seemed somehow to have changed. I gathered, however, that in their outer manner towards me they were pretending not to be different from before.

That evening I went to Tsurukawa's room and complained about the change that had come over people's attitude to me in the temple. At first he cocked his head to one side and tried to make me believe that nothing was wrong; but he was no good at concealing his feelings and before long he was gazing at me with a guilty expression.

"I heard about it from that other boy," he said, naming our fellow acolyte, "and he only knows about it from hearsay, because he also was at school when it happened. Anyhow, it seems that something strange happened while you were away."

I felt a vague apprehension and pursued my inquiry. Tsurukawa made me promise to keep the story secret. Looking fixedly into my eyes, he began to talk.

On the afternoon of the day in question, a girl had visited the temple and asked to speak to the Superior. She was wearing a red overcoat and was clearly a prostitute who catered to foreigners. The Deacon came to see her at the entrance in place of the Superior. The girl had abused the Deacon and told him that he'd better let her see the Superior if he knew what was good for him. At the moment the Superior unfortunately happened to be coming along the corridor. Noticing the girl, he came out to the entrance. The girl told him that about a week before, on the morning after it had been snowing, she had visited the temple with a foreign soldier. The soldier had

102

knocked her down and one of the temple acolytes had tried to curry favor with him by trampling on her stomach. That evening she had a miscarriage. Under the circumstances, she felt justified in demanding some money from the temple. If they wouldn't give her any, she was going to expose the misconduct that had taken place in the Rokuonji and would make her claim publicly.

The Superior gave her some money, without saying a word, and had her go home. Everyone knew that it was I who had acted as guide that day, but the Superior said that since there were no witnesses in the temple who had seen my misconduct, the matter should never be mentioned to me. He himself intended to shut his eyes to it all. But everyone else in the temple immediately suspected that I was the culprit when they heard the story from the Deacon.

Tsurukawa took my hand. I could see that he was almost in tears. He gazed at me with his clear eyes and appealed to me with his forthright, boyish voice: "Did you really do a thing like that?"

I confronted my own gloomy sentiments. Tsurukawa had made me confront them by pressing this question on me. Why did he ask me that? Was it out of friendship? Did he realize that by asking me such a question he was abandoning his true duty? Did he know that by this question he was betraying me in the deepest part of my being?

I must already have said it again and again: Tsurukawa was my positive picture. If Tsurukawa had fulfilled his duty faithfully, he would have pressed no questions on me, he would have asked me nothing, but would, instead, have taken my gloomy sentiments exactly as they were and translated them into cheerful sentiments. Then the lie would have become truth, and the truth a lie. If Tsurukawa had followed his characteristic method—his method of turning all shadows into light, all nights into days, all moonlight into sunlight, all the dampness of the night moss into the daytime rustling of shiny young leaves—then I myself might well have stuttered out a confession. But on just this occasion he did not do so.

Accordingly, my gloomy sentiments gained in strength.

I laughed ambiguously. Deep night in the fireless temple. Cold knees. The great ancient pillars of the temple towered round us as we sat there huddled in our secret conversation.

I was dressed in nothing but my night clothes and perhaps it was because of the cold that I was shivering. But the pleasure of lying openly to my friend for the first time was quite sufficient to make my knees tremble.

"I didn't do anything," I said.

"Really?" said Tsurukawa. "So that girl was lying. Damn her! To think that even the Deacon believed it!"

Tsurukawa's righteous indignation grew apace, until he declared that he was definitely going to speak to the Superior for me the next day and explain what had happened. At that moment the image flashed through my mind of the Superior's shaven pate that had looked like some boiled vegetable. Then I saw his pink, nonresistant cheeks. For some reason I was suddenly overcome by extreme repugnance for this image.

It was essential that I bury Tsurukawa's righteous indignation in the earth before it came to light.

"But do you really think the Superior believes that I did it?" I asked.

"Well," said Tsurukawa, immediately perplexed by this new idea.

"The others can speak badly about me behind my back as much as they want. So long as the Superior sees through the story, I feel perfectly at ease. That's how I think about it."

Thus I succeeded in making Tsurukawa believe that by trying to vindicate me he would, in fact, only be making people more suspicious than they already were. It was, I said, precisely because the Superior believed in my innocence, that he had chosen to remain quiet and to ignore the entire affair. As I spoke, joy rose in my heart, and gradually this joy took firm root within me. It was a joy that said: "There is *no* eyewitness. *No one* can be called in evidence against you."

I did not for a moment believe that only the Superior

trusted my innocence. Rather, it was the other way round: it was he alone who was absolutely certain of my guilt. The fact of his choosing to ignore the matter was in itself evidence of this presumption. Perhaps he had already seen through it all when I had handed him those two cartons of Chesterfields. Perhaps the reason that he had passed things over in silence was that he was waiting quietly in the distance for me to come and make my confession to him voluntarily. Not only that. Perhaps his recommending me for a university course was simply a bait to extract my confession: if I did not confess, he would withdraw his recommendation as a punishment for my dishonesty; if I did confess, however, and if he was convinced that I had truly repented, he might well be intending, as a special mark of favor, to continue recommending me for entrance.

The greatest trap of all lay in the fact that the Superior had told the Deacon not to mention the matter to me. If I were really innocent, I could then live serenely day after day, without knowing or feeling that anything particular had happened. If, on the other hand, I had committed the crime, I should (assuming that I had my wits about me) be able to make a good pretence of living in a state of peaceful purity that bespeaks innocence—the state, in other words, of someone who has nothing to confess. Well, I had better make the pretence. That was the best method for me, that was the only way in which I could establish my innocence. The Superior was hinting as much. This was the trap that he had prepared for me. At this thought, I was seized with rage. For it was not as though I had no excuse for my actions. If I had not stepped on that girl, the American might well have reached for his revolver and threatened me. After all, one could not resist the Occupation forces. What I had done, I had been forced to do.

But the feel of the girl's stomach against the sole of my rubber boot; the feel of her body that seemed to flatter me with its resilience; its groans; the way in which it felt like a crushed flower of flesh that is coming into bloom; that certain reeling or staggering of my senses; the sensation

105

which passed at that moment like some mysterious lightning from the girl's body into my own—I cannot pretend that it was compulsion that had made me enjoy all these things. I still cannot forget the sweetness of that moment. And the Superior knew what I felt to the very core; he knew that sweetness to the core!

During the year that followed, I was like a bird trapped in a cage. The cage was constantly before my eyes. Resolved as I was never to confess, I experienced no relief during my daily life. It was strange. That deed of mine, which at the time had aroused no guilt feelings in me, that deed of trampling on the girl's stomach, had gradually begun to glitter in my memory. This was not simply because I knew that as a result the girl had suffered a miscarriage. For my deed had settled like gold dust within my memory and had begun to give off a glittering light that constantly pierced my eyes. The glitter of evil. Yes, that was it. It may have been a very minor evil, but I was now endowed with the vivid consciousness that I had in fact committed evil. This consciousness hung like some decoration on the inside of my breast.

So far as practical matters were concerned, there was nothing for me now, until I took the entrance examinations for Otani University, but to live in a state of perplexity, trying my best to guess what the Superior's real intentions towards me might be. The Superior never once said anything to counter his promise about having me attend the university. On the other hand, he never said anything about promoting arrangements for my entrance examinations. How I waited for the Superior to say something to me, whatever it might be! But spitefully he kept his silence and subjected me to a drawn-out torture. For my own part, perhaps out of fear, perhaps out of a sense of resistance, I hesitated to ask the Superior about his intentions. Formerly I had regarded Father Dosen with normal respect, and at times I had looked at him critically. But now he gradually began to assume monstrous proportions, until I could no longer believe that his figure harbored an ordinary human heart. However often I tried to avert my eyes from it, this figure lurked before me like some weird castle.

It happened late in autumn. The Superior had been asked to the funeral of an old parishioner, and since it took two hours by train to reach the place, he had announced on the previous evening that he would be leaving the temple at half past five in the morning. The Deacon was going to accompany him. To be ready for the Superior's departure, we had to get up at four o'clock, do the cleaning, and prepare breakfast. As soon as we were up, we started our "morning task" of reciting the sutras, while the Deacon helped the Superior with his preparations. From the dark cold yard, came the uninterrupted creaking-sound of the well bucket. We hurriedly washed our faces. The crowing of the cock in the yard pierced the dark autumn dawn; there was a freshness and a whiteness about the sound.

We gathered up the sleeves of our robes, and hurried to congregate before the altar in the visitors' hall. In the chill of the early dawn, the straw mats of the great hall, on which no one ever slept, had a special feel about them, as though they were repelling one's touch. The altar candles flickered. We made our reverences. First we bowed standing up; then we knelt on the mats and bowed to the sound of the gong. We repeated the procedure three times.

I was always aware of a freshness in the male voices as they recited the sutras in unison during the morning task. The sound of those morning sutras was the strongest of the whole day. The strong voices seemed to scatter all the evil thoughts that had gathered during the night, and it was as though a black spray were gushing from the vocal chords of all the singers and being splashed about. I do not know about myself. I do not know, but it heartened me strangely to think that my voice was scattering away the same masculine evil thoughts as the others.

Before we had finished our "gruel session," the Superior was ready to leave. According to custom, we all lined up at the entrance to see him off. It was still night. The sky was full of stars. In the starlight the stone pavement stretched out faintly as far as the Sammon Gate, but the shadows of the great oaks, plum trees, and pines sprawled over the ground, and one shadow melted into the next so that they occupied the entire surface. My sweater was full of holes and the cold dawn air bit into my elbows.

Everything was done in silence. We bowed to the Superior without a word and he made some almost imperceptible response. Then the sound of the Superior's and the Deacon's clogs died away quietly as they walked away from us along the stone pavement. It is customary in the Zen sect to wait until the person whom one is seeing off has completely disappeared in the distance. As we now gazed at the two retreating figures, we could not see them in their entirety. All that we could see was the white hems of their robes and their white socks. At a certain point they seemed to have disappeared completely. But that was only because they were hidden under the trees. After a while, the white robes and the white socks emerged once more, and for some reason the echo of their footsteps seemed actually louder than before. We stood there gazing fixedly at them as they left, and it seemed ages until the two figures had gone through the main gate and finally disappeared.

It was at this point that a strange impulse was born in me. Just as when some important words were trying to break free from my mouth and were blocked by my stuttering, this impulse was held burning in my throat. The impulse was a sudden desire for release. At this moment, my previous ambitions—my desire to enter university, and still more, the hope suggested by Mother that I might succeed to the Superior's post—ceased to exist. I wanted to escape from some wordless force that controlled me and imposed itself on me.

I cannot say that I was lacking in courage at that moment. The courage required to make a confession was a trifling matter. For one such as I, who had lived in silence for the past twenty years, the value of confession was slight indeed. People may think that I am exaggerating. But the fact is that by setting myself up against the Superior's silence and refusing to confess, I had until then been experimenting with the single problem: "Is evil possible?" If I were to persist until the end in not confessing, it would prove that evil, albeit merely a petty evil, was indeed possible. But as I caught glimpses through the trees of the Superior's white skirt and white socks disappearing into the darkness of the dawn, the force that was burning in my throat became almost irresistible and I wanted to make a complete confession. I wanted to run after the Superior and cling to his sleeve and tell him in a loud voice everything that had happened on that snowy morning. It was certainly not any respect for the man that had inspired me with this wish. The Superior's force was like some strong physical power.

Yet the thought that if I should confess, the first petty evil of my life would collapse, held me back and I felt that something was tugging firmly at my back. Then the Superior's figure had passed under the main gate and disappeared under the still dark sky.

Everyone was suddenly relieved and ran noisily to the front door of the temple. As I stood there absently, Tsurukawa tapped me on the shoulder. My shoulder awoke. That lean shabby shoulder of mine regained its pride.

As I have already mentioned, I did in the end enter Otani University despite all these complications. I did not have to make any confession. A few days afterwards, the Superior had summoned Tsurukawa and me and told us briefly that we were to start preparing for our exams and that we should be excused from our temple duties while we were busy with these studies.

Thus I succeeded in entering the university. Yet this did not serve to settle all the difficulties. The Superior's attitude really told me nothing of what he was thinking about the incident on the snowy day; nor could I make out what his intentions were concerning his successor.

Otani University represented a turning-point in my life. It was here that for the first time in my life I became familiar with ideas, with ideas that I myself had deliberately chosen. Otani had its origins at a time almost three hundred years before, when in 1663 the university dormitory of the Chikushi Kanzeon Temple was moved to the Kikoku mansion in Kyoto. Ever since then it had served as the monastery for the followers of the Otani Sect of the Honganji. At the time of the Fifteenth Patriarch of the Honganji, an adherent of the temple, Soken Takagi by name, who lived in Naniwa, had made a large contribution. They had settled on the present site at Karasumaru-gashira in the northern part of the capital and established the university there. The grounds consisted of only ten acres and were small for a university. Yet it was here that so many young men, not only of the Otani Sect, but of every branch of Buddhism, had studied and been trained in the essentials of Buddhist philosophy.

An old brick gate separated the university grounds from the street and its streetcar lines. The gate faced west towards Hiei Mountain. From the gate a graveled drive led to the *porte-cochère* of the main building, a dark, gloomy, two-storied structure. On top of the roof at the entrance, a great copper tower soared into the air. It was neither a clock tower nor a bell tower; under a slender lightning-conductor, a useless square window cut out a corner of the blue sky.

Next to the entrance grew an old lime tree, whose magnificent leaves used to glow like red copper in the sun. The university, which had originally consisted of just the main building, had been expanded time after time, and the various parts were joined together without any particular order. For the greater part, it was an old, wooden, one-story structure. One was not allowed to wear shoes inside the building and the various wings were connected with endless corridors made of bamboo floor-boards. The floor had begun to crack with age. Occasionally the broken parts were repaired, and when one walked from one wing to another, one's feet passed over an entire mosaic of dark and light wood, as one extremely ancient floor-board was followed by a very new one.

Whenever one starts in a new school or university, it is the same: though one arrives each day with a fresh feeling, one is conscious of a certain vague, incoherent quality in things. So it was with me now during my early days at Otani University. Since Tsurukawa was the only person I knew, I found myself willy-nilly speaking to him and to no one else. After a few days, however, I began to think that there was little point in our having emerged with such trouble into this new world if we continued to see only each other. Tsurukawa evidently felt this also, and thereafter we made a point of not staying together during recreation hours and each of us tried to develop new friendships for himself. With my stuttering, however, I lacked Tsurukawa's courage, and as the number of his friends increased, I became more and more isolated.

The preparatory year's course at the university consisted of ten subjects—morals, Japanese, Sino-Japanese, Chinese, English, history, Buddhist scriptures, logic, mathematics, and gymnastics. From the outset I had the greatest trouble in the lectures on logic. One day during the noon recess that followed such a lecture, I decided to approach one of the students with some questions. For some time I had been hoping to become acquainted with this young man. He always used to sit by himself and eat his box lunch next to the flower beds in the back garden. This custom of his was like a sort of ritual and none of the other students used to approach him, especially since there was something exceedingly misanthropic about the way in which he looked disgustedly at his food as he ate. He, for his part, never spoke to any of his fellow students and seemed to reject the idea of making friends with anyone.

I knew that he was called Kashiwagi. His most striking characteristic was that he had two rather powerful-looking clubfeet. His way of walking was most elaborate. He always seemed to be walking in mud: when finally he had managed to pull one foot out of the mud, the other foot would appear to be stuck. At the same time there was a sprightliness about his whole body. His walk was a sort of exaggerated dance, utterly lacking in anything commonplace.

It stood to reason that I should have noticed Kashiwagi since my very first day at the university. I was relieved at the sight of his deformity. From the outset his clubfeet signified agreement with the condition in which I found myself.

Kashiwagi had opened his lunch box on a patch of clover in the back garden. This garden lay next to a dilapidated building, which housed the rooms where we practiced the *karate* form of self-defense and also ping-pong; hardly a single pane of glass was left in the windows. A few meager pines grew in the garden and some small wooden frames covered the empty nursery beds. The blue paint of the frames had begun to peel; it was rough and wrinkled like withered artificial flowers. Next to the nursery beds was a stand with a few shelves for arranging potted dwarf trees, a pile of tiles and pebbles, and also a bed of primroses and a bed of hyacinths.

It was pleasant to sit on the clover. The light was absorbed by its soft leaves and the surface of the clover was full of little shadows, so that it looked as if the entire patch were floating lightly above the earth. Kashiwagi was no different from the other students as he sat there; it was only when he walked that his abnormality appeared. There was a certain severe beauty in his pale face. Physically he was a cripple, yet there was an intrepid beauty about him, like that of a lovely woman. Cripples and lovely women are both tired of being looked at, they are weary of an existence that involves constantly being observed, they feel hemmed in; and they return the gaze by means of that very existence itself. The one who really looks is the one who wins. Kashiwagi was looking down as he ate his lunch; but I felt that his eyes were thoroughly scrutinizing the world about him.

He was self-sufficient as he sat there in the light. This was the impression that struck me. By just looking at him in the spring light amid the flowers, I could tell that he suffered from none of that shyness, none of that underhand guilt which I felt. He was a shadow that asserted itself, or rather, he was the existent shadow itself. Certain it was that the sun could never penetrate that hard skin of his.

112

The box lunch that he ate with such absorption and with such evident distaste was poor, but scarcely inferior to the one that I used to prepare for myself in the mornings out of leftovers from the temple breakfast. It was 1947 and unless one could afford to buy food on the black market, it was impossible to eat properly. I stood next to Kashiwagi with my notebook and my box lunch in my hands. My shadow fell on his food and he looked up. He glanced at me, then turned his eyes down and resumed his monotonous chewing, like a silkworm chewing mulberry leaves.

"Excuse me," I said, stuttering terribly, "I wanted to ask you about a couple of points I didn't understand in that last lecture." I spoke in the standard Tokyo accent, since I had decided not to use the Kyoto dialect after entering university.

"I can't understand a word you're saying," said Kashiwagi. "All I hear is a lot of stuttering."

I felt my face flush. Kashiwagi licked the end of his chopsticks and continued: "I know very well why you started talking to me. Mizoguchi—that's your name, isn't it? Well, if you think that we ought to become friends just because we're both cripples, I don't mind. But compared to what's wrong with me, do you really think your stuttering is such an important affair? You make too much of yourself, don't you? As a result, you make too much of your stuttering as well as of yourself."

Later, when I found out that Kashiwagi came from a Zen family, belonging to the same Rinzai Sect, I realized that in these initial questions and answers of his he was more or less assuming the characteristic approach of a Zen priest; but there was no denying the powerful impression that his remarks made on me at the time.

"Stutter!" he said. "Go ahead and stutter!"

I listened in utter amazement to his peculiar way of expressing himself.

"At last you've come across someone to whom you can stutter at your ease. That's right, isn't it? People are all like that, you know. They're all looking for a yoke-fellow. Well now, are you still a virgin?"

113

I nodded, without even smiling. The way in which Kashiwagi asked the question was that of a doctor and it made me feel that it would be better for me not to lie.

"Yes, I thought so," he said. "You're a virgin. But you're not a beautiful virgin. There's nothing beautiful about you at all. You have no success with girls and you don't have the courage to have professional girls. That's all there is to it. But if you thought when you started speaking to me that you are going to make friends with another virgin, you were quite mistaken. Would you like to hear about how I lost my virginity?"

Without waiting for my answer, Kashiwagi continued.

"I'm the son of a Zen priest in Sannomiya and I was born clubfooted. When you hear me start off like this, I suppose you'll imagine that I'm some poor sick fellow who doesn't mind who he's talking to so long as he can pour out his heart about himself. Well, I'm not. I wouldn't talk like this to just anyone who happened to come along. I'm rather embarrassed to say it, but the fact is that I deliberately chose you from the very beginning to hear my story. You see, it occurred to me that you'd probably get more benefit than anyone else from knowing what I'd done. The very best thing for you might be to do exactly what I did. As you know, that's how religious people smell out fellow believers and that's how teetotalers smell out their fellow teetotalers.

"Well then, I used to be ashamed about the conditions of my existence. I thought that to reconcile myself to those conditions, to live on good terms with them, represented a defeat. If I wanted to start bearing grudges, of course, there was no lack of material. My parents should have arranged for me to have an operation on my feet when I was small. Now it's too late. But I'm utterly unconcerned about my parents and the idea of bearing a grudge against them just bores me.

"I used to believe that women could never possibly love me. As you probably know yourself, this is a rather more comfortable and peaceful belief than most people imagine. There was not necessarily any contradiction between this belief and my refusal to be reconciled to the conditions of

114

my existence. You see, if I had believed that women could love me looking as I did, that is to say, in the actual conditions of my existence, then to the extent that I believed it, I'd have been reconciled to those conditions. I realized that the two types of courage—the courage to judge reality exactly as it was, and the courage to fight that judgment—could very easily be reconciled with each other. Without stirring, I could easily get the feeling that I was fighting.

"Since this was my state of mind, it was only natural that I should not have tried to lose my virginity by consorting with professional women as so many of my friends did. What stopped me, of course, was the fact that professional women don't go to bed with their customers because they like them. They'll have anyone as a customer, doddering old men, beggars, one-eyed men, good-looking men—even lepers, so long as they don't know they're lepers. This egalitarian approach would put most ordinary young men at their ease and they'd merrily go ahead and buy the first women they met. But I didn't appreciate this egalitarianism myself. I couldn't bear the idea that a woman should treat a perfectly normal man and someone like myself on a basis of equality. It seemed to me like a terrible self-defilement. You see, I was possessed by the fear that if my clubfooted condition was overlooked or ignored, I would in a sense cease to exist. It was the same fear that you're suffering from now, wasn't it? For my condition to be completely recognized and approved, it was essential that things should be arranged for me far more luxuriously than most people require. Whatever happened, I thought, that was how life had to turn out for me.

"No doubt it would have been possible to get over my terrible feeling of dissatisfaction—dissatisfaction that the world and I had been placed in a relationship of antagonism. It would have been possible by changing either myself or the world. But I hated dreaming about such changes. I loathed preposterous dreams of this kind. The logical conclusion that I reached after much hard thought was that if the world changed, I could not exist, and if I changed, the world could not exist. And paradoxically enough, this conclusion represented a type of reconciliation, a type of compromise. It was possible, you see, for the world to co-exist with the idea that looking as I did, I could never be loved. And the trap into which the deformed person finally falls does not lie in his resolving the state of antagonism between himself and the world, but instead takes the form of his completely approving of this antagonism. That's why a deformed person can never really be cured.

"Well, it was at this point in my life, when I was in the bloom of my youth—I use the phrase advisedly—that something unbelievable happened to me. There was a girl from a wealthy family who were parishioners of our temple. This girl had graduated from the Kobe Girls' School and she was well known for her looks. One day she happened to let out the fact that she loved me. For a while I could not believe my own ears. Due to my unfortunate condition, I was an expert in fathoming other people's psychology. For this reason, I did not perversely dismiss the whole affair, as many people would, by attributing this love of hers to mere sympathy. I was thoroughly aware that no girl would love me just out of sympathy. Instead, I guessed that the cause of this girl's love was her very exceptional sense of pride. This girl was fully aware of her own beauty and of her own value as a woman, and it was impossible for her to accept any suitor who showed signs of self-confidence. She couldn't bear the idea of putting her own pride on the scales against the conceit of some self-confident young man. She had the chance of numerous so-called good matches, but the better they were, the more she disliked them. In the end, she fastidiously rejected any love that involved some form of balance—on this point she was completely faithful—and set her eyes on me.

"I already knew what answer I would give her. You may laugh at me, but I told her quite simply: 'I don't love you.' What else could I have said? This answer was honest and utterly unaffected. If, instead, I'd decided not to miss a good opportunity and had answered her declaration by

116

saying: 'I love you too,' I'd have appeared worse than ridiculous—I'd almost have appeared tragic. People with comic looks like me are extremely adept at avoiding the danger of appearing tragic by mistake. I knew very well that if I once began to appear tragic, people would no longer feel at ease when they came into contact with me. It was especially important for the souls of other people that I should never appear to be a wretched figure. That's why I made a clean break of it and said: 'I don't love you.'

"The girl wasn't taken back by my answer. Without hesitation, she said that I was lying. It was a real spectacle to see how she then tried to win me over, while at the same time being extremely careful not to hurt my pride. This girl couldn't possibly imagine that there might be a man in this world who wouldn't love her if he had the chance. If there should be such a person, he could only be deceiving himself. And so she embarked on a thorough analysis of me and finally arrived at the conclusion that I had in fact been in love with her for some time. She was a clever girl. Assuming that she really did love me, she must have realized that she loved someone who was peculiarly hard to reach. Almost anything that she said would be wrong. If she pretended that I had an attractive face when in fact I don't, she would have annoyed me. If she said that my clubfeet were beautiful, that would have annoyed me even more. And if she made some remark about not loving me for my outer appearance, but because of what she felt was inside me, she'd really have made me angry. Anyhow, being clever, she took all this into account and simply continued saying: 'I love you.' And according to her analysis, of course, she had discovered a feeling within me that corresponded to this love of hers.

"I could not accept this sort of illogicality. At the same time, I was gradually being overcome with a violent desire for the girl, but I did not think that desire would ever bring her and me together. It occurred to me that if she really did love me and no one else, it must mean that I must have some individual characteristic that distinguished me from other people. And what could this

117

be but my clubfeet? So it came down to the fact that, though she didn't say so, she loved my clubfeet. Now this was completely unacceptable so far as my own thinking was concerned. If my individuality had not in fact existed in my clubfeet, this love might perhaps have been acceptable. But if I were to recognize my individuality—my reason for existing—as lying somewhere other than in my clubfeet, it would involve a sort of supplementary recognition. Then I would inevitably come to recognize other people's reasons for existence in this same supplementary way, and this in turn would lead to my recognizing a self that was thoroughly wrapped up within the world. So love was impossible. Her thinking that she was in love with me was simply an illusion, and I could not possibly love her. Therefore I kept on repeating: 'I don't love you.'

"Strangely enough, the more I told her that I didn't love her, the more she succumbed to the illusion that she was in love with me. And finally one evening she ended by throwing herself at me. She offered me her body, and I may say that it was a dazzlingly beautiful body. But I was completely impotent when it came to the point.

"This terrible failure of mine solved everything quite simply. At last she seemed to have a convincing proof that I really did not love her. She left me.

"I was ashamed at my impotence, but compared to my shame at having clubfeet, nothing else was worth mentioning. What really bothered me was something else. I knew the reason that I had been impotent. It was the thought, when the time came, of my deformed clubfeet touching her beautiful bare feet. And now this discovery utterly destroyed the peace within me that had been part of my belief that I would never be loved by a woman.

"At that moment, you see, I had felt an insincere kind of joy at the thought that by my desire—by the satisfaction of my desire—I would prove the impossibility of love. But my flesh had betrayed me. What I had wanted to do with my spirit, my flesh had performed in its place. And so I was faced with yet another contradiction. To put it in a rather vulgar way, I had been dreaming about love in the firm belief that I could not be loved, but at the final stage I had substituted desire for love and felt a sort of relief. But in the end I had understood that desire itself demanded for its fulfillment that I should forget about the conditions of my existence, and that I should abandon what for me constituted the only barrier to love, namely the belief that I could not be loved. I had always thought of desire as being something clearer than it really is, and I had not realized that it required people to see themselves in a slightly dreamlike, unreal way.

"From then on, my flesh began to attract my attention more than my spirit. But I could not become an incarnation of pure desire. I could only dream about it. I became like the wind. I became a thing which cannot be seen by others, but which itself sees everything, which lightly approaches its objective, caresses it all over and finally penetrates its innermost part. If I speak of the self-consciousness of the flesh, I expect that you will imagine a self-consciousness that relates to some firm, massive, opaque object. But I was not like that. For me to realize myself as a single body, a single desire, meant that I became transparent, invisible, in other words, like the wind.

"But my clubfeet instantly proved themselves to be the great obstacle. They alone would never become transparent. They seemed less like feet than like a couple of stubborn spirits. There they were—far firmer objects than my flesh itself.

"People probably think that they can't see themselves unless they have a mirror. But to be a cripple is to have a mirror constantly under one's nose. Every hour of the day my entire body was reflected in that mirror. There was no question of forgetting. As a result, what is known in this world as uneasiness could only strike me as child's play. There could be no uneasiness in my case. That I existed in this form was a definite fact, as definite as that the sun and the earth existed, or that beautiful birds and ugly crocodiles existed. The world was immobile like a tombstone.

"Not the slightest uneasiness, not the slightest

foothold—therein lay the basis of my original way of living. For what purpose do I live? At such thoughts people feel uneasy and even kill themselves. But it did not bother me. To have a pair of clubfeet—such was the condition of life for me, such was its reason, its aim, its ideal, such was life itself. Just to exist was more than enough to satisfy me. In the first place, doesn't uneasiness about one's existence spring precisely from a sort of luxurious dissatisfaction at the thought that one may not be living fully?

"I began to notice an old widow who lived by herself in our village. She was said to be sixty or, according to some people, even older. At the anniversary service of her father's death, I was sent to recite the sutras at her house in place of my father. None of her relatives had come to the service, and the old woman and I were alone at the altar. When I had finished the sutras, she served me some tea in another room. As it was a hot summer day, I asked her if it would be all right for me to wash myself. I took off my clothes and the old woman poured cold water over my back. I noticed her looking sympathetically at my feet, and immediately a plan occurred to me.

"I finished washing and returned to the room where we had been sitting before. While drying myself, I told her in a serious tone that when I was born, Buddha had appeared to my mother in a dream and announced that if this child should grow to be a man, the woman who sincerely worshipped his feet would be reborn in Paradise. As I spoke, the pious old widow gazed into my eyes intently and fingered her rosary. I lay naked on my back like a corpse; my hands were clasped on my breast, holding a rosary, and I murmured some spurious sutra. I closed my eyes. My lips kept on reciting the sutra.

"You can image how I was stifling my laughter! I was filled with laughter. And I was not dreaming in the slightest about myself. I was aware that the old woman was engaged in the most intent worship of my feet as she recited her sutra. My entire mind was occupied with my feet and I was suffocating with amusement at this ridiculous situation. Clubfeet, clubfeet—that was all I

120

could think of, that was all I could see in my mind. This monstrous formation of my feet. This condition of utmost ugliness in which I had been placed. The wild farce of it! And to make things even funnier, the old woman's stray locks brushed against the soles of my feet as she bowed time after time in prayer, and tickled me.

"It appeared that I had been mistaken about my feelings of lust ever since the time that I had touched that girl's beautiful feet and become impotent. For in the midst of this ugly service, I realized that I was physically excited. Yes, without dreaming about myself in the slightest! Yes, under these most ruthless of all conditions!

"I sat up and abruptly pushed the old woman over. I didn't even have time to think it strange that she showed no surprise at my action. The old widow lay there where I had pushed her, with her eyes shut tight and still reciting her sutra. Strangely enough, I vividly remember that the sutra she was reciting was one chapter of the Great Compassion Darani: '*Ikī ikī. Shino shinō. Orasan. Furashirī. Haza haza furashaya.*' You know how this passage is explained in the commentary, of course: 'We implore thee, we implore thee. For the pure substance of flawless purity in which the Three Evils of greed, anger, and stupidity are all annihilated.'

"Before my eyes, the face of an old woman in her sixties—a sunburned face without any make-up—seemed to welcome me. My excitement did not abate in the slightest. Therein lay the ultimate absurdity of the entire farce, but quite unconsciously I was being *led on* by it. Or rather, I wasn't unconscious—I saw everything. The special quality of hell is to see everything clearly down to the last detail. And to see all that in the pitch darkness!

"The old woman's wrinkled face had nothing beautiful about it and nothing holy. Yet her ugliness and her age seemed to provide a constant affirmation for that inner condition of mine in which there were no dreams. Who could say that if one were to look without dreaming at any woman, however beautiful she might be, her face would not be transformed into the face of this old woman? My clubfeet and this face. Yes, that was it. To look at reality itself maintained my state of physical excitement. Now for the first time I was able to believe in my own lust with a feeling of friendliness. And I realized that the problem lay not in trying to shorten the distance between myself and the object, but in maintaining this distance so that the object might remain an object.

"It is good to look at one's object. At that moment I discovered the logic of my eroticism from the cripple's logic that while he is at a standstill, he has also arrived—from the logic that he can never be visited by uneasiness. I discovered the pretense in what people normally call infatuation. Physical desire was like the wind or like some magic cloak that hides its wearer. And the union born of such desire was no more than a dream. At the same time as looking, I must subject myself to being thoroughly looked at. Then and there, I threw out of my world both my clubfeet and my women. My clubfeet and my women all stayed at the same distance from me. Reality lay there; desire was merely an apparition. And as I looked, I felt myself tumbling down endlessly into that apparition and at the same time being ejaculated onto the surface of the reality at which I was looking. My clubfeet and my women would never touch each other, would never come together; yet together they would be hurled out of the world. Desire rose up endlessly within me. Because my clubfeet and those beautiful feet would never in all eternity have to touch each other.

"Do you have trouble understanding me? Do my words require some explanation? But I am sure you understand that after that I was able to believe with perfect peace of mind that 'love was impossible.' I was released from uneasiness. I was released from love. The world had come to a permanent standstill and at the same time it had arrived. Do I have to elucidate this by saying 'our world'? Thus in a single phrase I can define the great illusion concerning 'love' in this world. It is the effort to join reality with the apparition. Presently I came to realize that my conviction—the conviction that I could never be loved—was itself the basic state of human existence. So now you know how I lost my virginity!"

Kashiwagi finished talking. I had been listening to him intently. Now at last I let out a sigh. I had been profoundly impressed by his talk and could not release myself from the painful sense of having been touched by a manner of thinking that had never occurred to me until then. A few moments after Kashiwagi finished, the spring sun woke up round me and the bright clover began to glitter. The sound of shouting from the basketball court at the back of the building also started again. But although it was still the same noontime on the same spring day, the meaning of all these things seemed to have changed completely.

I could not stay silent. I wanted to chime in, to add to his words. I stuttered out an awkward remark: "You must have been very lonely since then."

Once more Kashiwagi made an unkind pretense of not understanding me and asked me to repeat what I had said. But in his reply he already showed some slight sign of friendliness.

"Lonely, you say? Why should I be lonely? You'll come to find out how I developed after that when you get to know me."

The bell rang for the afternoon lectures. I was about to get up when Kashiwagi, who was still sitting on the grass, roughly pulled me by the sleeve. My university uniform was the same one that I had used at the Zen school. Only the buttons were new; the material was patched and threadbare. Besides, it was far too tight and it made my meager body look even smaller than it really was.

"The next class is Sino-Japanese, isn't it? That's deadly dull. Let's go for a walk instead." With these words, he stood up. It required the most terrible effort: first he seemed to dismember his entire body and then he had to assemble it all again. It reminded me of the camel that I had once seen standing up in a film.

Until then I had never missed a single lecture, but I did not want to lose this chance of hearing more about Kashiwagi. We set off in the direction of the main gate.

After we had passed the main gate, I suddenly became aware of Kashiwagi's really peculiar way of walking and was overcome with a feeling akin to embarrassment. It was curious that I should thus have connived at the commonplace feelings of the world and should have been ashamed to walk with Kashiwagi.

It was Kashiwagi who clearly let me know the whereabouts of my shame. At the same time it was he who had urged me on towards human life. The entire shamefaced side of my nature and all the wickedness in my heart had been healed by his words and had turned into something fresh. Perhaps it was because of this that, as I walked along the gravel past the main gate, Mount Hiei, which I saw ahead of me in the distance, hazy in the spring sun, looked as if I were seeing it for the very first time. And it also seemed to have reappeared there in front of me after renewing its own meaning, in the same way that so many things about me which had slept had now renewed their meaning. The top of the mountain was pointed, but the foothills round its base spread out endlessly, just like some theme of music that lingers in the air. As I gazed at Mount Hiei beyond the rows of low roofs, only the folds in its sides stood out clearly and seemed very close; the springlike shades of the rest of the great mountain were buried in a dense dark blue.

There were not many people walking outside the main gate of Otani University and there were hardly any cars. Only occasionally one could hear the sound of a streetcar clattering along the line that ran from the front of Kyoto Station to the front of the streetcar shed. On the other side of the street the old gateposts of the university stood facing the main gate on our side, and a row of gingko trees with fresh spring leaves stretched out to the left.

"Let's walk round the grounds for a while!" said Kashiwagi.

I led the way over the streetcar tracks to the other side of the street. Kashiwagi lurched heavily across the almost deserted street, his entire body convulsed with violent movement. The university grounds were quite extensive. In the distance several groups of students who had no lectures to attend or who had decided to miss them were playing catch; closer at hand a few boys were practising for a marathon race. The war had only been over for a couple of years, but young people were once more thinking of ways to exhaust their energy. I thought of the poor food that we were given at the temple. We sat on a half-rotten swing and looked absently at our fellow students as they ran towards us and then ran away across the elliptical playing-field, practising for their marathon. Missing class like this had a feel about it like a new shirt against one's skin; the surrounding sunlight and the slight breeze impressed this feel on me. A group of runners moved slowly towards us, breathing heavily; as they became tired, they fell out of step; then they moved into the distance, kicking up a cloud of dust.

"Fools," said Kashiwagi. "That's what they are!" His words did not smack in the least of sour grapes. "What on earth are they putting on that spectacle for? They say it's for their health, I suppose. But what possible good does it do to make a public display of one's health like that? They put on sport shows everywhere, don't they? It's really a sign that we've reached the latter days of decadence. What should be displayed in public is something that's never shown. What the public really should see are—executions! Why don't they put on public executions?"

Kashiwagi paused for a moment, then continued in a dreamy tone: "How do you suppose they managed to keep peace and order during the war if it wasn't by staging public exhibitions of violent death? The reason that they stopped having public executions was, I gather, because they were afraid it would make people bloodthirsty. Damned stupid if you ask me! The people who cleared away the dead bodies after the air raids all had gentle, cheerful expressions. To see human beings in agony, to see them covered in blood and to hear their death groans, makes people humble. It makes their spirits delicate, bright, peaceful. It's never at such times that we become cruel or bloodthirsty. No, it's on a beautiful spring afternoon like this that people suddenly become cruel. It's at a moment like this, don't you think, while one's vaguely watching the sun as it peeps through the leaves of the trees above a well-mown lawn? Every possible nightmare in the

125

world, every possible nightmare in history, has come into being like this. But as one sits there in the clear daylight, it's the idea of bloodstained figures fainting in agony that gives a clear outline to the nightmare and that helps to materialize the dream into reality. The nightmare is no longer our own agony, but the violent physical suffering of other people. And we are not obliged to feel the pain of others. Ah, what a relief that is!"

This sanguinary dogmatism of Kashiwagi's had its charm for me, to be sure, but what I now wanted to hear about was the pilgrimage that he had taken after losing his virginity. For, as I have already mentioned, I was earnestly looking to Kashiwagi for life. I managed to break in and to hint at my interest.

"You mean women?" he said. "Hm. I've come to the point that these days I can accurately tell by intuition whether or not a woman is the type that will like a man with clubfeet. There are such types, you know! It is possible that such a woman may keep her liking for clubfooted men hidden during her entire life. She may even not hesitate to take the secret with her to her grave. This may be the only lapse of taste that this sort of woman has, this may be her only dream. . . . Well let's see. How do you tell the type of woman who likes clubfooted men? As a rule, she's a beauty of the first water. She has a cool tapered nose. But there's something a little loose about her mouth. . . ."

Just then a girl came walking in our direction.

126

CHAPTER FIVE

She was not walking in the university grounds. Outside the grounds there was a road that ran past a block of residential houses. The road was about two feet below the

127

level of the grounds. It was here that she was walking.

The girl had come out of an impressive Spanish-style house. This house gave a rather fragile impression, with its two chimneys, its slanting lattice-work windows and the glass roof that covered its large greenhouse; but the general effect was rather marred by the high wire fence which towered up by the university grounds on the other side of the road, and which had no doubt been put there at the insistence of the owner of the house.

Kashiwagi and I were sitting on the swing outside the fence. I looked at the girl's face and was struck with astonishment. Her noble features were exactly those that Kashiwagi had described in talking about the type of woman who "likes clubfooted men." When later I thought back on the surprise that I had experienced at that moment, I felt rather foolish about it and wondered whether Kashiwagi hadn't been familiar with that face from long before and whether he hadn't dreamt about it.

We sat there waiting for the girl. Under the full rays of the spring sun, the dark-blue peak of Mount Hiei rose in the distance, while, closer at hand, the girl came gradually towards us. I had still not recovered from the sense of excitement which Kashiwagi's recent remarks had given me—his remark that his clubfeet and his women were dotted about the world of reality, like two stars in the sky, without ever touching each other, and his strange words about being able to accomplish his desire while he himself remained constantly buried in a world of apparitions. Just then the sun was covered by a cloud: Kashiwagi and I were wrapped up in a thin shadow and it seemed as if our world had suddenly displayed that aspect of itself which consists of apparitions. Everything was vague and gray and my own existence, too, seemed vague. It seemed as though only the purple peak of Mount Hiei and that graceful girl who was walking towards us were shining in the world of reality and possessed any real existence.

The girl was certainly walking toward us. But as the moments passed, time became like a growing agony, and the closer that she came to us, the more another face grew clear—the face of someone who bore no relation to her.

128

Kashiwagi stood up and whispered heavily in my ear: "Start walking! Just as I tell you."

I was obliged to walk as he directed. We both walked along the stone wall, about two feet above the level of the road, parallel to where the girl was walking and in the same direction.

"Now jump down there!" said Kashiwagi, prodding me in the back with his sharp fingers. I stepped over the low stone wall and jumped onto the road. I had no trouble at all in managing the two-foot jump. But no sooner had I jumped, than Kashiwagi collapsed next to me with a terrible noise. Having tried to jump on his clubfeet, he had actually fallen over. Looking down, I saw the black back of his uniform undulating on the ground. As he lay there on his face, he did not look like a human being; for a moment he seemed to me like some huge, meaningless black smudge, like one of the turbid puddles that one sees on the road after it has rained.

Kashiwagi had fallen down directly in front of where the girl was walking. She stood there, rooted to the spot. When I knelt down to help Kashiwagi to his feet, I looked up at the girl; and as I saw her cool, high-bridged nose, her mouth with its slight suggestion of looseness about the lips, her cloudy eyes—as I saw all her features, there appeared before me for a flash the figure that I had seen in the light of the moon, the figure of Uiko.

The illusion vanished at once and now I saw a girl who could not yet be in her twenties looking down at me with a scornful expression. I could tell that she was about to walk past us. Kashiwagi was even more sensitive than I about feeling such things. He started shouting. His terrible shout echoed through the deserted residential street.

"You callous creature! Are you going to leave me here like this? It's because of you I'm in this state!"

The girl turned round. She was trembling and with her slender, dry fingers she seemed to be rubbing her colorless cheeks. After a while she turned to me and said: "What shall I do?"

Kashiwagi looked up and stared intently at the girl. Then he spoke, giving each word distinct emphasis:

"Do you mean to say that you don't even have any medicine in your house?"

For a moment the girl stood there silently. Then she turned round and started walking in the direction from which she had come. I helped Kashiwagi to stand up. Until he was on his feet, he was extremely heavy and his breath came in painful gasps. But when I offered him my shoulder as we started to walk, I saw that he was moving ahead with extraordinary ease.

I ran to the streetcar stop in front of the Karasumaru streetcar shed and jumped onto a streetcar. Not until the streetcar started in the direction of the Golden Temple could I breathe freely. My hands were covered with perspiration.

As soon as I had helped Kashiwagi through the gate of that Spanish-style house, I had become absolutely terrified. I had left him standing there with the girl in front of him and, without even looking back, had run away. I did not have time to stop at the university, but rushed along the deserted streets, past pharmacies, confectionaries, and electric shops. I remember seeing out of the corner of my eye something purple and crimson fluttering in the breeze. Probably when I had passed in front of the Kotoku Church of the Tenrikyo, I had noticed the lanterns with their plum-blossom crests standing out against the black wall and the purple curtains hanging over the gate with the same plum-blossom crest. I had no idea where I was rushing. When the streetcar gradually approached Murasakino, I realized that my flurried heart was taking me back to the Golden Temple.

We were now in the midst of the tourist season and, although it was a weekday, there were tremendous crowds visiting the Golden Temple. The old guide looked at me suspiciously as I pushed my way through the people and hurried to the temple.

And then I was there—standing in front of the Golden Temple, which on this springtime afternoon was surrounded by the swirling dust and by the hideous crowds. While the guide's voice boomed away, the temple always seemed half to hide its beauty and to feign a certain ignorance. Only the shadows on the pond were bright. But if one looked at them in a certain direction, the clouds of dust seemed like the golden clouds that envelop the Bodhisattvas in that painting of the descent of the saints in which Amida Buddha is shown coming down to earth surrounded by all the Bodhisattvas; in the same way, the form of the Golden Temple, as it stood there hazy in the dust, was like old, faded pigment and a worn-out design. It was in no way strange that the surrounding noise and confusion should enter into the form of the temple's delicate pillars, and that they should be absorbed into the whitish sky toward which the little Kukyocho and the phoenix on top of the roof reached as they soared into the air, gradually becoming thinner. This temple, by just standing there as it did, was a controlling force, a regulating force. The more that the surrounding noise increased, the more the Golden Temple—that asymmetrical, delicate structure, with the Sosei on one side, and above it the Kukyocho, which abruptly tapered off at the top—acted like a filter that transforms muddy into clear water. The temple did not reject the merry chattering of the sight-seers, but instead filtered those sounds, so that they entered in between those permeable pillars and finally became part of the stillness and of the clarity. Thus it accomplished on earth exactly what the shadows of the motionless pond accomplished on the water.

My heart became calm and finally my fear ebbed away. For me, beauty must be of something of this nature. Beauty such as this could cut me off from life and protect me from life.

"If my life is to be like Kashiwagi's, protect me. For I do not think that I could possibly bear it." Such was the prayer that I almost uttered as I stood there facing the temple.

What Kashiwagi had suggested to me in his talk and what he had directly enacted before me could only mean that to live and to destroy were one and the same thing. Such a life lacked everything natural, and it also lacked

131

the beauty of a building like the Golden Temple; indeed, it was little more than a sort of painful convulsion. It is true that I was greatly attracted by such an existence and that I recognized in it my own direction; yet it was terrible to think that one must first bloody one's hands with the thorny fragments of life. Kashiwagi despised instinct and intellect to the same degree. Like some oddly shaped ball, his existence itself rolled round and round and tried to smash the wall of reality. It did not even involve a single deed. The life that he had suggested to me was, in short, a dangerous burlesque with which one tried to smash the reality that had deceived one by means of an unknown disguise, and with which one cleaned the world so that it might never again contain anything unknown.

I know all this from later having seen a poster in the room of Kashiwagi's lodging-house. It was a beautiful lithograph issued by a travel agency and showing the Japanese Alps. On the white mountain peaks, which soared into the blue sky, were printed the words: "We invite you to an unknown world!" Kashiwagi had crossed out this message with brush strokes in poisonous red ink, and next to it in his characteristic dancing form of script, which reminded one of his clubfooted walk, he had scribbled: "I can't stand an unknown life."

I was worrying about Kashiwagi when I went to the university on the following day. In retrospect, it did not seem very friendly of me to have run away and left him, and although I did not feel any particular responsibility, I was uneasy at the possibility of his not appearing in the lecture hall that morning. Just when the lecture was about to start, however, I saw Kashiwagi strut into the room with his usual unnatural gait.

During the break after the lecture I immediately took Kashiwagi by the arm. Such a lighthearted gesture was in itself unusual for me. Kashiwagi smiled out of the corner of his mouth and accompanied me to the corridor.

"You aren't badly hurt, are you?" I said.

"Hurt?" said Kashiwagi, looking at me with a pitying smile. "When should I have got hurt? Eh? What on earth

132

made you take it into your head that I was hurt?"

I was dumbfounded by his words. Having worked me up thoroughly, Kashiwagi explained his secret: "That was all an act. I've practised falling down on that road dozens of times, until I can now give such a convincing performance of having a bad fall that anyone would think I'd broken a bone. I must confess that I hadn't counted on the girl starting to walk past us with the look of complete indifference on her face. But you should have seen what happened. The girl's already beginning to fall in love with me. Or rather, I should say she's falling in love with my clubfeet. You see, she painted my legs with iodine herself."

He pulled up his trouser leg and showed me his shin, dyed yellow. I felt that I now saw through his ruse. It was natural enough that he should have purposely fallen on the road in order to attract the girl's attention; but hadn't he also tried to hide his clubfeet by the pretense of having hurt himself? But this doubt of mine, far from making me despise him, served on the contrary to increase my feelings of friendship. Besides, I had the feeling—a very adolescent feeling, to be sure—that the more his philosophy was full of ruses, the more it proved his sincerity towards life.

Tsurukawa did not approve of my relationship with Kashiwagi. He gave me some extremely friendly advice on the subject, but it only annoyed me. I went so far as to answer his objections by saying that it was perfectly possible for someone like himself to find good friends, but that in my case Kashiwagi was a suitable companion. With what violent regret was I later to recall the unspeakably sad expression that came into Tsurukawa's eyes at that moment!

In May, Kashiwagi made plans for an excursion to Arashiyama in the outskirts of Kyoto. In order to avoid the weekend crowds, he decided to take a day off from the university during the week. Characteristically he announced that he would not go if the weather was good, but only if it was an overcast gloomy day. He was going to take the young lady from the Spanish-style house, and he arranged to bring along a girl from his lodging-house for me.

We were to meet at Kitano Station on the Keifuku electric line. Fortunately it was an unusual day for the time of the year—as cloudy and depressing as Kashiwagi could have wanted.

It happened at this time that Tsurukawa was having some family trouble and that he had taken a week's holiday to go to Tokyo. This worked out rather well for me. Although Tsurukawa was certainly not the type who would have told on me at the temple, I was just as pleased not to have to give him the slip after having come to the university with him in the morning.

Well, my memories of that excursion are bitter ones. The four of us who set out for Arashiyama were all young, and it seemed as though the entire day was colored by the gloom, the irritability, the uneasiness, the nihilism that belong to youth. Kashiwagi had no doubt anticipated it all and purposely chosen a day when the weather was so gloomy. There was a southwesterly wind; just as one was expecting that it was going to blow with full force, it would suddenly die down, to be followed by uneasy gusts. The sky was overcast, but occasionally the sun would glare through. Part of the clouds shone white, like the white breast of a woman that one can vaguely make out under numerous layers of clothes; but further back, the whiteness became indistinct and, although one could still tell where the sun was, it blended with the even, dull color of the sky.

Kashiwagi had not been lying when he told me about the excursion. He duly appeared at the wicket in the station flanked by two young girls. One of them was, indeed, the girl that we had seen. A beautiful girl, with a cool, high-bridged nose and a loose mouth; she carried a water flask over the shoulder of her dress, which, as I could see, was made of imported material. Next to her, the plump girl from the lodging-house was inferior both in dress and in appearance. Only her little chin and her lips, which looked as if they were buttoned up, had an attractive girlish quality about them.

The holiday mood, which should have been a pleasant one, had already begun to break down on the train. I could not hear clearly what Kashiwagi and his young lady were saying to each other, but they were quarreling the entire time. Now and then she would bite her lips as if to repress the tears. The girl from the lodging-house seemed utterly indifferent to everything and sat there softly humming some popular tune. Then suddenly she turned to me and told me the following story: "There's a very pretty woman living near us who teaches flower arrangement. The other day she told me a really sad tale. She had a boy friend during the war. He was an officer in the army and finally the time came for him to go overseas. They only had time for a short farewell meeting at the Nanzen Temple. Their parents didn't recognize their relationship, but this had not stopped them and, shortly before, the girl had become pregnant. She had a still-born child, poor thing! The officer was terribly upset about this. When he saw her on their final day, he said that if they could not have their child, at least he would like to drink the milk from her breast. They didn't have time to go anywhere else, so then and there she squeezed the milk out of her breast into a cup of tea and gave it to him to drink. About a month later, the man was killed in the war. Ever since then, she's been living by herself and hasn't had a single love-affair. She's really an attractive woman and still quite young."

I could hardly believe my ears. That unbelievable scene which I had witnessed with Tsurukawa towards the end of the war from the top of the gate of the Nanzen Temple sprang up in my mind. I made a point of not mentioning my memories to the girl. For I felt that if I were to tell her about them, the emotion that I had experienced now on hearing her story would betray that sense of mystery which had overcome me on that day in the temple. By not telling her, it seemed as if her story, far from solving the riddle of that mystery, would in fact reinforce the mystery and make it still deeper.

The train was passing near the great bamboo grove by

the Narutaki Pond. Since it was May, the leaves of the bamboos were turning yellowish. The wind rustled through the branches, blowing the dry leaves down onto the thickly strewn surface of the grove; but the lower parts of the bamboos seemed to have no connection with all this, and stood there sunk quietly into themselves, with their great joints promiscuously entwined. Only when the train rushed past, the nearby bamboos made a great show of bending and shaking. One shiny young bamboo stood out among them all. The painful manner in which it bent gave me the impression of some strange, bewitching movement; I caught it with my eyes, then it moved away into the distance and disappeared.

When we reached Arashiyama, we walked towards the Togetsu Bridge and came to the grave of Lady Kogo, which none of us had ever noticed before. Many hundreds of years in the past, this lady had hidden herself in Sagano for fear of incurring the displeasure of Taira no Kiyomori. Minamoto no Nakakuni had set out to search for her on the orders of the Emperor, and had discovered her hiding-place from the faint sound of the harp that he had heard on a moonlit autumn night. The tune that she was playing had been "Loving Thoughts of A Husband." In the No play *Kogo* it was written: "When he emerged into the night, filled with yearning for the moonlight, he came to Horin and here it was that he heard the harp. He knew not whether it was the storm breaking over the mountaintops or the wind whistling through the pines. When he enquired what tune it might be that this lady was playing, he was told that it was 'Loving Thoughts of A Husband.' And he rejoiced greatly; for this betokened that the player was thinking lovingly of her husband." The Lady Kogo had spent the last part of her life in Sagano, praying for the future salvation of Emperior Takakura.

The grave, which was at the end of a narrow path, was merely a small stone pillar planted between a huge maple and a withered old plum tree. Kashiwagi and I recited a sutra in pious memory of the dead lady. There was something extremely blasphemous about the solemn way in which Kashiwagi spoke the sacred words. His manner

136

infected me, and soon I was reciting the sutra in the same high-spirited way in which students hum tunes through their noses. This bit of desecration served to release my spirits to an extraordinary degree and made me feel quite lively.

"There's something very shabby about a noble grave like this, isn't there?" said Kashiwagi. "Political power and the power of wealth result in splendid graves. Really impressive graves, you know. Such creatures never had any imagination while they lived, and quite naturally their graves don't leave any room for imagination either. But noble people live only on the imaginations of themselves and others, and so they leave graves like this one which inevitably stir one's imagination. And this I find even more wretched. Such people, you see, are obliged even after they are dead to continue begging people to use their power of imagination."

"You mean that nobility only exists in the power of imagination?" I said, merrily joining in the conversation. "You often speak of reality. What do you consider to be the reality of nobility?"

"It's this!" said Kashiwagi, slapping the top of the moss-covered pillar. "It's stone or bone—the inorganic residue that people leave after they are dead."

"You're damned Buddhist in your views, aren't you?" I said.

"What's it got to do with Buddhism or any stuff like that?" said Kashiwagi. "Nobility, culture, what people consider aesthetic—the reality of all those things is barren and inorganic. It isn't the Ryuan Temple that you see, but simply a pile of stones. Philosophy, art—it's all a lot of stones. The only really organic concern that people have is politics. It's a shame, isn't it? One can almost say that human beings are no more than self-defiling creatures."

"What about sexual desire? Where does that fit in?"

"Sexual desire? Well, that's halfway between. It's a matter of going round and round in a vicious circle from human beings to stone and back to human beings, like a game of blind man's buff."

I instantly wanted to add something to refute the beauty

137

in his thoughts, but the two girls had become tired of our discussion and had started back along the narrow path. We turned around and followed them. One could see the Hozu River from the path. We were exactly by the dam north of the Togetsu Bridge. The Ranzan hills on the opposite bank were heavy with gloomy green, but at just that point a vivid white streak of foam stretched across the river and the air was full of the water's roar.

We walked along the river until we reached the Kameyama Park at the end of the road. There was a good number of boats on the river, but when we entered the park gate, we found that the only thing scattered about was wastepaper: it was clear that there were very few visitors that day.

At the gate we turned back and looked once more at the Hozu River and at the green foliage of Arashiyama. One could see a small waterfall on the other side of the river.

"Beautiful scenery is hell, isn't it?" said Kashiwagi.

I felt that when Kashiwagi spoke like this, he was talking at random. Yet I tried to look at that scenery with Kashiwagi's eyes and to recognize that it was, as he said, hell. My effort was not in vain. For now I could see that hell was indeed quivering in that quiet, casual scene that lay before me, wrapped in its fresh foliage. It seemed that hell could appear day or night, at any time, at any place, simply in response to one's thoughts or wishes. It seemed that we could summon it at our pleasure and that instantly it would appear.

The cherry trees in Arashiyama, which were said to have been transplanted in the thirteenth century from the famous trees on Mount Yoshino, had entirely lost their blossoms and were already putting forth their foliage. When the cherry-blossom season was finished, these trees could only be called by the name that one gives dead beauties.

In Kamayama Park most of the trees were pines, and here the colors did not change with the seasons. It was a large, hilly park. The trees were all tall and they had no leaves until fairly high up. There was something disquieting about the sight of this park with all its countless, naked tree trunks crossing each other irregularly. A wide path led round the park; it was full of uneven slopes, and when one thought that it was going to rise, it would instead go down. Here and there I noticed tree stumps, shrubs, and little pines. Near where the great white rocks emerged from the ground in which they were half buried, the azaleas blossomed with a profusion of purple. Under the cloudy sky their color looked as if it harbored some evil design. We climbed up a small hill and sat down to rest under an umbrella-shaped arbor. Below us on an incline was a swing, on which a young couple was seated. From where we were, we could see the entire park spread out to the east, and in the west we could look down through the trees onto the waters of the Hozu River. The constant creaking of the swing reached us in the arbor like the grinding of teeth.

Kashiwagi's young lady opened the package that she was carrying. He had been right in saying that we did not need to go and have lunch. For the package contained enough sandwiches for four people, as well as imported biscuits, which were still so hard to obtain, and even a bottle of Suntory whisky, which at that time could only be bought on the black market, since the supply was all officially allotted to the Occupation forces. Kyoto was supposed to be the center of black-market activities in the Osaka-Kyoto-Kobe area.

I had great difficulty in drinking spirits, but when the girl offered Kashiwagi and me our little glasses, I joined my hands reverently and accepted mine. The two girls drank tea from a canteen. I was still rather dubious about how Kashiwagi and his companion had come to be on such close terms. I could not understand why this girl, who looked so hard to please, should have become friendly with a penniless, clubfooted student like Kashiwagi. After he had drunk a few glasses of whisky, he started to speak, as if in answer to the question that was in my mind.

"You remember that we were quarreling earlier in the train, don't you?" he said. "It's because this girl's family is insisting that she get married to a man whom she doesn't

139

like at all. It looked as if she was going to be weak-minded about the matter and give in to them at any moment. So I've been consoling her and threatening her and telling her that I'd go all out to stop this marriage."

This was hardly something that he should have said in front of the girl herself, but Kashiwagi spoke quite nonchalantly, as though she were not there at all. The girl did not change her expression in the slightest. She was wearing a necklace of blue porcelain beads round her lithe neck. Her features stood out almost too distinctly against the cloudy sky, but they were softened by her abundant black hair. Her eyes were set very deep and they alone gave one a fresh, naked impression. As usual, her loose mouth was slightly open. In the narrow space between her lips, her thin, sharp teeth looked fresh and dry and white. They were like the teeth of a little animal.

"Oh, it hurts, it hurts!" cried Kashiwagi all of a sudden, bending his body and grasping his legs. I rushed over excitedly and tried to help him, but he pushed me away and at the same time gave me a curious derisive grin. I withdrew my hand.

"Ouch, it hurts!" he groaned in an utterly convincing tone. At that moment I happened to glance at the young lady beside me. A remarkable change had come over her face. Her eyes had lost their composure, and her mouth was quivering impetuously. Only her cool, high-bridged nose seemed to be unmoved by what was happening and provided a curious contrast with the rest of her features; the harmony and balance of her face had been completely destroyed.

"Oh, I'm sorry!" she said, "I'm so sorry! I'll make you better, though. I'll make you better at once." This was the first time that I had heard her speak in this shameless, high-pitched voice, as though she were alone with the man. She raised her long, graceful neck and looked vaguely about for a moment. Then she knelt down at once on the stone in the arbor and embraced Kashiwagi's legs. She put her cheek against his feet and finally began to kiss them.

I was horror-struck, as I had been once before. I turned

140

to the girl from the lodging-house. She was looking in a different direction and was humming a tune to herself.

It seemed at that moment as if the sun had broken through the clouds, but it may have been a mere illusion on my part. Yet the entire composition of the park had lost its harmony. I felt that tiny cracks had begun to open up over all the surface of the picture in which we were contained—that pellucid picture which included the pine forest, the shining reflection of the river, the hills in the distance, the white surface of the rocks, the azaleas scattered here and there.

Evidently the expected miracle had occurred and Kashiwagi gradually stopped groaning. He raised his head, and as he raised it, he once more cast a derisive grin in my direction.

"I'm all right now," he said. "You've cured me. Strange, isn't it? When it starts hurting and you do that to me, the pain invariably stops."

He took the girl's hair in both hands and lifted up her face. She looked up at him with the expression of a faithful dog and smiled. At that moment the white clouded light made this beautiful girl's face look exactly like the face of that old woman in her sixties about whom Kashiwagi had once told me.

Having accomplished his miracle, Kashiwagi was in high spirits. He was in such high spirits, indeed, as to be almost demented. He laughed loudly, lifted the girl onto his knees and began kissing her. His laughter echoed in the branches of the pine trees at the bottom of the hill.

"Why don't you make love to that girl?" he said to me as I sat there quietly. "I brought her along especially for you, you know. Or are you shy because you think she'll laugh at you if you stutter? Go ahead—stutter, stutter! For all you know, she may fall in love with a stutterer."

"Do you stutter?" said the girl to me, as though this was the first time that she had realized it. "Well, well, almost all the deformities are represented today!"

Her words struck me violently and made me feel that I could no longer stay where I was. But, strangely enough, the hatred that I felt for the girl was transformed into a sudden desire for her and I was overcome with a sort of dizziness.

"Why don't we split up?" said Kashiwagi, looking down at the young couple, who were still sitting on the swing. "We'll each take our partners to some secluded place and we'll meet here again in two hours."

I left Kashiwagi and his companion and, accompanied by the girl from the lodging-house, went down the hill and then walked up a gentle slope to the east.

"He's gone and made that girl think she's a saint. It's his usual trick."

"How do you know?" I said, stuttering badly.

"Well, I've had an affair with Kashiwagi myself, you see."

"It's finished between you two now, isn't it?" I said. "And yet you can take it all so lightly."

"Yes, I take it lightly, all right. With a deformed fellow like that, it can't be helped."

This time her words, instead of angering me, filled me with courage and my question emerged smoothly: "You loved his deformed feet, didn't you?"

"Stop it!" she said. "I don't want to talk about those frog-feet of his. But I do think he has lovely eyes."

At this, I once more lost my self-confidence. Whatever Kashiwagi might believe, this girl loved some good point of his that he himself had not noticed; and, as I now realized, my own arrogant conviction that there was nothing about myself of which I was not aware resulted from my having singled myself out as the one person who could have no such good points whatsoever.

When we reached the top of the slope, we came to a small, peaceful field. In the distance through the pines and the cedars one could vaguely make out Daimonjiyama, Nyoigatake, and other mountains. A bamboo thicket stretched from the hill where we were and down the slope which led to the town. At the edge of the thicket stood a single late-blossoming cherry tree which had still not shed its blossoms. These were indeed late blossoms, and I wondered whether it wasn't because they had kept on stuttering when they first opened up that they were thus delayed.

I had an oppressive feeling in my chest and my stomach was heavy. But it was not because of what I had drunk. Now that the crucial moment was approaching, my desire increased in weight, became an abstract structure separated from my own body and descended onto my shoulders. It felt like a heavy, black piece of iron machinery.

As I have already mentioned many times, I appreciated the fact that Kashiwagi, whether out of kindness or out of malice, had urged me on toward life. I had already long since recognized that I, who in my middle-school days had deliberately scratched the scabbard of my schoolmate's sword, was not qualified to enter life through its bright surface. It was Kashiwagi who had first taught me the dark by-way along which I could reach life from the back. At first sight this appeared to be a method that could only lead to destruction; yet it was replete with unexpected stratagems, it transformed baseness into courage, it could even be called a sort of alchemy that restored what is known as immorality to its original state of pure energy. And this indeed was life of a kind. It was a life that advanced, that captured, that changed, that could be lost. It would hardly be called typical life, yet it was endowed with all the functions of life. Assuming that in some invisible place we are confronted with the premise that every form of life is meaningless, then this life that Kashiwagi had shown me must increasingly assume a value equivalent to the more commonplace types of life.

It could not be said, I thought, that Kashiwagi himself was free of intoxication. I had long since realized that in any form of knowledge, however gloomy, there lurked the intoxication of knowledge itself. And what, after all, served to intoxicate people was alcohol.

The girl and I sat down next to some faded, worm-eaten irises. I could not understand why she should want to associate with me in this way. I could not understand—and I use this cruel expression intentionally—what impulse drove her to this *desire for contamination*. In this world of ours there should be a nonresistance that is full of shyness and gentleness; but this girl simply let my hands gather on her own small, plump hands, like flies gathering on someone who is taking a nap. Yet the drawn-out kiss and the feel of the girl's soft chin awakened my feeling of lust. This was what I was supposed to have been dreaming about for so long, but the feeling itself was thin and shallow. My lust did not seem to advance directly, but to run round a circuitous track. The cloudy white sky, the rustling of the bamboo grove, the strenuous efforts of the ladybird as it crawled up the leaf of an iris—all these things remained as they had been before, scattered and without order.

I tried to escape by thinking of the girl in front of me as the object of my lust. I must think of this as being life. I must think of this as the one barrier in the way of my advancing and my capturing. For, if I were to miss this chance, life would not come visiting me indefinitely. The memories raced through my mind of all the countless times when my words had been blocked by stuttering and been unable to issue from my mouth. At this moment I should resolutely have opened my mouth and said something, even if it meant stuttering. Thus I could have made life my own. Kashiwagi's brutal bidding, that blunt shout of his: "Stutter, stutter!" echoed in my ears and put me on my mettle. Finally I slipped my hand up the girl's skirt.

Then the Golden Temple appeared before me.

A delicate structure, gloomy and full of dignity. A structure whose gold foil had peeled off in different places, and which looked like the carcass of its former luxury. Yes, the Golden Temple appeared before me—that strange building which, when one thought it was near, became distant, that building which always floated clearly in some inscrutable point of space, intimate with the beholder, yet utterly remote. It was this structure that now came and stood between me and the life at which I was aiming. At first it was as small as a miniature painting, but in an instant it grew larger, until it

144

completely buried the world that surrounded me and filled every nook and cranny of this world, just as in that delicate model which I had once seen the Golden Temple had been so huge that it had encompassed everything else. It filled the world like some tremendous music, and this music itself became sufficient to occupy the entire meaning of the world. The Golden Temple, which sometimes seemed to be so utterly indifferent to me and to tower into the air outside myself, had now completely engulfed me and had allowed me to be situated within its structure.

The girl from the lodging-house flew away into the distance like a tiny speck of dust. Inasmuch as the girl had been rejected by the Golden Temple, my efforts at finding life, too, were rejected. How could I possibly stretch out my hands towards life when I was being thus enwrapped in beauty? Perhaps beauty also had the right to demand that I relinquish my earlier aim. For clearly it is impossible to touch eternity with one hand and life with the other. Assuming that the meaning of those actions which we direct at life is that we may pledge devotion to a certain instant and make that instant stand still, then perhaps the Golden Temple was fully aware of this and had for a time suspended its usual attitude of indifference towards me. It seemed as though the temple had assumed the form of a single instant of time and had visited me here in this park so that I might know how empty was my longing for life. In life, an instant that assumes the form of eternity will intoxicate us; but the Golden Temple knew full well that such an instant is insignificant compared with what happens when eternity assumes the form of an instant, as the temple itself had now done. It is at such times that the fact of beauty's eternity can really block our lives and poison our existences. The instantaneous beauty that life lets us glimpse is helpless against such poison. The poison crushes and destroys it at once, and finally exposes life itself under the light-brown glare of ruin.

It was only for a short time that I was completely embraced by this vision of the Golden Temple. When I returned to myself, the temple was already hidden. It was merely a building that still stood far to the northeast in Kinugasa and that I could not possibly see from here. The moment of illusion, in which I had imagined myself being accepted and embraced by the Golden Temple, had passed. I was lying on the top of a hill in Kameyama Park. There was nothing near me but a girl who lay there sprawled lasciviously amid the grass and the flowers and the dull fluttering of the insects' wings. At my sudden exhibition of timidity, the girl sat up and looked at me blankly. I saw her hips moving as she turned her back on me and took a pocket-mirror out of her bag. She did not say a word, but her scorn pierced my skin through and through, like the burrs that stick to one's clothes in the autumn.

The sky hung low. Tiny raindrops began to beat against the surrounding grass and the leaves of the iris. We stood up hurriedly and returned along the path to the arbor.

It was not only because the excursion had ended so wretchedly that this day left such an exceptionally gloomy impression. That evening, before the "opening of the pillow," the Superior received a telegram from Tokyo. The contents were immediately announced to everyone in the temple.

Tsurukawa was dead. The telegram simply said that he had died in an accident, but later we heard the details. On the previous evening Tsurukawa had gone to visit an uncle of his in Asakusa and had drunk a good deal of saké. He was not used to drinking and it had evidently gone to his head. On his way back he had been knocked down by a truck that had suddenly come out of a side street near the station. He had suffered a skull fracture and died instantly. His family had been at their wits' end and it was not until the following afternoon that they had realized that they ought to telegraph the temple.

Although I had not cried at Father's death, I cried now. For Tsurukawa's existence seemed to have a closer connection than my father's with the problems that beset me. I had been rather neglecting Tsurukawa since I had come to know Kashiwagi, but now, having lost him, I

146

realized that his death severed the one and only thread that still connected me with the bright world of daylight. It was because of the lost daylight, the lost brightness, the lost summer, that I was crying.

Though I wanted to hurry to Tokyo to pay a visit of condolence to Tsurukawa's family, I did not have the money. I only received five hundred yen a month from the Superior for pocket money. My mother, of course, was indigent. It was the most she could do to send me two or three hundred yen a couple of times a year. The reason that she had been obliged to go and live with an uncle in Kasagun after settling matters in Father's temple was that she could not manage to live on the five hundred yen a month that the parishioners contributed and on the minute grant offered by the prefecture.

How could I possibly make sure of Tsurukawa's death in my mind without having seen his corpse and without having attended his funeral? The problem tormented me. That white-shirted stomach of his that I had once seen shimmering in the rays of the sun as they poured through the trees had been turned to ashes. Who could imagine this boy's flesh and spirit, which had been made only for brightness and which was only suitable to brightness, lying buried in a grave? He had not carried the slightest mark of being destined for a premature death, he had been constitutionally free of all uneasiness and grief and had born no element that even vaguely resembled death. Perhaps it was precisely because of this that he had died so suddenly. Perhaps it had been impossible to save Tsurukawa from death just because he was composed of only the pure ingredients of life and had the frailty of a pure-blooded animal. In this case it would seem that I, on the contrary, was fated to live to a cursed old age.

The transparent structure of the world in which he lived had always been a deep mystery for me, but now with his death the mystery became still more fearful. That truck had crushed his transparent world, just as though it had run into a sheet of glass that is invisible because it is transparent. The fact that Tsurukawa had not died of illness fitted in perfectly with this image. It was suitable

147

that he, whose life had been so incomparably pure a structure, should suffer the pure death of an accident. In that collision, which had lasted no more than a second, there had been a sudden contact and his life had merged with his death. A swift chemical action. Without doubt it was only by such a drastic method that this strange, shadowless young man could join both his shadow and his death.

The world that Tsurukawa had inhabited was overflowing with bright feelings and good intentions. Yet I can definitely affirm that it was not thanks to his misunderstandings or to his sweet, gentle judgments that he lived there. That bright heart of his, which did not belong to this world, was backed by a strength and by a powerful resiliency, and it was these that had come to regulate his actions. There was something superbly accurate about the way in which he had been able to translate each of my dark feelings into bright feelings. Sometimes I had suspected that Tsurukawa had actually experienced my own feelings, just because his brightness corresponded so accurately to my darkness, because the contrast between our feelings was so perfect. But no, it was not so! The brightness of his world was both pure and one-sided. It had brought into being its own detailed system, and it possessed a precision which might also have approached the precision of evil. If that young man's bright, transparent world had not constantly been supported by his untiring bodily power, it might instantly have collapsed. He had been running forward full tilt. And the truck had run over that running body of his.

Tsurukawa's cheerful looks and carefree body, which were the source of the favorable impression that he made on others, led me, now that they had been lost to this world, to embark on mysterious reflections concerning the visible side of human beings. I thought of how strange it was that something, by simply existing and reaching our eyes, could exercise so bright a force. I thought of how much must be learned from the body in order that the spirit might possess so simple a sense of its own existence. It is said that the essence of Zen is the absence of all particularities, and that the real power to see consists in the knowledge that one's own heart possesses neither form nor feature. Yet the power to see, which is capable of properly envisaging the absence of feature, must be exceedingly keen in resisting the charm of formal appearances. How can a person who is unable to see forms or features with selfless keenness so vividly see and apprehend formlessness and featurelessness? Thus the clear form of a person like Tsurukawa who emitted brightness by the mere fact of his existence, of a person who could be reached by both hands and eyes, who could in fact be called life for life's sake, might, now that this person was dead, serve as the clearest possible metaphor to describe unclear formlessness; and his sense of his own existence might become the most real, existent model of formless nihility. It seemed, indeed, as though he himself might now have become nothing more than such a metaphor. For example, the aptness and suitability of the juxtaposition between Tsurukawa and May flowers was precisely the aptness and suitability of those flowers which, as a result of his sudden May death, had been thrown onto his coffin.

My own life possessed no such firm symbolism as Tsurukawa's. For this reason I needed him. And what I envied most about him was that he managed to reach the end of his life without the slightest conscience of being burdened with a special individuality or sense of individual mission like mine. This sense of individuality robbed my life of its symbolism, that is to say, of its power to serve, like Tsurukawa's, as a metaphor for something outside itself; accordingly, it deprived me of the feelings of life's extensity and solidarity, and it became the source of that sense of solitude which pursued me indefinitely. It was strange. I did not even have any feeling of solidarity with nothingness.

Once again my solitude had started. I did not see the girl from the lodging-house again and my relations with Kashiwagi became less friendly than before. Kashiwagi's way of life still exerted a powerful fascination on me, but I felt that I would be carrying out my final service to Tsurukawa if I made some slight effort to resist this fascination and tried, however unwillingly, to keep my distance. I wrote my mother clearly that she should not come to visit me again until I had attained my independence. I had already told her this verbally, but I did not feel that I could rest easy until I had committed it to writing in the strongest terms. Her answer was couched in awkward phrases. She told me about how hard she was working at Uncle's farm and followed this by a few sentences that smacked of elementary admonitions. Then she had appended the following sentence: "I don't want to die until I have seen you with my own eyes as a priest in the Golden Temple." I hated this part of the letter and for some days after it made me feel uneasy.

Even during the summer I did not once visit the place where Mother was making her home. Due to the poor food at the temple, the summer heat was a great strain on me. In the middle of September there was a report of a possible typhoon. Someone had to stand night watch and I volunteered for the job.

I think that it was about this time that a delicate change started in my feelings concerning the Golden Temple. It was not hatred, but a premonition that at some time or other a situation would inevitably arise in which the thing that was slowly germinating within me would be utterly incompatible with the Golden Temple. This feeling had been emerging ever since that incident at Kameyama Park, but I had been afraid to put a name to it. Yet I was happy to know that during this one night's watch the temple would be entrusted to me and I did not conceal my pleasure.

I was given the key to the Kukyocho. This third story of the temple was regarded as especially valuable. A few feet above the floor an impressive tablet inscribed by the Emperor Go-Komatsu was hanging against one of the beams.

The wireless was reporting that the typhoon would be with us momentarily, but there was still not a sign of it. It had been raining intermittently during the afternoon, but now it had cleared up and a bright full moon appeared in the night sky. The various inmates of the temple had strolled into the garden and were examining the sky. I heard someone say that this was the quiet before the storm.

The temple fell asleep. Now I was alone in the Golden Temple. When I wandered into a part of the building where the light of the moon could not enter, I was entranced at the thought that the heavy, luxurious darkness of the temple was enveloping me. Slowly, deeply, I became immersed in this very real feeling, until it grew into a sort of hallucination. Suddenly I realized that I had now actually entered that vision which had separated me from life that afternoon in Kameyama Park.

I was there alone, and the Golden Temple—the absolute, positive Golden Temple—had enveloped me. Did I possess the temple, or was I possessed by it? Or would it not be more correct to say that a strange balance had come into being at that moment, a balance which would allow me to be the Golden Temple and the Golden Temple to be me?

After about half past eleven, the wind grew stronger. I switched on my flashlight and climbed the stairs of the temple. When I reached the top, I put my key to the door of the Kukyocho.

I was leaning against the railings of the Kukyocho. The wind came from the southeast. Yet so far the sky had remained unaltered. The moon was reflected on the water in the interstices between the duckweed. The air was full of the chirping of insects and the croaking of frogs.

When the powerful wind first struck me square on the cheek, an almost sensual shiver ran through my body. The wind grew stronger and stronger until it became a great gale. Now it seemed to be a sort of omen that I was to be destroyed together with the Golden Temple. My heart was within that temple and at the same time it rested on that wind. The Golden Temple, which prescribed the very structure of my world, had no curtains to shake in the wind, but stood there calmly bathing in the moonlight. Yet there was no doubt that the great wind, that evil intention of mine, would eventually shake the temple, awaken it and, at the moment of destruction, rob it of its arrogance.

That is how it was. I was enwrapped in beauty, I was certainly within that beauty; yet I doubt whether I was so consummately wrapped up in the beauty as not to be supported by the will of that ferocious wind, which was endlessly gathering force. Just as Kashiwagi had commanded me: "Stutter! Stutter!" so now I tried to spur on the wind by shouting the words with which one encourages a galloping horse: "Stronger, stronger!" I shouted. "Go faster! Put more strength into it!"

The forest started to rustle. The branches of the trees round the pond brushed against each other. The night sky had lost its usual indigo color and taken on a turbid hue of purple gray. The chirping of the insects had not abated and gave a lively air to the surrounding scene. From the distance the mysterious, flute-like sound of the wind approached; it seemed to be losing some of its earlier fury.

I watched the multitudinous clouds scudding across the moon. One after another they rose up from behind the hills in the south like great battalions. There were thick clouds. There were thin clouds. There were huge expanded clouds. There were countless little tufts of cloud. They all appeared from the south, crossed the surface of the moon, passed over the Golden Temple, and rushed off to the north as though they were hurrying to some important business. I seemed to hear the screech of the golden phoenix above my head.

Suddenly the wind died down; then it regained its strength. The forest responded sensitively to these changes: it became quiet, then it rustled wildly. The reflection of the moon on the pond also changed, becoming dark and light by turns; sometimes it would draw together its scattered beams of light and sweep swiftly across the water. The great cumuli of clouds stretched out tortuously beyond the hills, and extended like a huge hand across the sky. It was terrifying to see how they squirmed and jostled against each other as they approached. Occasionally a small clear area would appear in the sky through the clouds, but almost instantly it

152

would be covered again. Now and then when a very thin cloud passed by, I could glimpse the moon through it, surrounded by a faint aureole.

Thus the sky moved during the entire night. There was no indication that the wind was going to grow any stronger. I slept by the railing. Early the next morning—a clear, bright morning—the sexton came and informed me that the typhoon had left the area, having fortunately missed Kyoto.

CHAPTER SIX

It was almost a year now that I had been in mourning for Tsurukawa. Once my solitude had started, I realized anew that it was easy for me to become accustomed to this state and that the most effortless existence for me was in fact one in which I was not obliged to speak to anyone. My fretful attitude to life left me. Each dead day had its charm.

The university library was my one and only pleasure resort. I did not read books on Zen, but such translations of novels and philosophical works as happened to be on hand. I hesitate to mention the names of those writers and philosophers. I am aware of the influence that they had on me and also of the fact that it was they who inspired me to the deed that I committed; yet I like to believe that the deed itself was my own original creation; in particular, I do not want this deed to be explained away as having been actuated by some established philosophy.

As I have already explained, the fact of not being understood by others had been my sole source of pride since my early youth, and I had not the slightest impulse to express myself in such a way that I might be understood. When I did try to clarify my thoughts and actions, I did so with no consideration whatsoever. I do not know whether or not this was because I wanted to understand myself. Such a motive is in accord with a person's real character and comes automatically to form a bridge between himself and others. The intoxication that I derived from the Golden Temple served to make part of my personality opaque; and, because this intoxication deprived me of all other forms of intoxication, I was obliged to resist it by making a deliberate effort to preserve the clear parts of my personality. I do not know about others, but in my own case, the clarity itself was I and, conversely, it was not a case of my being the owner.

It was now the time of the spring holidays in 1948, my second year in the university. The Superior went out one evening. As I had no friends, the only way in which I could profit from his absence was by taking a walk by myself. I left the temple and walked out through the Sammon Gate. Outside, the gate was bordered by a ditch, next to which stood a notice board. I had been seeing this old board for a long time, but now I stopped before it and idly began reading the characters, which were bathed in the moonlight:

NOTICE

1. *No alterations may be carried out on these premises without special permission.*
2. *Nothing may be done that can in any way affect the preservation of these premises.*

The attention of the public is directed to these regulations.
Any breach of these regulations will be punished according to the law.

MINISTRY OF THE INTERIOR. *March 31, 1928*

The notice clearly referred to the Golden Temple. Yet it was impossible to gather any definite allusion from the abstract words themselves. I could not help feeling that a notice board like this existed in an utterly different world from that inhabitied by the immutable, indestructible temple. The notice itself anticipated some inscrutable or impossible deed. The man who had drafted these regulations and who had thus given a summary description of this sort of deed must have been someone who had hopelessly lost his bearings. For this was a deed that only a madman could plan; and how could one possibly scare a madman in advance by threatening to punish his deed? What was probably needed was a special form of writing that could be understood only by madmen.

I was engaged in such empty thoughts when I noticed a form approaching along the wide road in front of the gate. At this hour there was not a trace of the crowds of sight-seers who came here during the day; only the moonlit pine trees and the glare of the headlights, as the cars passed to and fro along the highway beyond where I stood, filled the night.

All of a sudden I recognized the form as Kashiwagi's. I could tell it was he by the way he walked. Then and there I decided to end the estrangement between us that I had chosen during the entire past year, and thought only of my gratitude towards him for having cured me in the past. For he had indeed cured me at the time. From the first day that I had met him he had cured my crippled thoughts by means of his ungainly clubfeet, by his unreserved and wounding words, by his complete confession. I should by all rights have perceived what joy there lay for me in being able for the first time to hold a conversation with someone on an equal footing. I should have relished that joy (which was akin to committing an act of immorality) of immersing myself into the very depths of the firm knowledge that I was both a priest and a stutterer. Yet all this had been expunged because of my relations with Tsurukawa.

I greeted Kashiwagi with a smile. He wore his student uniform and carried a long, narrow bundle.

"Are you going somewhere?" he said.

"No."

"It's good that I met you," he said. He sat down on some stone steps and unwrapped his bundle.

"You see," he said, showing me two dark, glossy tubes which formed a *shakuhachi* flute, "an uncle of mine in my home town died recently and left me this flute as a keepsake. But I still have the one he gave me long ago when he was teaching me how to play. This one seems to be a rather finer instrument, but I prefer the one that I'm used to and there's no point in my having two of these things. So I've brought this one along to give you."

For someone like me who never received a present from anyone, it was a great joy to be given something, whatever it might be. I picked up the flute and examined it. There were four holes in front and one in back.

"I belong to the Kinko school of flute-playing," continued Kashiwagi. "Since there was a good moon tonight for a change, I thought I'd come along to the Golden Temple and play it here. At the same time I thought I might give you a lesson."

"You've chosen a good time," I said. "The Superior has gone out, you see. Besides, the lazy old caretaker hasn't finished his sweeping yet. They don't close the temple gates until the sweeping has been done."

His appearance at the gate had been abrupt, and so, too, had been his suggestion that he wanted to play the flute in the temple because the moon was so beautiful that night. It all bespoke the Kashiwagi whom I knew. Besides, in my monotonous life the mere fact of being surprised was a pleasure. With my new flute in my hand, I led Kashiwagi to the Golden Temple.

I have no clear recollection about what we discussed that night. I don't believe that we talked about anything very substantial. Kashiwagi gave no sign of wanting to indulge in his usual eccentric philosophy and barbed paradoxes. Perhaps he had come on purpose to reveal a side of himself whose existence I had so far never suspected. And that night, indeed, this young man with his stinging tongue, who usually seemed interested in beauty only in so far as he could defile it, showed me a truly delicate aspect of his nature. He had a far, far more accurate theory about beauty than I did. He did not tell it to me in words, but with his gestures and his eyes, with the music that he played on his flute, and with that forehead of his which emerged in the moonlight.

We leaned against the railing of the second story of the Golden Temple, the Choondo. The corridor under the gently curving eaves was supported from below by eight brackets in the Tenjiku style and seemed to rise up from the surface of the pond, where the moon was lodged. First Kashiwagi played a short piece called the "Palace Carriage." I was amazed at his skill. I tried to copy him and put my lips to the mouthpiece, but I could produce no sound. He then carefully taught me how to hold the flute from above with my left hand and how to put my fingers to the proper openings; he also showed me the tricks of how to open one's mouth to hold the mouthpiece and of how to blow air in against the wide metal foil. Yet, though I tried again and again, no sound emerged. My cheeks and eyes were tense, and, although there was no wind, I had the feeling that the moon on the pond was shattering into a thousand fragments.

After a while I was exhausted, and for a moment I suspected that Kashiwagi might be imposing this penance

159

on me purposely in order to make fun of my stuttering. The effort, however, of trying to force out a sound that would not come seemed to purify that usual mental energy of mine with which I tried my very best to avoid stuttering by pushing the first words smoothly out of my mouth. I felt as if those sounds that still would not emerge already actually existed somewhere in this quiet, moon-bathed world. I was quite content if only I could reach and awaken those sounds after various lengthy efforts.

How could I reach that sound—that mysterious sound like the one which Kashiwagi was blowing out of his flute? It was skill alone that made it possible. Beauty was skill. A thought came to me and filled me with courage: just as Kashiwagi could attain such beautiful clear sounds despite his clubfeet, so I could attain beauty by means of skill. But I also recognized something else: Kashiwagi's playing of the "Palace Carriage" sounded so beautiful not only because of the lovely moonlit background, but because of his hideous clubfeet.

Later when I came to know Kashiwagi more intimately, I understood that he disliked lasting beauty. His likings were limited to things such as music, which vanished instantly, or flower arrangements, which faded in a matter of days; he loathed architecture and literature. Clearly he would never think of visiting the Golden Temple except on a moonlit night like this.

Yet how strange a thing is the beauty of music! The brief beauty that the player brings into being transforms a given period of time into pure continuance; it is certain never to be repeated; like the existence of dayflies and other such short-lived creatures, beauty is a perfect abstraction and creation of life itself. Nothing is so similar to life as music; yet, although the Golden Temple shared the same type of beauty, nothing could have been farther from the world and more scornful of it than the beauty of this building. As soon as Kashiwagi had finished playing the "Palace Carriage," music—that imaginary life—expired, and nothing was left there but his ugly body with its gloomy thoughts, all unscathed and unaltered.

It was certainly not consolation that Kashiwagi sought

in beauty. I understood that much without the slightest discussion. What he loved was that, for a short while after his breath had brought beauty into existence in the air, his own clubfeet and gloomy thinking remained there, more clearly and more vividly than before. The uselessness of beauty, the fact that the beauty which had passed through his body left no mark there whatsoever, that it changed absolutely nothing—it was this that Kashiwagi loved. If beauty could be something like this for me too, how light would my life become!

I kept on trying time after time according to Kashiwagi's instructions. My face became red and my breath came in gasps. Then, just as if I had suddenly become a bird, and as if a bird's cry had escaped my throat, the flute emitted a single daring note.

"There you are!" shouted Kashiwagi with a laugh. It was certainly not a beautiful note, but the same sound emerged time after time. Then I fancied that this mysterious sound, which did not seem to emanate from me, was the voice of that golden copper phoenix above our heads.

Thereafter I used the instruction manual that Kashiwagi had given me and worked hard every evening to improve my playing. In time I was able to play tunes like the "Rising Sun Dyed Red on a White Background," and my former feelings of friendship for Kashiwagi revived.

In May it occurred to me that I ought to give Kashiwagi something to show him my appreciation for the flute. But I had no money to buy him a present. I spoke to Kashiwagi frankly about my predicament. He told me that he didn't want anything that cost money. Then, screwing up his mouth in a strange way, he said: "Well, since you've gone out of your way to mention this matter, there actually is something that I'd like. I've been wanting to do some flower arrangement these days, but flowers are far too expensive for me. Now I believe this is just the time when the iris and sweet flag are in bloom at the Golden Temple. Do you think you could possibly bring me a few irises—one or two in bud, a couple that are just beginning to blossom, and a couple in full bloom? You could also let me have a few cattails. Tonight will be all right. What about bringing them to my lodging-house this evening?"

It was only after I had lightly agreed to his suggestion that I realized that he was actually putting me up to theft. In order for me not to lose face it was, in fact, essential that I become a flower thief.

We had no rice for supper that evening, only boiled vegetables and heavy black bread. Fortunately it was a Saturday and a number of people from the temple had already gone out in the afternoon. Saturday was known as the "inner opening curtain": one could leave the temple early and did not have to be back until eleven o'clock; besides, the following morning was called "sleeping oblivion" and we were allowed to stay in bed late. The Superior had already gone out.

The sun finally set at half past six. It began to be windy. I waited for the sound of the first bell of the night. At eight o'clock the high clear sound of the Ojikicho bell at the left of the center gate announced the first watch of the night; it rang eighteen times and its echo hung for a long time in the air.

Near the Sosei, a small waterfall, half surrounded by a weir, carried the water from a lotus pond into the large Kyoko Pond. It was here that the irises grew in the greatest profusion. They were exceptionally beautiful at that time. As I approached, I heard the clusters of irises rustling in the night wind. The lofty purple petals trembled within the quiet sound of the water. It was very dark in that part of the garden: the purple of the flowers and the dark green of the leaves looked equally black. I tried to pick a few of the irises; but in the wind the flowers and the leaves managed to avoid my hands, and one of the leaves cut my finger.

When I finally arrived at Kashiwagi's lodging-house with an armful of irises and cattails, he was lying down reading a book. I was afraid of meeting the girl who lived here and who had come on the picnic, but fortunately she seemed to be out.

My small theft had made me feel cheerful. The first

things that my contact with Kashiwagi always produced were small acts of immorality, small desecrations, small evils. These always made me cheerful; but I did not know whether a steady increase in the quantity of this evil would produce a corresponding increase in my cheerfulness.

Kashiwagi was delighted with my present. He went to the landlady's room to borrow a bucket and various other utensils needed for his flower arrangement. The lodging-house was a one-storied building; Kashiwagi lived in a small room in an outhouse.

I picked up his flute, which was leaning against the alcove, put my lips to the mouthpiece and tried playing a small étude. I managed extremely well, much to the surprise of Kashiwagi, who just then returned to his room. But the Kashiwagi whom I met that evening was not the same one who had visited the Golden Temple.

"You don't stutter at all when it comes to the flute, do you? When I taught you how to play, I was hoping to hear what stuttering music sounded like!"

With this single remark he pulled us back to the situation that had existed when we first met. He recovered his own position. Thereupon I was able to ask nonchalantly what had happened to the young lady from the Spanish-style house.

"Oh, that girl?" he replied simply. "She got married ages ago. I didn't leave a stone unturned, though, in showing her how to hide the fact that she was no longer a virgin. But her husband is a healthy, innocent type of fellow and things seem to have gone all right."

As he spoke, he removed the irises one by one from the bowl of water where they had been soaking and examined them carefully. Then he put the scissors into the bowl and cut the stems in the water. Each time that he held an iris in his hand, the large shadow of the flower would move across the straw-matted floor of the room. Then suddenly he said: "Do you know the famous words in the chapter of Popular Enlightenment in the *Rinsairoku?* 'When ye meet the Buddha, kill the Buddha! When ye meet your ancestor, kill your ancestor! . . .' "

" 'When ye meet a disciple of Buddha,' " I continued, " 'kill the disciple! When ye meet your father and mother, kill your father and mother! When ye meet your kin, kill your kin! Only thus will ye attain deliverance.' "

"That's right. And that was the situation, you see. That girl was a disciple of Buddha."

"And so you delivered yourself?"

"Hm," said Kashiwagi, arranging some of the irises that he had cut and gazing at them. "There's more to killing than that, you know."

The flower bowl was full of limpid water; it was painted silver on the inside. Kashiwagi examined the flower holder and carefully adjusted one of the spikes that was slightly bent. I felt ill at ease and tried to fill the silence by chatting away.

"You know the problem about Father Nansen and the kitten, don't you? Immediately after the war ended, the Superior called us all together and gave us a sermon about it."

"Oh, 'Nansen Kills a Kitten'?" said Kashiwagi, while he determined the length of a cattail and held it against the flower basin. "That's a problem that crops up several times in a person's life, always in a slightly different form. It's a rather eery problem, you know. Each time that you come across it at some turning-point in your life, it's changed both in appearance and in meaning, though the problem itself is always the same. First let me tell you that the kitten which Father Nansen killed was a rascally creature! She was beautiful, you know, incomparably beautiful. Her eyes were golden, her fur was glossy. Every pleasure and beauty in this world was flexed taut like a spring within that little soft body of hers. Most of the commentators have forgotten to mention the fact that the kitten was a bundle of beauty. Except for me, that is. The kitten jumped out of a clump of grass all of a sudden. Her gentle, cunning eyes were shining and she was caught by one of the priests—just as if she had done it all on purpose. And it was this that resulted in the quarrel between the two halls of the temple. Because, although beauty may give itself to everyone, it does not actually

164

belong to anybody. Let me see.

"How shall I put it? Beauty—yes, beauty is like a decayed tooth. It rubs against one's tongue, it hangs there, hurting one, insisting on its own existence. Finally it gets so that one cannot stand the pain and one goes to the dentist to have the tooth extracted. Then, as one looks at the small, dirty, brown, blood-stained tooth lying in one's hand, one's thoughts are likely to be as follows: 'Is this it? Is this all it was? That thing which caused me so much pain, which made me constantly fret about its existence, which was stubbornly rooted within me, is now merely a dead object. But is this thing really the same as that thing? If this originally belonged to my outer existence, why—through what sort of providence—did it become attached to my inner existence and succeed in causing me so much pain? What was the basis of this creature's existence? Was the basis within me? Or was it within this creature itself? Yet this creature which has been pulled out of my mouth and which now lies in my hand is something utterly different. Surely it cannot be *that*?'

"You see," continued Kashiwagi, "that's what beauty is like. To have killed the kitten, therefore, seemed just like having extracted a painful decayed tooth, like having gouged out beauty. Yet it was uncertain whether or not this had really been a final solution. The root of the beauty had not been severed and, even though the kitten was dead, the kitten's beauty might very well still be alive. And so, you see, it was in order to satirize the glibness of this solution that Joshu put those shoes on his head. He knew, so to speak, that there was no possible solution other than enduring the pain of the decayed tooth."

This interpretation of Kashiwagi's was completely original, but I could not help wondering whether he himself, having seen into my inmost heart, was not being the satirist at my expense. For the first time I became really frightened of him. I was afraid to remain silent and hastened to ask: "So which of the two are you? Father Nansen or Joshu?"

"Well, let's see. As things are now, I am Nansen and you're Joshu. But some day you might become Nansen and I might become Joshu. This problem has a way of changing—like a cat's eyes."

While Kashiwagi was talking, his hands had been moving delicately, first arranging the little, rusty flower holder in the bowl, then inserting the cattail, which occupied the role of Heaven in the arrangement, next adding the irises, which he had adjusted into a three-leaf set. Gradually a flower arrangement of the Kansui school had taken shape. A pile of tiny, well-washed pebbles, some white and some brown, lay next to the bowl, waiting to be used for the finishing touches.

The movement of Kashiwagi's hands could only be described as magnificent. One small decision followed another, and the effects of contrast and symmetry converged with infallible artistry. Nature's plants were brought vividly under the sway of an artificial order and made to conform to an established melody. The flowers and leaves, which had formerely existed *as they were,* had now been transformed into flowers and leaves *as they ought to be.* The cattails and the irises were no longer individual, anonymous plants belonging to their respective species, but had become terse, direct manifestations of what might be called the essence of the irises and the cattails.

Yet there was something cruel about the movement of his hands. They behaved as though they had some unpleasant, gloomy privilege in relation to the plants. Perhaps it was because of this that each time that I heard the sound of the scissors and saw the stem of one of the flowers being cut I had the impression that I could detect the dripping of blood.

The Kansui flower arrangement was now complete. On the right-hand side of the bowl, where the straight line of the cattail blended with the pure curve of the iris leaves, one of the flowers was in bloom and the other two were buds that were about to open. Kashiwagi placed the bowl in the alcove; it filled almost the entire space. Soon the water in the bowl became still. The pebbles concealed the flower holder, and at the same time gave precisely the pellucid impression of a water's edge.

"Magnificent!" I said. "Where did you learn it?"

"There's a woman living nearby who gives lessons in flower arrangement. She'll be coming here any minute now, I expect. I've struck up a friendship with this woman and at the same time she's been teaching me flower arrangement. But now that I can make this sort of arrangement by myself, I'm getting a bit bored with it all. She's still quite young, this teacher, and good-looking. I understand that during the war she had an affair with an officer and became pregnant. The child was still-born and the lover was killed in the war. Since then she's been constantly running after men. She's got a snug little nest of money of her own and evidently only gives these lessons as a hobby. Anyhow, if you want to, you can take her out somewhere this evening. She'll go anywhere."

As I heard this, I was overcome with the most confused feelings. When I had seen her from the top of the gate of the Nanzen Temple, Tsurukawa had been next to me. Now, three years later, she was to appear before me and I was to see her, instead, through Kashiwagi's eyes. Hitherto I had viewed this woman's tragedy with a bright look of mystery; but from now on I would see it with the dark look of someone who believed in nothing. For the stark reality was that her breast, which I had seen in the distance like a white moon in the daylight, had since then been touched by Kashiwagi's hands, and that her legs, enveloped then in that magnificent, flowing kimono, had been touched by Kashiwagi's clubfeet. The reality was that she had already been defiled by Kashiwagi, that is to say, by knowledge.

This thought tormented me greatly and made me feel that I could no longer stay where I was. Yet curiosity kept me from leaving. I could, in fact, hardly wait for the arrival of this woman, whom I had originally seen as a reincarnation of Uiko, but who was now to appear as the discarded mistress of a crippled student. For, having become Kashiwagi's accomplice, I was prepared to indulge in the illusory pleasure of defiling my precious memories with my own hands.

When the woman arrived, I did not feel the slightest

tremor of excitement. I still vividly remember that moment. That faintly husky voice of hers, her ceremonious manners and her formal way of speaking, which contrasted so strikingly with the wild expression that flashed in her eyes, the sadness that emerged from her tone when she spoke to Kashiwagi, despite her obvious embarrassment at my presence—I saw all this and then for the first time I understood why Kashiwagi had asked me to his room that evening: he intended to use me as a barrier.

There was no connection between this woman and the heroine of my vision. She gave me the impression of a completely different individual whom I was seeing for the first time. Although she did not alter her polite manner of speech, I could tell that she was gradually becoming distraught. She did not pay the slightest attention to me.

Finally her misery seemed to become unbearable, and I had the impression that she had decided for a while to abandon her efforts to make Kashiwagi change his mind. She made a pretense of having suddenly calmed down, and looked round the room. Although she had been there for half an hour, she now evidently for the first time noticed the flower arrangement that was so conspicuously installed in the alcove.

"That's a wonderful Kansui arrangement," she said. "You've really done it well, you know."

Kashiwagi, who had been waiting for her to say this, now brought things to their conclusion.

"Not too bad, is it?" he said. "Now that I've reached this point, there's really nothing more that you can teach me. I don't need you any longer. Yes, I mean it!"

Kashiwagi spoke with formal emphasis. I noticed the color draining from the woman's face and I turned away. She seemed to be laughing slightly; but still she did not abandon her ceremonious manner as she advanced on her knees towards the alcove. Then I heard her say: "What? What sort of flowers are these? Yes, what are they?" In a moment, the water had all been spilled on the floor, the cattails had fallen over, the blossoms of the open irises had been torn to shreds: all the flowers that I had procured by my theft lay in utter disorder. I had been kneeling on the floor, but now I automatically jumped to my feet. Not knowing what to do, I leaned against the window. I saw Kashiwagi seize the woman by her slender wrists. Then he grasped her hair and slapped her across the cheek. Kashiwagi's succession of rough actions revealed exactly the same quiet cruelty that I had observed not long before when he was cutting the leaves and the stems of the flowers; they seemed, indeed, to be a natural extension of his earlier movements.

The woman covered her face with both hands and ran out of the room. As for Kashiwagi, he looked up at me as I stood there with a stupefied expression. He gave me a strangely childish smile and said: "Now's your chance. Run after her! Try to console her! Go on, quick!"

I do not know whether it was because I was impelled by the authority of Kashiwagi's command or because in my heart I felt some sympathy for the woman, but my legs instantly started to move and I chased the girl. I caught up with her a few houses away from the lodging-house. It was in a corner of Itakuramachi behind the Karasumaru streetcar shed. Under the cloudy night sky I could hear the rattle of a streetcar as it entered the shed, and the light purple sparks shaded off into the darkness. The woman hurried away from Itakuramachi towards the east and went up a back street. Without saying a word, I walked along beside her. She was crying. Before long she noticed that I was there and came close to me. Then, in a voice made even huskier than usual by her tears, she began to complain to me at great length about Kashiwagi's misdeeds.

How long she and I walked together through the streets that night! As she drummed Kashiwagi's misdeeds into my ears and told me of all the cloying sordidness of his behavior towards her, the single word that I heard resounding in the night air was—"life." His cruelty, his little plots, his betrayals, his heartlessness, his tricks for extorting money from women—all this merely served to explain his subtle charm. The only thing in which I myself needed to believe was Kashiwagi's sincerity regarding his clubfeet.

After Tsurukawa's sudden death I had existed for a long time without touching life itself. Then finally I had been stimulated by touching a new form of life—a darker, yet less unhappy, life that involved constantly hurting other people as long as one lived. Kashiwagi's simple words: "There's more to killing than that!" came to life once more and captivated me. And what I also recalled at that moment was the prayer which I had uttered when I had climbed the mountain behind the temple at the end of the war and looked down at the multitudinous city lights: "Let the darkness that is in my heart become equal to the darkness of the night that surrounds those innumerable lights!"

The woman was not walking back to her house. Instead she wandered aimlessly through the back streets, where there were few passers-by and she could talk freely. When finally we arrived in front of the house where she lived by herself, I had no idea what part of the city we were in.

It was already half past ten. I wanted to return to the temple, but the woman persuaded me not to leave her and so I went into the house with her. She led the way and turned on the light.

"Have you ever cursed someone and wished he was dead?" she said abruptly.

"Yes," I answered at once. Strangely enough, I had not thought about it until that moment, but now it was clear to me that I had been hoping for the death of the girl in the lodging-house, who had been a witness of my shame.

"It's a terrible thing," she said, collapsing on the straw-matted floor and placing herself in a sideways position. "I have too."

Her room was lit with a brilliance that was unusual in these days of power restriction. The bulb must have been about one hundred watts, three times as strong as that in Kashiwagi's room. For the first time I saw the woman's body clearly illuminated. Her Nagoya-style sash was a brilliant white, and the purple mist of the wisterian trellis

170

that formed the pattern of her Yuzen kimono stood out clearly.

The top of the gate at the Nanzen Temple was separated from the Tenjuan guest room by a distance that only a bird could cover, but now I felt that during all these years I had gradually been moving across this distance and that now I was finally approaching the destination. Since that afternoon on the gate I had been chopping time into minute particles and now I was really approaching the meaning of that mysterious scene in the Tenjuan. It had to be like this, I thought. It was inevitable that this woman should have changed, just as the features of this earth are changed by the time that the light from a distant star has finally reached it. If at the time when I saw her from the gate of the Nanzen Temple she and I had been joined in anticipation of today's meeting, such changes as had taken place in her since then could be effaced; with only a few small alterations, things could be restored to their earlier state and the former *I* could come face to face with the former *she*.

Thereupon I told her the story. I told it breathlessly and with constant stuttering. As I spoke, the green leaves once more began to glitter, and the angels and the fabulous Hoo bird that were painted on the ceiling of the temple sprang back to life. A fresh color came into the woman's cheeks and the former wild light in her eyes changed to an uncertain and confused expression.

"So that's what happened?" she said. "My goodness! So that's really what happened, is it? What a strange karma! Yes, that's what a strange karma means."

As she spoke, her eyes filled with tears of proud joy. She forgot her recent humiliation and instead cast herself back into memories. From one excitement she had moved directly into another excitement, and she became almost crazed. The bottom of her kimono with its wisteria pattern was in complete disorder.

"I don't have any milk now," she said. "Oh, my poor little baby! No, I don't have any milk, but all the same I'll do for you now what I did that other time. Since you've loved me ever since then, I'll consider that you are the

171

same as that man. So long as I can think that, I have nothing to be ashamed of. Yes, really, I'll do exactly what I did that time."

She spoke as if she were handing down a great decision. Her action that followed seemed to come from an overflow of ecstasy, or else from an overflow of despair. I suppose that consciously it was ecstasy that drove her to that passionate deed, but that the real impelling force was the despair which Kashiwagi had given her, or at least a persistent after-taste of that despair.

Thus it was that she unfastened her sash-bustle before my eyes and untied the various cords. Then with a silky shriek the sash itself came undone, and, released from this constriction, the neck of her kimono opened up. I could vaguely make out the woman's white breasts. Putting her hand into her kimono she scooped out her left breast and held it out to me.

It would be untrue to say that I did not feel dizzy. I looked at her breast. I looked at it with minute care. Yet I remained in the role of witness. That mysterious white point which I had seen in the distance from above the temple gate had not been a material glove of flesh like this. The impression had been fermenting so long within me that the breast which I now saw seemed to be nothing but flesh, nothing but a material object. This flesh did not in itself have the power to appeal or to tempt. Exposed there in front of me, and completely cut off from life, it merely served as a proof of the dreariness of existence.

Still, I do not want to say anything untrue, and there is no doubt that at the sight of her white breast I was overcome by dizziness. The trouble was that I looked too carefully and too completely, so that what I saw went beyond the stage of being a woman's breast and was gradually transformed into a meaningless fragment.

It was then that the wonder occurred. After undergoing this painful process, the woman's breast finally struck me as beautiful. It became endowed with the sterile and frigid characteristics of beauty and, while the breast remained before me, it slowly shut itself up within the principle of its own self. Just as a rose closes itself up within the essential principle of a rose. Beauty arrives late for me. Other people perceive beauty quickly, and discover beauty and sensual desire at the same moment; for me it always comes far later. Now in an instant the woman's breast regained its connection with the whole, it surmounted the state of being mere flesh and became an unfeeling, immortal substance related to eternity.

I hope that I am making myself understood. The Golden Temple once more appeared before me. Or rather, I should say that the breast was transformed into the Golden Temple.

I recalled the night of the typhoon at the beginning of autumn when I had stood watch in the temple. Much as the building may have been exposed to the moonlight, a heavy, luxuriant darkness had settled over it and this darkness had penetrated into the nocturnal temple, into the shutters, into the wooden doors, under the roof with its peeling gold-foil. And this was only natural. For the Golden Temple itself was simply a nihility that had been designed and constructed with the most exquisite care. Just so, although the outside of this breast gave forth the bright radiance of flesh, the inside was filled with darkness. Its true substance consisted of the same heavy, luxuriant darkness.

I was certainly not intoxicated by my understanding. My understanding was trampled underfoot and scorned; naturally enough, life and sensual desire underwent the same process. But my deep feeling of ecstasy stayed with me and for a long time I sat as though paralyzed opposite the woman's naked breast.

I was sitting there when I met the woman's cold, scornful look. She put her breast back into the kimono. I told her that I must leave. She came to the entrance and closed the door after me noisily.

Until I returned to the temple, I remained in the midst of ecstasy. In my mind's eye I could see the Golden Temple and the woman's breast coming and going one after the other. I was overcome with an impotent sense of joy.

Yet when the outline of the temple began to emerge

173

through the dark pine forest, which was soughing in the wind, my spirits gradually cooled down, my feeling of impotence became predominant and my intoxication changed into hatred—a hatred for I knew not what.

"So once again I have been estranged from life!" I thought. "Why does the Golden Temple try to protect me? Why does it try to separate me from life without my asking it? Of course it may be that the temple is saving me from falling into hell. But by so doing, the Golden Temple is making me even more evil than those people who actually do fall into hell, it is making me into 'the man who knows more about hell than anyone.' "

The main temple gate was black and quiet. In the side gate, the light, which was never extinguished until the morning bell, was shining dimly. I pushed the side gate. Inside I could hear the sound of the old, rusty iron chain as it pulled up the weight. The door opened. The gatekeeper had already gone to sleep. On the inner side of the gate there was a sign saying that the last person who returned after ten o'clock was responsible for locking the gate. Two of the wooden nameplates indicated that their owners were still not back. One of the plates was the Superior's; the other was the old gardener's.

As I walked towards the temple, I noticed a number of wooden boards about five yards long, which were being used for some reconstruction work. Even in the night one could see the light grain of the wood. When I came closer, I saw that sawdust was scattered about the place like little yellow flowers; the fascinating smell of wood drifted through the darkness. Before entering the kitchen, I turned back and went to have a final look at the Golden Temple. I walked down the path towards it and gradually the building became visible. It was surrounded by the rustling of trees and stood there utterly motionless, yet wide awake, in the midst of the night. As though it were the guardian of the night itself. Although the residential part of the Rokuonji slept at night, I had never seen the Golden Temple sleep. This uninhabited structure was able to forget sleep. The darkness that dwelt within it was completely absolved from human laws.

Then in a tone that was almost like a curse I addressed the Golden Temple roughly for the first time in my life: "One day I shall surely rule you. Yes, one day I shall bring you under my sway, so that never again will you be able to get in my way."

My voice echoed hollowly in the night shadows of the Kyoko Pond.

CHAPTER SEVEN

A type of cipher seemed to operate in my general experience of life. As in a corridor of mirrors, a single image is reflected again and again to an endless depth.

Things that I had seen in the past were clearly reflected on those that I encountered for the first time, and I felt that I was being led by such resemblances into the inner recesses of the corridor, into some fathomless inner chamber. We do not collide with our destiny all of a sudden. The man who later in his life is to be executed is constantly—every time that he sees a telegraph pole on his way to work, every time that he passes a railway crossing—drawing an image in his mind of the execution site, and is becoming familiar with that image.

In my experience, therefore there was nothing in the nature of accumulation. There was no thickness of the kind that could form a mountain by piling one stratum upon another. I felt no intimacy with anything in the world except the Golden Temple; indeed, I was not even on intimate terms with my own past experiences. Yet one thing I knew was that among all these experiences certain small elements—elements that were not swallowed up in the dark sea of time, elements that did not subside into meaningless and interminable repetition—would be linked together and would come to form a certain sinister and disagreeable picture.

Which, then, were these particular elements? I thought about it on and off. Yet these scattered, shining fragments of experience were even more lacking in order and meaning than the shining pieces of a broken beer bottle that one sees by the roadside. I was unable to believe that these fragments were the shattered pieces of what had in the past been shaped as a thing of perfect beauty. For, in their meaninglessness, in their complete lack of order, in their peculiar unsightliness, each of these discarded fragments still seemed to be dreaming of the future. Yes, mere fragments though they were, each lay there, fearlessly, uncannily, quietly, dreaming of the future! Of a future that would never be cured or restored, that could never be touched, of a truly unprecedented future!

Indistinct reflections of this type sometimes gave me a kind of lyrical excitement that I could not help finding unsuitable for myself. On such occasions, if by good chance there happened to be a moon, I would take my flute and play it next to the Golden Temple. I had now reached the point of being able to play Kashiwagi's tune, the "Palace Carriage," without looking at the music. Music is like a dream. At the same time it is, on the contrary, like a more distinct form of consciousness than that of our normal waking hours. Which of the two really was music, I used to wonder? Music had the power at times to reverse these two contrary things. And sometimes I was easily able to embody myself, as it were, into the tune of the "Palace Carriage" that I was playing. My spirit was familiar with the joy of embodying itself in music. For in my case, unlike that of Kashiwagi, music was truly a consolation.

Whenever I finished playing my flute, I used to wonder: "Why does the Golden Temple disregard this action of mine? Why does it not blame me or interfere with me when I embody myself like this into music? Never once has the temple disregarded me when I have tried to embody myself in the happiness and pleasures of life. On every such occasion it has been the fashion of the temple to block my effort instantly and to force me to return to myself. Why will the Golden Temple only permit intoxication and oblivion in the case of music?"

At these thoughts, the charm of the music would fade owing to the mere fact that the Golden Temple allowed me this particular pleasure. For inasmuch as the temple gave me its tacit approval, music, however closely it might resemble life, became an imaginary and spurious form of life; and, much as I might try to embody myself within it, that embodiment itself could only be something temporary.

I do not want to give the impression that I resigned myself and retired from the field as a result of my two setbacks with women and with life. Until the end of 1948 I had several more such opportunities, as well as Kashiwagi's guidance; and, nothing daunted, I set myself to the task. But the result was always the same.

Between the girl and myself, between life and myself,

there invariably appeared the Golden Temple. Whereupon the thing that touched my hand as I tried to grasp it would instantly turn to ashes and the prospect before me would change into a desert.

Once when I was resting from some work in the field behind the kitchen, I happened to observe the manner in which a bee visited a small, yellow summer chrysanthemum. It came flying through the omnipresent light on its golden wings, then from among all the numerous chrysanthemums chose one flower and hovered in front of it. I tried to look at the flower through the bee's eyes. The chrysanthemum stood there with its proper petals spread out, yellow and flawless. It was just as beautiful as a little Golden Temple and just as perfect as the temple; but it did not become transformed into the temple and remained in the state of being a single summer chrysanthemum. Yes, it continued to be a steadfast chrysanthemum, one flower, a single form without any metaphysical connotations. By thus observing the rules of its own existence, it emitted an abundant charm and became a suitable object for the bee's desire. What a mysterious thing it was to lurk there, breathing, as an object for that shapeless, flying, flowing, moving desire! Gradually the form becomes more rarefied, it looks as if it is going to crumble, it quivers and trembles. This is quite natural, for that proper form of the chrysanthemum has been fashioned in terms of the bee's desire and its very beauty has blossomed forth in anticipation of that desire. Now is the instant when the meaning of the flower's form is going to shine within life. The form itself is a molding of life, which flows constantly and which has no form; at the same time, the flight of formless life is the molding of all forms in this world. . . . Thus the bee thrust its way deep into the flower and, covered with pollen, sank into intoxication. The chrysanthemum, having welcomed the bee into its body, became itself like a luxurious, armor-clad, yellow bee, and I watched it shake itself violently as if at any moment it were going to fly away from its stem.

The light, and this act performed under the light, almost made me dizzy. Then, just as I left the bee's eyes and returned to my own eyes, it occurred to me that my eyes which had been gazing at this scene were exactly in the position of the eyes of the Golden Temple. Yes, this is how it was. In the same way that I had reverted from the bee's eyes to my own eyes, so at those instants when life approached me I abandoned my own eyes and made the eyes of the Golden Temple into mine. And it was precisely at such moments that the temple would intrude between me and life.

I returned to my eyes. In this vast, vague world of objects the bee and the summer chrysanthemum only remained to be "put in order," as it were. The flying of the bee and the shaking of the flower did not differ in the slightest from the rustling of the wind. In this still, frozen world everything was on an equal footing, and that form which had emitted so powerful a charm was extinct. The chrysanthemum was no longer beautiful because of its form, but because of that vague name of "chrysanthemum" that we give it and because of the promise contained in that name. Because I was not a bee, I was not tempted by the chrysanthemum and, because I was not a chrysanthemum, no bee yearned after me. I had been aware of a sense of fellowship with the flow of life and with all the forms in it, but now this feeling disappeared. The world had been cast away into relativity and only time was moving. I do not want to labor my point. All I wish to say is that, when the eternal and absolute Golden Temple appeared and when my eyes changed into the temple's eyes, the world about me was transformed in the way that I have described, and that in this transformed world only the Golden Temple retained its form and possessed beauty, turning everything else back into dust. Ever since I trampled on the body of that prostitute in the temple garden, and especially since Tsurukawa's death, I had kept on repeating to myself the question: "Is evil nevertheless possible?"

One Saturday in January of 1948, I took advantage of having a free afternoon to visit a third-class cinema theater. After the film I walked through the Shinkyogoku by myself for the first time in ages. Among the crowds I suddenly found myself next to a very familiar face, but before I could remember who it was, the face was swallowed up in the sea of pedestrians and disappeared behind me.

The man had been wearing a felt hat, an elegant overcoat, and a scarf, and had been walking with a girl in a rust-vermilion coat, who was obviously a geisha. The man's pink, plump face, his air of baby-like cleanliness, so different from that of most middle-aged gentlemen, his lengthy nose— yes, all these were the distinguishing traits of the Superior, Father Dosen, and it was only the felt hat that had disguised them for a moment. Though I had nothing to feel ashamed of myself, my immediate reaction was fear that I might have been seen. For instantly I felt that I must avoid being a witness to my Superior's surreptitious expedition and thus becoming silently involved in a relationship of trust or mistrust with him.

Then a black dog walked through the crowds. He was a large, shaggy dog and was obviously used to walking in crowded places, for he picked his way skillfully between the feet of the women in their colorful coats and the men in their military uniforms, and occasionally stopped in front of a shop. I noticed the dog stopping to sniff outside a souvenir shop that had not altered since the time of Shogoin Yatsuhashi. Now for the first time I could see the dog's face in the light of the shop. One of his eyes had been crushed, and the blood and solidified mucus in the corner of the eye looked like a ruby. The uninjured eye was looking directly down at the ground. The shaggy hair on his back was conspicuously bunched together and had a hardened look.

I am not quite sure why this dog should have attracted my attention. Perhaps it was because, as this dog wandered about, he stubbornly carried within himself a world that was totally different from this bright, bustling street. The dog walked through a dark world that was dominated by a sense of smell. This world was superimposed on that of human streets, and in effect the lights of the city, the songs that come from gramophone records, and the sound of human laughter were all being threatened by persistent, dark smells. For the order of smell was more accurate, and the smell of urine that clung to the dog's damp feet was accurately connected with the faint, unpleasant odor that emanated from the internal organs of human beings.

It was extremely cold. A small group of young men, who looked like black-market operators, walked down the street, plucking at the New Year pine tree decorations, which were still standing outside some of the houses even though the holiday period had finished. They opened the palms of their leather gloves to see who had been able to collect most. One of the men had only a few leaves; another had an entire small pine branch. The young man laughed and disappeared from sight.

I found that I was following the dog. For a moment I thought that I had lost him, but he instantly reappeared. He turned into the road leading to Kawaramachi. I walked along after him and came to the road where the streetcars run. It was rather darker here than in Shinkyogoku. The dog disappeared. I stopped and looked in every direction for him. I went to the corner of the street and continued searching for the dog. Just then a chauffeur-driven hired car with a glossy chassis stopped in front of me. The chauffeur opened the door and first of all a girl stepped in. I found myself looking at her. A man was about to get in after the girl, but, when he noticed me, he stood there rooted to the spot.

It was the Superior. I don't know by what chance it was that the Superior, who had passed me earlier on the street and who had made a detour with the girl, should have run into me again like this. Anyhow, there he was, and the coat of the girl who had entered the car was the rust-vermilion one that I remembered.

This time there was no avoiding him. But I was thoroughly upset by the encounter and I could not say a word. Before I could utter anything, stuttering sounds began to boil in my mouth. In the end my face assumed an expression that I had not intended. In fact, I did something that was entirely irrelevant to the situation: I burst out laughing at my Superior.

I cannot explain this laugh of mine. It was as if it had come from the outside and suddenly adhered to my mouth. But when the Superior saw me laughing, his look changed.

"You little fool!" he said. "Are you trying to follow me?"

Then he stepped into the car and slammed the door in my face. As the car drove away, I realized that the Superior had definitely noticed me when we had passed each other earlier in Shinkyogoku.

On the following day I waited for the Superior to call me in for a scolding. This would be an opportunity for me to explain myself. But, just as after that previous occasion when I had trampled on the prostitute, the Superior now began to torture me by passing the matter over in silence.

It was just then that I had another letter from Mother. She ended with her usual remark about living in the hope of seeing me become the master of the Golden Temple.

"You little fool, are you trying to follow me?"—as I thought about the words that the Superior had roared at me, they seemed more and more inappropriate. If he had been a more typical Zen priest, more open-minded and with a greater sense of humor, he would never have addressed such a vulgar reproof to his pupil. He would have made some more pithy, effective remark. Now, of course, the Superior could not take back what he had said; but I felt sure that at the time he had mistakenly believed that I had followed him on purpose and had sneered at him as though I had caught him out in some grave misdemeanor; as a result he had become flustered and automatically made a vulgar display of anger.

Whatever the facts of the matter may have been, the Superior's silence again became a source of uneasiness that pressed on me day after day. The Superior's existence had become a great force, it had become like the shadow of a moth that flutters annoyingly before one's eyes.

It was customary for the Superior to take along one or

two of the acolytes when he was asked to attend services outside the temple. In the past the deacon had invariably been in attendance on these occasions, but recently, as part of the so-called process of democratization it had become normal for five of us—the deacon, the sexton, myself, and two other apprentices—to take turns in accompanying the Superior. The superintendent of the dormitory, whose strictness had become proverbial among us, had been conscripted and killed in the war. His duties were now exercised by the middle-aged sexton. Following Tsurukawa's death, another apprentice had taken his place in the temple.

Just then the Superior of a temple (which belonged to the Sokokuji sect and which had the same historical lineage as the Rokuonji) died and our Superior was invited to attend the installation of his successor. It happened to be my turn to accompany him. Since the Superior did nothing to avoid my going with him, I expected that there would be a chance for an explanation between us on the way to the temple or back. On the night before the installation ceremony, however, it was arranged that the new apprentice would be added to our party and my hopes were seriously shaken.

Readers who are familiar with Gosan literature will no doubt recall the sermon that was delivered when Ishimuro Zenkyu entered the Manju Temple in Kyoto in the first year of the Koan era (1361). The beautiful words that the new priest spoke on arriving at the temple and as he proceeded from the main gate to the Earth Hall, then to the Hall of Ancestors, and finally to the Abbot's chamber have been handed down to us. Pointing to the main gate, he had spoken proudly in words that were charged with joy at the thought of assuming his new religious duties: "Within the Tenjo Kyuchu, before the gate of Teijo Manju. Empty-handed I open the lock, barefooted I climb the sacred Mount Konron."

The incense ceremony began. First, the priest performed the Shihoko in honor of the great religious leader, Shiho. In former times, when the Zen religion had not yet been captured by convention and when the spiritual awakening of the individual was valued above all else, it had been customary for the pupil to select his teacher, rather than for the teacher to select his pupil. In those days the pupil received religious "approval" not only from the priest who had first instructed him, but from a variety of different teachers; and during the Shihoko incense ceremony he would make public the name of the teacher to whose mission he devoutly aspired to succeed.

While I watched this impressive incense ceremony, I wondered whether, when the time came for me to attend the succession ceremony at the Golden Temple, I would announce the name of the Superior as custom demanded. Perhaps I would break the seven-hundred-year-old custom and announce some other name. The coldness of the Abbot's chamber on this early spring afternoon, the redolent odor of the five types of incense, the diadem that glittered behind the Three Utensils and the resplendent halo that surrounded the main Buddha, the brightness of the surplices worn by the officiating priests . . . and what if one day I should find myself here performing the Shihoko incense ceremony? I imagined myself in the form of a priest undergoing this ceremony of inauguration. Inspired by the stringent atmosphere of the early spring, I should betray the old custom cheerfully. The Superior would be in attendance; hearing my words, he would be speechless with amazement and pale with anger. For I should pronounce a name other than his. Another name? But who is this other teacher who has instructed me in the true way of enlightenment? I am stuck for his name. It is blocked by my stuttering and will not issue from my mouth. I stutter; and, as I stutter, that other name begins to come out—"Beauty," I start to say, and "Nihility." Then all who are present burst out laughing, and I stand there awkwardly rooted to the spot amidst their laughter.

I abruptly awoke from my daydream. The Superior had some office to perform and I, as his acolyte, had to assist him. It was a proud thing for an acolyte to be present at an occasion like this; this was especially so in my case, since the Superior of the Golden Temple was the main guest among those officiating at the ceremony. When my Superior had finished burning the incense, he struck a blow with the mallet known as the "white hammer," thus attesting to the fact that the priest who had today been installed as the Superior of this temple was not a *ganfuto*, that is to say, a clerical impostor. He intoned the traditional formula and struck a loud blow with the white hammer. Then I realized afresh the miraculous power that this Superior of mine possessed.

I could not stand the way in which the Superior passed over the recent event in silence, especially since I had no idea of how long this silence would continue. If I myself was endowed with some form of human feeling, why should I not expect corresponding human feelings from people, like the Superior, with whom I was in contact? Whether they be feelings of love or of hate. I now got into the wretched habit of examining the Superior's expression on every possible occasion, but never once could I detect any special feelings in that face of his. His absence of expression was not even equivalent to coldness. It may have signified contempt, but, if so, this was not a contempt for me as an individual, but rather something universal, something, for instance, that he directed towards humanity in general or even towards various abstract conceptions.

From about this time I forced myself to conjure up the image of the Superior's animalian head and of the indecent physical functions that he performed. I imagined him in the process of defecating, and also pictured him as he slept with that girl in the rust-vermilion coat. I saw his expressionless features relax and a look, which could be one of either laughter or pain, appear on his face as it became languid from physical pleasure.

The appearance of his soft, sleek body as it melted into the equally soft, sleek body of the girl and as the two became virtually indistinguishable. The way in which his swollen stomach pressed against the girl's swollen stomach. Yet, strangely enough, however vigorous my imagination became, the Superior's expressionless features were always instantly linked in my mind with the animalian expression that belongs to defecation and to sexual intercourse, and nothing ever emerged to fill the space between the two. One extreme was transformed directly into the opposite extreme, without any of the intervening rainbow-like shadings of everyday life to connect them. The only thing that provided the slightest connection was the rather vulgar rebuke that the Superior had addressed to me on that afternoon: "You little fool, are you trying to follow me?"

After I had become exhausted from thinking and from waiting, I was finally seized by an obstinate desire: it was simply to catch a distinct look of hatred on the Superior's face. The plan that I formulated in consequence was mad, childish, and quite clearly to my disadvantage; but I was no longer able to control myself. I did not even take account of the fact that this prank of mine would merely confirm the Superior's previous misunderstanding of me when he thought that I had been following him on purpose.

I met Kashiwagi at the university and asked him the name and address of the shop. Kashiwagi gave me the information without even enquiring about my purpose. I promptly went to the shop and examined numerous photographs of post-card size showing the famous geishas from the Gion district. At first the girls' faces with their heavy make-up all looked the same, but after a while a variety of tones began to emerge vividly from the pictures. Through the identical masks of powder and rouge I could now distinguish the delicate shades of their respective natures—gloominess or brightness, nimble wits or beautiful dullness, ill-humor or irrepressible gaiety, misfortune or luck. Finally I came on the picture for which I was searching. Owing to the bright electric light in the shop, the reflection of the image glittered on the glossy paper and it was hard to get a good view of the photograph, but as the reflection settled down in my hands, I could see that this was indeed the face of the girl in the rust-vermilion coat.

"I should like this one," I said to the shopkeeper.

My peculiar boldness at this time corresponded precisely to the fact that, since I had embarked on this plan of mine, I had changed completely and become light-hearted and full of an inexplicable joy. My original idea had been to choose a time when the Superior was away and thus to conceal from him who had done the deed; but my new spirited mood now led me to carry out the plan boldly in such a way that there would be no mistaking my responsibility.

It was still my duty to deliver the morning newspaper to the Superior's room. One morning in March, when the air was still chilly, I went as usual to the entrance of the temple to fetch the paper. My heart was pounding as I extracted the photograph of the Gion geisha from my pocket and inserted it into the newspaper.

The morning sun shone down on the sago palm that grew in the center of the courtyard surrounded by a circular hedge. The rough bark of the palm's trunk was vividly shaded off in the sunlight. On the left was a small lime tree. A few belated finches on the branches made a soft chirping that sounded like the rubbing of rosary beads. It seemed strange that there should still be finches at that time of the year, but that minute expanse of yellow down, which I could see by the rays of the sun that pierced through the branches, could belong to no other type of bird. The white pebbles lay peacefully on the courtyard.

I made my way carefully along the corridor so as not to wet my feet in the puddles that remained here and there from the recent mopping. The door of the Superior's office in the Great Library was firmly closed. It was still so early in the morning that the whiteness of the paper sliding-door shone brightly.

I knelt down outside in the corridor and said as usual: "May I enter, Father?" At the word of acknowledgment from the Superior, I pushed open the sliding-door, entered the room and placed the lightly folded newspaper on a corner of the desk. The Superior was busy with a book and did not look into my eyes. I retired from his presence, closed the door, and walked slowly along the corridor back to my room, making a special effort to remain calm.

When I reached my room, I sat down and gave myself over entirely to my throbbing excitement until the time came for me to leave for the university. Never had I looked forward to anything in my life with such anticipation. Though I had made my plan with the expectation of arousing the Superior's anger, the scene that I now envisaged was filled only with the dramatic passion of the moment when two human beings come to understand each other.

Perhaps the Superior would suddenly burst into my room and forgive me. And if he forgave me, perhaps for the first time in my life I should reach that pure, bright state of feeling in which Tsurukawa had always lived. The Superior and I would embrace each other, and all that would remain thereafter would be our regret that we had not arrived sooner at a mutual understanding.

This dream did not last long, but it seems quite inexplicable that even for a short time I should have given myself over to such *idiotic* fancies. When I thought about it calmly, I realized that, while I had been incurring the Superior's anger by this act of utter folly, thus removing my name from the list of possible candidates for succession, and thus, in turn, myself paving the way for a situation in which I could never possibly hope to become the master of the Golden Temple—during all this time I had been so absorbed with my immediate objective that I had actually forgotten my lifelong devotion to the Golden Temple itself.

My attention was concentrated on listening for any sound that might come from the Superior's room in the Great Library. I could hear nothing.

Now I began to wait for the Superior's violent rage, for the thunderous shout that he would roar out. I felt that there would be no regrets on my part even if I were assaulted, kicked onto the floor, and made to shed blood. But there was complete silence in the direction of the Great Library; not a sound approached me as I sat waiting in my room.

When finally the time came for me to leave the temple and set out for the university, my heart was utterly worn out and desolate. I was unable to concentrate on the lecture and, when the instructor asked me a question, I gave a completely inappropriate answer. Everyone laughed at me. I glanced at Kashiwagi and saw that he alone was indifferent to all this and was gazing out of the window. He was undoubtedly aware of the drama that was taking place within me.

When I returned to the temple, nothing had changed. The dark, musty eternity of the temple life was so well established that there could be no possible discrepancy between one day and the next.

Lectures on the Zen canon were held twice a month and this happened to be one of the days. Everyone in the temple congregated in the Superior's quarters to hear him deliver his lecture. It occurred to me that he might well use his talk on the *Mumonkan* scriptures as a pretext to censure me in front of all the others. I had a special reason for believing this. From the fact of my sitting directly opposite the Superior at his lecture that evening, I felt that I was inspired by an exceedingly incongruous type of manly courage. It seemed to me that the Superior would respond to this by himself displaying a manly virtue: he would break through all hyprocrisy and confess his deed before everyone in the temple and, having done this, would censure me for my own shabby action.

The immates of the temple all foregathered under the dim electric light with copies of the *Mumonkan* text in their hands. It was a cold night, but the only form of heating was a small brazier placed next to the Superior. I could hear people sniffing. They sat there, young and old, with the shadows making gradations of light on their bent-down faces; and there was something ineffably powerless about their expressions. The new apprentice, who worked as a primary-school teacher during the daytime, was a near-sighted young man and his spectacles kept on slipping down the bridge of his meager nose.

I alone was conscious of power in my body. At least that is what I imagined. The Superior opened his text and looked round at us all. I followed his gaze. I wanted him to see that I was most certainly not casting down my eyes. But when his eyes, surrounded by their fleshy wrinkles, came to me, they showed not the slightest interest and moved on to the next person.

The lecture started. I was only waiting for the moment when suddenly it would be turned to my problem. I listened intently. The Superior's high-pitched voice droned on. Not a sound came from his inner feeling.

I could not sleep that night. As I lay awake, I was filled with scorn for the Superior and with a desire to make fun of him for his hypocrisy. Gradually, however, a sense of regret awoke within me and began to modify my arrogant feelings. My scorn for the Superior's hypocrisy became connected in a strange way with the gradual weakening of my spirit, and finally I came to the point of thinking that, inasmuch as I now realized what a nonentity the Superior really was, my asking his forgiveness would in no way represent a defeat. My heart, having climbed to the top of a steep slope, was now swiftly running downhill.

I decided that I would go and make my apologies on the following morning. When the morning came, I decided that I would apologize some time during the course of the day. I noticed that the Superior's expression had not changed in the slightest.

It was a windy day. On my return from the university, I happened to open my drawer. I saw something wrapped in white paper. It was the photograph. Not a word was written on the paper. Evidently the Superior had intended to make an end of the matter by this method. He did not mean to overlook my action entirely, but to let me realize its futility. The curious way in which he had returned the photograph, however, brought a host of images flocking into my mind.

"So the Superior has been suffering also!" I thought. "He must have gone through the most extraordinary anguish before hitting on this method. Now he must surely hate me. It is probably not because of the photograph itself that he hates me, but because I have made him behave in such an ignoble way. As a result of this single photograph, he has been made to feel that he must behave surreptitiously in his own temple. He had to walk stealthily along the corridor while no one else was about, then he had to enter the room of one of his apprentices where he had never set foot before and had to open the drawer exactly as if he were committing some crime. Yes, now he has ample reason to hate me."

At these thoughts an indescribable joy flooded through me. Then I set myself to a pleasant task. I took a pair of scissors and cut the photograph into little pieces. Then I wrapped it securely in a strong sheet of paper from my notebook and, grasping it firmly in my hand, walked to a place next to the Golden Temple. The temple, filled with its usual gloomy equilibrium, towered into the windy, moonlit sky. The slender pillars stood close together; as the moon shone down on them, they looked like harpstrings and the temple itself looked like some huge, peculiar musical instrument. This particular impression depended on the height of the moon. Tonight there was no mistaking it. Yet the wind blew vainly through the spaces between those soundless harpstrings.

I picked up a stone, wrapped it in the paper and pressed the package tightly together. Then the tiny fragments of the girl's face, weighed down by the stone, sank into the center of the Kyoko Pond. The ripples spread out freely and soon reached the edge of the water where I was standing.

My sudden flight from the temple in November of that year came as an accumulation of all these things. When I thought about it later, I realized that this flight of mine, which seemed so sudden, had in fact been preceded by considerable reflection and hesitation. I preferred, however, to believe that I had been driven by some abrupt impulse. Since I was essentially lacking in anything impulsive, I was addicted to a form of spurious impulsiveness. In the case of a man who, for example, has been planning to visit his father's grave on the following day, but who, when the day comes and he finds himself in front of the station, suddenly changes his mind and decides to go and visit a drinking-companion of his, can one say that this shows any genuine impulsiveness? Is not his sudden change of mind a sort of revenge that he takes on his own will? Is it not, in fact, something more *conscious* than his long-standing preparations to visit the grave?

The immediate motive for my flight lay in what the Superior had clearly revealed to me on the previous day: "There was a time when I planned to make you my successor here. But I can now tell you quite plainly that I have no such intention."

This was the first time that I had heard anything of the sort from him, but I should really have been expecting and preparing for the announcement. I cannot pretend that it came to me as a bolt from the blue or that I was dumbfounded and panic-stricken. Even so, I like to believe that my flight was detonated by the Superior's words and caused by a sudden impulse.

After I had made sure of the Superior's anger by means of my trick with the photograph, I started to neglect my studies at the university. This was quite obvious. In my preparatory year's course, I had the best results in Chinese and History, scored eighty-four marks in those two courses and a total of seven hundred and forty-eight marks, thus ranking twenty-fourth in a class of eighty-four students. Out of four hundred and sixty-four hours I was absent for only fourteen. In my second year I made a total of only six hundred and ninety-three marks and sank to the rank of thirty-fifth out of seventy-seven students. It was in my third year, however, that I really began to neglect my studies—not because I had any money to waste my time with, but simply from the joy of being idle. And it so happened that the first term of the third year started just after the photograph incident.

When the first term finished, the university sent a report to the temple and I was reprimanded by the Superior. The reason for this reprimand was that my marks were poor and that I had been absent for so many hours, but what particularly irked the Superior was that I had missed the special classes in Zen practice, which were only held for three days during the term. These classes in Zen practice were held for three days before the beginning of the summer, winter, and spring holidays—nine days in all during the year—and were conducted in the same form as those given in the various specialized seminaries.

On the occasion of this scolding the Superior summoned me to his private room, which in itself was a rare event. I stood there silently with my head bowed. In my heart I was waiting for his words to move onto a certain subject; but he made not the slightest reference to the incident of the photograph, nor did he go back and mention the prostitute and her blackmail.

It was from this time that the Superior's attitude toward me became noticeably cold. This was, so to say, the very upshot that I had desired, the very evidence that I had longed to see; and it represented a sort of victory for me. Yet the only thing that had been necessary to achieve it had been idleness on my part. In the first term of my third year I had been absent for sixty hours—about five times as much as my total absences for the entire first year. During all those hours I did not read any book, nor did I have money to spend on amusements. Sometimes I would talk to Kashiwagi, but most of the time I stayed by myself doing nothing. Yes, I stayed silently by myself doing nothing, and my memories of Otani University are intimately mixed with memories of inactivity. This sort of inactivity was perhaps my own special form of Zen practice and, while I was engaged in it, I was never for a single moment conscious of any boredom.

Once I sat for hours on the grass watching a colony of ants engaged in transporting minute particles of red earth. It wasn't a matter of the ants having aroused my interest. On another occasion I stood for ages outside the university, staring like a dolt at the thin wisp of smoke that rose from a factory chimney at the back. It wasn't that the smoke had caught my fancy. At such times I felt as though I was drenched up to my neck in the existence that was *myself*. The world outside me had cooled down in parts and had then been reheated. How shall I put it? I felt that the outside world was spotted and again that it was striped. My inner being and the outer world slowly and irregularly changed places. The meaningless scene that surrounded me shone before my eyes; as it shone, it forced its way into me and only those parts of the scene that had not entered continued to glitter vividly in a place beyond. Those glittering parts could be either the flag on a factory, or an insignificant spot on the wall, or an old, discarded clog that lay on the grass. Moment by moment they sprang to life within me—these and every other sort of thing—and then they died away. Or should I say, every other sort of shapeless thought? Important things joined hands with the most trivial things, and the political development in Europe about which I had read in the morning paper became inextricably connected with the old clog that lay at my feet.

I spent a long time thinking about the acute angle formed by the tip of a certain blade of grass. Perhaps the word "thinking" is not quite appropriate. That strange, trifling conception of mine was no continuing process, but reappeared persistently, like some refrain. Why did that acute angle have to be so acute? If instead it were obtuse, would the classification "grass" be lost and would nature inevitably be destroyed from that one corner of its totality? When a single tiny cog is removed from nature, is not nature itself being entirely overthrown? Then my mind would aimlessly examine the problem from one point of view after another.

The Superior's reprimand soon became known among the people in the temple and their attitude towards me became visibly more hostile. My fellow apprentice who had been so envious of my having been recommended for the university course now gave a triumphant chuckle whenever he saw me.

I continued my life in the temple during the summer and the autumn, and hardly spoke to anyone. On the morning of the day before my flight the Superior had the deacon summon me to his room. It was the ninth of November. Since I was about to leave for the university, I was wearing my student uniform.

The Superior's plump face was normally cheerful, but in the anticipation of having to tell me something unpleasant, it had become strangely congealed. So far as I was concerned, however, it was quite agreeable to see the Superior looking at me as though he were observing a leper. This was precisely the expression that I had wanted to see in him—a look of human feeling.

The Superior turned away from me. As he spoke, he rubbed his hands together over the brazier. The soft flesh of his palms made only a slight sound, yet it was jarring to my ears and seemed to destroy the clarity of the winter-morning air. The contact of the priest's flesh against his flesh produced an unnecessarily intimate feeling.

"How sad your late father would be to know about this!" he said. "Look at this letter! They've written again from the university in the strongest terms. You'd better start thinking about what will happen if things go on like this." And then he passed directly to those other words of his: "There was a time when I planned to make you my successor here. But I can now tell you quite plainly that I have no such intention."

I remained quiet for a long time. Then I said: "So you aren't going to back me up any longer?"

"Did you really expect that I'd go on backing you up after this?" asked the Superior after a pause.

I did not answer his question, but presently I heard myself stuttering out something on quite a different subject: "You know me down to the last detail, Father. I think I know about you, too."

"And what if you do know?" said the Superior, a gloomy look coming into his eyes. "It amounts to nothing. It's all quite useless."

Never before had I seen a human being's face that had so utterly deserted the present world. Never had I seen a man who, though he sullied his hands with money and women and every other detail of material life, so thoroughly despised the present world. I was filled with hatred, as if I were in the presence of a corpse that was still warm and of healthy complexion.

And that moment a violent desire came over me to get away from all my surroundings, even if only for a short time. After I had withdrawn from the Superior's room, the desire became still stronger and I could think of nothing else.

I took my *furoshiki* wrapper and made a bundle of my Buddhist dictionary and the flute that Kashiwagi had given me. As I set out for the university, carrying this bundle and my satchel, my mind was absorbed with the idea of departure.

On entering the university gate, I was pleased to see Kashiwagi walking ahead of me. I pulled him by the arm and took him to the side of the road. I asked him to lend me three thousand yen, and to take the dictionary and the flute to use in any way that he saw fit. There was no sign now on his face of that usual expression which he showed when he made his paradoxical remarks—that expression which one might describe as a look of philosophic exhilaration. He glanced at me with narrowed, hazy eyes.

"Do you remember the advice that Laertes gives his son in *Hamlet?* 'Neither a borrower nor a lender be. For a loan oft loses both itself and friend.' "

"I don't have a father any more," I replied. "But if you can't do it, it doesn't matter."

"I didn't say I couldn't," said Kashiwagi. "Let's talk it over. I'm not sure whether I can scrape three thousand yen together or not."

I wanted to charge Kashiwagi with what I had heard about him from the woman who taught flower arrangement—with his way of squeezing money out of women—but I managed to restrain myself.

"First we'd better think about how to dispose of this dictionary and flute."

So saying, Kashiwagi turned round abruptly and walked back to the gate. I also turned round and accompanied him, slowing my pace down to his. He began talking about our fellow student who was president of a credit society known as the Hikari Club, and who had been arrested on suspicion of dealing in some financial black-market activities. He had been released in September, and thereafter he had evidently been in difficulties, since his reputation had suffered a serious blow. Since about April, Kashiwagi had been extremely interested in this president of the Hikari Club and we often used to talk about him. We had both firmly believed that he was still socially influential and we had certainly not expected that only a fortnight later he would kill himself.

"What do you want this money for?" said Kashiwagi abruptly. It seemed an odd question for him to ask.

"I want to go off somewhere. I have no particular object in mind."

"Will you be coming back?"

"Probably."

"What are you running away from?"

"I want to get away from all my surroundings. From the smell of powerlessness that everyone round me gives off so strongly. The Superior is powerless. Terribly powerless. I've understood that, too."

"You want to get away from the Golden Temple also?"

"Yes indeed! From the Golden Temple also."

"Is even the Golden Temple powerless?"

"No, the Golden Temple certainly isn't powerless! It's the root of everyone else's powerlessness."

"Yes, that's the sort of thing you would think," said Kashiwagi and, as he walked along with his exaggerated dancing gait, he clicked his tongue cheerfully. I followed him into a chilly little antique shop, where he sold the flute. He could only get four hundred yen for it. Next we stopped at a second-hand bookshop and managed to sell the dictionary for one hundred yen. For the remaining twenty-five hundred yen Kashiwagi took me to his lodging-house. Having lent me the money, he made a peculiar suggestion. The flute, he explained, was a borrowed object that I had returned to him and the dictionary could be regarded as a gift. Accordingly I had done nothing but hand over to him what he actually owned, and the five hundred yen realized from the sale belonged to him. When one added the twenty-five hundred yen, the amount of the loan naturally became three thousand. On this three thousand yen Kashiwagi wished to receive monthly interest of ten per cent until the debt was repaid. Compared to the thirty-four per cent charged by the Hikari Club, this was such a low rate of interest, according to Kashiwagi, that the entire transaction was virtually a favor on his part. He took out a piece of thick Japanese paper and an inkstone and solemnly inscribed the terms of the loan. Then he had me make my thumbprint on the document. Since I disliked thinking about the future, I instantly put my thumb on the ink pad and pressed it onto the bond of debt.

My heart was pounding with impatience. On leaving Kashiwagi's lodging-house with the three thousand yen in my pocket, I took a streetcar as far as Funaoka Park. I ran up the stone steps that led round to the Kenkun Shrine. I planned to draw a sacred *mikuji* lot in order to obtain some suggestion about my journey. At the foot of the stairs one could see the main building of the Yoshiteru Inari Shrine painted gaudily in vermilion, and also a pair of stone foxes surrounded by wire netting. Each fox had a scroll in its mouth and even the insides of their sharp, raised ears were painted in vermilion.

It was a chilly day. Occasionally the wind fluttered between the thin rays of the sun. The weak sun broke through the trees and made the steps look as if fine ash had been scattered over them. Dirty ash, it looked like, because the light was so weak.

I ran up the steps without pausing for breath and, when I reached the large open courtyard in front of the Kenkun Shrine, I was covered with perspiration. Ahead of me was another flight of steps leading to the shrine itself. The even-tiled roof reached towards the steps. On both sides of the approach to the shrine small pines stretched out tortuously under the winter sky. The old wooden building of the shrine office stood to the right and on the door hung a sign with the words: "Research Institute for the Study of Human Fate." Between the shrine office and the main hall of worship was a white godown, and beyond it some sparse cedars grew under the cold, opalescent clouds which were scattered above me full of a mournful light.

From here one could get a view of the mountains to the west of Kyoto.

The principal deity worshipped at the Kenkun Shrine was the great feudal warrior, Nobunaga. His eldest son, Nobutada, was also enshrined as an associate deity. It was a simple shrine and the only touch of color was the vermilion of the railing that surrounded the main hall of worship.

I climbed the steps and paid my respects to the gods. Then I picked up the old hexagonal box that stood on a shelf next to the offertory chest. I shook the box. A finely carved bamboo stick emerged from the hole on top of the box. On it was written in India ink the figure "14." I turned round.

"Fourteen, fourteen," I muttered to myself as I walked down the steps. The sound of the syllables seemed to coagulate on my tongue and gradually to assume some meaning.

I went to the entrance of the shrine office and announced my presence. A middle-aged woman appeared. She had evidently been doing some washing and she was busily wiping her hands on her apron. Without the slightest expression on her face, she accepted the standard ten-yen fee that I handed to her.

"What's your number?" she asked.

"Number fourteen."

"Wait over there, please."

I sat down on the open veranda and waited. It occurred to me how meaningless it was that my fate should be determined by the wet, chapped hands of this woman. Yet it did not matter, since I had come to the shrine precisely with the intention of risking such meaninglessness. On the other side of the paper sliding-door I could hear the clinging sound of the metal ring on an old drawer as the woman evidently tried to pull it open with considerable difficulty. Then I heard a piece of paper being torn off and a moment later the sliding-door was pulled ajar.

"Here you are," said the woman, holding out a thin sheet of paper, and then once again she closed the door.

The woman's wet finger had left a damp mark on one corner.

I read the paper. "Number Fourteen—unlucky," it said. *"If thou beest here, the Myriad Gods will utterly destroy thee.*

"Prince Okuni, having undergone the burning stones, the plunging arrows, and other tortures, departed this Province according to the instructions of his Ancestral Gods. Herein lies a portent for thee of secret flight."

The interpretation printed underneath dealt with all manner of hardships and with the uncertainty that lay ahead. It did not frighten me. I looked among the various points that were listed on the lower half of the paper and found the item on travel.

"Travel—unlucky. Especially avoid traveling in a north-western direction."

On reading this, I decided to make my journey to the northwest.

The train for Tsuruga left Kyoto Station at five to seven in the morning. The time for getting up at the temple was half past five. On the morning of the tenth when I got up and changed directly into my student uniform, no one showed any suspicion. They were all in the habit of pretending not to see me.

Things were always a bit confused during the period of morning twilight in the temple. Some people were busy with sweeping, others with mopping. The hour until half past six was devoted to cleaning-activities. I went out and began sweeping the front courtyard. I planned to set out on my journey directly from the temple without taking anything along, as if I had suddenly been spirited away. My broom and I moved along over the pebbled path, which shone faintly in the early dawn light. Suddenly the broom would fall down, I would disappear and nothing would remain in the dim light but the white pebbles on the path. That is how I imagined that my departure must be.

It was for this reason that I did not bid the Golden Temple farewell. It was essential that I should be abruptly snatched away from my entire environment—and this environment included the Golden Temple. Gradually I directed my sweeping towards the main gate. Through the branches of the pines I could see the morning stars.

My heart was pounding. Now I must *leave*. The word almost seemed to be fluttering in the air. Whatever happened, I must leave—leave my surroundings, leave my conception of beauty which so shackled me, leave the isolated obscurity in which I lived, leave my stuttering and all the other conditions of my existence.

My broom fell from my hands into the darkness of the grass like a ripe fruit falling from a tree. I made my way stealthily towards the main gate, concealing myself behind the trees. As soon as I had passed the gate, I started running as fast as my legs would carry me. The first streetcar of the morning rattled along. I stepped aboard. There were only a few people in the streetcar; they looked like workers. I let the electric light pour over me with full force. I felt as if I had never been in such a bright place.

I vividly recall the details of my journey. I had not left without a destination. I had decided on a district that I had once visited on a school excursion in my middle-school days. Yet as I gradually approached the place, my feelings of *departure* and of *release* were so strong that I felt as if I were moving toward an unknown destination.

I was traveling on the familiar railway line that led to my home town, but never before had this sooty old carriage looked so strange to me as it did now and never had it appeared in such fresh colors. The station, the whistle, even the grating voice on the loudspeaker that echoed in the early dawn air, all reiterated a single feeling, reinforced it, and spread a dazzling, lyrical prospect before my eyes. The morning sun cut the great platform into sections. The sound of shoes running along the platform, the persistent, monotonous ringing of the station bell, the sound of a wooden clog splitting, the color of a tangerine that one of the platform venders picked out of his basket and held up—everything appeared to me as suggestions or portents of that vast thing to which I had now entrusted myself.

Every single fragment of the station, however minute it might be, was focused on my dominant feeling of separation and departure. Courteously and with the utmost serenity, the platform began to move away from me. I could feel it. Yes, I could feel how that expressionless concrete surface was illumined by the object that moved away from it, that separated, that left.

I relied on the train. This is a strange manner of expressing it, but there is no other way to secure the incredible thought that my position was gradually moving and drifting away from Kyoto Station. Night after night as I had lain in the temple I had heard the whistle of the goods trains as they passed near the temple grounds, and I could not help finding it strange that I should now myself be seated in one of those trains that day and night without fail had rushed past in the distance.

Now we were speeding along next to the Hozu River, which I had seen long ago when I had been on this train with my ailing father. The area between here and Sonobe, to the west of the Atago mountain range and of Arashiyama, had a completely different climate from the city of Kyoto. This was probably a result of air currents. During the last three months of the year a mist would invariably arise from the Hozu River at about eleven o'clock at night and cover the entire area until about ten o'clock the following morning. There would hardly ever be a break in the mist as it floated away from the river.

The fields opened up hazily on both sides of the train, and the parts that had been harvested had the color of green mold. A few scattered trees, all differing in size and height, grew on the ridges between the rice fields. All the lower branches and leaves had been cut away and straw matting (known in this district as "steam cages") had been wrapped round the slender trunks, so that, as the trees emerged one after another out of the fog, they looked like the ghosts of trees. Once a huge willow tree appeared with striking clarity very close to the train window. In the background was the gray, almost invisible expanse of rice fields; the wet leaves of the willow hung

204

down ponderously and the whole tree was shaking slightly in the mist.

My spirits, which had been so cheerful when I left Kyoto, had now been drawn into memories of dead people. As I recalled Uiko and my father and Tsurukawa, an ineffable tenderness arose within me, and I wondered whether the only human beings whom I was capable of loving were not, in fact, dead people. Be that as it might, how easy dead people were to love compared to those who were still alive!

The third-class carriage was not very crowded. There they sat—the people who were so hard to love—busily puffing away at their cigarettes or peeling tangerines. Next to me sat an old official who belonged to some public organization. He was talking loudly to another man. Both men wore old, shapeless suits, and I noticed a piece of torn striped lining peeping out of one of their sleeves. Once again I was struck by the fact that mediocrity did not wane in the slightest when people grew old. Those wrinkled, sunburned, peasant faces, those voices of theirs rendered husky by drink, could be said to represent the essence of a certain type of mediocrity.

They were discussing whom they should get to make contributions to their public organization. One bald old man sat there with a self-possessed look on his face. He did not join in the conversation, but kept on wiping his hands on a cotton handkerchief, which had originally been white, but which had now turned yellow from countless washings.

"Look at these hands of mine!" he muttered. "They get filthy from the soot while I just sit here. It's really annoying!"

"You wrote a letter to the papers once about the soot, didn't you?" said another man, who now joined in the conversation.

"No," said the bald man. "But it really makes me annoyed—all this soot!"

Though I was not listening, I could not help hearing. Hearing that the Golden Temple and the Silver Temple kept on appearing in the men's conversation. They were all agreed that they should obtain substantial contributions from these two temples. The income of the Silver Temple was only half that of the Golden Temple, yet it was a very considerable amount. The annual income of the Golden Temple, said one of the men by way of example, was probably over five million yen. The actual cost of running the temple on the ordinary lines of a Zen establishment, including the cost of electricity and water, could not exceed two hundred thousand. Well, what happened to the balance? Quite simple! The Superior let the acolytes and the apprentices feed on cold rice while he went out every night by himself and spent the money on geishas in the Gion District. And with all that, the temples were tax-exempt. It was just as if they had extraterritorial rights. Yes, those temples should be dunned mercilessly for contributions!

So their conversation went. When they came to an end, the old bald-headed man, who was still wiping his hands on his handkerchief, said: "It's really annoying!" and this summed things up for everyone. There was not a trace of soot on his hands; they had been thoroughly wiped and polished and they gave forth the luster of an ornamental *netsuke* carving. Those ready-made hands of his were really more like a pair of gloves than anything else.

It may seem strange, but this was the first time that I had ever come into contact with public criticism. In the Golden Temple we all belonged to the world of priests, and the university, too, was part of that world. It never happened that we exchanged criticisms concerning the temple. Yet this conversation of the old officials did not surprise me in the slightest. Everything that they had said struck me as self-evident. We ate cold rice. The Superior visited the Gion district. All this was quite normal. But what filled me with inexpressible rage was that I myself should be understood by the method of understanding which these old officials displayed. It was intolerable that I should be understood by *their words*. For *my words* were of a different nature. Please do not forget that even when I

206

saw the Superior walking with that Gion geisha I was not overcome by the slightest degree of moral hatred.

For these reasons the conversation of the old officials flew away from my mind, leaving only a faint hatred and a lingering odor of mediocrity. I had no intention of seeking public support for my thoughts. Nor did I intend to provide a frame for my ideas which might make them more comprehensible to the world. As I have said again and again, the fact of not being understood was the very reason for my existence.

The carriage door opened and a vendor appeared with a large basket hanging from his neck. He announced his wares in a hoarse voice. It suddenly occurred to me that I was hungry and I bought one of his box lunches. The meal consisted of green vermicelli in which seaweed had evidently been used instead of rice. The mist had cleared, but there was no brightness in the sky. At the foot of the Tamba mountains I could see the mulberry trees growing on the barren earth, and the houses in which people worked at paper-manufacturing came into sight.

Maizuru Bay. The name moved me now just as it had in the past. I am not quite sure of the reason. Ever since my childhood days in the nearby village of Shiraku, "Maizuru" had become a sort of generic term for a sea that cannot be seen, and in the end it came to represent an actual foreboding of the sea.

That invisible sea could be clearly seen from the top of Mount Aoba, which rose behind the village of Shiraku. I had climbed that mountain twice. On the second occasion I had seen the combined squadron, which happened to be anchored in Maizuru Naval Harbor. The ships which rode at anchor in the glittering bay may well have been part of some secret disposition of forces. Everything surrounding this squadron pertained to secrecy and one could hardly help wondering whether the fleet really existed at all. As a result, the combined squadron that I saw in the distance appeared like a flock of majestic black water-birds which one has known by name and so far only seen in photographs. They looked as if they were enjoying a secret swim in the bay, under the watchful eye of one fierce old bird and seemed blissfully unaware that they were being observed.

I was pulled back to the present by the voice of the conductor, who came in and announced the next station, West Maizuru. Among the passengers there was now not a single one of those sailors who in the past had hurriedly put their kit on their shoulders. The only people who were getting ready to leave the train, apart from myself, were a few men who looked like black marketeers.

Everything had changed. It had become a foreign harbor. English-language street signs flourished menacingly at the intersections and American troops were walking about in great numbers. Under the cloudy winter sky a cold, salt-laden breeze blew down the road, which had been built especially wide for military purposes. It had the inorganic smell of rusty iron rather than the waft of a sea breeze. The narrow strip of sea that led like a canal deep into the center of the town, the dead surface of the water, the small American war vessel that lay tied to the shore—there was a sense of peace about it all, to be sure, but an exaggerated policy of hygiene had robbed the port of its former disorderly, physical vigor and made the whole town seem like a sort of hospital.

I did not expect that I should encounter the sea here on any intimate terms, although of course a jeep might come along from behind and push me into the sea for fun. When I think about it now, I realize that the impulse which had made me travel had contained an intimation of the sea; it had not, however, been an artificial harbor sea like the one at Maizuru, but a rough sea that still retained its newborn vigor, like the sea with which I had come into contact during my childhood in my home on Cape Nariu. Yes, it had been the irritable, rough-grained sea, always so full of rage, that one finds along the coast of the Sea of Japan.

I therefore decided to go to Yura. In the summer the beach was crowded with bathers, but at this season it must be deserted and there would be nothing but the sea and

208

the land struggling against each other with dark power. From West Maizuru to Yura was a little over seven miles. My feet vaguely remembered the road.

The road followed the lower part of the bay west from Maizuru, crossed the Miyazu Line at right angles, went over the Takajiri Pass and came out at the Yura River. Then, after crossing Okawa Bridge, it followed the Yura River northward along the west bank. From then on, it simply followed the course of the river and led to the mouth at the sea.

I left the town and began walking along the road. As I walked, my legs became tired and I asked myself: "What shall I find at Yura? What kind of proof do I expect to run into that I exert all this effort? Surely there is nothing there but a stretch of the Sea of Japan and a deserted beach?" But my legs showed no tendency to slow down. I was trying to reach a destination, it did not matter where. The name of the place for which I was headed had not the slightest meaning. I was inspired by courage—by an almost immoral courage—to confront my destination, whatever it might be.

Now and then the soft beams of the sun would glisten fitfully and its gentle rays would shine invitingly through the branches of the great *keyaki* trees by the side of the road. Yet for some reason I felt that I could not procrastinate. There was no time for me to rest.

Instead of finding a gentle slope that led down to a wide river valley, I suddenly saw the Yura River from a narrow pass in the mountain. The water was blue and, though the river was wide, it flowed along dully under the cloudy sky and it looked as if it was crawling along reluctantly towards the sea.

When I reached the west bank of the river, there were no longer any cars or pedestrians on the road. Occasionally I noticed an orange grove by the roadside, but there was not a soul to be seen. As I passed a little hamlet called Kazue, I heard the sound of the grass being pushed aside. It was a dog, and only its face emerged from the grass. The hair at the tip of its nose was black.

I knew that this area was famous for being (according to a rather doubtful tradition) the site of the residence of that ancient squire, Sansho Dayu; but I had no intention of stopping at the place and I passed by without even noticing it. For I was only looking at the river. In the middle of the river was a great island surrounded by bamboo. Although there was not the slightest breeze on the road, the bamboo on the island was prostrating itself before the wind. The island had four or five acres of rice field, which were irrigated by rain water, but I could not see a single farmer. The only person in sight was a man who stood there with his back to me, holding a fishing-line. I had not seen anyone for quite a long time and I felt a certain friendliness for him. It looked as if he was fishing for gray mullet. In that case, I thought, I could not be very far from the mouth of the river.

Then the great rustling of the bamboo as it prostrated itself in the wind drowned out the sound of the river. What seemed to be a mist rose over the island: it must have been the rain that was starting. The raindrops dyed the desiccated riverbank on the island and, before I knew it, they began to fall on me. As I stood looking at the island and gradually becoming wet, I noticed that there was now no sign of rain over there. The man who was fishing had not changed his position in the slightest from when I had first seen him. Soon the shower passed from where I was standing, too.

At every turning of the road the rushes and the autumn flowers covered my field of vision. But I was soon coming to the place where the mouth of the river would open up before my eyes. For an exceedingly cold sea wind had struck me on the nose. As the Yura River neared its end, it displayed a number of desolate islands. The river water was certainly approaching the sea and already it was being attacked by salt water, but the surface itself became calmer and calmer and showed no portent of what was coming—just like a person who has fainted and who dies without recovering consciousness.

The mouth of the river was unexpectedly narrow. The sea lay there indistinctly mingled with the dark cumuli of clouds, melting into the river, assaulting it. In order to get a tactile perception of this sea, I still had to walk a considerable distance with the wind blowing fiercely on me from across the plains and the rice fields. The wind was drawing its patterns over the entire surface of the sea. It was because of the sea that the wind was thus wasting its violent energy on these deserted fields. And the sea was a sea of vapor that covered this wintry area, a peremptory, dominant, invisible sea.

Beyond the mouth of the river the waves folded onto themselves, layer upon layer, and gradually revealed the extension of the sea's gray surface. An island shaped like a Derby that floated on the river. This was Kammuri Island, which was preserved as the habitat for the rare *omizunagi* birds.

I decided to go into one of the fields. I looked round. It was a desolate land. At that moment some sort of meaning flashed through my mind. But no sooner was I aware of this flash than it disappeared and I lost the meaning. I stood there for a while, but the icy wind that blew against my body robbed me of all thought. I began walking into the wind. The meager fields merged into stony, barren land. The grass was withered; the only unwithered green was that of some moss-like weeds which clung to the ground, and those weeds, too, had a crushed, shrunken look. Already the earth was mixed with sand.

I heard a dull, quivering sound. Then I heard human voices. It was when I turned my back to the fierce wind and gazed up at the peak of Yuragatake in the back that I heard them.

I looked round for the sight of human beings. A small path led down to the beach along the low cliffs. I knew that work was gradually being carried out to protect those cliffs against the extensive erosion. Concrete pillars lay here and there like white skeletons and there was something curiously fresh about the color of the new concrete against the sand. The dull, quivering sound came from the concrete mixer, which shook the cement as it was poured into the frame. A group of workmen with bright-red noses looked at me curiously as I walked past in my

211

student's uniform. I glanced in their direction. Such was the extent of our human greetings to each other.

The sea subsided conically and abruptly from the beach. As I walked across the granite sand towards the edge of the water, I was seized with joy at the thought that I was without doubt moving step by step toward the single meaning that had flashed through my mind a short time before. The wind was bitterly cold and, since I was not wearing any gloves, my hands were almost frozen, but I did not mind in the slightest.

Yes, this was really the coast of the Sea of Japan! Here was the source of all my unhappiness, of all my gloomy thoughts, the origin of all my ugliness and all my strength. It was a wild sea. The waves surged forward in an almost continuous mass, hardly letting one see the smooth, gray gulfs that lay between one wave and the next. Piled up over the open sea, the great cumuli of clouds revealed a heaviness and, at the same time, a delicacy. For that heavy, undefined accumulation of cloud had for its edging a line as light and cold as that of the most delicate feather, and in its center it enveloped a faint blue sky of whose actual existence one could not be sure. Behind the zinc-colored waters rose the purple-black mountains of the cape. Everything was imbued with agitation and immobility, with a dark, ever-moving force, with the coagulated feeling of metal.

Abruptly I remembered what Kashiwagi had said to me on the day that we first met. It is when one is sitting on a well-mowed lawn on a beautiful spring afternoon, vaguely watching the sun as it shines through the leaves and makes patterns on the grass—it is at such times that cruelty suddenly springs up within us.

Now I was confronting the waves and the rough north wind. There was no beautiful spring afternoon here, no well-mowed lawn. Yet this desolate nature before me was more flattering to my spirits, more intimately linked with my existence, than any lawn on an early spring afternoon. Here I could be self-sufficient. Here I was not threatened by anything.

Was the notion that now occurred to me a *cruel* notion

212

in Kashiwagi's sense of the word? I do not know, but in any case this notion which suddenly came to life within me revealed the meaning that had flashed through my mind earlier, and it made me shine brightly inside. I still did not try to think it out deeply, but was merely seized by the notion, as though I had been struck by light. Yet that idea, which until then had never once occurred to me, began to grow in strength and size as soon as it was born. Far from containing the idea, I myself was wrapped up in it. And this was the notion that enwrapped me: "I must set fire to the Golden Temple."

CHAPTER EIGHT

Meanwhile I continued walking and came to the front of the Tango-Yura Station on the Miyazu Line. When I had come here on the school excursion from the East Maizuru

Middle School, we had followed the same course and had taken the train from this station. There was hardly anyone on the road in front of the station and it was easy to tell that this was a place where people depended for their living on the short summer season when visitors came in considerable numbers.

I decided to stay at a little inn where I saw a sign saying: "Yura Hall—Inn for Bathers." I opened the sliding glass window at the entrance and announced my presence, but there was no reply. There was dust on the steps. The shutters were closed and it was dark inside the house. There was not a soul to be seen.

I went to the back door. There was a simple little garden with some withered chrysanthemums. A bucket stood on a high shelf. This was for the benefit of the summer visitors, who used it as a shower to wash off the sand that was sticking to them when they returned from their swimming.

At a short distance from the main building was a small house, where the owner of the inn evidently lived with his family. I could hear the sound of a radio through the closed glass doors. There was a certain hollowness about the unnecessarily loud sound, which made me feel that in fact there was no one at home. A few pairs of wooden clogs lay scattered at the entrance. I stood outside and announced my presence each time that there was a lull in the noise from the radio. But, as I had expected, there was no reply from this building either.

A shadow appeared in the back. The sun soaked faintly through the cloudy sky. I did not notice it until I happened to see the grain of the wooden clog-box at the entrance turning brighter. A woman was looking at me. She was of a fatness that made the contours of her white body bulge out gently, and her eyes were so narrow that one could hardly tell whether she had any. I asked her for a room. The woman did not even ask me to follow her, but turned on her heels without a word and walked towards the hotel entrance.

I was given a small corner room on the second story, facing toward the sea. The room had been closed up for a long time and the feeble fire from the brazier, which the woman had brought for me, rapidly filled the air with fumes and made it almost unbearably musty. I opened the window and exposed myself to the north wind. In the direction of the sea the clouds were pursuing that leisurely, ponderous game of theirs, which they did not mean anyone to see. These clouds seemed to be a reflection of some aimless impulse of nature. In certain parts of them one could see fragments of the sky—small, blue crystals of clear intelligence. The sea itself was invisible.

Standing by the window, I began to pursue my earlier notion. I wondered why I had not arrived at the idea of killing the Superior before I had thought of setting fire to the temple. The possibility of killing the Superior had, I now realized, flitted through my mind; but I had instantly understood how useless it would be. For even if I should succeed in killing the Superior, his shaven priest's head and that evil of his, which was compounded of powerlessness, would keep on reappearing endlessly from the dark horizon. In general, things that were endowed with life did not, like the Golden Temple, have the rigid quality of existing once and for all. Human beings were merely allotted one part of nature's various attributes and, by an effective method of substitution, they diffused that part and made it multiply. If the purpose of a murder was to destroy the once-and-for-all quality of one's victim, then that murder was based on a permanent miscalculation. Thus my thoughts led me to recognizing more and more clearly that there was a complete contrast between the existence of the Golden Temple and that of human beings. On the one hand, a phantasm of immortality emerged from the apparently destructible aspect of human beings; on the other, the apparently indestructible beauty of the Golden Temple gave rise to the possibility of destroying it. Mortal things like human beings cannot be eradicated; indestructible things like the Golden Temple can be destroyed. Why had no one realized this? There was no doubting the originality of my conclusion. If I were to set fire to the Golden Temple, which had been designated as a National

Treasure in 1897, I should be committing an act of pure destruction, of irreparable ruin, an act which would truly decrease the volume of beauty that human beings had created in this world.

As I continued thinking on these lines, I was even overcome by a humorous mood. If I burn down the Golden Temple, I told myself, I shall be doing something that will have great educational value. For it will teach people that it is meaningless to infer indestructibility by analogy. They will learn that the mere fact of the Golden Temple's having continued to exist, of its having continued to stand for five hundred and fifty years by the Kyoko Pond, confers no guaranty upon it whatsoever. They will be imbued with a sense of uneasiness as they realize that the self-evident axiom which our survival has predicated on the temple can collapse from one day to another.

The continuity of our lives is preserved by being surrounded by the solidified substance of time which has lasted for a given period. Take, for example, a small drawer, which the carpenter has made for the convenience of some household. With the passage of time, the actual form of this drawer is surpassed by time itself and, after the decades and centuries have elapsed, it is as though time had become solidified and had assumed that form. A given small space, which was at first occupied by the object, is now occupied by solidified time. It has, in fact, become the incarnation of a certain form of spirit. At the beginning of the *Tsukumogami-ki*, a medieval book of fairy tales, we find the following passage: "It is written in the Miscellany on the cosmic forces, Yin and Yang, that, after a hundred years have passed and objects have been transformed into spirits, the hearts of men are deceived; and this is given the name of Tsukumogami, the year of the mournful spirit. It is the custom of the world to remove one's old household utensils each year before the advent of Spring and to throw them into the alley; and this is known as the house-sweeping. In the same way, every hundred years men must undergo the disasters of the Tsukumogami."

Thus my deed would open the eyes of men to the

disasters of the Tsukumogami and save them from those disasters. By my deed I should thrust the world in which the Golden Temple existed into a world where it did not exist. The meaning of the world would surely change.

The more I thought about it, the more cheerful I became. The end and downfall of the world—of that world which now surrounded me and lay before my eyes—were not far off. The rays of the setting sun lay across the land. The Golden Temple was shining in their light, and the world that contained the Golden Temple was assuredly slipping away moment by moment, like sand trickling between one's fingers.

My stay at the Yura Hall was brought to an end after three days, when the landlady, who was suspicious of me because I had not taken a single step out of the inn during this time, went and fetched a policeman. When I saw him enter my room in his uniform, I was frightened that he would detect my plan, but I realized at once that I had no grounds for such fear. In reply to his questions, I told him exactly what had happened—that I had wanted to get away from my temple life for a short time and that I had fled. Then I showed him my university identification papers, and later I made a special point of settling my bill in full while he was watching. The policeman consequently adopted a protective attitude. He immediately telephoned the temple to make sure that my story was correct and then informed me that he would take me back there himself. To avoid any possible damage to "my future," as he called it, he took the trouble to change out of his uniform for the journey.

While we waited for the train at Tango Yura Station, there was a shower and, since the station had no roof, it immediately became wet. The policeman, now dressed in his ordinary clothes, accompanied me into the station office, where he took particular pride in showing me that the station master and the other employees were his personal friends. Nor was that all, for he introduced me to everyone as his nephew who had come to visit him from Kyoto.

I understood the psychology of revolutionaries. These

country officials, the station master and the policeman, who now sat chatting round the red embers of the iron brazier, did not have the slightest presentiment of the great alteration of the world that was advancing before their very eyes, of the destruction of their own order of things that was so close at hand.

When the Golden Temple has been burned down—yes, when the Golden Temple has been burned, the world of these fellows will be transformed, the golden rule of their lives will be turned upside down, their train timetables will be thrown into utter confusion, their laws will be without effect. It made me happy to think that these people were completely unaware that the young man who sat there next to them, warming his hands over the brazier with an unconcerned look, was a prospective criminal.

A lively young station official was telling everyone in a loud voice about the film that he was going to see on his next free day. It was a splendid film which could not fail to bring tears to one's eyes and which at the same time was full of action. Yes, on his next free day he would be off to the pictures! This youthful fellow, who was so much sturdier than I, so much more full of life, was going to the pictures on his next free day; he would sit there with his arm round some girl and then he would go to bed. He kept on teasing the station master, telling jokes, and receiving mild rebukes from his superiors, while at the same time he bustled about the place, putting charcoal on the brazier and writing figures on the blackboard. For a moment I felt that I was on the verge of being caught up once more in the charm of life or in an envy for life. It was still possible for me to refrain from setting fire to the temple; I could leave the temple for good, give up the priesthood and bury myself in life like this young fellow. But instantly the dark forces brought me back to myself and abducted me from such ideas. Yes, I must burn the Golden Temple after all. Only then could a new life begin that was made specially to order for myself.

The station master answered the telephone. Then he went up to the mirror and carefully adjusted his gold-braided cap. He cleared his throat, threw out his chest and strutted onto the platform, as though he were entering a ceremonial hall. It had stopped raining. Soon one could hear the clear, wet noise of the train as it ran along the tracks that were cut through the cliff, and a moment later it glided into the station.

I reached Kyoto at ten minutes to eight and the plain-clothed policeman took me to the main gate of the temple. It was a chilly evening. As I emerged from the dark row of pines and approached the obdurate gate, I saw that my mother was standing there. She happened to be standing next to the sign on which was written: "Any breach of these regulations will be punished according to the law." In the light of the lamp on the gate, her disheveled head looked as if each individual white hair were standing on end. The reflection of the lamplight made her hair look much whiter than it actually was. Surrounded by this bristling white mass, her little face was motionless.

Mother's small body seemed luridly distended. Behind her stretched the darkness of the courtyard, which I could see through the open gate. Her huge form loomed up in front of the darkness; she was foolishly attired in a shabby kimono, which was much the worse for wear, and over this she had tied her best gold-embroidered sash which was now thoroughly worn out. She looked like a dead person as she stood there.

I hesitated to approach her. At the time I could not understand how she happened to be there, but later I found out that, on discovering my departure, the Superior had made enquiries at Mother's place; she had been greatly upset and had visited the temple, where she had stayed until my return.

The policeman pushed me forward. Strangely enough, as I approached Mother's body, it gradually became smaller. Her face was below mine and, as she looked up at me, it was grotesquely twisted.

I was hardly ever deceived by my instinctive feelings and the sight of her small, cunning, sunken eyes now brought home to me how justified I had been in my hatred for Mother. Drawn-out hatred over the fact that she

221

should have given birth to me in the first place, memories of that deep affront to which she had exposed me—an affront which, as I have already explained, did not leave me any room for planning my revenge, but instead simply isolated me from Mother. Those bonds had been hard to break. Yet now, while I sensed that she was half immersed in maternal grief, I abruptly felt that I had become free. I do not know why, but I felt that Mother could never again threaten me.

There was a sound of wild sobbing, as of someone being strangled to death. Then Mother's hand reached out and began slapping me feebly across the cheek.

"You undutiful son! Have you no sense of your obligations?"

The policeman looked at me in silence as I received my slaps. Mother's fingers lost their co-ordination and all the power seemed to leave her hand; as a result, the tips of her nails clattered against my cheek like hailstones. I noticed that, even while she was striking me, Mother did not lose her look of supplication, and I averted my eyes.

After a while she changed her tone. "You've been—you've been and gone all that way," she said. "How did you manage for money?"

"Money? I borrowed it from a friend, if you want to know."

"Really?" said Mother. "You didn't go and steal it?"

"No, I didn't steal it."

Mother gave a sigh of relief, as if this was the only thing that had been worrying her.

"Really? So you haven't done anything wrong?"

"No, nothing."

"Really? Well, that's good anyway. Of course, you'll have to make your humble apologies to the Superior. I've apologized myself, but now you'll have to go and beg him from the bottom of your heart to forgive you. The Superior is a broadminded man and I think he'll let the matter pass. But you're going to have to turn over a new leaf this time, or it'll be the death of your poor old mother! I mean it, Son! It'll be the death of me if you don't change yourself. And you've got to become a great priest . . . But the first thing is to go and make your apologies."

The policeman and I followed Mother in silence. Mother was so excited that she had even forgotten to address a conventional word of greeting to the policeman. She walked along with quick, short steps. As I gazed at her soft sash, which hung down in the back, I wondered what it was that made Mother so particularly ugly. Then I understood. What made her ugly was—hope. Incurable hope, like an obstinate case of scabies, which lodges, damp and reddish, in the infected skin, producing a constant itching, and refusing to yield to any outer force.

Winter came. My decision became more and more firm. Again and again I had to postpone my plan, but I did not grow tired of this steady prolongation. What worried me during that half-year period was something entirely different. At the end of each month Kashiwagi would demand that I repay the loan which he had made me. He would notify me of the total amount, taking the full interest into account, and would then torment me with all sorts of foul abuse. But I no longer had any intention of repaying the money. So long as I stayed away from the University, I did not have to meet Kashiwagi.

It may seem strange that I do not give an account of how, having once made this decision, I soon became unsettled and began to waver back and forth. The fact is that such waverings were now a thing of the past. During this period of half a year my eyes were fixed steadfastly on a single point in the future. It may well have been that at this time I knew the meaning of happiness.

In the first place, my life at the temple became pleasant. When I thought that, whatever happened, the Golden Temple was going to be burned down, unbearable things became quite bearable. Like someone who is anticipating his death, I now began to make myself agreeable to the other people in the temple. My manner became pleasant and I tried to reconcile myself to everything. I even became reconciled to nature. Each morning when the birds came to peck at what was left of the holly, I looked at their downy breasts with a feeling of real friendliness.

I even forgot my hatred for the Superior! I had become free—free of my mother, free of my companions, free of everything. But I was not foolish enough to believe that this new-found comfort in my daily life was the result of my having transformed the world without even laying hands on it. Anything can become excusable when seen from the standpoint of the result. In making myself view things from the standpoint of the result, in feeling that the decision to bring about this result rested in my own hands—here lay the basis for my sense of freedom.

Although my decision to set fire to the Golden Temple had been such a sudden one, it fitted me perfectly, like a suit that has been carefully made to measure. It was as though I had been planning it ever since my birth. At least, it was as though the idea had been growing within me, waiting for the day of its full flowering, since I had first visited the Golden Temple with Father. The very fact that the temple should have struck a young boy as so incomparably beautiful contained the various motives that were eventually to lead him to arson.

On March 17, 1950, I completed the preparatory course at Otani University. Two days later I had my twenty-first birthday. My record for the three years of the preparatory course was quite splendid. Among seventy-nine students I had managed to rank seventy-ninth. My lowest marks were in Japanese, for which I received the grand total of forty-two. I had been absent for two hundred and eighteen hours out of six hundred and sixteen—in fact, more than one third of the time. Yet since everything at this university was based on the Buddhist doctrine of mercy, there was no such thing as failure and I was allowed to advance into the regular course. The Superior gave his tacit approval to this step.

I continued to neglect my studies, and during the lovely days from late spring until early summer I spent my time visiting various shrines and temples that one could enter without paying. I used to walk as long as my legs would carry me. I remember one such day.

I was walking along the road in front of the Myoshin

Temple when I happened to notice a student striding ahead of me at the same pace as mine. He stopped at a little tobacco shop which was housed in a building with ancient eaves, and I noticed his profile as he stood there in his student's cap buying a pack of cigarettes. It was a sharp, white profile with narrow eyebrows. From his cap I could tell that he came from Kyoto University. He glanced at me out of the corner of his eyes. It was as though dark shadows had drifted together. I knew intuitively that he was a pyromaniac.

It was three o'clock in the afternoon—hardly the time for arson. A butterfly fluttered from the asphalt road where the buses passed, and clung to a drooping camellia that stood in a vase at the front of the tobacco shop. The withered parts of the white flower looked as though they had been burned by a brown fire. It was a long time before a bus came. The clock that hung over the road had stopped.

I do not know why, but I was convinced that the student was moving step by step toward arson. I suppose it was just that he looked so unequivocally like a pyromaniac. He had resolutely chosen the broad daylight, the most difficult time of all for arson, and now he was directing his steps slowly towards the destination on which he had firmly resolved. In front of him lay fire and destruction; behind was the world of order that he had abandoned. There was something stern about the back of his uniform which made me feel this. Perhaps I had for some time been imagining that this was how the back of a young pyromaniac would look. His black serge back, on which the sun shone down, was full of unhappiness and anger.

I slowed down and decided to follow the student. As I walked behind him and observed that he carried one of his shoulders a little lower than the other, I felt that his back was, in fact, my own. He was far more beautiful than I, but I had no doubt that he was being impelled to commit the same act as myself because of the same loneliness, the same unhappiness, the same confused thoughts about beauty. As I followed him, I began to feel that I was witnessing my own deed in anticipation.

Such things are liable to happen on a late spring afternoon, because of the brightness and the languid air. I became double and my other self imitated my actions in advance, thus clearly showing me the self that I should not be able to see when the time came for me to put my plan into execution.

The bus still did not come. There was no one on the road. Gradually the great South Gate of the Myoshin Temple approached. The doors were wide open and the gate seemed to have taken in every possible type of phenomenon. Within its magnificent frame, as I observed it from my particular angle of vision, it combined the overlapping of the pillars of the Imperial Messengers' Gate and the two-storied Sammon Gate, the tiles of the Buddhist Hall, numerous pine trees, a part of the blue sky, which had been vividly cut off from the rest, and numerous tufts of faint cloud. As I approached the gate, more was constantly being added—the stone paving that ran lengthwise and crosswise within the vast temple precincts, the walls of the pagoda building, and endless other things. And once one had passed through the gate, one realized that this mysterious structure contained the entire blue sky within itself and every single cloud in that sky. Such was the nature of a cathedral.

The student passed through the gate. He went round the outside of the Imperial Messengers' Gate and stopped by the lotus pond in front of the Sammon Gate. He then stood on the Chinese-style stone bridge that crossed the pond and looked up at the Sammon Gate, which towered above him. That gate, I thought, must be the object of his intended arson.

The superb Sammon Gate was indeed suited for being wrapped in flames. On such a clear afternoon the fire would probably be invisible. The smoke would coil about the gate and rise into the air; but the only way in which one could tell that those invisible flames were licking the sky would be to observe how the blue heavens were bent and trembling. As the student approached the Sammon Gate, I went to one side, where I could not be seen, and watched him closely. It was the time at which the mendicant priests returned to the temple, and I noticed a group of three of them approaching along the path. They walked side by side over the stone paving, wearing straw sandals and carrying their wicker hats in their hands. As they passed me, they turned to the right. They walked along in complete silence, observing the rule of mendicant priests according to which they must not look more than a few feet ahead until they were back in their cells.

The student still hovered hesitantly by the Sammon Gate. Finally he leaned against one of the pillars and took out of his pocket the pack of cigarettes that he had just bought. He looked round nervously. It occurred to me that he was undoubtedly going to set fire to the gate on the pretext of having a smoke. As I had envisaged, he next put a cigarette into his mouth, moved his face forward, and struck a match.

For an instant the match gave forth a small, clear flash. It looked as if the color of the flame were invisible even to the student. This was because at that moment the afternoon sun had enveloped three sides of the gate, leaving only my side in the shadow. For only an instant the match produced something like a bubble of fire, which flared up next to the face of the student as he stood there leaning against the pillar of the gate by the lotus pond. Then he shook his hand violently and extinguished it.

Even when the match was extinguished, the student did not seem satisfied. He threw it onto one of the foundation stones and assiduously rubbed his foot on it. Then, cheerfully smoking his cigarette, he crossed the bridge and strolled past the Imperial Messengers' Gate, utterly oblivious of the disappointment that I felt as I stood there alone and deserted. Finally he disappeared past the South Gate, through which one could see the main road and vaguely make out a row of houses stretching into the distance.

This was no pyromaniac, but simply a student who had gone out for a walk. In all probability, a rather bored, rather poor, young man.

I had stood watching his actions in detail and I may say

that everything about him displeased me—his cowardice, which had made him look round so nervously—not because he was going to commit arson, but simply because he was going to break the rules and smoke a cigarette; the mean pleasure, so typical of students, which he obviously derived from breaking these rules; the way in which he had been so careful to rub his foot on the match although it was already extinguished; and, most of all, his "civilized culture." It was thanks to this trashy sort of culture that his little flame had been safely brought under control. He probably took great pride in the idea that he himself was the controller of his match, the perfect, prompt controller who protected society from the dangers of fire.

One boon of this culture was that since the Meiji Restoration the old temples in and about Kyoto had hardly ever burned down. Even on those rare occasions when fires did accidentally break out, the flames were immediately cut up, divided, and controlled. It had never been like that in the past. The Chion Temple had burned down in 1431 and had suffered from fire numerous times thereafter. The main building of the Nanzen Temple had caught fire in 1393, with the loss of the Buddha Hall, the Hall of Rites, the Diamond Hall, the Great Cloud Hermitage and other structures. The Enryaku Temple was turned to ashes in 1571. The Kenjin Temple was laid waste by fire during the warfare in 1552. The Sanjusangen Hall was burned down in 1249. The Honno Temple was destroyed by fire during the fighting of 1582.

In those days the fires used to be on intimate terms with each other. The fires were not divided into little fragments and looked down on, as they are nowadays, but were allowed to join hands with each other in such a way that countless separate fires could unite into a single grand blaze. The people of the time were probably like that also. Wherever a fire might be, it could call to another fire and its voice would immediately be heard. The reason that the temple fires mentioned in the old records were never attributed to arson, but were always described as accidental fires, spreading fires, or fires caused by warfare, is that even if there had been someone like myself in the old days, all he would have had to do was to hold his breath and wait somewhere in hiding. Every temple was bound to burn down sooner or later. Fires were abundant and unrestrained. If only he waited, the fire, which was watching for its opportunity, would break out without fail, one fire would join hands with another fire and together they would accomplish what had to be accomplished. It was truly by the rarest chance that the Golden Temple had escaped being burned down. For Buddhist principles and law had strictly governed the world—fires broke out naturally, destruction and negation were the order of the day, the great temples that had been built were inevitably burned down. Even if there were pyromaniacs, they would be bound to make so natural an appeal to the forces of fire that no historian could bring himself to believe that the ensuing destruction was the result of arson.

The world had been an uneasy place in those days. Now, in 1950, the world was no less uneasy. Assuming that the various temples had been burned down as a result of this uneasiness, what reason was there that the Golden Temple should not be burned down now?

Although I was avoiding the lectures, I used to go quite often to the library and one day in May I ran into Kashiwagi, whom I had been carefully avoiding. When he saw me trying to avoid him, he pursued me with an amused expression. The realization that, if I ran away from him, he could not possibly catch up with me on his clubfeet, prevented me from moving. Kashiwagi caught me by the shoulder. He was out of breath. The lectures had finished for the day and I should estimate that it was about half past five. In order not to meet Kashiwagi, I had gone round the back of the university building after leaving the library, and had taken the path between the high stone wall and the barracks which housed the classrooms. Wild chrysanthemums grew in abundance on the waste land, interspersed with scraps of paper and empty bottles that people had thrown away. Some children had sneaked into the grounds and were playing catch.

Their raucous voices drew one's attention to the emptiness of the classrooms, which one could see through the broken windows. All the students had left and row after row of dusty desks stood there silently.

I passed the barracks and came to the other side of the main university building. I stopped outside a little hut on which the flower-arrangement department had hung a sign saying "Studio." The sun shone on the row of camphor trees that grew along the wall and the delicate shadow of the leaves was reflected across the roof of the hut onto the red brick wall of the main building. The red bricks looked gay in the evening sun.

Kashiwagi supported his body against the wall. He was breathing heavily. The shadow of the leaves of the camphor trees lit up his cheeks, which looked as haggard as ever, and gave them a peculiarly lively air of motion. Perhaps it was the reflection of the red brick wall, so unsuited to Kashiwagi, that produced this impression.

"It's five thousand one hundred yen, you know!" he said. "Five thousand one hundred yen at the end of this month. You're making it harder and harder for yourself to pay me back."

He extracted my bond of indebtedness from his breast pocket, where he always carried it, and spread it out before me. Then, evidently fearing that my hand might reach out for the document and tear it to pieces, he hurriedly folded it up again and put it back in his pocket. Nothing remained in my vision but an after-image of a poisonous, red thumbprint. It looked exceedingly cruel, that thumbprint of mine.

"Pay me back quickly!" said Kashiwagi. "It's to your advantage. Why don't you use your tuition fee or something to pay off the debt?"

I did not answer. Was one obliged to pay back one's debts in the face of a world catastrophe? I was tempted to give Kashiwagi the tiniest hint of what was in my mind, but I stopped myself.

"I can't understand you if you won't say anything," said Kashiwagi. "What's wrong? Are you ashamed of your stuttering? Surely you've got over that. Everyone knows

230

you're a stutterer—even this. Yes, even this!" He struck the red brick wall, on which the evening sun was reflected. His fist was dyed with brownish-yellow powder.

"Even this Hall knows. There's not a person in the university who doesn't know about it!"

Still I stood facing him in silence. At that moment one of the children missed the ball and it came rolling between us. Kashiwagi began to bend down in an effort to pick up the ball and throw it back to them. Seeing this, I was overcome by a perverse desire to observe how Kashiwagi would manage to move the ball with his clubfeet from where it lay about a foot away, so that he could reach it with his hand. My eyes seemed to turn unconsciously towards his feet. Kashiwagi perceived this with almost uncanny speed. Before one could tell whether he had really tried to bend down, he pulled himself up straight and stared at me with a look of passionate hatred in his eyes that was most unlike him. One of the children approached us timidly, picked up the ball from where it lay between us and ran away. Finally Kashiwagi said to me: "All right. If that's your attitude, I know what to do. Before I go home next month, I'll get as much of my money back as I can. You'll see! You'd better be prepared."

In June the important lectures became more and more infrequent and the students began to make preparations for returning to their home-towns. June 10 was a day that I shall never forget. It had been raining steadily since the morning, and in the evening it became a torrent. After supper I was reading a book in my room. At about eight o'clock I heard steps approaching along the corridor between the guest hall and the Great Library. It was one of the rare evenings on which the Superior had not gone out. Evidently he had a guest. There was something strange about those footsteps. They sounded like scattered raindrops beating against a wooden door. The steps of the novice who was conducting the guest to the Superior's quarters were soft and regular, and were almost drowned by the guest's drawn-out steps, which made the old floor boards of the corridor creak in a most peculiar fashion.

The temple was charged with the sound of rain. The night rain poured down on the large, ancient temple and the endless, vacant, musty rooms were replete with its sound. In the kitchen, in the deacon's residence, in the sexton's rooms, in the guest hall, there was nothing but the sound of rain. Now I thought of the rain that had captured the Golden Temple. I partly opened the sliding-door of my room. The little central courtyard, which consisted only of stones, was overflowing with rain water and I could see the black, glossy back of the water as it ran along from stone to stone.

The novice returned from the Superior's quarters and stuck his head into my room.

"There's a student in there called Kashiwagi who's come to see the Superior. Isn't he a friend of yours?"

I was overcome by uneasiness. The novice, who wore glasses and who worked as a primary-school teacher during the day, was about to leave, but I stopped him and asked him into my room. I was imagining all sorts of things about the conversation that was going on in the library and I could not bear to be alone.

A few minutes passed. Suddenly the sound of the Superior's hand-bell rang out. With its commanding peal it pierced the noise of the rain; then it stopped abruptly. The apprentice and I looked at each other.

"It's for you," he said. I forced myself to stand up.

When I reached the Superior's room, I knelt down outside. I could see the document with my thumbprint lying on his desk. The Superior raised one end of the piece of paper and showed it to me. He kept me kneeling outside the room.

"Is this really your thumbmark?" he asked.

"Yes."

"Well, this is a fine thing you've done, isn't it! If I have any more trouble of this sort from you, I shan't be able to keep you here any longer. You'd better wake up to the fact. This isn't the first time . . ." Perhaps because Kashiwagi was in the room, the Superior broke off. "I'll pay back the money myself," he continued, "so you can leave now."

At these words I was able to look at Kashiwagi for the first time. He was sitting on the floor with the look on his face of someone who has behaved in a most laudable manner. He did, however, avert his eyes. When Kashiwagi had done something evil, he always had an air of the greatest purity, as though, quite unbeknown to himself, the very essence of his nature had been extracted. It was I alone who knew this about him.

When I returned to my room, I was conscious that tonight, in the fierce sound of the rain, in my solitude, I had been released.

"I shan't be able to keep you here any longer"—for the first time I had heard the Superior tell me this, for the first time he had given me this pledge. Suddenly it all became clear. The Superior was already contemplating my expulsion from the temple. *I must hurry to carry out my decision.*

If Kashiwagi had not acted as he did that night, I should probably not have had an opportunity to hear those words from the Superior and my plan would have been further postponed. At the thought that it was Kashiwagi who had given me the strength to break through my inertness, I was overcome by a strange sense of gratitude for him.

The rain gave no sign of letting up. It was chilly for June and my little back room, surrounded by its wooden boards looked desolate in the feeble light of the electric bulb. This was my dwelling, from which I should probably soon be expelled. There was not a single ornament in the room. The black edge of the faded straw-matting on the floor had been torn and twisted, and one could plainly see the hard threads. Often when I entered my dark room and turned on the light, my toes would catch on the torn edge of the mat, but I made no effort to repair it. My zeal for life had no concern with straw mats.

Now that summer was approaching, my little room was redolent with the acrid odor of my body. It seemed funny that though I was a priest, my body should have the smell of an ordinary young man. This smell had penetrated the old, glossy black pillars in the four corners of the room

233

and even the wooden walls. Now the unpleasant odor of a young man oozed out between the grain of the wood, to which age had managed to give a certain patina. The pillars and the walls had been transformed into living things—immovable, yet exuding a raw, fishy smell.

Then the strange footsteps that I had heard before approached along the corridor. I stood up and went into the corridor. Kashiwagi was standing there, like a mechanical device that has abruptly come to a stop. Behind him the light from the Superior's quarters lit up the Sailboat Pine Tree in the garden and I could see the wet, blackish-green prow of the tree raising itself high in the darkness.

A smile came to my face, and it gave me great satisfaction to realize that when Kashiwagi saw this smile he displayed for the first time an expression that was close to fear.

"Won't you drop in for a while?" I said.

"Well, well. Don't try to frighten me! You're an odd fellow, aren't you?"

Kashiwagi came into my room, and eventually he managed to lower himself sideways onto the floor with that usual slow movement of his that made one think he was trying to crouch. He raised his head and looked round the room. Outside, the sound of the rain closed us in like a thick curtain. Amid the splash of the water on the open veranda one could hear the raindrops bouncing back from the paper sliding-doors in different parts of the building.

"Well," said Kashiwagi, "you mustn't hold it against me, you know. After all, it's your own fault that I had to go about it this way. Well, so much for that!" He extracted from his pocket an envelope, on which I could see the imprint of the temple, and counted the bank notes that were inside. There were only three thousand-yen notes—brand-new ones that had clearly been issued since January.

"The bank notes at this temple are nice and clean, aren't they?" I said. "Our Superior is so fastidious that he makes the Deacon go to the bank every three days to get clean money for all our small change."

"Look at this!" said Kashiwagi. "Only three of them. You've got a really stingy priest running this temple, don't you? He says he won't recognize the interest on loans between fellow students. Though he's profited to his heart's content from that sort of thing himself."

To see Kashiwagi overcome by this unexpected disappointment cheered the cockles of my heart. I laughed without reserve and Kashiwagi joined in. For a moment there existed a sort of harmony between us, but almost at once Kashiwagi stopped laughing and, fixing his eyes somewhere about my forehead, spoke as if he was casting me off. "I know," he said. "You've got some destructive scheme in your mind these days, don't you?"

I had the greatest difficulty in supporting the weight of his gaze. Then I realized that his understanding of "destructive" was entirely different in nature from what I was planning, and I regained my composure. There was not the trace of a stutter in my reply. "No, nothing," I said.

"Really? You're a strange fellow. You're about the strangest person I've ever met."

I knew that this remark was inspired by the friendly smile that still did not fade from my mouth. It was quite certain that Kashiwagi would never realize the meaning of the gratitude that had sprung up within me, and this thought made my smile spread even further of its own accord.

"Will you be going back to your home town now?" I asked in a manner that normal friends might use in speaking to each other.

"Yes, I'm going home tomorrow. Summer in Sannomiya. It's pretty boring there too, though."

"Well, we shan't be seeing each other at the university for some time."

"What? You're never there yourself anyway."

As he spoke, Kashiwagi hurriedly unbuttoned the front of his uniform and felt for the inside pocket.

"I decided to bring you these before I left for home," he said. "I thought they'd please you. You had such an absurdly high opinion of him, didn't you?"

235

He dropped a small bundle of letters on my table. I was amazed to read the sender's name on the envelope.

"Please read them," said Kashiwagi in a matter-of-fact tone. "They're a memento from Tsurukawa."

"Were you friends with Tsurukawa?" I asked.

"Well, let's see. Yes, I suppose I was a friend in my own way. Tsurukawa himself hated to be thought of as my friend. At the same time I was the only person to whom he ever confided. He's been dead three years now, so I suppose it's all right to show these letters to people. You were so friendly with him that I thought I'd let you see them and no one else. I've been meaning to let you look at them some day."

The dates on the letters were all from the period in May 1947 just before his death. They had been written from Tokyo almost every day and were addressed to Kashiwagi. He hadn't sent me so much as a single letter, but he had written Kashiwagi regularly from the day after he returned to Tokyo. The letters were certainly from Tsurukawa—there was no mistaking the square, childish writing. I felt slightly envious. Tsurukawa, who had never seemed to make the slightest effort to hide his transparent feelings from me, who had sometimes spoken badly about Kashiwagi and who had tried to discourage my friendship with him, had himself been carrying on this secret relationship.

I started reading the letters in the order of their dates. They were written in small characters on thin sheets of note paper. The style was peculiarly clumsy. His thought seemed to bog down constantly and it was hard to follow. Yet from behind his confused sentences a vague suffering soon began to emerge, and when I reached the final letters the agony that Tsurukawa had experienced stood before me in all its clarity. As I continued reading, the tears came to my eyes, and at the same time I was astounded at the banal nature of Tsurukawa's unhappiness.

It had been no more than a commonplace, little love affair—the unhappy love of an inexperienced young man for someone of whom his parents did not approve. Then a certain passage in the letter brought me up short. It may have been an unintentional exaggeration on Tsurukawa's part in describing his feelings, but the effect was none the less startling.

"When I think of it now," he had written, "this unhappy love of mine may have been the direct result of my own unhappy nature. I was born with a gloomy nature. I do not think I have ever known what it is to be cheerful and at ease."

The final letter broke off on a tumultuous note and when I read it I was struck by a suspicion that had never occurred to me until then.

"Could he possibly . . ." I began.

Kashiwagi nodded and interrupted me: "Yes, indeed. It was suicide. I'm quite sure it must have been. His family probably smoothed things over to save appearances and came out with that story about the truck and the rest of it."

"You wrote him an answer, didn't you?" I was stuttering with indignation as I pressed this question on Kashiwagi.

"Yes, but I understand that it didn't arrive until he was dead."

"What did you write?"

"I wrote that he mustn't die. That's all."

My deep-seated conviction that I could never be betrayed by my own feelings had proved to be false. Kashiwagi gave this illusion of mine its quietus.

"Well, what does it feel like?" he said. "Have these letters changed your outlook on life? Your plans have all been smashed now, haven't they?"

It was clear to me why Kashiwagi had shown me these letters now after three years. Yet, despite my shock, a certain memory still remained with me—the memory of the morning sun streaming through the trees and dappling the white shirt of the young man who lay there in the thick summer grass. Tsurukawa had died and three years later he had been transformed like this. It might have seemed that what I had entrusted to him would have vanished with his death, but instead at that very moment it was reborn with a new type of reality. It had come about that I believed in the substance of the memory, rather than in its actual meaning. And the conditions of my belief were such that, if I were now to stop believing in that memory, life itself would automatically collapse. As Kashiwagi stood there looking down on me, however, he was full of satisfaction at having so boldly carried out this butchery of my feelings.

"What about it?" he said. "Something broke inside you just now, didn't it? I can't bear to see a friend of mine living with something inside him that is so easy to break. My entire kindness lies in destroying such things."

"And what if it still hasn't broken?" I asked.

"Enough false pride!" said Kashiwagi with a scornful smile. "I just wanted to make you understand. What transforms this world is—knowledge. Do you see what I mean? Nothing else can change anything in this world. Knowledge alone is capable of transforming the world, while at the same time leaving it exactly as it is. When you look at the world with knowledge, you realize that things are unchangeable and at the same time are constantly being transformed. You may ask what good it does us. Let's put it this way—human beings possess the weapon of knowledge in order to make life bearable. For animals such things aren't necessary. Animals don't need knowledge or anything of the sort to make life bearable. But human beings do need something, and with knowledge they can make the very intolerableness of life a weapon, though at the same time that intolerableness is not reduced in the slightest. That's all there is to it."

"Don't you think there's some other way to bear life?"

"No, I don't. Apart from that, there's only madness or death."

"Knowledge can never transform the world," I blurted out, skirting along the very edge of confession. "What transforms the world is action. There's nothing else."

Just as I had expected, Kashiwagi parried my statement with a chilly smile, which looked as if it had been plastered on his face.

"There you go!" he said. "Action, you say. But don't you see that the beauty of this world, which means so much to you, craves sleep and that in order to sleep it must be protected by knowledge? You remember that story of "Nansen Kills a Kitten" which I told you about once. The cat in that story was incomparably beautiful. The reason that the priests from the two halls of the temple quarreled about the cat was that they both wanted to protect the kitten, to look after it, to let it sleep snugly, within their own particular cloaks of knowledge. Now Father Nansen was a man of action, so he went and killed the kitten with his sickle and had done with it. But when Choshu came along later, he removed his shoes and put them on his own head. What Choshu wanted to say was this. He was fully aware that beauty is a thing which must sleep and which, in sleeping, must be protected by knowledge. But there is no such thing as *individual* knowledge, a *particular* knowledge belonging to one special person or group. Knowledge is the *sea* of humanity, the *field* of humanity, the general condition of human existence. I think that is what he wanted to say. Now you want to play the role of Choshu, don't you? Well, beauty—beauty that you love so much—is an illusion of the remaining part, the excessive part, which has been consigned to knowledge. It is an illusion of the "other way to bear life" which you mentioned. One could say that in fact there is no such thing as beauty. What makes the illusion so strong, what imparts it with such a power of reality, is precisely knowledge. From the point of view of knowledge, beauty is never a consolation. It may be a woman, it may be one's wife, but it's never a consolation. Yet from the marriage between this beautiful thing which is never a consolation, on the one hand, and knowledge, on the other, something is born. It is as evanescent as a bubble and utterly hopeless. Yet something is born. That something is what people call *art*."

"Beauty . . ." I said and broke off in a fit of stuttering. It was a limitless thought. The suspicion had just crossed my mind that it might be my very conception of beauty that had given birth to my stuttering. "Beauty, beautiful things," I continued, "those are now my most deadly enemies."

"Beauty is your most deadly enemy?" said Kashiwagi, opening his eyes wide. Then the usual philosophical, exhilarated look returned to his flushed face. "What a change to hear that from you! I really must re-focus the lenses of my understanding."

We continued to talk for a long time. It was the first time for ages that we had exchanged our views in such an intimate way. The rain still had not stopped. As he was leaving, Kashiwagi told me about Sannomiya and Kobe Harbor. I had never been to any of these places and he now described the great ships leaving the harbor in summertime. The scenes came alive for me as I recalled Maizuru. For once our opinions coincided. We two indigent students shared the same daydreams and agreed that nothing, neither understanding nor action, was likely to equal the joy of sailing away into the distance.

Komatsu

CHAPTER NINE

It was probably no mere chance that, instead of admonishing me as he usually did, the Superior should now, at the very time when admonition was called for, have granted me a favor. Five days after Kashiwagi had come to collect his debt, the Superior called me to his study and handed me three thousand four hundred yen for my university fees during the first term, three hundred and fifty yen for my transport and five hundred yen for my stationery expenses. It was a rule at the University that we had to pay our fees before the summer holidays, but after what had happened I had not for a moment imagined that the Superior would give me the money. Even if he decided to pay the fees. I thought that, knowing as he now did how little I was to be trusted, he would send the money directly to the University.

I knew better than he that, even though he handed me the money now, his confidence in me was false. In a certain way this favor that the Superior accorded me without saying a word reminded me of his soft, pink flesh. Flesh that is replete with falsehood, flesh that trusts what deserves to be betrayed and that betrays what deserves to be trusted, flesh that is attacked by no corruption, warm, light-pink flesh that propagates itself in silence.

Just as when I had seen the policeman in the inn at Yura I had been terrified of being found out, now I was overcome by the fear, which came close to being a delusion, that the Superior had seen through my plans and was trying to make me miss my opportunity for decisive action by giving me money. I felt that I could never possibly sum up the courage to commit my action so long as I was nursing that sum of money which he had given me. As soon as possible I had to find some way to spend the money. I had to find some way of spending it so that, if the Superior should find out what I had done, he could not possibly avoid being overcome with rage and expelling me from the temple on the spot.

It was my turn to work in the kitchen that day. While I was washing up the dishes after supper, I happened to look in the direction of the dining-room. Everyone had left and the room was quiet. At the entrance was a sooty pillar which gave out a black luster. A sign, almost entirely discolored by soot, was stuck to the pillar. I read the words:

A - TA - KO   HOLY SIGN

Beware of Fire

In my mind I could see the pale form of the captive fire that was imprisoned by this amuletic sign. Something that had once been gay hovered now behind this sign, wan and debilitated. I wonder whether I shall be believed when I say that during these days the vision of fire inspired me with nothing less than carnal lust. Yet was it not natural that, when my will to live depended entirely on fire, my lust, too, should have turned in that direction? My desire molded the supple figure of the fire; and the flames, conscious that they were being seen by me through the shining black pillar, adorned themselves gracefully for the occasion. They were fragile things—the hands, the limbs, the chest of that fire.

On the evening of June 18 I stole out of the temple with the money in my pocket and made my way to the North Shinchi district, which is usually known as Gobancho. I had heard that it was cheap there and that they were friendly to temple novices and other such customers. Gobancho was about half an hour's walk from the temple. It was a humid evening. The moon shone dimly through a sky that was overcast with thin clouds. I was wearing a jumper, a pair of khaki trousers, and some wooden clogs. In all probability I should be returning after a few hours in exactly the same clothes. How could I have convinced myself of the idea that the I who was contained in those clothes would be an entirely different person?

It was certainly in order that I might live that I was planning to set fire to the Golden Temple, but what I was now doing was more like a preparation for death. In the same way that a man who has determined to kill himself might first pay a visit to a brothel in order to lose his virginity, so I was now setting out for the gay quarters. But please rest assured. When such a man visits a prostitute it is like putting his signature to a prescribed form and, even though he may lose his virginity, he will never become a "different person."

Now I did not have to stand in fear of that frustration—that frustration which I had so often experienced at the crucial moment when the Golden Temple intervened between me and the woman. For I no longer had any dreams or any aim of participating in life by means of a woman. My own life was now firmly fixed on that other thing; all my actions hitherto had merely been the cruel and gloomy processes that had brought me to my present state.

So I told myself as I walked towards Gobancho. But then Kashiwagi's words rose within me: "Professional women don't go to bed with their customers because they like them. They'll have anyone as a customer, doddering old men, beggars, one-eyed men, good-looking men—even lepers, so long as they aren't aware of the fact. This egalitarian approach would put most men at their ease and they'd go ahead quite happily and buy the first woman they came across. But this sort of egalitarianism didn't appeal to me in the slightest. I couldn't bear the idea that a woman should treat a perfectly normal man and someone like myself as if they were equal. It seemed to me like a terrible self-defilement."

It was unpleasant for me now to recall these words. My case was not, however, the same as Kashiwagi's. Apart from my stuttering, I did not suffer from any actual deformity, and there was no reason that I should not regard my lack of physical charm as being merely a conventional sort of ugliness.

All the same, I wondered, wouldn't any woman's intuition make her recognize the marks of a born criminal on my ugly forehead? This foolish thought immediately filled me with uneasiness and my pace slowed down. Finally I became weary of thinking and I really was no longer sure whether I was intending to lose my virginity so that I could set fire to the Golden Temple or whether I was planning to burn the Golden Temple in order to lose my virginity. Then without rhyme or reason the noble phrase *tempo kannan* ("the troubles that lie in store for the world") rose in my mind and as I walked along I kept on murmuring *tempo kannan, tempo kannan*. Before long I approached a place where the bright, bustling pinball parlors and drinking establishments gave way to a stretch of quiet darkness illuminated at regular intervals by fluorescent lights and faint, white paper lamps. From the moment that I had left the temple, I had been overcome by the fancy that Uiko was still alive and that she was living in seclusion in this particular place. This fancy filled me with strength. Since I had resolved to set fire to the Golden Temple, I had returned to the fresh, undefiled condition of my youth and I felt that it would now be all right for me to come across the people and the things that I had met at the beginning of my life.

From now on I should be *living*. Yet, strangely enough, all sorts of ominous thoughts gathered force within me day by day and I felt that at any moment I might be visited by death. I only prayed that death might spare me until I had set fire to the Golden Temple. I had hardly ever been ill and I showed no signs of illness now. Yet I felt more and more strongly every day that control over the various conditions which kept me alive rested on my shoulders alone; I alone had to bear the weight of this responsibility of continuing to live.

The day before, when I had been sweeping, I had hurt my finger with a bamboo whisk from my broom and even this minute wound had been sufficient to make me uneasy. I recalled the poet whose death had resulted from pricking his finger with a rose thorn. The commonplace people about me would never die from such causes. But I had become a precious person and there was no telling what fateful death might not be in store for me. Fortunately my finger did not fester, and today when I had pressed on it I had only felt the slightest pain.

I need hardly say that I had taken every sanitary precaution prior to my visit to Gobancho. On the previous day I had gone to a chemist's in some fairly distant part of the city where I was not known and had bought myself a packet of rubber prophylactics. The powdery membranes of these objects had a truly powerless, unhealthy color. In the evening I had taken one of them out and tried it on.

As my member stood there amid the other objects in my room—the Buddhist painting on which I had scribbled with a red crayon, the calendar from the Kyoto Tourist Association, the Buddhist texts for use in Zen temples which happened to be open precisely at the Butcho-Sonsho incantation, my dirty socks, the split straw-matting—it looked like some inauspicious image of the Buddha, smooth, gray, devoid of both eyes and nose. Its unpleasant form reminded me of the atrocious religious act known as "cutting the member," which nowadays only remains in certain records that have been handed down from the past.

I entered a side street which was lined with paper lanterns. The hundred or more houses along the street were all built in the same style. It is said that if a fugitive from justice put himself in the hands of the boss who managed this district, he could easily be hidden. Evidently when the boss pressed a button, a bell would ring in each of the brothels and the criminal would be warned that the police were coming.

Each house had a dark lattice window at the side of the entrance and each had two stories. The heavy, ancient tiled roofs which extended into the distance under the humid moon were all of the same height. Dark-blue curtains with the characters *Nishijin* dyed in white hung over each entrance, and behind them one could see the madams of the respective brothels dressed in their white aprons and bending forward to observe who was passing on the street.

I did not have the slightest notion of pleasure. I felt as though the regular order of things had abandoned me, as though I had been separated from the ranks all by myself; and now I seemed to be dragging my weary legs through some area of utter desolation. The desire that lodged within me squatted down hugging its knees and showed me its sullen back. All the same, I thought, it was my duty to spend the money in this place. I should use up all the money that I had received for my university fees and thus I should give the Superior a perfectly reasonable excuse for expelling me from the temple. It did not occur to me

246

that there was any peculiar contradiction in this thought; yet if this was my true motive, it meant that I must love the Superior.

Possibly it was still rather early for the crowds to visit the Gobancho. In any case there were curiously few people on the street. My wooden clogs echoed clearly in the night air. The monotonous voices of the madams as they called out to the occasional passers-by seemed to crawl through the moist, low-hanging air of the rainy season. My toes firmly clasped the thongs of my clogs, which had become loose. And these were my thoughts. Amid those multifarious lights that I had seen from the top of Mount Fudo on that night when the war ended, I must have been gazing at the lights of this very street.

In the place where my legs now led me Uiko must be waiting. At one of the crossroads I noticed an establishment called Otaki. I chose this place at random and went in through the blue curtains. Abruptly I found myself in a room with a tiled floor. Three girls sat at the opposite end of the room. They looked exactly as if they were sitting wearily waiting for a train. One of them was dressed in a kimono and had a bandage round her neck. The other two wore Western clothes. One girl was bending over; she had pulled down her stocking and was busily scratching her calf. Uiko was out. The fact of her being out put me at ease.

The girl who had been scratching her leg looked up like a dog that has been called. The heavy white powder and rouge had been applied to her round, puffed-up face with the sort of harsh clarity that one sees in a child's drawings. Yet, though this may seem a strange thing to say, she looked at me with an expression that was truly well-intentioned. It was precisely the look that one might give to some fellow human-being whom one passes at a street corner. Her eyes showed not the slightest recognition of the desire that lay within me.

As Uiko was not there, it did not matter which girl I had. I was still moved by the superstition that any choice or anticipation on my part would mean failure. Just as the girls could not choose their customers, so it was better that I should not choose my girl. I must make sure that the terrifying concept of beauty, which makes people powerless to act, would not now intervene between me and my intention.

"Which girl would you like?" said the madam. I pointed to the girl who had been scratching her leg. The slight itching on that girl's leg—an itching which probably remained from the bite of one of the mosquitoes that was prowling about the tiled floor—was the bond that linked me to her. Thanks to that itch of hers, she would earn the right thereafter to act as a witness when it came to officially investigating my deed. The girl stood up and came over to me. She lightly touched the sleeve of my jumper. I noticed that her lips were turned up in a smile.

As I climbed the old, gloomy stairs to the second story, I again thought about Uiko. I thought about how she had gone out from this hour, from the world that existed in this hour. Inasmuch as she had gone away from this place, I should certainly not find her wherever I might look. It seemed as if Uiko had gone outside this world of ours to have a bath or something simple of the sort.

While Uiko was still alive, I had felt that she was able to go freely in and out of a double world of this kind. Even at the time of that tragic incident, just when she seemed to be rejecting the world, she had once more accepted it. Perhaps for Uiko death had been merely a temporary incident. The blood that she had left on the gallery of the Kongo Temple had perhaps been something like the powder that remains from a butterfly's wings when one opens the window in the morning and it instantly flies away.

In the center of the second story an openwork balustrade surrounded an area where the draught came up from the courtyard; a clothesline stretched from one part of the eaves to the next and on it hung a red petticoat, a few articles of woman's underwear, and a nightgown. It was very dark and the indistinct outline of the nightgown looked like a human figure.

A girl was singing in one of the rooms. The girl's song

flowed along smoothly; occasionally it was joined by the discordant voice of a man. The song came to an end and there was a short silence. Then the girl started to laugh as if a string had been broken off.

"It's Haruko," said the girl who was with me, turning to the madam.

"It's always like that," said the madam, "always." And she obstinately turned her square back toward the room from where the laughter was coming. I was shown into a tasteless little room. A sort of stand took the place of the usual alcove and on it someone had haphazardly placed an image of the lucky Hotei god and a figure of a beckoning cat. A detailed notice of regulations had been pasted on the wall and a calendar also hung there. The room was illuminated by a single, dim light bulb. Through the open window one could occasionally hear the footsteps of passers-by as they wandered through the streets in their search for pleasure.

The madam asked me whether I wanted to stay for a short time or to spend the night. The cost for a short visit was four hundred yen. I asked for some saké and some rice biscuits. The madam went downstairs to fetch what I had ordered, but still the girl did not come next to me. It was only when the madam returned with the saké and told the girl to sit next to me that she joined me on the straw mat. Now that I could observe her close at hand I saw that her upper lip had been rubbed so that it was slightly red. Evidently the girl was in the habit of killing the time by rubbing and scratching not just her legs but all over her body. Then it occurred to me that this slight redness might be simply a smudge from her thick rouge. Please do not be surprised that I should have observed everything so minutely. After all, this was my first visit to a brothel and I was eager to search out proofs of pleasure in every item that met my eyes. I saw everything as clearly as in an etching; each detail was pasted in all its clarity at a fixed distance before my eyes.

"I've seen you before, Sir, haven't I?" said the girl, who had introduced herself as Mariko.

249

"It's my first time, you know."

"Really? This is the first time you've been to a place like this?"

"Yes, the very first time."

"Yes, I suppose it is. That's why your hand is trembling."

It wasn't until she said this that I realized that the hand in which I held my saké cup was shaking violently.

"If that's true, Mariko," said the madam, "you're in luck tonight, aren't you?"

"Well, I'll soon know if it's true or not," said Mariko casually. There was nothing in the least sensual about the way she spoke, and I perceived that Mariko's spirit was disporting itself in a place that had no connection with my body or with her body, like a child that has been separated from her playmates. Mariko was wearing a light green blouse and a yellow skirt. I looked at her hands and saw that just her thumbs were painted red. Perhaps she had borrowed some nail polish from one of her friends and had painted her thumbs for fun.

Soon we went into the bedroom. Mariko put one foot on the bed roll, which was spread out on the straw matting, and pulled the long cord that hung from the side of the lamp shade. The bright colors of the printed cotton quilt showed up clearly in the electric light. A French-style doll was ensconced in the elegant alcove.

I undressed clumsily. Mariko put a robe of light pink toweling over her shoulders and skillfully removed her clothes underneath it. There was a pitcher of water by the bedside and I gulped down a couple of glasses. Mariko, who was facing the other way, heard the sound of the water.

"Oh, so you're a water drinker!" she said laughingly.

When we got into bed and lay facing each other, she put her finger lightly on the tip of my nose and said: "Is this really your first time?" She laughed.

Even in the dim light of bedside lamp I did not neglect to look. Because the act of looking was a proof that I existed. Besides, this was the first time that I had ever seen another person's eyes so close to me. The law of distance that regulated my world had been destroyed. A stranger had fearlessly impinged on my existence. The heat of a stranger's body and the cheap perfume on its skin combined to inundate me by slow degrees until I was completely immersed in it all. For the first time I *saw* that someone else's world could melt away like this.

I was being handled like a man who is part of a universal unit. I had never imagined that anyone would handle me like this. After I had taken off my clothes, many more layers were taken off me—my stuttering was taken off and also my ugliness and my poverty. That evening I certainly attained physical satisfaction, yet I could not believe it was I who was enjoying that satisfaction. In the distance a feeling that had so far shunned me gushed up and presently collapsed. I instantly separated my body from the girl's and put my chin on the pillow. One part of my head was numb with cold and I tapped it lightly with my fist. Then I was overcome by the feeling that everything had left me in the lurch. Yet it was not sufficient to make me weep.

After we had finished, we lay next to each other talking. I vaguely heard the girl telling me about how she had drifted to this place from Nagoya. But my own thoughts were all directed towards the Golden Temple. They were really abstract reflections about the temple, quite different from my usual sluggish, heavily sensual thoughts.

"You'll come here again, won't you?" said Mariko, and from her words I felt that she must be a few years older than I. Yes, she was surely older than I. Her breasts were directly in front of me and they were moist with perspiration. They were plain flesh, those breasts of Mariko's, and would never undergo any such strange processes as being transformed into the Golden Temple. I touched them timidly with the tip of my finger.

"I suppose these must seem strange to you," said Mariko. Then she sat up in bed and, looking intently at one of her breasts, shook it lightly as if she were playing with a little animal. The gentle rocking of her flesh reminded me of the evening sun over Maizuru Bay. The way in which the sun had so quickly changed seemed to fuse in my mind with the quickly changing quality of the girl's flesh. And it comforted me to think that, like the evening sun which is presently buried in the many-layered clouds, the quivering flesh before my eyes would soon be lying deep in the night's dark grave.

The next day I visited the same shop and asked for the same girl. This was not only because I still had a good deal of money left over. The act, when I had first committed it, had seemed terribly poor in comparison with the ecstasy that I had imagined, and it was essential for me to try once more and to bring it slightly closer to my imagined ecstasy. One of the many ways in which I differ from other people is that the acts which I perform in my real life are inclined to end as faithful copies of what is in my imagination. Or, rather, I should say not imagination but the memory of my own wellsprings. I could never get over the feeling that every single experience that I might enjoy in my life had already been experienced by me previously in a more brilliant form. Even in the case of a physical act like this, I felt that at some time and at some place which I could no longer remember—perhaps with Uiko—I had known a more violent form of carnal joy, a sensuality that had made my entire body seem numb. This provided the source of all my later joys, and indeed those joys were merely tantamount to scooping handfuls of water from the past.

Truly I felt that at some time in the distant past I had somewhere witnessed a sunset glow of incomparable magnificence. Was it my fault that the sunsets which I had seen thereafter had always appeared more or less faded?

Yesterday the girl had treated me too much as if I were some ordinary customer and so on my visit today I took a book along in my pocket. It belonged to a collection and I had bought it a few days before at a second-hand bookshop. The book was *Crime and Punishment* by Bequaria. This work by an Italian criminal lawyer of the eighteenth century had turned out to be a sort of *table d'hote* dinner consisting of standard helpings of enlightenment and rationalism, and I had thrown it aside after reading a few pages. It occurred to me, however, that the girl might possibly be interested in the title.

Mariko greeted me with the same smile as yesterday. The smile was the same, but "yesterday" had not left the slightest trace. Her friendliness towards me was the friendliness that people show to a stranger they happen to glimpse at some street corner. Perhaps it was because this girl's body was itself like a street corner.

I sat in a little room with Mariko and the madam. We had some saké to drink and I was fairly skillful in my manner of exchanging cups according to the traditional custom.

"You turn the cup round properly when you hand it to your partner, don't you?" said the madam. "You may be young but I can see you know your etiquette!"

"But if you come here every day like this," put in Mariko, "won't your Superior scold you?"

So they had seen through me, I thought; they knew that I belonged to a temple.

"Don't think I didn't catch on to that!" said Mariko, noticing my look of surprise. "All the young men nowadays wear their hair long in the Regency style. If you see a fellow with close-cropped hair like yours, you can tell at once that he belongs to some temple. We know all about them in houses like this. Because this is where the men who've now become famous priests used to come when they were young. Well, what about having a song?" And abruptly Mariko started to sing a popular song about the various doings of some woman from the harbor.

Presently we went to the bedroom and I managed everything smoothly and with perfect ease in those surroundings that had now become familiar. This time I actually felt that I had had a glimpse of pleasure; yet it was not the sort of pleasure that I had imagined, but merely the slovenly satisfaction of feeling that I was adapting myself to the conditions of carnal pleasure.

When it was over, Mariko gave me a sentimental lecture, which bespoke the fact that she was older than I. For a short while it had a rather chilling effect on me.

"I think it'll be better for you if you don't come too

often to this sort of place," Mariko said. "You're a serious fellow. I'm sure of that. You mustn't get taken up with this kind of thing, you know. You should be putting all your energy into your work. That's much the best thing for you. Of course I like having you come here to see me. But you understand why I'm speaking to you like this, don't you? I feel you're like my younger brother, you see."

Mariko had probably picked up this sort of conversation from a story in some cheap women's magazine. Her words were not spoken with any particular depth of feeling. Mariko was simply concocting a little story, using me as the object and expecting that I would enter into the emotions that she had created. The ideal thing from her point of view would be that I should respond by bursting into tears.

But I did not do so. Instead, I abruptly snatched the copy of *Crime and Punishment* from the bedside and thrust it under her nose. Mariko obediently turned over the pages of the book. Then without a word she put it back to where it had lain. The book had already left her memory.

I only wished that Mariko would experience some premonition from the fateful fact of having met me. I wished that she would come just a little closer to the knowledge that she was lending a hand in the destruction of the world. After all, this should not be a matter of indifference even to this girl. I became impatient and finally blurted out something that I should not have said: "In a month—yes, in a month from now there'll be lots about me in the papers. Please remember me when that happens."

My heart was throbbing violently when I finished speaking. Mariko, however, burst out laughing. She laughed so hard that her breasts shook; then she glanced at me and tried to restrain herself by biting her sleeve, but once more she was convulsed with laughter so that her whole body shook. I felt sure that Mariko herself would be unable to explain why she was so amused. She noticed my expression and stopped laughing.

"What is so funny?" I asked. It was a stupid question.

"You're a real liar, aren't you? Oh, it's really too funny! What a terrible liar you are!"

"I'm not telling any lies."

"Oh, you must stop!" said Mariko, bursting into laughter once again. "I'll die if I go on laughing like this. You're killing me! It's all a pack of lies. And you can keep a perfectly straight face the whole time."

I looked at her laughing. Perhaps what amused her was simply the fact that I had stuttered so strangely when I made my emphatic remarks about the future. The fact remained that she did not believe a word I had said.

Mariko was devoid of belief. If there had been an earthquake directly before her eyes, she would not have believed it. If the entire world were to collapse, this girl alone would probably be spared. For Mariko believed only in things that happened according to her own private logic. This logic did not allow for any collapse of the world and accordingly nothing could possibly provide an opportunity for Mariko to think of such a thing. In this way she resembled Kashiwagi. Mariko was a female Kashiwagi, a Kashiwagi who did not think.

As the conversation had come to an end, Mariko sat up in bed with her breasts still naked and began humming. Her humming blended with the buzzing of a fly that was flying round her head. After a while the fly happened to settle on one of her breasts.

"Oh, it's tickling!" she said but made no effort to chase it away.

Once the fly had alighted on her breast, it stuck there closely. To my surprise, Mariko did not seem to find it altogether unpleasant to be caressed in this way by an insect.

I could hear the rain on the eaves. It sounded as if it were only raining on this particular spot. To my ears the rain seemed petrified with fear, as though it had wandered astray in this particular part of the town and had utterly lost its way. The sound of the rain was cut off from the vast night, just as I was; it was a sound that belonged to a circumscribed world, like the little world that was illuminated by the dim light of the bed lamp.

Inasmuch as flies love putrefaction, had Mariko begun to putrefy? Did the girl's total absence of belief connote putrefaction? Was it because she inhabited an absolute world of her own that the fly had visited her? It was hard for me to understand.

Then I noticed that all of a sudden Mariko had fallen asleep. She lay there like a corpse and on the roundness of her bosom, which was illuminated by the bed lamp, the fly, too, was motionless and had evidently dozed off.

I never returned to the Otaki. I had accomplished what I had to do. All that remained now was for the Superior to realize how I had used my university fee and to expel me from the temple.

Nevertheless, I did not give the Superior any hint about what I had done with the money. It was not necessary for me to confess; the Superior must ferret out my action for me without any confession on my part.

It was hard for me to explain to myself why I wanted to go to this length in relying, as it were, on the Superior's strength. Why should I want to borrow this strength of his? Why should I allow my final decision to depend on being expelled by the Superior? For, as I have already said, I had for a long time been aware of the Superior's essential powerlessness.

A few days after my second visit to the brothel, I had an opportunity to observe this particular aspect of the Superior's nature. Early that morning, before the grounds were open, the Superior went for a walk round the temple. This was a most unusual thing for him to do. He came up to me and the other young priests who were sweeping the grounds and made some conventional remark to thank us for our efforts. Then in his cool-looking white robes he walked up the stone steps that led to the Yukatei. Evidently he was going to sit up there by himself preparing some tea and clearing his mind.

The sky bore the traces of a violent sunrise. Here and there clouds, still reflecting a red glow, moved across the blue background. It was as though the clouds had not yet been able to get over their shyness.

When we had finished our sweeping, the other members of my group returned to the main building. I alone took the path that led past the Yukatei to the rear of the Great Library. It was my duty to sweep the grounds behind the Library. I picked up my broom and climbed the stone steps, which were bordered by a bamboo fence. The steps led to a point next to the Yukatei teahouse. The trees were still wet from the rain that had been falling until the previous evening. The morning glow was reflected on the dewdrops which were abundantly speckled on the surrounding shrubs and it looked as though red berries had started to grow there out of season. The cobwebs that stretched from one dewdrop to the next were also slightly red and I noticed that they were quivering.

As I gazed at it all, I was filled with a sort of wonder at the thought that the objects on this earth could so sensitively reflect the colors of the heavens. Even the moisture of the rain which shrouded the compound of the temple derived its quality entirely from the sky above. Everything was dripping wet, as if it had received some bounteous blessing from heaven, and it was exuding a smell in which putrefaction was blended with freshness. For the objects on this earth did not know the means of rejecting anything.

Next to the Yukatei Pavilion stood the famous Tower of the North Star, whose name originated from the passage: "The North Star bideth in this place and all the myriad stars do render service unto it." The present Tower of the North Star, however, was not the same as that which had stood here when Yoshimitsu held power. It had been reconstructed some one hundred years before in the round shape favored for teahouses. Since the Superior was not to be seen in the Yukatei, he must be in the Tower of the North Star.

I did not want to confront the Superior alone. I walked silently along the hedge, bending my body so that I could not be seen from the other side.

The Tower of the North Star was open. In the alcove I could see the usual scroll of Maruyama Okyo. The alcove also contained the small, delicately wrought Buddhist

257

shrine, which was made of sandalwood, but which had turned black during the hundreds of years since it had been brought over from India. On the left I could see the Rikyu-style shelf made of mulberry wood; I also noticed the painting on the sliding-door. Everything was there as I had expected, except for the figure of the Superior. Instinctively I raised my head over the hedge and looked round.

In a dark part of the room next to the pillar I saw something that looked like a large white packet. When I looked carefully, I saw that it was the Superior. His white-robed figure was bent to the utmost possible extent and he crouched there with his head between his knees and his face covered with his long sleeves.

The Superior remained in the same position. He was utterly immobile. But I who stood there watching him was attacked by a surge of shifting feelings.

My first thought was that the Superior had suddenly fallen ill and was having some sort of a paroxysm. I should go up at once and offer him my help. No sooner had this occurred to me, however, than something held me back. I felt not the slightest love for the Superior, and any day now I should be carrying out my intention to set fire to the Golden Temple. To offer him my help under such circumstances would be sheer hypocrisy. Moreover, there was the danger that, if I did help him, I might become the object of his gratitude and love and that as a result my resolution might weaken.

Now that I observed the Superior carefully, he did not appear to be ill. Whatever may have happened to him, his figure as he crouched there in the little teahouse was utterly devoid of pride and dignity. There was something ignoble about it, like the figure of a sleeping animal. I noticed that his sleeves were quivering slightly and it was as if some invisible weight was pressing against his back.

What could it be—this invisible weight? Was it suffering? Or again, was it the Superior's unbearable knowledge of his own powerlessness?

As I became accustomed to the quiet, I realized that the Superior was murmuring something in a very subdued voice. It sounded like a sutra, but I could not recognize it. Suddenly I was struck by a thought which shattered my pride—the thought that our Superior possessed a dark spiritual life of which we knew nothing and that, compared with this life, the little evils and sins and negligences that I had so assiduously attempted were trivial beyond words.

And then I realized it. The Superior's present crouching position was precisely like that of the "garden waiting," that is, of the itinerant priest whose request to enter the temple has been refused and who sits on his sack all day long by the entrance with his head bowed. If a prelate as high-ranking as our Superior was really imitating the religious discipline practised by a newly arrived traveling priest, he must be endowed with a fantastic degree of modesty. But to what was this modesty of his directed? Just as the modesty of the blades of grass, of the leaf tips on the trees, of the dew that lodged on the spider's web was directed towards the morning glow in the heavens, so perhaps the Superior was directing his modesty towards the original evils and offences of the world, which did not belong to himself; perhaps he was allowing these things to be reflected naturally on his person as he sat there crouched like an animal.

But no, his modesty was not directed at any such universal force. It was to me, I suddenly perceived, that he was displaying this humble attitude. There could be no doubt about it. He had known that I was going to pass this place and he had adopted this posture for my benefit. The Superior had fully perceived his own powerlessness and he had finally hit upon this fantastically ironical method of admonishing me, of silently tearing my heart to pieces, of awakening pity in me, of making me bend my knees in prayer.

While I watched the Superior crouching there in what I had taken to be an attitude of humility, I only narrowly escaped being attacked by emotion. Although I was trying to reject it with all my strength, the fact was that I was on the verge of succumbing to affection for him. But the thought that he had adopted this posture for my special benefit turned everything into reverse and made my heart

259

even harder than it had been before.

It was at this moment that I resolved to go ahead with my plans without depending on any preliminary condition such as being expelled by the Superior. The Superior and I had become the inhabitants of two different worlds and no longer had any influence on each other. I was free from all trammels. Now I could carry out my decision how I liked and when I liked, without expecting anything from an outside power.

The morning glow faded from the sky; at the same time the clouds gathered and the clear sunlight withdrew from the Tower of the North Star. The Superior stayed there in his crouched position. I hurriedly left the place.

On June 25 the Korean War broke out. My premonition that the world was going to rack and ruin had come true. I had to hurry.

Komatsu

CHAPTER TEN

On the day after my visit to Gobancho I had already
carried out an experiment. I had pulled out a couple
of nails, which were about two inches long, from

the wooden door at the back of the Golden Temple.

There are two entrances to the Hosui-in on the ground floor of the Golden Temple. Both are folding-doors, one to the east, the other to the west. The old guide used to go up to the Golden Temple every night. First he would close the west door from the inside, then he would close the east door from outside and lock it. I knew, however, that I could enter the Golden Temple without a key. For there was an old wooden door at the back which was no longer in use. This door could easily be removed if one took out about half a dozen nails from the top and bottom. The nails were all loose and it was quite simple to pull them out with one's fingers. I had therefore taken out a couple of the nails as an experiment. I had wrapped them in a piece of paper and placed them carefully in the back of my drawer. A few days went by. No one seemed to have noticed. A week passed. There was still no sign that anyone had observed that the nails were missing. On the evening of the twenty-eighth I stealthily entered the temple and put them back in their former place.

On the day that I had seen the Superior crouching in the teahouse and had finally decided that I was not going to depend on anyone else's strength, I had gone to a pharmacy near the Nishijin police station in Chimoto Imaidegawa and bought some arsenic. First I was given a small bottle which could not have contained more than thirty pills. I asked for a larger size and finally paid one hundred yen for a bottle of a hundred pills. Then I went to an ironmonger's south of the police station and bought a pocketknife, which had a blade about four inches long. Together with the case it cost me ninety yen.

I walked back and forth in front of the Nishijin police station. It was evening and several of the windows were brightly lit. I noticed a police-detective hurrying into the building. He was wearing an open-neck shirt and was carrying a briefcase. No one paid any attention to me. No one had paid any attention to me during the past twenty years and under present conditions this was bound to continue. Under present conditions I was still a person of no importance. In this country of Japan there were people by the million, by the tens of millions, who were tucked away in corners and to whom no one paid any attention. I still belonged to their ranks. The world felt not the slightest concern as to whether these people lived or died and for this reason there was something reassuring about them. The police-detective was therefore reassured and did not bother to give me a second look. The red, smoky light of the lamp illuminated the stone sign of the Nishijin Police Sation, the character for *jin* had fallen out and no one had bothered to replace it.

On my way back to the temple I thought about the purchases which I had made that evening. They were exciting purchases. Although I had bought the drugs and the knife for the remote eventuality of having to die, I was so pleased with them that I could not help wondering whether this was not how a man must feel who has acquired a new house and who is making plans for his future life. Even after I had returned to the temple I did not tire of looking at my two acquisitions. I took the pocketknife out of its case and licked the blade. The steel immediately clouded over and the clear coolness against my tongue was followed by a remote suggestion of sweetness. The sweetness was faintly reflected on my tongue from within the thin steel, from within the unattainable essence of the steel. The clarity of form, the luster of iron like the indigo color of the deep sea—it was they that carried this limpid sweetness which coiled itself securely round the tip of my tongue together with my saliva. Finally the sweetness receded from me. Happily I imagined the day when my flesh would be intoxicated by a great outburst of that sweetness. Death's sky was bright and seemed to me like the sky of life. My gloomy thoughts all left me. This world was now devoid of agony.

After the war an automatic fire alarm of the latest model had been installed in the Golden Temple. It was so designed that when the temperature inside the temple reached a certain point, the warning-bell would ring in the corridor of the building where we lived. On the evening of June 29 something went wrong with the alarm. It was the old guide who discovered the fault. I happened to be in the kitchen at the time and I heard the old man report the matter to the deacon's office. I felt that I was listening to an encouragement from heaven.

On the following morning, however, the deacon telephoned the factory that had installed the equipment and asked them to send a repairman. The good-natured guide went out of his way to inform me of this development. I bit my lip. Last night had been the golden opportunity for carrying out my decision and I had missed it.

In the evening the repairman came. We all stood round curiously watching him at work. It took a long time to carry out the repairs. The man inclined his head to one side with a vague air of discouragement and his audience began to leave one by one. In due course I also left. Now I had to wait for the repairs to be completed and for that signal of despair when the alarm bell would ring out loudly through the temple buildings as the man tested it. I waited. The night pushed its way up the Golden Temple like a rising tide, and I could see the repairman's little light flickering inside the dark building. There was no sound of an alarm. The repairman gave up and said that he would return on the following day to finish the job.

He broke his word, however, and failed to come on July 1. The temple authorites were aware of no particular reason to speed up the repairs.

On June 30 I went once again to Chimoto Imaidegawa and bought some sweet bread and some bean-jam wafers. Since we were never given anything to eat between meals at the temple, I had occasionally come to this place and bought a few sweets out of my meager pocket money.

But my purchases on the thirtieth were not inspired by hunger. Nor did I buy the bread to help me swallow the arsenic. If I must give a reason, I should say that uneasiness caused me to buy that food.

The relationship between me and that full paper bag

which I carried in my hand. The relationship between that perfect and isolated deed that I was about to undertake and the shabby bread in my bag. The sun oozed out from the cloudy sky and shrouded the old houses along the street like a sweltering mist. The perspiration began to run stealthily down my back as if a cold thread had suddenly been pulled along it. I was terribly tired.

The relationship between me and the sweet bread. What could it be? I imagined that when the time came and I was face to face with the deed, my spirit would be buoyed up by the tension and concentration of the moment, but that my stomach, which would be left in its usual state of isolation, would still demand some guaranty of this isolation. I felt that my internal organs were like some shabby dog of mine that could never be properly trained. I knew. I knew that however much my spirit might be enlivened, my stomach and my intestines—those dull, stolid organs lodged within my body—would insist on having their own way and would start dreaming some banal dream of everyday life.

I knew that my stomach was going to dream. It was going to dream about sweet bread and bean-jam wafers. While my spirit dreamed about jewels, my stomach would obstinately dream about sweet bread and bean-jam wafers. In any case, this food of mine would provide a fitting clue when people started to rack their brains about the reason for my crime. "The poor fellow was hungry," people would say. "How very human!"

The day came. July 1, 1950. As I have already mentioned, there was no prospect that the fire alarm would be repaired during the course of that day. This was confirmed at six o'clock in the evening. The old guide telephoned the factory once again and urged them to complete the repairs. The mechanic replied that he was unfortunately too busy to come that evening, but that he would finish the job on the following day without fail.

There had been about a hundred visitors at the temple during the day, but since the gates closed at half past six, the waves of human beings were already beginning to recede. When the old guide had finished telephoning, he stood at the entrance of the kitchen looking absently at the little field outside. He had completed his work for the day.

It was drizzling. There had been several showers since the morning. There was also a slight breeze and it was not too sultry for the time of year. I noticed the flowers of the pumpkin plants scattered here and there in the field under the rain. The soybeans, which had been planted in the previous month, had begun to sprout along the black, glossy ridges on the other side of the field.

When the guide was engaged in thinking, he used to bring his badly fitting false teeth together with a resounding clang. Every day he gave forth the same information to the temple visitors, but owing to his false teeth it was steadily becoming harder to understand him. He paid absolutely no attention to the various suggestions that he should have them repaired. The old man was muttering to himself as he gazed at the field. He paused for a moment and I could hear his dentures clattering. Then he started muttering again. He was probably grumbling about the delay in repairing the fire alarm. As I listened to his incomprehensible murmur, I felt he was saying that it was now too late for any repair—either to his teeth or to the fire alarm.

The Superior had an unaccustomed visitor that evening. It was Father Kuwai Zenkai, the head of the Ryuho Temple in Fukui Prefecture, who had been a friend during his seminary days. Since Father Zenkai had been a friend of the Superior's, he had also been friendly with my father.

The Superior was out when Father Zenkai arrived. Someone telephoned him and told him that he had a visitor; he said that he would be back in about an hour. Father Zenkai had come to Kyoto to spend a day or two at our temple.

I remembered that Father had always spoken happily about this priest and I knew that he had a very high opinion of him. He was extremely masculine both in appearance and in character and was a model of the rough-hewn type of Zen priest. He was almost six feet tall, with dark skin and bushy eyebrows. His voice was like thunder.

When one of my fellow apprentices came to tell me that Father Zenkai wanted to talk to me until the Superior returned, I felt rather hesitant. I was afraid that the priest's clear pure eyes would see through my plan, which was now so rapidly nearing the moment of execution.

I found him sitting cross-legged in the large visitor's hall in the main building. He was drinking saké, which the deacon had sensibly brought him, and munching some vegetarian tidbits. My fellow apprentice had been serving him until I arrived, but I now took his place and, sitting down formally in front of the priest, began to pour his saké for him. I sat with my back to the darkness of the silent rain. Father Zenkai therefore had two gloomy prospects before his eyes—the dark garden, which was sodden from the rainy season, and my face. But he was not a man to be enmeshed by this or anything else. Although it was our first meeting, he spoke brightly and without hesitation. One remark followed another. "You look just like your father." "You've really grown up, haven't you?" "How very sad that your father should have died!"

Father Zenkai had a simplicity that was alien to the Superior and a strength that my father had never possessed. His face was sunburned, his nostrils were extremely wide, the folds of flesh round the heavy brows of his eyes bulged toward each other, so that his face looked as if if it had been modeled after the Obeshimi masks used for goblins in Nō plays.

He certainly did not have regular features. There was too much inner power in Father Zenkai. This power revealed itself just as it pleased and entirely destroyed any regularity that there might have been. His protruding cheekbones were precipitous like the craggy mountains depicted by Chinese artists of the Southern School.

Yet there was a gentleness in the priest's thundering

267

voice that found an echo in my heart. It was not a usual sort of gentleness, but the gentleness of the harsh roots of some great tree that grows outside a village and gives shelter to the passing traveler. His gentleness was rough to the feel. As we talked, I had to be on my guard lest tonight of all nights my resolution should be blunted by contact with this gentleness. The suspicion occurred to me that the Superior might have asked Father Zenkai especially for my benefit, but I realized that he would hardly have had him come all the way from Fukui Prefecture just for me. No, this priest was merely a peculiar guest, who by chance was going to be witness to a supreme cataclysm.

The white earthenware saké bottle held over half a pint, but Father Zenkai had already emptied it. I excused myself with a formal bow and went to the kitchen to fetch another bottle. As I returned with the heated saké, I was overcome by a feeling that I had never known until then. The desire to be understood by others had so far never occurred to me, but now I wished that Father Zenkai alone would understand me. He should have noticed that as I again knelt there before him pouring out his saké my eyes gleamed with a sincerity that they had not had a little while before.

"What do you think of me, Father?" I asked.

"Hm, I should say that you look like a good serious student. Of course I don't know what kind of debauchery you go in for on the sly. But there, I've forgotten. Things aren't like they used to be, are they? I don't suppose you young fellows nowadays have enough money for debauchery. When your father and I and the Superior here were young, we used to do all sorts of wicked things."

"Do I look like an ordinary student?" I asked.

"Yes," replied Father Zenkai, "and that's the best way to look. To look ordinary is by far the best thing. People aren't suspicious of you then, you see."

Father Zenkai was devoid of vanity. High-ranking prelates, who are constantly being used to judge everything from human character to paintings and antiques, are apt to fall into the sin of never giving a positive judgment on anything for fear of being laughed at later in case they have been wrong. Then, of course, there is the type of Zen priest who will instantly hand down his arbitrary decision on anything that is discussed, but who will be careful to phrase his reply in such a way that it can be taken to mean two opposite things. Father Zenkai was not like that. I was well aware that he spoke just as he saw and just as he felt. He did not go out of his way to search for any special meaning in the things that were reflected in his strong, pure eyes. It made no difference to him whether there was a meaning or not. And what more than anything else made Father Zenkai seem so great to me was that when he looked at some object—at me for instance—he did not try to assert his individuality be perceiving something that he and no one else could see, but saw the object just as anyone else would see it. The mere objective world itself had no meaning for this priest. I understood what he was trying to tell me and gradually I began to feel at ease. So long as I looked ordinary to other people, I really was ordinary and, whatever strange actions I might bring myself to commit, this ordinariness would remain, like rice that has been sifted through a winnow.

Without any conscious effort, I had come to imagine myself as a quiet little bushy tree planted in front of Father Zenkai.

"Is it all right, Father," I said, "to act according to the pattern that people expect of one?"

"It's not always so easy. But if you start acting in a different way, people soon come to accept that as being normal for you. They're very forgetful, you see."

"Which personality is really lasting?" I asked. "The one that I envisage myself or the one that other people believe I have?"

"Both will soon come to an end. However much you may convince yourself that your personality is lasting, it is bound to cease sooner or later. While the train is running, the passengers stay still. But when the train stops, the passengers have to start walking from that point. Running comes to an end and resting also comes to an end. Death seems to be the ultimate rest, but there's no telling how long even that continues."

"Please see into me, Father," I said finally. "I am not the sort of person you imagine. Please see into my heart."

The priest put his saké cup to his mouth and looked at me intently. The silence weighed down on me like the great, black, rain-drenched roof of the temple. I shuddered. Then suddenly Father Zenkai spoke in a laughing voice that was extraordinarily clear: "There's no need to see into you. One can see everything on your face."

I felt that I had been completely understood down to the deepest recess of my being. For the first time in my life I had become utterly blank. Just like water soaking into this blankness, courage to commit the deed gushed up in me afresh.

The Superior returned to the temple. It was nine o'clock. As usual, a group of four set out to make the final inspection for the night. There was nothing out of the ordinary. The Superior sat drinking saké with Father Zenkai. At about half past twelve one of my fellow apprentices came to conduct the visitor to his bedroom. Then the Superior had his bath—or "entered the waters," as it was called in the temple—and by one o'clock on the morning of the second, when the night watch was finished, the temple was completely quiet. Outside it continued to rain silently.

My sleeping-roll was spread out on the floor. I sat there by myself and contemplated the night that had settled on the temple. Gradually the night became denser and heavier. The large pillars and the wooden door of the little room where I sat looked austere as they supported this ancient night.

I stuttered silently inside my mouth. As usual, a single word appeared on my lips much to my irritation; for it was just like when one vainly searches for something in a bag and instead keeps on coming across some other object that one does not want. The heaviness and density of my inner world closely resembled those of the night and my words creaked to the surface like a heavy bucket being drawn out of the night's deep well.

It wouldn't be long now, I thought; I must just remain patient for a short while. The rusty key that opened the door between the outer world and my inner world would turn smoothly in its lock. My world would be ventilated as the breeze blew freely between it and the outer world. The well bucket would rise, swaying lightly in the wind and everything would open up before me in the form of a vast field and the secret room would be destroyed. . . . Now it is before my eyes and my hands are just about to stretch out and reach it. . . .

I was filled with happiness as I sat there in the darkness for about an hour. I felt that I had never been as happy in my entire life. Abruptly I arose out of the darkness.

I made my way stealthily to the back of the library and put on the straw sandals that I had carefully placed there beforehand. Then in the drizzling rain I walked along the ditch behind the temple in the direction of the workroom. There was no lumber in the workroom, but the floor was strewn with sawdust whose rain-sodden smell wandered helplessly about the place. The workroom was also used for storing straw. It was usual to buy forty bundles of this straw at a time, but that night only three bundles remained from the last lot.

I picked up the three bundles and returned along the edge of the field. All was hushed in the kitchen. I made my way round the corner of the building and reached the rear of the Deacon's quarters. Suddenly a light shone in the lavatory window. I crouched down.

I could hear someone clearing his throat in the lavatory. It sounded like the Deacon. Then I heard him relieving himself. It seemed to go on for ever.

I was afraid that the straw might get wet in the rain, and I protected it with my chest as I crouched there next to the building. The smell from the lavatory had been intensified by the rain and now it settled heavily over the clumps of ferns. The splashing in the toilet bowl stopped and then I heard a body bump against the wooden wall. Evidently the Deacon was not fully awake and he was still unsteady on his feet. The light in the window went out. I picked up the three bundles of straw and set out for the rear of the library.

My property consisted only of a wicker basket, in which I kept my personal belongings, and a small, old trunk. I intended to burn all of it. Earlier in the evening I had packed my books, my clothes, my robes, and the various other odds and ends in these two pieces of luggage. I hope that people will recognize how carefully I went about everything. Such things as my mosquito-net rod that were apt to make a noise while I carried them, and also noninflammable objects, like my ash tray, my cup and my ink bottle, which would leave evidence of my deed, I had packed between some soft cushions and wrapped up in a cloth. I had put these apart from my other possessions. In addition, I had to burn one mattress and two quilts. I moved all this bulky luggage piece by piece to the rear of the library and piled it up on the ground. Then I went to the Golden Temple to remove the back door that I mentioned earlier.

The nails came out one after another as easily as if they had been stuck in a bed of soft earth. I supported the slanting door with my entire body and the wet surface of the rotten wood swelled out to rub gently against my cheek. It was not as heavy as I had expected. Having removed the door, I laid it down on the ground next to the building. Now I could look into the interior of the Golden Temple. It was replete with darkness.

The door was just wide enough so that one could enter the temple sideways. I soaked my body into the darkness of the Golden Temple. Then a strange face appeared before me and made me tremble with fear. As I was holding a lighted match, my face was reflected on the glass case that contained the model of the temple.

This was hardly an appropriate time for such activities,

but I now stopped and gazed intently at the miniature Golden Temple which stood inside its case. This little temple was illuminated by the moonlight of my match, its shadow flickered and its delicate wooden frame crouched there full of uneasiness. Almost immediately it was swallowed up by the darkness. My match had burned out.

Strangely enough, the red glow that dotted the end of the match made me nervous and I carefully stamped it out, just like that student whom I had once seen at the Myoshin Temple. Then I struck another match. I passed in front of the Sutra Hall and the statues of the three Buddhas and came to where the offertory box stood. The box had numerous wooden slats, between which the coins were dropped, and now as the light of my match flickered in the darkness the shadows of those slats rippled like waves. Inside the offertory box there was a wooden statue of Ashikaga Yoshimitsu, which was classed as a National Treasure. It was a sitting figure dressed in a priestly robe whose sleeves stretched out at both ends; a scepter rested in its hands. The eyes of the little shaven head were wide open and the neck was buried in the wide sleeves of the robe. The eyes of the statue glittered in the light of my match, but I was not afraid. It was really horrible, that little statue of Yoshimitsu. Though it was enshrined in a corner of the building that he had himself constructed, he seemed long since to have abandoned all ownership and control.

I opened the western door which led to the Sosei. As I have already mentioned, this was a hinged door which one could open from the inside. The rainy night sky was lighter than the inside of the Golden Temple. With a subdued grating sound the wet door let in the breeze-filled dark-blue night air.

Yoshimitsu's eyes, I thought as I bounded out of the door and ran back to the rear of the library. Those eyes of Yoshimitsu's. Everything would be performed in front of those eyes. In front of those unseeing eyes of a dead witness.

As I ran, I noticed that something was making a sound

in my trouser pocket. It was the rattling of my matchbox. I stopped and stuffed a paper handkerchief under the lid of the box. This ended the rattle. No sound came from the other pocket, where my bottle of arsenic and my knife were securely wrapped in a handkerchief. Nor, of course, was there any sound from the sweet bread, the bean-jam wafers, and the cigarettes, which lay in the pocket of my jumper.

Then I embarked on some mechanical work. It took me four journeys to move all the things that I had piled up outside the library to their destination in front of the statue of Yoshimitsu in the Golden Temple. First I carried the mattress and the mosquito net, from which the rod had been removed. Then I took the two quilts. Next the trunk and the wicker basket, and after that the three bundles of straw. I piled all these things up in disorder, putting the straw bundles between the mosquito net and the bedding. The mosquito net seemed to be the most inflammable of all the objects and accordingly I stretched part of it over the rest of my luggage.

Finally I returned to the rear of the library and fetched the bundle in which I had wrapped the various things that were hard to burn. This time I took my load to the edge of the pond at the east of the Golden Temple. From here I could see the Yohaku Rock directly ahead of me. I stood under a cluster of pine trees and barely managed to protect myself from the rain.

The reflection of the night sky gave a dim whiteness to the surface of the pond. The dense duckweed made it look as if it were solid land and it was only from the occasional interstices between this thick covering that one could tell that water lay beneath. Where I stood it was not raining hard enough to make any ripples. The pond steamed in the rain and seemed to stretch out endlessly into the distance. The air was full of moisture.

I picked up a pebble and dropped it into the water. There was a splash of such exaggerated loudness that the air about me seemed to have cracked. For a while I crouched in the darkness without a sound, hoping by my silence to eradicate the noise that I had accidentally produced.

I put my hand into the water and the lukewarm duckweed clung to my fingers. First I let the mosquito-net rod slip into the water from my moist fingers. Then I entrusted my ash tray to the pond, as though I were rinsing it out. In the same way I dropped my cup and my ink bottle. That took care of all the things that had to be thrown into the water. All that remained beside me was the cushion and the cloth in which I had wrapped these objects. Nothing was left for me now but to take these two things in front of Yoshimitsu's statue and then finally to fire the temple.

The fact that at this moment I was abruptly overcome by hunger accorded too much with what I had expected and, far from gratifying me, made me feel that I had been betrayed. I was still carrying the sweet bread and the bean-jam wafers, which I had started eating on the previous day. I wiped my wet hands on the end of my jumper and devoured the food greedily. I was not aware of the taste. My stomach cried out loudly for food and did not care in the slightest about any sense of taste. It was a good thing that I was able to concentrate on stuffing the sweet bread hurriedly into my mouth. My heart was pounding. When I had finished swallowing the food, I scooped some water out of the pond and drank.

I was on the very threshold of my deed. I had completed all the preparations that led to the deed and now I was standing on the further edge of those preparations with nothing left to do but to hurl myself into the actual deed. With only the slightest effort I should be able to attain that deed.

I did not imagine for a moment that a gulf great enough to swallow my entire life was opening up between me and what I intended to do.

For at that moment I gazed at the Golden Temple to bid it a last farewell. The temple was dim in the darkness of the rainy night and its outline was indistinct. It stood there in deep black, as though it were a crystallization of the night itself. When I strained my eyes, I managed to make out the Kukyocho, the top story of the temple, where the entire structure suddenly became narrow, and also the forest of narrow pillars that surrounded the Choondo and the Hosui-in. But the various details of the temple, which had moved me so greatly in the past, had melted away into the monochrome darkness.

As my remembrance of the beauty grew more and more vivid, however, this very darkness began to provide a background against which I could conjure up my vision at will. My entire conception of beauty lurked within this somber, crouching form. Thanks to the power of memory, the various aesthetic details began to glitter one by one out of the surrounding darkness; then the glittering spread wider and wider, until gradually the entire temple had emerged before me under that strange light of time itself, which is neither day nor night. Never before had the Golden Temple showed itself to me in so perfect a form, never had I seen it glitter like this in its every detail. It was as though I had appropriated a blind man's vision. The light that emanated from the temple itself had made the building transparent, and standing by the pond I could vividly see the paintings of angels on the roof inside the Choondo and the remains of the ancient gold foil on the walls in the Kukyocho. The delicate exterior of the Golden Temple had become intimately mingled with the interior. As my eyes took in the entire prospect, I could perceive the temple's structure and the clear outline of its motif, I could see the painstaking repetition and decoration of the details whereby this motif was materialized, I saw the effects of contrast and of symmetry. The two lower stories, the Hosui-in and the Choondo, were of the same width and, though there was a slight difference between them, they were protected by the same extensive eave; one story rested on top of its companion, so that they looked like a pair of closely related dreams or like memories of two very similar pleasures that we have enjoyed in the past. These twin stories had been crowned by a third story, the Kukyocho, which abruptly tapered off. And high on top of the shingled roof the gilt bronze phoenix was facing the long, lightless night.

Yet even this had not satisfied the architect. At the west of the Hosui-in he had added the tiny Sosei, which projected from the temple like an overhanging pavilion. It was as if he had put all his aestheic powers into breaking the symmetry of the building. The role of the Sosei in the total architecture was one of metaphysical resistance. Although it certainly did not stretch very far over the pond, it looked as though it were running away indefinitely from the center of the Golden Temple. The Sosei was like a bird soaring away from the main structure of the building, like a bird that a few moments before had spread its wings and was escaping toward the surface of the pond, toward everything that was mundane. The significance of the Sosei was to provide a bridge that led between the order which controls the world and those things, like carnal desire, which are utterly disordered. Yes, that was it. The spirit of the Golden Temple began with this Sosei, which resembled a bridge that has been severed at its halfway point; then it formed a three-storied tower; then once more it fled from this bridge. For the vast power of sensual desire that shimmered on the surface of this pond was the source of the hidden force that had constructed the Golden Temple; but, after this power had been put in order and the beautiful three-storied tower formed, it could no longer bear to dwell there and nothing was left for it but to escape along the Sosei back to the surface of the pond, back to the endless shimmering of sensual desire, back to its native land. Every time in the past that I had looked at the morning mist or the evening mist as it wandered over the pond I had been struck by this same thought—the thought that this was the dwelling-place of the abundant sensual power that had originally constructed the Golden Temple.

And beauty synthesized the struggles and the contradictions and the disharmonies in every part of this building—and, furthermore, it was beauty that ruled over them all! The Golden Temple had been built with gold dust in the long, lightless night, just like a sutra that is painstakingly inscribed with gold dust onto the dark-blue pages of a book. Yet I did not know whether beauty was, on the one hand, identical with the Golden Temple itself or, on the other, consubstantial with the night of nothingness that surrounded the temple. Perhaps beauty was both these things. It was both the individual parts and the whole structure, both the Golden Temple and the night that wrapped itself about the Golden Temple. At this thought I felt that the mystery of the beauty of the Golden Temple, which had tormented me so much in the past, was halfway towards being solved. If one examined the beauty of each individual detail—the pillars, the railings, the shutters, the framed doors, the ornamented windows, the pyramidal roof—the Hosui-in, the Choondo, the Kukyocho, the Sosei—the shadow of the temple on the pond, the little islands, the pine trees, yes, even the mooring-place for the temple boat—the beauty was never completed in any single detail of the temple; for each detail adumbrated the beauty of the succeeding detail. The beauty of the individual detail itself was always filled with uneasiness. It dreamed of perfection, but it knew no completion and was invariably lured on to the next beauty, the unknown beauty. The adumbration of beauty contained in one detail was linked with the subsequent adumbration of beauty, and so it was that the various adumbrations of a beauty *which did not exist* had become the underlying motif of the Golden Temple. Such adumbrations were signs of nothingness. Nothingness was the very structure of this beauty. Therefore, from the incompletion of the various details of this beauty there arose automatically an adumbration of nothingness, and this delicate building, wrought of the most slender timber, was trembling in anticipation of nothingness, like a jeweled necklace trembling in the wind.

Yet never did there come a time when the beauty of the Golden Temple ceased! Its beauty was always echoing somewhere. Like a person who suffers from ringing of the ears, I invariably heard the sound of the Golden Temple's beauty wherever I might be and I had grown accustomed to it. If one compared this beauty to a sound, the building was like a little golden bell that has gone on ringing for five and a half centuries, or else like a small harp. But what if that sound should stop?

I was overcome by intense weariness.

Above the Golden Temple that existed in the darkness I could still vividly see the Golden Temple of my vision. It had not yet concluded its glittering. The railing of the Hosui-in at the water's edge withdrew with the greatest modesty, while on its eaves the railing of the Choondo, supported by its Indian-style brackets, thrust out its breast dreamily towards the pond. The eaves were illuminated by the pond's reflection and the flickering of the water reflected itself uncertainly against them. When the Golden Temple reflected the evening sun or shone in the moon, it was the light of the water that made the entire structure look as if it were mysteriously floating along and flapping its wings. The strong bonds of the temple's form were loosened by the reflection of the quivering water, and at such moments the Golden Temple seemed to be constructed of materials like wind and water and flame that are constantly in motion.

The beauty of the Golden Temple was unsurpassed. And I knew now where my great weariness had come from. That beauty was taking a last chance to exercise its power over me and to bind me with that impotence which had so often overcome me in the past. My hands and my feet flinched from what lay before me. A few moments before, I had been only one step from my deed, but now once again I had retreated far into the distance.

"I had made all my preparations," I murmured to myself, "and was only one step from the deed. Having so completely dreamed the deed, having so completely lived that dream, is there really any need to act it out physically? Wouldn't such action be quite useless at this stage?

"Kashiwagi was probably right when he said that what changed the world was not action but knowledge. And there was also the type of knowledge that tried to copy the action to the utmost possible limit. My knowledge is of this nature. And it is this type of knowledge that makes the action really invalid. Does not the reason, then, for all my careful preparations lie in the final knowledge that *I would not have to act in earnest?*

"Yes, that's it. Action is now simply a kind of superfluity for me. It has jutted out of life, it has jutted out of my own will, and now it stands before me, like a separate, cold steel mechanism, waiting to be put in motion. It is as if there is not the slightest connection between me and my action. *Up to this point* it has been I, from here on it is not I. How can I dare to stop being myself?"

I leaned against the bottom of the pine tree. The wet, cool skin of the tree bewitched me. I felt that this sensation, this coolness was—myself. The world had stopped just as it was; no longer was there any desire and I, too, was utterly satisfied.

What should I do with this terrible weariness, I thought? Somehow I felt feverish and languid and my hands would not move where I intended. Surely I must be ill.

The Golden Temple was still glittering before me, just like the view of the Jissokan that Shuntokumaru had once seen. Within the black night of his blindness Shuntokumaru had seen the setting sun playing lambently on the Sea of Namba. He had seen Awaji Eshima, Suma Akashi, and even the Sea of Kii reflecting the evening sun under a cloudless sky.

My body seemed to be paralyzed and the tears flowed incessantly. I did not mind staying here just as I was until the morning came and I was discovered. I should not offer a word of excuse.

Until now I had been speaking at great length about how impotent my memory had been since the time of my childhood, but I must point out that a memory which is suddenly revived carries a great power of resuscitation. The past does not only draw us back to the past. There are certain memories of the past that have strong steel springs and, when we who live in the present touch them, they are suddenly stretched taut and then they propel us into the future.

While my body seemed benumbed, my mind was groping somewhere within my memory. Some words floated up to the surface and then vanished. I seemed to reach them with the hands of my spirit and then once again they were hidden. Those words were calling me. They were trying to approach me in order to put me on my mettle.

"Face the back, face the outside, and if ye meet, kill instantly!"

Yes, the first sentence went like that. The famous passage in that chapter of the *Rinsairoku*. Then the remaining words emerged fluently: "When ye meet the Buddha, kill the Buddha! When ye meet your ancestor, kill your ancestor! When ye meet a disciple of Buddha, kill the disciple! When ye meet your father and mother, kill your father and mother! When ye meet your kin, kill your kin! Only thus will ye attain deliverance. Only thus will ye escape the trammels of material things and become free."

The words propelled me out of the impotence into which I had fallen. All of a sudden my whole body was infused with strength. One part of my mind still kept on telling me that it was now futile to perform this deed, but my new-found strength had no fear of futility. I must do the deed precisely because it was so futile.

I rolled up the cloth that lay beside me and tucked it under my arm together with the cushion. Then I stood up. I looked towards the Golden Temple. The glittering temple of my vision had begun to fade. The railings were gradually swallowed up in the darkness and the forest of slender pillars lost its clarity. The light vanished from the water and its reflection on the back of the eaves also vanished. Soon all the details were concealed in the darkness and the Golden Temple left nothing but a vague, black outline.

I ran. I ran round the north of the temple. My feet

became accustomed to their task and I did not stumble. The darkness opened up before me successively and guided me on my way.

From the edge of the Sosei I leaped into the Golden Temple through the hinged door at the western entrance, which I had left open. I threw the cushion and the cloth onto the pile that I had already prepared.

My heart was throbbing merrily and my wet hands were trembling. Moreover, my matches were wet. The first one wouldn't light. The second one was about to light when it broke. The third one burst into flames and as I held out my hand against the wind it illuminated the spaces between my fingers.

Then I had to search for the bundles of straw. For, although I had dragged the three bundles in here myself and placed them in different parts of the building, I had completely forgotten where I had put them. By the time that I had found them, the match had burned out. I crouched down by the straw and this time struck two matches together.

The fire delineated the complex shadows of the piles of straw and, giving forth the brilliant color of the wild places, it spread minutely in all directions. As the smoke rose into the air, the fire hid itself within its white mass. Then, unexpectedly far from where I was standing, the flames sprang up, puffing out the green of the mosquito net. I felt as if everything round me had suddenly become alive.

At this moment my head became completely clear. There was a limit to my supply of matches. I ran to another corner of the room, and, carefully striking a match, set fire to the next bundle of straw. The new flames that sprang up heartened me. In the past when I had been out with my companions and we had made campfires I had always been particularly adept at the job.

Within the Hosui-in a great flickering shadow had arisen. The statues of the Three Holy Buddhas, Amida, Kannon, and Seishi were lit up in red. The wooden statue of Yoshimitsu flashed its eyes; and in the back its shadow fluttered.

I could hardly feel the heat. When I saw that the steadfast flames had moved to the offertory box, I felt that everything was going to be all right.

I had forgotten about the arsenic and the pocketknife. Suddenly I had the idea of dying in the Kukyocho surrounded by the flames. Then I fled from the fire and ran up the narrow stairs. It did not occur to me to wonder why the door leading up to the Choondo was open. The old guide had forgotten to close the second-story door.

The smoke swirled toward my back. As I coughed, I gazed at the statue of Kannon that was atrributed to Keishin and at the music-playing angels painted on the ceiling. Gradually the drifting smoke filled the Choondo. I ran up the next flight of stairs and tried to open the door of the Kukyocho. The door would not open. The entrance to the third story was firmly locked.

I knocked at the door. It must have been a violent knocking, but the sound did not impinge on my ears. With all my might I knocked at the door. I felt that someone might open the door to the Kukyocho for me from the inside. What I dreamed of finding in the Kukyocho was a place to die, but since the smoke was already pursuing me I knocked impetuously at the door as though I were instead seeking a refuge. What lay on the other side of that door could only be a little room. And at that moment I poignantly dreamed that the walls of the room must be fully covered with golden foil, though I knew that in actual fact they were almost completely defoliated. I cannot explain how desperately I was longing for that radiant little room as I stood there knocking at the door. If only I could reach it, I thought, everything would be all right. If only I could reach that little golden room.

I knocked as hard as I could. My hands were not strong enough and I threw my whole body against the door. Still it would not open.

The Choondo was already filled with smoke. Beneath my feet I could hear the crackling sound of the fire. I choked in the smoke and almost lost consciousness. As I coughed, I kept on knocking. But still the door would not open.

When at a certain moment there arose in me the clear consciousness of having been refused, I did not hesitate. I dodged the stairs. I ran down to the Hosui-in through the swirling smoke; I must have passed through the fire itself. When finally I reached the western door, I threw myself out into the open. Then I started to run like a shot, not knowing where I was going.

I ran. It was fantastic how far I ran without stopping to rest. I can't even remember what places I passed. I must have left by the back gate next to the Kyohoku Tower in the north of the temple precincts, then I must have passed by the Myoo Hall, run up the mountain path that was bordered by bamboo grass and azalea, and reached the top of Mount Hidari Daimonji. Yes, it was surely on top of Mount Hidari Daimonji that I lay down on my back in the bamboo field in the shadow of the red pines and tried to still the fierce beating of my heart. This was the mountain that protected the Golden Temple from the north.

The cry of some startled birds brought me to my senses. Or else it was a bird that flew close to my face with a great fluttering of its wings.

As I lay there on my back I gazed at the night sky. The birds soared over the branches of the red pines in great numbers and then thin flakes from the fire, which were already becoming scarce, floated in the sky above my head.

I sat up and looked far down the ravine towards the Golden Temple. A strange sound echoed from there. It was like the sound of crackers. It was like the sound of countless people's joints all cracking at once.

From where I sat the Golden Temple itself was invisible. All that I could see was the eddying smoke and the great fire that rose into the sky. The flakes from the fire drifted between the trees and the Golden Temple's sky seemed to be strewn with golden sand.

I crossed my legs and sat gazing for a long time at the scene.

When I came to myself, I found that my body was covered in blisters and scars and that I was bleeding profusely. My fingers also were stained with blood, evidently from when I had hurt them by knocking against the temple door. I licked my wounds like an animal that has fled from its pursuers.

I looked in my pocket and extracted the bottle of arsenic, wrapped in my handkerchief, and the knife. I threw them down the ravine.

Then I noticed the pack of cigarettes in my other pocket. I took one out and started smoking. I felt like a man who settles down for a smoke after finishing a job of work. I wanted to live.

A Note about the Author

The late Yuko Mishima was the most spectacularly talented young writer in Japan. He was born in Tokyo in 1925. Upon his graduation from the Peers' School in 1944, he received a citation from the Emperor as the highest honor student. He was graduated from Tokyo Imperial University School of Jurisprudence in 1947, and his first novel was published in 1948. He wrote constantly after that: more than a dozen novels, many successful plays, and a travel book. He once remarked that his "lesser writings" included fifty short stories, ten one-act plays, and several volumes of essays.

His first novel published in the United States was *The Sound of Waves* (1956); under its original title, *Shiosai*, it had won the 1954 Shinchosha Literary Prize. In 1957, when his *Five Modern No Plays* was translated by Donald Keene and published here, he spent six months in the United States. His work has been translated into several European languages, and one of his *Nō Plays* has been presented on German television. He was married and, until his tragic suicide in late 1970, lived in Tokyo.

MORE BERKLEY *MUST* TITLES
FOR YOUR LIBRARY